"Takes readers into the black depth testament to the strength of the hu to heal even the deepest wounds."

—Linda Howard, *New York Times* bestselling author

"Incredibly awesome . . . I love Maya Banks and I love her books."

—Jaci Burton, *New York Times* bestselling author

"Really dragged me through the gamut of emotions. From . . . 'Is it hot in here?' to 'Oh my GOD' . . . I'm ready for the next ride now!"　　—*USA Today*

"[A] one-two punch of entertainment that will leave readers eager for the next book."　　—*Publishers Weekly*

"Any book by Maya Banks is a book well worth reading."

—Once Upon a Twilight

"For those who like it naughty, dirty and do-me-on-the-desk HAWT!"

—Examiner.com

"Hot enough to make even the coolest reader sweat!"　　—Fresh Fiction

"Definitely a recommended read."　　—Fallen Angel Reviews

"[For] fans of Sylvia Day's *Bared to You*."　　—Under the Covers

"Grabbed me from page one and refused to let go until I read the last word."　　—Joyfully Reviewed

"An excellent read that I simply did not put down . . . Covers all the emotional range."　　—The Road to Romance

"The sex is crazy hot."　　—Scandalicious Book Reviews

KEPT

THE ENFORCERS

Maya Banks

BERKLEY
New York

BERKLEY
An imprint of Penguin Random House LLC
375 Hudson Street, New York, New York 10014

Copyright © 2016 by Maya Banks

Library of Congress Cataloging-in-Publication Data

Names: Banks, Maya, author.
Title: Kept / Maya Banks.
Description: First Edition. | New York : Berkley, [2016] | Series: The enforcers ; 3
Identifiers: LCCN 2016030006 (print) | LCCN 2016037165 (ebook) | ISBN 9780425280676
(paperback) | ISBN 9780698191839 (ebook)
Subjects: LCSH: Man-woman relationships—Fiction. | Sexual dominance and submission—
Fiction. | BISAC: FICTION / Romance / Contemporary. | FICTION / Contemporary Women. |
FICTION / Romance / General. | GSAFD: Erotic fiction.
Classification: LCC PS3602.A643 K47 2016 (print) | LCC PS3602.A643 (ebook) |
DDC 813/.6—dc23
LC record available at https://lccn.loc.gov/2016030006

First Edition: October 2016

Printed in the United States of America
1 3 5 7 9 10 8 6 4 2

Cover photo: ball and chain © Africa Studio / Shutterstock
Cover design by Rita Frangie

KEPT

1

Hayley Winthrop walked morosely down the busy Manhattan side-walk, her spirits sinking lower as she registered just how far she'd walked from her old apartment and the school of music in which she was enrolled part-time—for now. She glanced surreptitiously up at the sky and sighed, thinking the sudden cloud cover that had rolled in, marring what had been an otherwise spectacular spring day, was a direct reflection of her spirits. She hadn't brought an umbrella because she hadn't intended to venture this far in her search of a new place to stay, and, well, the forecast hadn't called for rain. Just her luck. Bad, as always. Being an eternal optimist was beginning to wear on her as she'd been treated to dose after dose of cold, hard reality.

In a few days, she'd have nowhere to live, and she'd had no luck find-ing another place she could afford on her meager budget. She'd known when she'd fortuitously found an apartment to house-sit for that it wouldn't be a permanent arrangement, but she had expected at least a few more months before being forced to move out. Unfortunately, the owners, a kindly elderly couple who were patrons of the music school that Hayley attended, had cut short their European tour because the wife had become ill and the husband wanted to bring her home to be attended by her own physician in the city.

They had been apologetic and had even offered their help in finding Hayley another suitable place to live, but it would be next to impossible to find something she could afford and she couldn't—wouldn't—accept any further help from them. They'd already been so kind to her, and the thought of taking advantage of their generosity made Hayley ill. She had pride. Perhaps more than was good for her, particularly given her desperate circumstances, but she was determined to make her own way and fulfill her promise to her dying father, the one she'd made him on his deathbed to pursue her dream of attending the prestigious school of music in New York City. A dream he thought he'd made possible for her by purchasing an insurance policy at exorbitant cost so that when he was gone, she would be provided for even when he was no longer alive to take care of her.

Tears stung her eyelids. Her father had had only the best of intentions, a pure and kind heart and so much pride in his only daughter, and he'd been taken in by a con artist who'd sold him a life insurance policy with more holes and exemptions in the nearly illegible fine print than a hunk of Swiss cheese. The only comfort she drew from the fact of his passing was that he would never know the shame and embarrassment of realizing that the money he couldn't afford to spend was for absolutely nothing. The worthless piece of human trash had taken advantage of her father and had promised him that he was absolutely doing the right thing, all the while siphoning every penny of her father's meager savings right from under his nose.

And while her father lay so sick in bed, dying a little more with each passing day, he'd exacted a promise from her that she would go to New York and pursue her dream of becoming a professional violinist, though she'd protested, telling him she refused to leave him and that they'd fight this. Together. She vowed never to leave his side and that nothing was more important than him fighting, overcoming and winning his battle. Then and only then would she pursue her dream. But not at the expense of his health and life. She'd work two, three jobs—whatever it took to give him the care he so desperately needed—but he wouldn't hear of it. He adamantly refused, telling her that it was what her mother would have wanted and that he'd promised her mother when she too lay dying that he would ensure their little girl's dream became a reality if it was the last thing he did.

In the end, she'd had no choice but to agree, though she'd hated the mere thought of moving to the city while her father had moved to hospice. She hadn't wanted to be away from him, but he hadn't wanted her to see him die, to continue to watch him waste away to nothing. Their final night together, he'd simply asked her to play for him, and so she'd stayed the entire night, playing her violin as he drifted between consciousness and unconsciousness, a smile on his face despite the crippling pain she knew he felt with every breath.

When morning came, she'd kissed his forehead, tears running freely down her face as she'd whispered her good-bye, and in a moment of rare strength and lucidity, he'd wrapped his arms around her, hugging her tightly to him, and told her in a gruff voice that he loved her and that she'd already made him proud, but now it was time for her to spread her wings and for her to pursue her dreams.

Two days after her arrival in New York City, her father's nurse had called to tell her he'd passed away and that his last words had been of her, how proud he was that she was following her dream and that he could rest easy and finally join his beloved wife now that their daughter was finally taken care of.

She bit her lip, fighting back the tears of grief that threatened to fall. She cast a wary eye to the skies to see that the gray clouds had now covered all hints of the formerly sunny day, but as of yet, not a single drop of rain had fallen. Maybe her luck would hold. She needed to turn back. It was a long walk back to her apartment and whenever possible, she walked everywhere, saving every precious cent. The subway wasn't exorbitant by any means, but she needed every penny.

Who was she kidding, spending days, hours, between her part-time school schedule and the many part-time and seasonal jobs she could pick up, pounding the pavement in search of an affordable apartment? There was no such thing as reasonable rent in Manhattan. And a roommate was out for her because the only time she had left to practice her beloved music was late in the night after she got off the late shift at one of her jobs, only stopping so she could get in a few precious hours of sleep before her early-morning classes the next day.

She was about to turn around and trudge back the way she'd come when she noticed a smaller building crammed between two imposing buildings, at least thirty floors high. It was obviously an apartment building, though modest, but surprisingly well-kept given its obvious age. It had five levels, perhaps six if there was a walk-out basement unit as so many buildings had.

There was no sign to indicate that there was a vacancy, but then most apartments—at least those in safer areas—had no need to advertise vacancies. They more often than not had waiting lists longer than both her arms. Oh well, what was the worst they could say that she hadn't already heard? Either there were no vacancies, or if there had been, the rent was so high, even for the smallest studio apartment, that even working six jobs, she'd never afford the rent on her own.

Still, she hesitated outside the entrance with a sign above it indicating that the management office was inside, wondering how much more disappointment she could take in one day. But the fact that she only had three more days until she was homeless made her spine straighten. She sucked in a deep breath and pressed the bell, opening the door when it buzzed to enter.

Her gaze swept the empty lobby, her eyes widening in surprise.

Despite the worn look of the exterior, the inside had an updated look that didn't scream modern. It was warm and comfortable, a place where someone could immediately feel at home.

Don't get your hopes up. You've been disappointed time and time again. Why would this time be any different?

When an older man appeared from the office just off the lobby, Hayley donned her most hopeful and warm smile but clenched her fingers together in front of her in an attempt to allay her hope and desperation.

Fresh from a shower, Silas sauntered through his living room, or command central as it was more appropriately deemed. Here he had a bird's-eye view of not only his entire apartment building but the streets surrounding the block. After Evangeline, his partner and brother's now-wife, had been abducted a few months earlier, he'd expanded his reach by installing street cams that extended well beyond the area immediately surrounding his domain.

He had slept past his usual time to wake, before dawn, because of a problem the night before that had taken him until well into the morning to handle. Thus, he was in a hurry to dress and report back to Drake that the issue had been taken care of. Something Drake would already know, but would want the details regardless.

He paused, coming to a complete halt when he caught sight of the monitor that gave him a view of the front office—and anyone who entered his building.

A young woman was standing in the small lobby, obviously nervous and ill at ease. Silas hurried to turn up the volume on the feed that recorded that area and took a seat, studying the woman more closely.

She was stunning. She had an arresting look that would make a man stop in his tracks and take a second and third look at her. Long, raven hair with startling blue eyes the color of the ocean at high noon on a cloudless day. And young. She looked far too young and innocent to even gain the notice of a man like Silas. He felt a hundred years old under the weight of all he'd seen and done in his lifetime just looking on the beautiful stranger.

"I-I was inquiring as to whether you had a vacant apartment for rent," the woman asked hesitantly.

Silas wondered if she even realized that she wore desperation like a flag and that yearning hope glowed in her eyes.

"As it happens, we have a basement unit with a walkout to the street," Miles, his property manager, said cheerfully. "It's small, but utilities are included and we have very good security. And there aren't any broker fees either."

Silas watched as the woman held her breath, battling against the burst of hope threatening to bloom on her expressive face.

"When would it be available? And how much is it?" she blurted.

Silas watched as her face whitened at the amount specified, her shoulders sagged in defeat and any vestiges of hope leached from her eyes, leaving her looking utterly lost.

"I see," she murmured. "I'm sorry to have wasted your time. It's far more than I can afford, but thank you anyway. I'll just be on my way. Again, my apologies for interrupting you."

She handed Miles a small card, grimacing as if she realized the futility of her action.

"If . . . if you should have something less expensive come available, will you call me?"

She turned, like an aged woman instead of the vibrant young girl Silas had witnessed upon her arrival, and shuffled toward the door, head bowed. He thought he caught a glimmer of tears on one cheek as her profile was briefly presented when she opened the door to slip out onto the busy sidewalk.

Silas bolted from his chair, fists gripped into tight balls at his sides as he watched her walk slowly down the street, tears trickling down her pale cheeks. In that instant, he threw sanity and caution to the wind and yanked up his phone, punching the button that would immediately connect him to his manager.

Miles answered on the first ring.

"Yes, sir," he said briskly. "What can I do for you, sir?"

"The woman who just left," Silas said hoarsely. "Find her. Give her the apartment to the right of mine but tell her she won't be able to move in until day after tomorrow. It will take that long to have the workers replace the wall dividing it from mine and to refurnish the apartment."

"Pardon?" Miles asked in a shocked voice.

"You heard me," Silas snarled. "Offer her a ridiculously low rent and let her know it comes fully furnished with utilities paid. Make up something. I don't care. Tell her construction was finished ahead of schedule and you only just received notice that it would be ready for a tenant just after she left. Just make damn sure you find her."

"Yes, sir. Right away, sir," Miles stammered.

"And have my driver offer her a ride home. I'll call him now."

2

Hayley dodged the first few raindrops and then cursed under her breath as she glanced again at the ever-darkening sky. Yep. Perfect foil for the day she'd had. The week she'd had, for that matter. At least she'd had sense enough to leave her violin at home instead of bringing it with her in her urgent search for a place to live.

Knowing it would cost her precious money she didn't have, she hurried in the direction of the nearest subway stop and dug into her pocket for enough to purchase a subway card to get home.

Her cell phone rang and for a moment she was tempted to ignore it, her focus more on getting out of the rain, but she'd left her number with every place she'd been to in her apartment search and couldn't afford to assume it was nothing more than a telemarketer.

With a sigh and admonishing herself for allowing herself foolish hope, she pulled up her cell and uttered a polite greeting.

"Miss Winthrop, this is Miles Carver. You left here a few minutes ago where you inquired about an apartment."

Hayley's spirits plummeted.

"Yes, sir, I remember you, of course."

"Hopefully I have good news for you, Miss Winthrop. You see, an upstairs unit has been undergoing renovation, and it was thought it wouldn't be ready for another few weeks, which is why I didn't mention it, but right after you left, the owner called and informed me that the apartment would be ready shortly. I called to see if you'd be interested."

Hayley closed her eyes, disappointment keen. It was as if fate were taunting her with opportunities she in no way could take advantage of.

"It's completely furnished and all utilities are included," the manager hurried on to say. "But it wouldn't be ready for you to move in until day after tomorrow. I hope that's not too late for you."

"No," Hayley said gently. "That wouldn't be a problem at all. The rent is the issue. I'm afraid it would be far more than I could afford."

Then the manager stunned her by stating a ridiculously low sum for the monthly rent. Her mouth fell open in a gasp, and her heart started pounding so hard that her knees threatened to buckle. She was so rattled she had to ask him to repeat himself. Against her will, a pulse of hope began to beat a furious tempo in her head. Surely she couldn't be this fortunate. Fully furnished, all utilities included *and* within her price range? It had to be a sick joke, or she was just imagining it all.

"It's small," the manager said. "Not quite as small as a studio but it does have one bedroom, an en suite bathroom, a small living room and a kitchenette."

"I'll take it," Hayley said breathlessly.

There was a momentary silence. "You don't want to come look at it first?"

"No," she said firmly. "It sounds perfect. And I'll be honest, Mr. Carver. I only have a few days remaining until I must move from where I currently reside, so as the old saying goes, beggars can't be choosers. Should I come right back to sign a lease?"

Again there was a pause, and then he said, "Yes, perhaps that's best, unless you're too far away now? It's begun to rain and I could offer you a ride home after you've completed the paperwork."

Hayley's mouth dropped open at the generous, kind offer.

"Oh no, I couldn't possibly put you out like that. I'll come by and fill out the paperwork, but there's no need for you to give me a ride home."

"I insist," the manager said firmly.

Delight fizzed in her veins even as she started rushing back toward the small apartment building.

"I'll be there in five," she said breathlessly.

Four minutes and a quick buzz of the door later, Hayley burst into the lobby, her cheeks flushed, her hair plastered wetly to the sides of her head. Her clothing was soaked through, but at the moment nothing could dim her excitement. Finally, one less worry on her shoulders. She had a place to live! One where she wasn't dependent on the kindness or charity of others.

The manager frowned when he took in her appearance and left the lobby only to return a moment later with a large, warm towel.

"Come into my office. It's warmer and more comfortable there," he directed.

He seated her in a leather chair across from his desk, then pushed a surprisingly small packet of papers toward her with a pen.

"Here's the application for the apartment you'll need to fill out, and then two copies of the lease to sign. You'll find it's straightforward. It's a standard one-year lease, and there is a guarantee that the current rate will not go up for the next five years upon renewal of this lease. No pets without the express written consent of the owner. No subletting and you are to be the sole occupant of the apartment."

Hayley nodded her head eagerly, thrilled that she must have unknowingly lucked into one of the city's highly coveted rent-controlled apartments—no wonder the rent was so low!—and began reading over the language in the contract. As Mr. Carver had stated, it was straightforward. No fine print. No tricky language. Just a basic agreement with the rules she was to follow and a place for her signature.

"If you'll come by in the morning day after tomorrow, I'll give you the keys and show you the apartment as well as give you your copy of the signed lease. You can begin moving in any time you wish after that."

Hayley rose. "I can't thank you enough, Mr. Carver. You have no idea what a godsend this is. I had no idea what I was going to do if I couldn't find a place to stay."

The manager looked discomfited by her gratitude, his face reddening.

"I'll just be on my way now," Hayley said. "I'll need to start packing!"

"I'll escort you to the car waiting out front," Mr. Carver said. "If you'll give the driver your address, he will see you home. It's pouring outside, and getting a taxi will be impossible."

Hayley flushed. "That isn't necessary. Truly. You've been far too kind as it is."

"On the contrary. The owner of the apartment insists."

Puzzled by his cryptic statement, Hayley allowed herself to be escorted outside and into a sleek, very expensive car that she didn't recognize the make of. As she slid inside, she nearly sighed at the buttery-soft leather as her body sank into its welcoming softness.

Silas downloaded the e-mail attachment sent to him by his manager and waited impatiently for the woman's application to finish printing. As soon as it was done, he snatched it up, temporarily shoving his pressing meeting with Drake to the back of his mind. He sank into his office chair and began scanning the form, absorbing every piece of information on the young woman who'd so inexplicably captivated him from the moment she'd appeared on his security monitor.

His lips twitched in ironic amusement. It wasn't lost on him that a similar thing had happened to Drake months ago when Evangeline had caught his attention the moment she'd entered his club and he'd seen her on the surveillance camera. The difference, however, was that

Silas didn't believe in love at first sight. Fascination, yes. Love, infatuation, even emotional interest, no.

He couldn't say why she'd intrigued him so much or why her obvious distress and desperation had touched a part of his black soul that had never once touched the sun in all the years of his existence. He could only say that the feeling was . . . exhilarating. A rush he hadn't expected and hadn't welcomed at all. And yet he had been unable to deny himself the opportunity to observe her unnoticed. He'd taken in every single detail. Her beauty hadn't escaped him, but what had stopped him in his tracks and made him take intense notice was the innocence and obvious, inherent goodness that shone from the depths of her soul, despite her weary, exhausted expression and the defeated look tugging at the delicate features of her face.

Perhaps he was just getting old and growing too soft, or maybe Evangeline was to blame for his instant keen sense of protectiveness when he'd laid eyes on the girl. No, not girl. A young woman, but hardly a girl. But it was easy to look at her and see Evangeline. Young, innocent and as of yet unjaded by life. For all practical purposes she had been Evangeline before Drake had swept into Evangeline's life and spoiled her and lavished attention and focus on her.

Hayley Winthrop was twenty-two years old according to the application, and she was a student at a music college he recognized. Small but prestigious. From what he knew, admittance was extremely competitive and only the brightest, most gifted musicians were accepted. He frowned, however, when he saw that she'd listed herself as a part-time student but that she had two full-time jobs as well as a variety of other temporary jobs. No wonder she'd been dismayed when Miles had given her the price of rent for the vacant studio apartment. She had no way of affording it.

She listed no family. Not even an emergency contact person. Was she completely alone in a strange city? Much as Evangeline had been? He shook his head. Yes, it had to be the parallels between her and Evangeline that had touched a part of his heart he would have sworn hadn't existed before meeting Evangeline. That was the only reasonable explanation.

Men like him certainly didn't give in to infatuation or even fascination, and they definitely didn't disrupt plans to renovate the entire upstairs into one huge apartment that would be his private domain where no one save him had access.

He sighed. It was done and there was no going back. He didn't want neighbors. He'd never rented out the two apartments lying vacant on either side of the one he resided in, having always planned to remodel it into his quarters. But he couldn't in good conscience rescind his offer to Hayley. Not when she was so obviously in need and had been so devastated when she'd realized she had no way of affording the usual rent. He could have simply had Miles inform Miss Winthrop that he'd misquoted the rent on the basement studio apartment, so she'd be as far from him as possible, but there were two problems with that. She would likely be suspicious over the drastic change in rent on the already-quoted unit, and, well, she wouldn't be next door to him, where he could monitor her comings and goings, and he knew he would be keeping a very close eye on his new neighbor.

He would just have to do so very discreetly.

He checked his watch with a soft curse, knowing Drake would be wondering where the hell he was and impatient to go over the results of Silas's task the night before. It wouldn't do to keep him waiting any longer.

3

Hayley sank further into the heated seat of the luxurious car as they sailed through traffic, and she smiled, unable to believe her good fortune. How fast things changed and how quickly she'd gone from desperation and resignation to excitement and optimism about her future.

Tears glittered and clung to her eyelashes.

I'm going to make it, Dad. Just like I promised. I've found a place I can afford to rent. I can continue school like you and Mom wanted. One day you'll see me playing with a prestigious symphony. This is all for you, Dad. For all you sacrificed for me. I only wish you were here to see me the first time I play with a symphony.

A fierce ache besieged her chest and she rubbed, blinking furiously to rid herself of the tears that burned her eyes. It was hard to accept that her biggest—only—supporter was gone. First her mom, whom she'd lost when she was but a child, but Hayley still clung to the fleeting memories she had of her mother. Every time she looked in the mirror she saw her mother's face. As her father often fondly remarked, she was the picture of her mother.

It was bad enough to lose one parent. Why did she have to lose both? The only two people she had in the world?

She leaned forward in the seat when she saw that they were approaching the street where her current residence was located.

"You can let me off at the corner," she said to the driver, who hadn't uttered a single word during the ride. "I'll walk from there. It's not far and the rain has stopped."

The man glanced in the rearview mirror, obviously staring intently at her, though she couldn't see his eyes behind the shades he wore despite the overcast day.

"I would feel better if I dropped you in front of your building," the man said, surprising her with the firmness of his statement.

Hayley smiled. "No, it's okay, truly. I'd like to walk so I can clear my head. It's been an eventful morning."

His lips tightened but he didn't argue further as he pulled to the corner and glided to a halt. When she would have opened her door to duck out, he sent her a look of reprimand that froze her in her tracks. He got out and unhurriedly stepped around the car to open the passenger door not facing the street.

She smiled at him again, ruefully this time, and offered her thanks, squeezing the hand he'd offered to help her out. To her shock, the staid, somber man's lips turned into a semblance of a smile, only the corners slightly tipping up.

"It was my pleasure," he offered formally before once more returning to the driver's seat.

Seconds later the car melted away into traffic and Hayley turned to walk the half block to her apartment, shaking her head at the most unexpected turn of events the day had offered.

She was so absorbed in the task of mentally packing and arranging the few remaining hours left before she had to report to work that she didn't notice Christopher standing in front of her building until she nearly bumped into him.

"Hayley! I've been waiting for you," he said in an angry tone, as if he expected her to be where he wanted at all times and had been put out by having to wait for her.

She winced inwardly and only barely managed to suppress a sigh of exasperation. She didn't have time to deal with a classmate who didn't get the hint, no matter how many times she gently gave it, that she had no interest in any sort of a personal relationship with him—or anyone. If anything it seemed to make him all the more determined.

"I've been busy, Christopher," she said quietly. "I only have a few days to find another place to live before I have to move out of this apartment."

His lips twisted, his expression becoming sullen. "You could move in with me. You know that. I have money. An inheritance. And I get the bulk of it once I graduate with this ridiculous music degree."

There was a gleam of satisfaction and greed, as if he expected her to be so impressed that she'd throw herself into his arms. But then at his mention of the "ridiculous degree," distaste glimmered in his eyes as though he found music repugnant. She was shocked by his reaction. Why on earth was he enrolled in the school if he found it—and music— so abhorrent?

She shook her head because she wasn't even going there. She didn't care. Wasn't going to ask, because she had no intention of doing anything to encourage him, and his *raisons d'etre* didn't matter to her. The only thing that mattered was that he finally get the message and move on to someone else. Hopefully someone more receptive.

"You wouldn't have to work or worry about a place to live. I'd take care of you. You're just being stubborn."

As kindly as she could when what she wanted to do was smack his head, she said, "I don't have time for this, Christopher. I go to school and work full-time. Aside from that, I have no desire to become involved in any relationship. I am quite capable of taking care of myself, and if you don't stop harassing me, I'm going to the police and swearing out a restraining order."

The last was said firmly, a hint of warning in her voice that she only had so much patience and that he was fast stretching the limits of it.

His face reddened and his eyes glittered with anger and something else that made her extremely uneasy. Before she could examine that other uneasy emotion and before he could say anything further, she moved quickly around him and escaped into her building, hurriedly punching in the code to gain access so he couldn't push his way in.

At least he had no idea where she was moving to, and she planned to keep it that way. There was something about him that made her nervous, made her afraid to be alone with him. It was bad enough to have to suffer his presence around others. But at least now, the only time she'd be forced to see him would be in the one class they shared. The one where he spared no opportunity to display his overwhelming arrogance and sense of self-worth.

Shaking off unpleasant thoughts of Christopher's persistence and the equally unpleasant thought that he wasn't one to give up so easily, she instead turned her attention to her new apartment and the manager's kindness. As a thank-you she would bake him her father's favorite dessert. Homemade triple-chocolate brownies. She'd bring them to him when she went in two days to pick up the keys and be let into her apartment. It wasn't much, but it was from the heart and hopefully he would appreciate the sweet treat.

Her apartment. Giddiness assailed her. Finally something of her own. She would be self-reliant and not dependent on the generosity and goodwill of strangers. Not that what the Forsythes had done hadn't been welcome and deeply appreciated. When she first arrived in the city, she hadn't the first clue of just how expensive housing was, and if it weren't for them, she would have been on the first bus back home. But now she could make her own way, and that instilled satisfaction deep within her. She was one step closer to fulfilling her dream—and the promise she'd given her father as he lay dying.

. . .

Silas strode into Drake's office, meeting Drake's look of surprise.

"You're late," Drake said unnecessarily.

Silas responded with a nod. "Something came up."

Drake lifted an eyebrow in question. "Anything wrong?"

"Nothing business related," Silas said vaguely, knowing Drake wouldn't pry even if his curiosity had been aroused.

"Any problems last night?" Drake asked, moving the conversation to the matter at hand.

Silas relaxed, easily shifting gears, effectively ridding himself of thoughts of a raven-haired young innocent and the fact that he'd acted on impulse, something he never, ever did. And he didn't want to delve into the reasons why, when his life had been a study of remaining in a state of complete control over every aspect of his life.

"Everything went according to plan. The Vanuccis are spooked and have fallen back to regroup. They're not happy about the alliance between you and the Luconis."

"That makes two of us," Drake said grimly.

Drake had always had a policy of not aligning himself with anyone, preferring to reserve his loyalty for his men, his brothers, and they for him. But his hand had been forced when Evangeline had been abducted and he'd had no choice but to ally himself with the Luconis in order to save her. His original plan had been to pit the two crime families against one another and watch them both fall. Now his focus was on keeping the Vanuccis in check while maintaining a civil relationship with the Luconis but at the same time keeping a very close eye on their dealings.

"They'll want revenge," Silas warned softly. "We can't afford to stand down or assume they're cowed by our alliance with the Luconis. They'll do what they can to pit us against the Luconis and vice versa, hoping for an eventual war, but while they aren't the sharpest tools in the shed, they're smart enough not to plant all their hopes on that eventuality. Nor are they that patient. They'll try to arrange partnerships with other smaller syndicates to build their power, and they'll bide their time, looking for an opportunity to strike when we least expect it. Which is why we have to expect it at all times and never relax our guard."

Drake's lips tightened, his expression going cold. Left unsaid was that Evangeline would most assuredly be a target given that she was Drake's greatest and only weakness. And now that she was pregnant, she was more vulnerable than ever.

To distract Drake from the paralyzing fear of losing his new wife, Silas leaned back with a smile and said, "So how is she doing? Still throwing up around the clock?"

Drake sighed, suddenly looking haggard, a different kind of worry darkening his gaze.

"Pretty much. It's driving me crazy. I've never felt so fucking helpless in my life. That shit's supposed to stop after the first trimester, but someone apparently needs to tell her that because I swear it's worse now than it was."

"Think she'll be up for our takeout date tomorrow?"

Evangeline was assigned one or more of Drake's men any time Drake wasn't with her. And when she and Drake went out, at least two of his men accompanied them. Her security measures were tight, but necessary given the inherent risk to her. She'd already been abducted once, and Drake was determined that no harm would ever come to her again.

Early on in Drake and Evangeline's relationship, Silas had formed a friendship with her, and he genuinely liked and respected her. They had a weekly takeout date where he would get her favorite takeout foods and bring them to Drake's apartment, and they'd eat together. Tomorrow was their scheduled date, but with Evangeline's sickness,

Silas wanted to make sure he wouldn't make things worse for her by choosing foods she couldn't eat.

"Even if she didn't feel like eating, she would want your company," Drake said with an indulgent smile. "She likes you and enjoys your time together. But here's a tip. Her current cravings are anything Thai, pickles, cookies-and-cream ice cream, and I swear she eats Wagyu steak every other day. A monster has been created."

"I thought pickles and ice cream was just a pregnancy cliché," Silas muttered. "Pregnant women actually do crave that shit?"

"Apparently so," Drake said ruefully. "I keep a stock in the apartment. Crazy woman gets up when she should be sleeping and has both. At the same time."

He emitted a shudder and Silas had to work to contain his own.

"Okay, then. Thai, pickles, ice cream and Wagyu steak it is," Silas said with a grin. "Surely that will earn me brownie points and at least one home-cooked meal."

Evangeline's cooking was off the charts and Drake's men, Silas included, employed any means to extort a meal from her.

"You show with all four and she'll likely be your culinary slave for a year at least," Drake said with a chuckle.

"I'm definitely bringing her enough, not only for our date tomorrow, but for leftovers several days after."

Drake rolled his eyes. "Don't overwork my woman just because you're addicted to her cooking. She has no business slaving over a hot stove when she's been feeling like shit." His face formed a scowl. "Damn woman needs to be off her feet and rest more, but she's declared war against sickness and fatigue and refuses to stay off her feet for any length of time."

"I'll make sure she sits her ass down and puts her feet up while I feed her tomorrow," Silas said with a scowl of his own.

Drake snorted. "Good luck with that."

"It's too fucking quiet," Silas said in an abrupt change of subject.

It had been burning in his gut for weeks, but now it was a steady fire, a sense of foreboding he couldn't ignore.

Drake glanced up, his features drawn in concern. He didn't question Silas. He never had. He above all people relied on Silas's instincts, and anything his enforcer said was met with absolute acceptance.

"Think they're planning something?" Drake asked in a low voice.

"They most assuredly have something up their sleeve," Silas mused. "They aren't the kind to suffer insult quietly, nor will they simply go away. What bothers me, though, is that I haven't heard of any plan, or scheme, or anything. The streets are quiet, and my sources are silent. No one is talking and that makes me nervous, because someone always has something to say."

Drake's expression became even more worried, and then he cursed viciously. "So help me God, if they go after what is mine, I'll kill every single one with my bare hands."

"With my help," Silas said by way of agreement.

Their mutual fear was a strike against Evangeline, but Silas worried that, in fact, Drake could very well be the target. The enemy would know by now just what Evangeline meant to Drake. And that she was pregnant with his child. They would know her security would be nearly impenetrable and their hope would be that Drake—and his men—would be so focused on protecting Evangeline that Drake's protection would be overlooked.

That wasn't going to happen, but it didn't mean an attempt wouldn't be made.

"You need to be careful," Silas said quietly. "I'm not convinced they won't try to go after you."

"I hope to hell they do," Drake said savagely.

"You have to think about Evangeline. And your child," Silas said patiently. "You no longer have no one, Drake. Think what it would do to Evangeline were something to happen to you. Your child growing up without his or her father. Alone. Unprotected. That's why you have to take care. I well know you'd like your shot at the bastards, but you can't take such a risk. It would devastate Evangeline, and I think that's the last thing you'd ever want to do."

Drake paused, anger still blazing in his eyes, and then resignation and acceptance of Silas's words crept in. He leaned back in his chair and blew out his breath.

"I don't like being put out of action," he said with distaste. "Like I'm hiding behind my men like a goddamn pussy."

"Your brothers," Silas corrected. "That's what we do. What you've done for us countless times. It's merely our turn to return the favor. For you. And for Evangeline. For your child."

"Fuck," Drake muttered in a tone he always used when Silas had scored a point Drake couldn't possibly counter.

Silas smiled. "I trust I won't have to worry about you taking any unnecessary risks, then?"

"Fuck you," Drake grumbled.

4

Hayley hoisted her purse over her shoulder and was careful not to drop the container of brownies as she neared the apartment building, tension mounting as she reached the door. Praying it hadn't been her imagination or that the manager hadn't changed his mind and rented the unit to someone else, she rang the bell and stepped inside once it unlocked, issuing a shy hello to the manager when he looked up from the reception desk.

A returning smile broadened Mr. Carver's face as he picked up a set of keys and hastened around the counter.

"Ready to see your apartment, Miss Winthrop?"

Oh God, it wasn't a dream. It was real! She had found an apartment in a safe part of the city, and the rent . . . She shook her head, sure some mistake had been made, that she'd heard wrong. But no, the amount had been outlined in the lease. An apartment that rented for this amount was simply unheard of. Even the worst accommodations in the seediest sections of the city rented for twice what she would be paying.

She flashed him her most brilliant smile, desperately trying to contain her overwhelming excitement. "Please, Mr. Carver, do call me Hayley. No one calls me Miss Winthrop. Well, except complete strangers, and as you and I will be seeing one another frequently now, you certainly can't be considered a stranger."

"Only if you'll agree to call me Miles," the older man said.

She beamed at him. "Miles it is."

"Shall I take you up? It's on the very top floor, but there are only five floors. Six counting the basement level, but only five floors aboveground."

"Yes, but first, I have something for you."

She ducked her head self-consciously when his eyebrow immediately arched in surprise. She fingered the plastic container and before she could lose her nerve she thrust it toward the manager.

"It's not much," she hedged. "But you were so kind to me and you didn't have to go to the trouble of calling me back when I'm sure you would have no problem renting out the apartment, but I wanted to do something to express my appreciation. So I baked you brownies. They were my father's favorite dessert. Triple-chocolate brownies."

Mr. Carver didn't take the brownies from her outstretched hand, and oddly, a look of intense discomfort entered his eyes. Had she offended him? Then he sighed and ran a hand through his hair.

"I shouldn't tell you this. It could mean my job, but I can't accept your very kind gift. It wasn't at my instigation, you see. The owner is the one who insisted I call you and offer you the apartment immediately. He is the one who is owed your gratitude. I merely oversee the day-to-day running of the building for him, but he is very much in charge and adopts a hands-on approach when it comes to all the tenants, their needs, any problems that arise and so on."

"Oh," Hayley said dumbly.

Thinking quickly after having such a surprise dumped on her, she looked back up at the manager. "Do you . . . do you have paper and a pen I could use? I'd like to write him a proper thank-you note, and would you ensure that he receives the brownies then, since you say I have him to thank?"

If anything the manager looked even more discomfited. He fidgeted and appeared very nervous, but eventually he gave in with a nod, returning behind the counter and then producing a single sheet of paper and a pen.

She set the brownies down on the counter and then picked up the pen, positioning the paper just so. Biting into her lip, she gave herself a brief moment to assemble her thoughts and figure out what to say, and then she began writing. A minute later, she folded the paper carefully and then set it atop the plastic container holding the brownies.

"Thank you for seeing that he gets this," she said softly.

"You're quite welcome, Miss . . . Hayley," he amended. "Now are you ready to see your apartment?"

Her smile was instantaneous. "Oh yes, I can't wait to see it. I'm already packed and ready to go. All I need are the keys and a quick look around, and then I'll go back and fetch my belongings and move in today."

He smiled indulgently and then gestured toward the bank of elevators just down a short hallway leading to a fire exit. Hayley was surprised to see two elevators when she wasn't sure if there would be even one. Some of the other apartment buildings she'd inquired into had more floors but only one elevator. It would appear the owner had the convenience of his tenants in mind when remodeling the building. It was an older building, but it only showed its age on the exterior, so it wasn't likely the original model had two elevators.

When they reached the elevators, she was further surprised to see a single elevator set off to the side away from the other two. Miles must have seen her perplexed look because he offered an explanation.

"It's strictly for the use of the owner," he explained without going into further detail or explanation.

He ushered her inside, and once more she was taken aback by the fact that the elevator appeared new and state-of-the-art. It was also fast. They zipped to the top floor in no time at all. So far Hayley was impressed greatly by her new home and she hadn't even been inside her apartment yet.

When they got off, Miles turned to the right but she saw two other units to the left, spaced wide apart. It appeared there were only three apartments on the fifth floor, and hers was the one all the way down the hall. An end unit. Even more wonderful. Less chance of disturbing any neighbors when she practiced her violin. Was this perfect or what? It certainly seemed too good to be true.

Miles inserted the key and explained that one key opened the regular lock while another was for the deadbolt. As soon as he opened the door, she was greeted by the smell of . . . new. New paint. New everything. He showed her how to operate the deadbolt and pointed out the chain, which appeared to be sturdy and not easily broken, a fact she was grateful for.

She sucked in her breath when they ventured farther into the apartment. He'd said small, but the living room was spacious. By New York apartment standards, at least. There was a galley kitchen, but she was fine with that. It was perfect for one person and she could cook and bake comfortably within the confines of the small kitchen. The living room was magnificent, though.

She walked from the kitchen into the living room and noted that the hardwood floors gleamed, obviously new and not cheap by a long shot. It was good-quality real wood, giving the place a homey, comfortable feeling.

The furniture, however, surprised her the most. It too was brand-new and extremely comfortable looking. Nothing like the often threadbare furniture that adorned so many furnished apartments, used who only knew how many times and abused in any number of ways. There was no musty smell to indicate old or dirty. Everything reeked of being brand-new and not just new but quality. High quality.

It puzzled her because with the insanely low rent being charged for the apartment, she wouldn't have expected it to be furnished at all. But so far everything was positively luxurious.

Miles looked expectantly at her. "Would you like to see the bedroom?"

In her awe over the kitchen and spacious living room she'd completely forgotten about the bedroom and the bathroom. She nodded eagerly and followed him through the doorway into the bedroom.

Once again her jaw dropped because the bedroom was nearly opulent. It looked . . . feminine. Almost as if it had been designed and furnished with a woman in mind. But surely that was impossible. How could they know whether their prospective renter would be male or female?

The bed was positively sumptuous and queen size! She sat on the mattress with a bounce and nearly groaned in pleasure as the softness immediately molded to the contours of her body. It was like sitting on a cloud. She couldn't imagine what it would be like to sleep on.

Her gaze scanned the rest of the furnishings to see a vanity and a wardrobe but also an open closet that was almost large enough to be considered walk-in, another oddity. There was no way she could fill all of the space provided for storage with her meager belongings.

Reluctantly she rose from the decadent mattress and walked toward the bathroom. By now, nothing should surprise her, but despite that thought, she was surprised. There was a claw-foot tub against the far wall as well as a separate shower stall that was huge. There was even a double sink and a tall cabinet against the opposing wall where towels and other necessities could be stored.

It was as if the owner had accounted for every possible need when renovating and furnishing the apartment. Why would he offer such a low rent when he could easily fetch four times as much—and even at four times the current amount, the apartment would be snatched up within hours.

She didn't have the answer to that question, but she wasn't about to overlook her sudden good fortune. With only three days until she would be homeless, her circumstances had certainly been dire, and to have this opportunity suddenly land in her lap was truly an answered prayer.

Reluctant to leave the confines of the apartment that was now hers, but knowing she needed to go collect her belongings so she could move in and settle, she walked back toward the living room.

"Thank you for showing me around, but I really need to go now. I need to get my things so I can move in."

"A driver is waiting outside to take you home. He will help carry your belongings out of your apartment and assist you in bringing them up to your new apartment," Miles said. "It's the same driver who took you home the other day."

Hayley flushed. "I couldn't possibly accept your offer. It's too much and I don't want to be a bother. I don't have much to move, so it won't take me long. I'll just get a taxi."

As before, Miles said the same thing.

"I insist," he said. "It's obvious you have no one to help you, and the owner was very specific that someone help you with your belongings."

Hayley's brow furrowed in confusion. Just who was this mysterious benevolent owner whose kindness befuddled her? Why would he care? And why would he insist on giving her a ride home, not once, but twice, the second time with instructions for the driver to help carry out all her things and then help her move them into her new apartment?

She shrugged, because again, she was looking a gift horse in the mouth, and she wasn't too proud to admit that she did indeed need help. Had needed help. And the mysterious owner had come through for her at a time when her need was at its greatest.

"When you pass along the brownies and my thank-you note, please express my sincerest gratitude for his going out of his way to have someone drive me to and from my apartment. Tell him I'll never be able to thank him enough."

"I'll do that, Hayley. Now come. The driver is waiting out front to take you back to your apartment."

5

When Silas's buzzer sounded, signaling a call from the front desk, his automatic reaction was to scowl over the unwanted intrusion. But once he realized this was the day Hayley Winthrop was to move into her apartment, his scowl disappeared as he strode toward the phone that was a direct line to the front desk or his manager's office. If there were any complications, he wanted his manager to deal with them. He paid his man quite a large salary to do just that. He didn't want to reveal himself to Hayley. He was too disoriented by his reaction to her, and he felt a rawness when thinking of her or picturing her that was completely alien to him.

"Yes," Silas said tersely into the phone.

There was a brief hesitation that annoyed Silas. Then his manager seemed to find his voice, and it was filled with discomfort.

"Mr. Goodnight, sir, uh, I have something for you. Shall I bring it up? I was asked to deliver it to you personally. There's a note as well," he added hastily.

Silas's brow furrowed. How the hell would anyone know to leave anything for him with the manager? It wasn't public knowledge that he owned the building. It wasn't even in his name, but rather under the name of one of the numerous dummy corporations he "owned."

"What is it?" Silas asked in an icy tone.

"It's a . . . gift," the manager said shakily.

"Bring it up."

He hung up, glaring at the phone, irritated that his solitude was being disrupted. He would reprimand his manager, who damn well knew Silas's order for him not to be interrupted unless under dire circumstances. Someone sending him a gift hardly constituted an emergency situation.

Still, his curiosity piqued, he waited impatiently for his manager to arrive. Then realization struck him. It was likely from Evangeline. She was forever doing nice things for him and Drake's other men. Then he frowned. Surely she hadn't dropped it by herself. No, if she had she would have come up herself. Besides, he would certainly have been apprised if Evangeline had planned an outing. She was under heavy guard, well into her pregnancy, not far from her due date. Her outings were few and far between these days because of Drake's paralyzing fear of something happening to her.

Drake had good reason, given the fact that his wife had been abducted just after New Year's when she was already two-plus months pregnant and no one had even known she was carrying a child. Drake had come perilously close to losing both the woman he loved *and* their child.

Perhaps she had merely arranged to have the gift delivered to him, which would explain why it had been left with his manager and not brought directly up to him.

When a knock sounded, Silas unlocked a series of deadbolts and then opened the door to see his manager, pale and sweaty, fear in his eyes. What the fuck? The man was holding a plastic container and he acted like it had a bomb inside it.

Mr. Carver thrust the container at him and then placed a folded piece of paper atop it.

"I'll just be getting back downstairs," he mumbled. "Have a good day, sir. If there is anything you require, just let me know."

Then he all but ran back to the elevator as if the hounds of hell were nipping at his ankles. Silas shook his head. Was he that much of an ogre that his own manager had been nearly paralyzed with fear over breaching Silas's privacy?

He smiled ruefully. He had been rather adamant in his demand for privacy. He shouldn't be surprised over his manager's fear. Silas had always instilled a healthy dose of fear in anyone he had any regular dealings with. He cultivated that fear and respect, found it useful, and it suited his purposes. If people feared him, then they tended to give him a wide berth so he never had to worry about anyone getting too close.

The only people who meant anything to him were his brothers and Evangeline. The wife of the man Silas had pledged his allegiance to. Silas was Drake's enforcer. He would die for all of them. Drake. Evangeline. His brothers. They were his . . . family. Evangeline had done that for them. Made them all see that they were more than a group of men who had sworn loyalty to one another and worked together under Drake.

He stared suspiciously at the container he held in his hand and at the note on top of the lid. Setting it aside, he carefully put every lock back into place and then went from bottom to top, unlocking and relocking, and then top to bottom once more as was his habit of ensuring the locks were all set and no mistake had been made.

The ritual set his mind at ease. It was a compulsion, just as was his carefully arranged and obsessively tidy apartment and his absolute adherence to his strict routine. Control was essential to him. No, not just essential. It was everything. He controlled every aspect of his life.

He controlled those around him. Everything had to be in perfect accord or he didn't sleep.

He glanced at the container he'd laid aside and opted to open the note first. When he realized who it was from, his heart jumped and sped up, an uncharacteristic event to say the least. He glanced over the elegant, feminine cursive, even brushing over the words with the tip of his finger as if to absorb them into his skin.

Something deep inside him began to thaw and warm as he took in the sweetly worded thank-you from Hayley Winthrop. Reverently he folded the paper back as it had been and then folded it over one more time so it would fit into his pocket. Then he slid it inside his jeans where it would be safe from damage and so it wouldn't be lost.

Then he opened the container and the aroma of rich chocolate wafted to him. He sniffed appreciatively and to his consternation, his hand trembled as he reached to pick up one of the neatly cut squares of the decadent-looking confection.

It was my father's favorite dessert.

One of the lines of her note came back to him as he bit into the brownie and savored the burst of flavor on his tongue. She'd referred to her father in the past tense. Was he no longer alive, then? Remembering that she'd listed no one on her application under the emergency contact section, he wondered if she was truly alone in the world. Like him.

But no, he wasn't completely alone. He had his family. Even if he preferred solitude most of the time. He could no longer get away with appearing when he was needed and then disappearing, staying away for days at a time. Evangeline would have none of that. In addition to their weekly takeout date, she insisted he and the others come to dinner, lunch, sometimes breakfast. Basically any time she deemed it was "family" time, they all gathered at Drake's apartment to be spoiled and pampered by Drake's wife.

Who did Hayley have? Did she have anyone at all to look out for her and watch over her? He had the sinking feeling that she didn't, and why that should bother him, he didn't know. He only knew it bothered him a hell of a lot. A girl like her alone in the city? A woman whose goodness and innocence shone from her eyes like a beacon? It might as well be a welcome sign for every predator within a ten-mile radius.

He cursed savagely. He was not taking her under his wing, damn it. But even as he made the fervent vow, he knew that he could no more turn away from her than he could ever turn away from Evangeline or any of his brothers. He didn't have to be close to her in order to protect her. Didn't have to be within touching distance.

Even if every part of him ached to be just that.

6

Silas opened his bedroom window as had become his habit during the last week and then settled onto his bed in a comfortable position, his gaze fixed to the ceiling as he waited.

And then it began. He closed his eyes as the first beautiful, heart-rending strains of the violin spilled into the night and slid into his bedroom, wrapping around him, capturing him in their sensuous web.

Hayley was extremely talented for one so young. He was well acquainted with fine music, and he knew talent when he heard it. This woman was destined for greatness, of that he was certain.

Every night since the night she'd first slept in the apartment next to his, she'd played her violin, her window open to allow the music to blend with the sounds of the city and the night. Before, Silas would have only heard the sounds of traffic, only slightly quieter this late at night, but now he only heard the exquisite melodies she played and the poignancy with which she captured every note.

He wondered if like him she seldom slept. She was rarely at home and only late at night, and then she spent hours practicing, her music soaring in power the longer she practiced. Some nights she didn't sleep at all because she played until the first streams of light bathed the sky and then he saw her leave the apartment building on the surveillance cameras he had installed when he'd first purchased the property.

He knew she only attended classes part-time. The rest of the time, it appeared she worked. He frowned at the unwanted distraction from the peace that had descended the moment she'd begun to play. She was always either attending class, working or practicing her violin. When did she sleep? When did she simply take time off to enjoy life? It didn't appear as though she had any sort of life beyond work, school and practice.

Yet she'd found the time to make him homemade brownies. Her father's favorite.

A peculiar sensation settled into the region of his heart, and it was habit to reach for the note she'd written him, one he'd taken out many times in the week since he'd received it. He handled it with utmost care, reading again her written words, tracing every line and curve of her letters with his fingers as if he were in some way touching her. Even now he simply rubbed the thin paper between his thumb and fingers. He found comfort in it and he was at a loss as to why.

No one had ever done something so unselfish for him. Except Evangeline, who was forever going out of her way to spoil all of Drake's men rotten. But apart from her, no one had ever made anything for him.

But this . . . from Hayley. It was different. He loved Evangeline like the sister he'd never had. Yes, he'd warned Drake that if he fucked up things with Evangeline again, he'd step in, take care of Evangeline and ensure that she never lacked for anything the rest of her life, but he hadn't meant in a romantic sense. And Evangeline's kindness, as well as her homemade gifts and her cooking, were for all of Drake's men. She didn't grant preferential treatment, though Silas knew that he and Maddox had a closer friendship with Evangeline than the rest of Drake's men did.

Hayley's gift was solely for him. Not something she'd done for others. And somehow he knew that it wasn't something she did often. It was an arrogant assumption but he clung to it, needing it to be true whether it was or wasn't. That she'd taken the time to make him something she'd said was her father's favorite, to write her sincere thank-you and to share something so special and intimate with him, made him feel ... worthy?

Even as the thought crossed his mind, he shook his head. He wasn't worthy. That was something that could ever be said of him. His soul had been damned when he was a mere child. A child who'd for all practical purposes died when he was but eleven years old, and from the ashes had arisen a monster, far older than his eleven years, with knowledge of evil no child should ever have. But when had he ever been just a child, innocent and filled with the knowledge that he was safe, cherished and loved?

He'd seen more as a child than most people ever saw in a lifetime. And since then he'd killed when necessary, never suffering a useless emotion such as remorse when the men he'd executed deserved far worse than his swift mercy. He did his job coldly and without emotion, knowing it was kill or be killed, knowing he must protect those he'd sworn to protect and also knowing that while his actions could hardly be justified and he would never receive absolution for his sins, the men who'd died by his hand deserved far, far worse than quick death.

They were animals. Undeserving of life and of the power they so carelessly and brutally wielded. They rose to power on the backs of countless men and women and on the suffering they so casually inflicted. The rare times Silas slept, he could hear their screams. The victims all crying for justice. They preyed on his mind and his consciousness, at night in the dreams that would forever torment him, but also during the day, always there, a weight he couldn't get rid of.

It was as though they were solidly ingrained in his psyche and silently judging his every action, holding him accountable for the deeds he'd done and the sins he'd committed in the name of brotherhood, loyalty and justice. No, his wasn't the kind of justice held up by polite society. He had his own brand of justice, a code he adhered to and never deviated from. He'd lived by his own set of rules ever since gaining freedom from the horrible slavery that was his childhood and from his very earliest memories of his life. Never again would he be in subjugation to another. Never would another wield such power over him. He was his own man first. Drake's enforcer second. Of all Drake's men—brothers—Silas was the only one Drake never gave orders to. He knew well the folly of doing so. Silas offered his loyalty and protection to Drake freely, and Drake knew that. He also knew that if at any time Silas was no longer content to remain in the shadows, an instrument for the kind of justice he and his brothers believed in, there was nothing Drake could or would do to stop him.

Silas's thoughts stilled and he tuned back in to the notes that flowed from the violin. She was playing something new. Not a melody he'd heard until now. A cold shiver slid down Silas's spine at the sheer, haunting ache that seemed instilled in every note. It wasn't a selection that was light and airy or even melancholy, as some of her choices were. What music poured through his window each night seemed to be a reflection of her current mood.

He sat up, drawn to the grief that almost seemed tangible in the air. The melody reverberated over the walls, over him, leaving him awash in the innate sadness the tune was heavy with. And yet it was the most beautiful song he'd ever heard. Nothing she'd played until now even compared, and everything she played was perfection. But this . . . this was so much more . . . personal. Yes, that was what he'd been grasping for, an explanation or rather description of what the music sounded—felt—like to him.

The grief and sadness embedded within each individual stroke of the bow were heavy and suffocating, blanketing his entire bedroom with the forlorn sound. Chill bumps erupted and prickled a path across his skin. Was she, like him, all alone in this world? Did she have no one to share her grief with? And who or what was she grieving for?

True, the song could be nothing more than a new song added to her repertoire, one assigned to her by one of her teachers. And yet he discounted that notion as soon as it crossed his mind. There wasn't a single mistake in its performance. No jarring notes to indicate a miscue. It was simply too smooth and too practiced, unlike the other songs she often played when practicing, when she'd sometimes miss a note or simply stop in the middle, only to begin again until it was perfected to her liking. He admired her for that. She was obsessively a perfectionist, never settling for simply good. She strove to be flawless.

But tonight's choice held no mistakes. The song seemed to pour from her very soul as if she'd practiced it a million times before and had memorized every single note, needing no sheet music before her. He imagined her sitting close to her window, violin up, resting against her cheek, her eyes closed as she played with all of the passion for music—and life—she seemed to possess.

It was deeply personal to her. He knew that like he knew so many of the other things he couldn't possibly be so certain of. He didn't know her. Had never even seen her face-to-face. It was ridiculous of him to think he knew anything at all about her, and yet his instincts never guided him wrong and he knew all of his assumptions about her were not assumptions at all. They were fact.

What pain did she hide from the world only to be released in the predawn hours of the night when no one was around her, when there was no one to hear her or see her? He knew if she realized that he could hear her playing, that he listened to her practice every night, she'd likely be appalled and embarrassed, and worse, she'd likely shut her window, never to open it again when she played. And he couldn't bear the thought of that.

Somehow, in the mere week since she'd taken up residence next door to him and had begun her nightly serenade, it had become necessary to him. Vital even that he be here each night at two in the morning when she began to play. Some days she practiced a few hours only, and then silence descended and Silas imagined them both drifting into sleep together and yet separated by one wall between them. Other nights she played well past dawn, only to hurriedly leave her apartment a few minutes later to either attend class or go to work.

When she played, he remained awake and listened. When she slept, he slept. Unwittingly, he'd fallen into her routine and kept it as his own, even going so far as to arrange his business obligations and priorities around the times he knew she would be playing.

He knew he wouldn't be able to do so forever. Inevitably something would crop up that prevented him from being just a few feet away from her while she sent her soul soaring into the night. There were always things that demanded his attention. The safety of his brothers, and especially Evangeline, superseded all else. And as long as evil existed, and it would never truly be eradicated, the people he cared about would always be in danger. The threat to them all existed everywhere and came from all directions.

Neither he nor his brothers were saints. Silas knew there was a thin line between his self-imposed code of justice and the very evil he kept his brothers safe from. At times the line seemed to disappear altogether, and it was at those times that Silas was more aware than ever that he was just as much of a monster as the ones he hunted down and meted out retribution on. It was senseless to grieve the fact that he wasn't in the least sorry for removing such vileness from the streets and the city he now called home. He knew what he was and what his job was, and he faced both with calm acceptance. The world was a better place without men like the Vanuccis, a crime family that had perpetuated so much violence against innocents that the very foundation of their homes must groan with the weight of so much blood.

Women, children, nothing held any regard or compassion in the Vanuccis' eyes, and they'd proven that over and over. It might take him a lifetime, but Silas was determined to bring every single one of them to justice, along with those who allied themselves with the Vanuccis. His justice, the permanent kind. He would be judge and juror and sentence them to death, where all the power, connections and money in the world held no sway or importance. After death, only your deeds and actions over your lifetime held any merit or weight.

He rubbed his head tiredly, uncharacteristic fatigue making his bones ache. Even the beautiful song of grief pouring into the night next door could no longer offer him solace. Not when he'd brought so much to the surface when it remained buried most of the time. Ridding the world of the Vanuccis wouldn't even put a dent in the threats to what he considered his own. His family. There was always someone else. Evil was pervasive, insidious. There was no cure for it. No way to ever destroy it permanently. The Vanuccis weren't the only murdering, raping sons of bitches in the city. They just happened to be the ones most prevalent in Silas's mind as he sought every day to keep his brothers, Drake and Evangeline safe. They were all targets. The Vanuccis had even placed a bounty on Drake *and* Evangeline. They were furious when Drake, in a very unexpected turn of events, had thrown his support and muscle behind the Luconis and had backed them as they prepared to dismantle the Vanucci family.

But Silas didn't fool himself. He was a realist. A cynic. Cold, harsh and unfeeling. He knew that getting rid of the Vanuccis would pave the way for more organized crime to grow and prosper, and indeed, it would become more prevalent than ever. The Vanuccis were worthless pieces of shit, the entire lot of them, but at least they were powerful enough to squelch and force down anyone else seeking to set up shop in the city. The only other factions with as much power as the Vanuccis, or more, were the Luconis and . . . Drake Donovan. And now that

Drake had allied with the Luconis, the Vanuccis were more desperate and unpredictable than ever.

With a heavy sigh, he closed his eyes and reached for the soothing balm of what he was certain was another's grief. She might be mourning the loss of something dear and her music was an outlet for that grief, but for him the song touched the deepest, darkest recesses of his being. Just for the span of a few moments, he knew peace, even as the song whispered to him of love and loss. For once he wanted to drift to sleep with her music still echoing in his ears, her presence here in his bedroom despite the distance separating them. Tonight he didn't feel quite so alone. Because she was here, sharing her grief and sharing her gift, providing comfort though she would never know that she had. Even as he allowed himself to drift away, held in the warm embrace of pure beauty, he wondered if Hayley felt as alone as he, and if she, like him, had nothing but her music to comfort her. Though he finally fell into sleep, he dreamed of Hayley. Bathed in the moonlight as she played the same song over and over. In his dream he saw the shimmer of tears escaping her closed eyes and silently trekking down her face. Then, since it was only a dream, he went to her, drawn by her pain and suffering, not able to keep from offering her the same comfort she gave him each night.

He drew her into his arms and gently kissed every single tear away. And he held her until finally she slept, whispering to her over and over that she wasn't alone.

7

"That stupid asshole McDuff just had to fuck everything up." Giovanni Vanucci seethed, allowing his temper to flare. He pounded his polished mahogany desk to emphasize his statement and then fixed his forceful stare at the gathered family members. His sentinels, his loyal soldiers, here at his demand.

It wasn't irregular for Giovanni to hold family meetings at his Connecticut home, one of the many places he owned. But here, away from the city and the possibility of surveillance, spies and secrets being exposed, was where he held family meetings, where there was no chance that anything would leak from his private office, a room even his wife and daughters didn't dare enter.

"He screwed up months of our planning and just when we're ready to move on the Luconis, he snatches Drake Donovan's woman and suddenly the bastard is allied with them?"

He knew his face was mottled with rage and likely red as a beet, judging by the concerned expression of his oldest son, Gabriel. He made a concerted effort to calm down so his blood pressure didn't soar dangerously high and he didn't suffer another stroke. The doctors had warned him he likely wouldn't survive another one. But regardless of the need to regain his composure, rage and an overwhelming thirst for revenge pervaded his every thought.

He turned to the only person in the room who wasn't related to him by blood. A man who'd proven loyal to him and had displayed more ambition and loyalty than Giovanni's own sons. His sons knew he favored the man referred to as Ghost and didn't even bother trying to hide their anger or resentment over having an outsider usurp their importance and their role in their father's organization.

As he turned to Ghost, planning to outline his plans and issue orders to him, he saw two of his sons cast belligerent looks in Ghost's direction, while Gabriel's lips merely tightened and his eyes went cold and flat as he continued to stare at his father.

Ghost couldn't possibly miss the animosity directed at him, but his expression never wavered and he looked bored and unbothered by Giovanni's sons' childish temper tantrums.

"There has to be a weak link in Donovan's organization," Giovanni muttered. "One of his men was a snitch for the police, and he disappeared shortly after the police raid on Donovan's club. It's too risky to go after his woman. With her about to deliver a child, the security net surrounding her is impossible to breach. So we have to find another weakness, another hole in their security. All of his men have vulnerabilities. We just have to discover them and take advantage of them. Can I trust you with this, Ghost?"

Ghost gave a clipped nod, but then he wasn't a man of many words, and when he spoke, the others listened. Even Giovanni's sons were too afraid of him to overtly defy him.

Giovanni then turned to his sons, Gabriel, Jacques and Paulo. He knew that in order for them to be competent, reliable assets to the family, he had to give them the opportunity to prove themselves. He just hoped to hell they didn't fuck up.

"I want all three of you on this. I want no angle uninvestigated.

Every lead pursued. And whatever you find, you are to report it immediately to Ghost."

His sons didn't look at all happy with the order to report to someone who wasn't even family, but they also understood the significance of their father asking them to do the duty he requested. It was their opportunity to prove themselves worthy of the name they bore and the chance to move up in the organization they would one day rule in their father's stead.

What they didn't realize was that if they failed him in any way, he'd ensure they never took over the helm. If he couldn't rely on them for such a simple task as this, how was he supposed to leave the running and care of the entire family on their shoulders?

Giovanni waved his hand in a clear signal of dismissal but motioned for Ghost to remain. When everyone was gone, Giovanni slumped back into his chair and rubbed a hand through his hair.

"I'm counting on you," he said wearily. "There has to be a way to strike at Donovan, to bring him to his knees. Without his support, the Luconis will be a piece of cake to take apart and destroy. But until I can remove Donovan from the picture, my hands are tied and every day that passes I lose more power. I will not stand by and allow that bastard to take everything I and my father, my grandfather and his father and his father's father worked our entire lives to build."

"Consider it done," the man called Ghost said in his usual calm voice, his face devoid of emotion.

Giovanni shivered. He would never admit it, but he was as afraid of this man as his sons were, and he had a very good suspicion that he had every reason to be.

8

Hayley walked through the door of her apartment complex and rolled her shoulders even as she attempted to stifle a jaw-cracking yawn. This was her first day off from work since she'd moved in two weeks ago and she was in desperate need of a nap. She'd spent too many nights practicing, forgoing sleep because one of the two jobs she worked required late hours and she often didn't get home until past one, and it was always closer to two in the morning before she started practicing.

A nice long nap would be next to heaven, and then she could cook herself a nice dinner and afterward get an earlier start on practice so she could get a few extra hours of sleep before tomorrow's first class.

As she punched the button to the elevator, the doors opened and a woman who looked to be in her late thirties or perhaps early forties was coming out. She stopped once she saw Hayley and gave her an assessing look.

"You must be new," she said cheerfully. "We've never met. I'm Patricia and I live on the fourth floor."

Hayley returned her smile, sticking a hand out to hold the elevator. "I'm Hayley. I live on the top floor."

The woman's eyes rounded with surprise. "You must live next to the owner, then. Wow. To my knowledge the top-floor units have never been rented out before. It's rumored the owner values his privacy very much."

Hayley was equally shocked. She'd never seen her neighbors, but then she kept such odd hours she wouldn't have had the opportunity. But the owner lived in the complex? That she hadn't known.

"Well, I was told a top-floor unit was undergoing renovation," Hayley explained. "When I first came in to inquire as to vacancies, only a basement unit was available. The manager called me shortly after and said the owner had just called to let him know that the top-floor unit was finished and to rent it out." She shrugged. "I guess I just happened to be in the right place at the right time."

The woman's expression was skeptical, but she didn't argue the point.

"Do you know which unit he lives in?" Hayley mused. "I live on the end and I've never seen anyone else on the top floor, but I'm not often at home."

"I believe he takes the middle unit, but I'm not certain. Like I said, the owner is very private. I don't recall actually ever seeing him." She frowned. "For that matter, I don't think anyone in the building has ever laid eyes on him."

Pondering that oddity, Hayley gave the woman a friendly wave and then pressed the number of her floor as the doors slid closed. She frowned as the elevator quickly soared to the top floor and she stepped off, eyeing the door to the middle unit, even pausing outside it, straining to hear if any sound came from within. But there was only silence. No sound of a television or movement. With a shake of her head she continued on to her apartment only wanting a nap and to snuggle into the luxurious bed that she'd barely spent any time in since she'd moved here.

Guilt nagged at her, though, twenty minutes later when fresh from a shower she'd curled up beneath the covers. She tossed and turned, mentally cursing the fact that she couldn't simply relax and sleep. Usually if she had difficulty resting, she'd simply play a few selections on her violin to settle her, and then she found she could sleep much better. But the violin wasn't what occupied her thoughts. Thoughts of her neighbor, the owner who'd been so kind to her, were what kept her from rest.

She owed him a great deal of gratitude. Had he gotten the brownies she'd baked for him? When she'd made them for the manager and he'd nervously informed her that it was the owner who deserved her thanks, she hadn't had time to compose a more heartfelt thank-you. Perhaps she could make him something else and this time write a more personalized note to him. She could even bring it over and knock on his door; after all, it was better to thank him personally.

Patricia's warning came to mind. The owner valued his privacy and none of the tenants had even seen him before? That seemed highly unlikely. But then Patricia had also seemed shocked that he had agreed to rent the top-floor apartments that flanked his. With the low amount he was charging for rent, maybe he needed the additional income.

Now that the idea had taken root, she knew it would be impossible to sleep. With a disgruntled sigh she scrambled out of bed, casting one last longing glance at the comfortable mattress. So much for a nice relaxing afternoon.

She took inventory of the groceries she'd stocked, mentally going over her repertoire of recipes and comparing them to the supplies she had on hand. The last thing she wanted was to make a trip to the market a few blocks away. It would take too much time.

Her eyes lighted on a can of condensed milk and a bag of toffee bits, remembering she'd bought the stuff to make her caramel pie on a whim. There was only one graham cracker pie crust and only enough whipped cream to make one pie, so she couldn't afford to screw it up.

It would take a few hours for the condensed milk to boil and become the thick caramel filling she used in the pie, so she started that first, filling a large pot with water and setting it to a low boil. After placing the can in the water, she pulled the rest of the ingredients from her small pantry and the fridge and laid out the cream cheese, heavy whipping cream, vanilla, pie crust and toffee bits on the counter. Realizing there was little she could do until the caramel was done and had cooled enough not to melt the chocolate-covered toffee bits, she decided to use the time to practice her violin. Perhaps instead of practicing late this night, she'd get in her practice now, finish the pie and take it to her neighbor, and then she'd have a simple dinner and go to bed early. The idea of an actual whole night's sleep was extremely enticing.

After putting the whipping cream back in the fridge, she left the cream cheese out to soften to room temperature, and then she went to open the window closest to the chair she sat in to play. She pulled the violin from the case and lovingly ran her fingers over the worn and faded wood, tears suddenly burning like acid in her eyes.

"Oh, Daddy, I miss you so much," she choked out.

For a moment she simply hugged the aged violin to her chest and bowed her head, allowing herself, for the first time in a very long time, to weep for her loss.

Silas let himself into his apartment on silent feet and then turned and began the comforting, necessary ritual of locking and unlocking the many deadbolts that guarded the entrance to his apartment. Satisfied they were secure, he then set about ensuring that his space—and the complex—was secure from threat. It was a habit ingrained in him, as necessary as breathing.

As he sat in his chair where security monitors surrounded him, a distant echo caught his attention. He became still, senses alert as he strained to discern the source. Then the muffled strains of the same haunting melody she'd played for the first time several nights ago barely reached his ears, but he knew instantly that she was home and playing.

He uncharacteristically shoved away from the monitors, not having completed his sweep of the premises, something he *never* did, and hurried into his bedroom, to his window, pushing it open to allow the beautiful music inside.

Before Hayley moved in, opening a window in his apartment was something he would have never even contemplated. It was a security risk. Someone could access his private domain, and he held his privacy and his space sacred. No one dared encroach on it. There were a hundred other risks he took by opening his window and making himself vulnerable, but he was simply unable to resist the call of her violin.

With his windows closed, they were nearly impenetrable. All were top of the line, bulletproof and shatterproof. It would take a high-powered bomb to penetrate the glass and provide someone access to his apartment. And yet now, he found himself easing onto the edge of his bed, the soft breeze blowing inside, concentrating on each note, the raucous noise of the city falling away as he narrowed his concentration only on the heavenly sound seemingly carried on the wind by angels' wings.

He shook his head, wondering if he was finally losing what was left of his mind. He wasn't a poetic man at all, even if he did have a preference for fine music, food and wine. He had promised himself many years ago, when he'd given up all dreams of being a normal child and living a normal life, that he would leave dirt and poverty behind. Never again would he go days without eating only to then rummage through garbage bins, so hungry it mattered little what he stuffed in his mouth, and then be chased away like vermin by angry store owners who thought he was there to cause trouble.

His self-worth had been stripped away long before he even knew what self-worth was or what it meant. He'd never been given the opportunity to be a human being, instead regarded as little more than an animal since his unfortunate birth. Hell, even animals were treated more humanely than he had been.

But he'd made a solemn vow to never again be moneyless or powerless, and by God, he'd followed through on that vow. He had more money than he would ever spend in a lifetime, and yet he had no one to leave his vast wealth to. He'd set his course, choosing a solitary existence, only embracing the men he called brothers, men like him who'd seen the darker side of humanity, men who'd been shaped and scarred from the travesty of growing up in appalling conditions, never knowing what it was like to have someone love or care about them. Drake was the exception. He was a fortunate man to have found a woman—Evangeline—who accepted the darkness that lived inside him, in them all. It hadn't been easy. Drake had very nearly destroyed—twice—the very woman who ended up saving him from the barren existence Silas and the rest of his brothers lived.

Such would never be for Silas. He carried too much darkness with him. Far more than Drake or any of his brothers. His demons were strong, alive and growing stronger all the time. His life was too dangerous to ever consider allowing anyone too close. They would only suffer because of him and the choices he'd made. He didn't regret those choices or choosing a life that was solely devoted to the protection of Drake and the others. He'd given his allegiance and loyalty freely to Drake, knowing that Drake would never betray him. But that was all Silas had room for, and it occupied his entire life. Every minute of his days—and nights—was filled with one aim. He'd give his life for any of his brothers, and now Evangeline, or Angel as Drake had so appropriately deemed her.

It was likely that one day he would indeed die for one or more of those he'd sworn his loyalty to, but he embraced this duty as he did everything else in his life. With calm acceptance and no regret. Drake had much reason to live now. He had a wife he loved beyond measure, and a child who would arrive in less than two months. For the first time, Drake's life had purpose and meaning beyond their group of brethren and the business of amassing wealth and power. And Silas would absolutely sacrifice himself to ensure that Drake never lost what he'd claimed as his, because without Evangeline and their child, Drake would no longer have any reason to live and their empire would crumble to dust. Silas would never allow that to happen while he had breath in his body. Drake needed him. Their brothers needed him. Evangeline and her unborn child needed his protection. And Evangeline was one of very few people in this world to whom Silas readily gave his regard, affection and unwavering support. She was the only person who could make him truly smile, and before her, he could not remember when he'd smiled at anyone, even himself.

A sudden and unwanted thought intruded upon his introspection. Would Hayley manage to give him a reason to smile? Could he ever be in her presence and *not* smile? He shook off the ridiculous notion, pissed beyond measure that he was fucking *obsessed* with a woman he'd never even met and her nightly gift of music. He had to break her hold on him. Had to get away during the times she practiced, or he feared losing his focus at a moment when he could not afford to have his concentration anything but absolute.

And yet the mere thought of not hearing her each night as he lay in his bed was more than he could bear. Even thinking of running, escaping, being somewhere else instilled something remarkably like panic deep within him, and he was not a man who ever panicked. He was cold, ruthless and had no emotion, good or bad, when performing his duties. Emotion had no place in his dealings. Emotion made people rash, hasty. It made people make mistakes, second-guess, or hesitate. And any of those possibilities meant the difference between living and dying, killing or being killed, protecting those he was sworn to protect or failing them. He could never live knowing he had failed the people he had vowed no harm would ever come to.

For how long Silas sat there, transfixed and soothed by the notes Hayley wove together, he didn't know. She was a magician, able to tame the beast when nothing or no one else could. Did she realize the extent of her gift? He was so lost in his thoughts and the oddity of *feeling*, just for a brief moment, of being at complete peace, something he couldn't remember ever experiencing, that he didn't realize the music had stopped until silence blanketed his bedroom, taking with it his ability to feel . . . joy, *contentment* and the brief respite from the rage that always simmered so close to the surface.

He bowed his head, feeling the loss as keenly as if his heart had been cut from his body. He curled his fingers into tight fists, angry that he *allowed* her this control over him. Her music. Even as he realized the futility in blaming her for what she had no knowledge of. Then the realization that he had no power over *allowing* or *not* allowing her anything instilled a feeling of helplessness and of being powerless, two things he'd vowed never to be again. No matter his fury or the vicious war he waged within himself, he was forced to acknowledge that he had no ability whatsoever to break the power she had over his emotions, thoughts and mood. And that made him feel more helpless and vulnerable—*defenseless*—than he'd felt since he was just a child.

He stood abruptly and stalked back to the living room, livid at himself for not completing his security sweep of the perimeter. It was a practice he *never* deviated from. Every time he left and then returned to his apartment, he always went over every single area his cameras kept a steady eye on. He had traps set inside his apartment, ways of knowing if anyone had been within, and yet he'd forgotten everything the moment he'd heard Hayley's violin.

He swore viciously, enraged with himself for being so easily distracted. Distractions were what got a person killed. He was the man Drake was depending on to keep him and Evangeline safe, and yet Silas wasn't even able to maintain his own security and see to his own safety thanks to his new neighbor, a woman he should have never softened toward. He should have never offered her the apartment adjoining his. To this day he was still bewildered by the sudden urge that had come over him when he saw the anguish and desperation in her face. It was so unlike him to ever give in to impulse and yet not only had he demanded that his manager offer her the apartment, but he'd also ordered him to have his driver see her home and then he'd paid the contractor an obscene amount of money to reconstruct the walls and make what had been one huge apartment spanning the entire top floor into two apartments so Hayley would have a place to live.

Stupid. Impulsive. Irrational.

And all three were a recipe for disaster and actions a man like him should never succumb to—had never succumbed to. Until now.

The only plausible explanation for his uncharacteristic behavior was that Hayley had reminded him far too much of Evangeline in that dark time when Drake had believed she had betrayed him, had betrayed them all, and had thrown her out of his life. Perhaps the incident wasn't as far removed from his memory as he'd thought. Yes, that had to be the only reason he'd acted on such impulse and refused to turn away a young woman who looked so vulnerable and desperate.

He meticulously checked the indicators that would let him know if anyone had entered his apartment during his absence. When he'd studied each one, three times in succession, he then went back to the monitors, disturbed and uneasy by the deviation in his routine. He always locked up first. Then he reviewed footage from each of the monitors, rewinding and watching until he was satisfied that there had been no intruders. Then and only then did he check his traps. After strict adherence to the routine that had become automatic—until now—then and only then would he see to his personal needs, but even those were carried out in exact order. Until fucking now. He cursed savagely, venting his frustration for the disruption, because *any* deviation from his routine greatly unsettled him and threatened his fragile hold on his sanity.

As a result of the change in the order of his tasks, and because his anxiety was so great he could barely breathe much less pull himself back together, he rewound the security footage once, twice and then a third time until he was finally satisfied that no one had trespassed on his private domain. Still tense, he went to his liquor cabinet and poured a drink in an effort to calm his rioting thoughts. He sank into the leather chair facing the monitors and ran a hand raggedly through his hair.

He had to do something about her. She couldn't remain so close. She was driving him to the brink of insanity. She was a huge distraction. One he couldn't afford. And yet the thought of making her leave and denying himself the healing balm of her music made him feel bereft. Lonely when he'd been alone his entire life, and before now it had *never* bothered him. He embraced solitude and isolation. He was far more uncomfortable in the presence of people than when he was alone. He *knew* how to be alone. He didn't know how to *not* be alone.

To his utter astonishment, shame and guilt suddenly plagued him. Shame he was well acquainted with, having lived it for the first eleven years of his life. Since then he'd refused to feel shame for any of his actions. But guilt? He was flabbergasted that for even a brief moment he had felt an emotion that wasn't just foreign to him. It was, quite simply, something he had never even imagined he was capable of.

He recognized his selfishness, though, and shame and guilt both accompanied that realization. He'd thought to get rid of Hayley, remove her from close proximity so he could go back to his well-ordered and disciplined existence, yet he couldn't deprive himself of those precious few stolen moments when her music gave him beauty and peace such as he'd never known. Were it not for that one thing, he likely would have his manager move her somewhere else, citing repairs that must be made. Having already been witness to the desperation and sorrow in her eyes, how could he be a complete bastard and turn her out when she'd unknowingly given so much to him? He knew damn well how much she needed the apartment he'd given her. He'd seen—hell, he'd *felt*—her joy and gratitude over his renting it to her. And yet, were it not for what she gave *him*, he'd put her out on the streets without anywhere to go and no way to protect herself from the evil he was only too well aware existed there. He truly *was* the monster he'd been deemed.

He slammed his empty whiskey glass down in frustration. She was driving him insane and they hadn't even met. In the two weeks she'd lived here, he'd felt all manner of things he'd never allowed into his mind before. Selfishness, shame and, worst of all, fucking guilt. He had to do *something* or she'd make him weak, defenseless and ineffective as the enforcer for the people he protected. Because how could he focus on his primary objective when his thoughts were consumed with a woman who didn't even know he existed?

He was so absorbed in self-loathing that at first he didn't register the knock at his door. When it sounded again, his head came up, nostrils flaring as anger seized him. Too much of his routine had already been destroyed today. And now some idiot was knocking on his door? If it was his manager again, he'd have his fucking head. The man knew not to ever disturb Silas and, above all, *never* come up unannounced to his apartment.

Never one to chance anything, he stood and slipped his gun into the shoulder holster he always wore. Then he secured his knives in their rightful places on his body. When he was fully armed, he threw on a light jacket but kept the front open so he could easily access his weapons. Then he went to the door, uneasiness gripping him. But when he glanced through the peephole, he nearly stumbled back in shock.

Hayley?

What the hell was she doing here? How had she even known he lived here?

He forced himself to calm his rapid breathing and still his racing pulse. Perhaps she didn't at all know who lived here. Perhaps she was merely being neighborly. Or maybe she had a problem or needed something—help.

His mind sorted through the various possibilities at the speed of a computer. She seemed to be every bit as much of a loner as he was. He never saw anyone at her apartment. She never entertained. Didn't seem to have friends, or at least no one she invited over. But then she was rarely at home. For that matter, what was she doing home so early today?

It was the thought of her needing help or having a problem that made Silas go against his every instinct and begin unlocking the series of deadbolts. If it had been anyone else, he would have simply ignored the knock and left whoever it was to conclude no one was home.

When he got to the last lock, he realized, to his consternation, that his hands were trembling. He took a step back, sucking in a deep breath to compose himself, and then he slowly rolled the doorknob in his palm and eased the door open.

9

Hayley swallowed her nervousness as she knocked a second time, deciding that if no one answered she would simply leave the pie on his doorstep with the thank-you card, and she'd simply write the instructions to promptly refrigerate the pie at the bottom of her note.

She was about to squat to set the pie to the side when she heard fumbling with the locks from the inside. She quickly rose, her mouth going dry. She wiped her free hand down the leg of her jeans to rid it of the clammy moisture and waited as she heard more locks being undone.

She frowned. How many locks did the owner have on his door? Was he aware of danger to the apartment building that she wasn't? Perhaps he was simply paranoid. She suspected he was an elderly man, perhaps even retired, and renting out the apartments to supplement his pension. She could hardly fault him for wanting to feel safe.

But when the door finally opened, Hayley's mouth fell open as she stared into the face of a man who wasn't remotely elderly or even middle-aged. She shivered at the cold flatness to his eyes and the fact that his expression portrayed irritation and surprise and was definitely not welcoming. In that moment, she knew she'd made a huge mistake by encroaching on his privacy. His irritation over the intrusion was plain to see on his face. If her feet had not been rooted to the floor in fear, she would have fled.

He was young. Or at least far younger than she'd imagined, having already conjured an elderly retired gentleman. Yet older than she was by at least ten years. Maybe more. It was hard to tell. He had a timeless look but upon closer examination, there were lines in his face that told of pain and a man aged beyond his years. He was also devastatingly handsome. Tall, very broad shouldered, his chest massive. Even his thighs, encased as they were in faded denim, bulged like tree trunks. There didn't appear to be an inch of spare flesh anywhere on him, and his thin T-shirt would certainly have betrayed such if there were.

His hair, perhaps the darkest black she could ever remember seeing, was a brilliant foil for the dark green eyes assessing her until she squirmed beneath his scrutiny. She could *feel* his gaze, an electric current, as it swept over her, and then when he finally met her gaze, she was thunderstruck. A full-body shiver rolled through her and chill bumps prickled and danced over every inch of her skin.

It was obvious she was intruding and equally obvious the intrusion wasn't welcome. Acute embarrassment seized her, and to her mortification, heat invaded her cheeks at the realization he could surely see the betraying flush.

"Uh, I'm sorry to b-bother you," she stammered awkwardly. "One of the other renters told me that y-you lived here, next door I mean, and I wanted to th-thank you—in person—for renting me the apartment. You have no idea how desperate I was to find an affordable place to live."

She was babbling and knew she should just shove the pie at him and scurry back to her apartment and never, ever bother him again, but she felt pinned motionless by his piercing stare. She felt naked and vulnerable, as if he could see inside her and was privy to her every thought. How insane was that?

Dear Lord, but the man was gorgeous. Mouthwateringly gorgeous. In her wildest fantasies, not that she indulged in many, she could have never conjured such a perfect male specimen. Her knees went positively weak as she took in every aspect of the man standing so rigidly in front of her and committed it to memory. At least she'd have a fantasy to indulge in now. Heck, he would forever be the mother of all fantasies. For the rest of her lifetime, any other man would pale in comparison. There was no comparison. She hadn't felt this shy and awkward since junior high, and here she was supposed to be a sophisticated urbanite embracing life away from the rolling mountains of East Tennessee.

Run. Flee. Escape. Before she made an even bigger fool of herself.

She thrust the pie forward and the man's eyebrow went upward in surprise. He stared suspiciously at the pie she held and then back up at her, wariness still lurking in the rich green pools that seemed so shadowed.

She let out an exasperated sigh, barely resisting throwing up her hands in frustration or surrender. Which one, she wasn't certain of. "Surely you don't think I poisoned it. It's just a thank-you. A more *personalized* thank-you, now that I know it was you and not the manager who was responsible for me renting the apartment next to you."

As she spoke, she slipped the small floral card from her pocket, wincing now at how ridiculous it was for her to have done this. But then she should have pondered the folly of her actions *before* giving in to impulse.

Then the most amazing thing happened. The man's expression, which she would have sworn she could crack a brick on and one that seemed likely more permanent than not, actually faltered as his lips moved upward in a semblance of a smile. Amusement replaced the coldness in those mesmerizing eyes, and all she could do was stare dumbfounded as the smile, small as it was, completely transformed his face. Wow, what would a full-on real smile look like on him?

He took the pie from her and then seemed to be staring at her expectantly. When her brow crinkled in confusion, the amusement in his eyes deepened and his smile grew just a tiny bit more. He had to stop now because if he smiled any more she wouldn't be able to walk the short distance back to her apartment. For that matter, if she didn't breathe soon, walking would be the least of her worries.

"Is the card for me as well?" he asked, his deep voice rumbling from his chest.

She looked down, having forgotten all about taking it from her pocket. She thrust it toward him as well, her hand trembling slightly. Hopefully he wouldn't notice, though he struck her as the type who noticed everything.

"What is this for?" he asked softly, his earlier gruffness fading.

She relaxed a little. "My name is Hayley. But I guess you know that, unless of course your manager oversees all the paperwork and stuff."

Damn it, but she was babbling again, and she never babbled. It was obvious she needed to get out more. Mix with people. Because she'd forgotten how to do something so simple as socialize.

"Anyway," she hastened to add before he could respond. "I wanted to bake you something as a thank-you and give you a card. Instead of a note, I mean." God, she was so lame.

His lips twitched suspiciously. "You already thanked me. The brownies were delicious. Thank you for making them for me."

"I know, but I didn't realize you lived here at the time and, well, I also didn't realize it was because of you I had the apartment, so I just wrote a few words because I was in a hurry, so I thought it was only right that I expressed my gratitude more, or rather properly."

To keep the groan of dismay from escaping her suddenly very busy lips, she gestured toward the pie. "You need to refrigerate it so the topping will set. If you try to eat it now, it will be too . . . messy. It will run everywhere. It's better to leave it refrigerated overnight, but if you absolutely must have some tonight, let it chill for several hours at least."

His lips twitched again and she could swear he was trying not to laugh. Then his expression became something else entirely and while she wasn't at all certain what he was thinking or what his expression meant, it made her feel . . . hunted and wary and yet electrified. Just as quickly his face softened and a glimmer of warmth entered his eyes.

"I'm Silas," he said in his deep voice. "Thank you for the pie. I'm sure I'll love it. I have a sweet tooth but I rarely indulge."

Yes, she could certainly surmise that much. The man was extremely fit.

"It was nice to meet you, Silas," she said, smiling back at him.

He went suddenly still, causing her smile to falter. She took a step back without even realizing that she had or why.

"You have nothing to fear from me, Hayley," he said quietly. "I will never hurt you."

What an odd thing for him to say. But maybe she had been a little frightened for a moment. Stranger still, the way he said it made her believe him, absolutely. Which made her certifiably nuts, since she knew nothing about the man.

"You're very talented."

Her brow furrowed in confusion at his abrupt change in topic. "I beg your pardon?"

"You play the violin. I can hear you at night. You're very talented. I've never heard anything so beautiful."

She blushed crimson. "I'm so sorry. I had no idea you could hear me. I should never have opened my window. It's just that the night, the sounds of the night . . . I find them comforting. They make me feel not quite so alone."

She closed her eyes in mortification at what she'd just shared with a complete stranger. God, she needed to get back to her apartment so she would shut up and avoid making an even bigger fool of herself.

"It won't happen again. I do hope you will forgive me for disturbing you."

His expression became fierce then, and she very nearly took yet another step back but was unable to because she was frozen solidly in place. What on earth had she done to upset him?

"No," he said sharply. "I didn't say that because you were disturbing me or to make you stop. I shouldn't have said anything at all. I enjoy listening to you play. It . . . soothes me, much as the sounds of the city soothe you. And like you, it makes me feel not so alone."

His admission seemed painfully wrung from him, as though sharing such a private thought was something he never did. In that moment, she could see a kindred spirit reflected in his eyes. So much loneliness and pain. Sorrow. Regret even.

"Please, leave your window open while you play," he asked softly. "If I didn't want to hear, I would have never opened my own."

That startled Hayley. That he'd sought out comfort in her music, that it meant something to him, just as it did to her. An outlet. Not just a creative outlet, but a way to express emotions she kept bottled up. Emotions she could never share with anyone else. There *was* no one else.

"Then I'll keep my window open when I practice," she promised, her voice as soft as his.

"Just make certain you always remember to close and lock it at all other times," he said, in what she thought to be an almost protective-sounding tone.

She simply nodded, and then, because she could bear the awkwardness, and her powerful awareness of him, no longer, she pointed to the pie.

"You need to get that into the fridge," she said in a husky voice. "And I need to get back to my apartment."

"It was very nice to meet you, Hayley," he said, gifting her once more with that small glimmer of a smile. "If there is ever anything you need, please don't hesitate to let me know."

She nodded, trying to find her tongue. "Likewise, Silas. And you've alrcady done far more than was necessary for me. Thank you. Perhaps I'll see you around sometime."

There was something in his gaze that made hcr nape prickle, the tiny soft hairs bristling, causing an itching sensation.

Before she lost the courage to walk away, she turned and nearly fled back to the door of her apartment, keenly aware that his gaze followed her until she disappeared inside. She swung it closed forcibly and then lunged for it so it didn't slam loudly, and then she turned her back to it, pressing her body against the wood, closing her eyes as she tried desperately to still the rapid beat of her heart.

10

Silas opened his refrigerator and took out the pie Hayley had made him and set it on the bar. He'd done as she asked and let it chill overnight and eaten the first piece the following morning for breakfast. Those who knew him would laugh if they knew he'd eaten dessert for breakfast when he rarely ate anything that wasn't deemed healthy. He took his body and its care very seriously. But he hadn't been able to resist the temptation of tasting the gift bestowed on him.

It had been delicious. Decadent even. Better even than the things Evangeline made for him. He'd waited all day until he returned, deciding to have another piece in his bedroom while he listened to the sweet strains of Hayley's violin.

He cut a small piece, placed it on a saucer and then collected a fork and went into his bedroom, knowing that Hayley would begin her practice any moment, and he didn't want to miss a single minute. Her schedule, like his, was extremely regimented. He knew when she left the apartment and when she returned. Knew her work schedule. He frowned because she worked far too many hours and that, coupled with her classes and her practice time, left her little time to sleep, if any. He had seen the fatigue in her eyes, but he'd seen something else as well that discomfited him. Grief. Something or someone had caused her pain. If he knew the source, he would destroy it. She deserved to be happy and carefree. She was young and yet she seemed to bear the weight of the world on her shoulders.

He ambled into his bedroom and propped himself against the headboard of his bed, taking the first bite of the delicious caramel pie. He checked his watch, frowning because it was ten minutes past the time she normally began her practice. Then he shook his head. She could have gotten off work a few minutes late, or she might be doing things around her apartment. It was ridiculous, this obsession with her and the fact that he monitored her every movement to the minute.

He forced his thoughts from the distraction she caused and finished the slice of pie, setting aside the saucer on the nightstand. Still, impatience simmered and tension grated on him. His nightly ritual had become a necessity. A need he couldn't explain.

He sat there for a long time, lost in his thoughts, going over the events of the day, the concerns he had about the Vanuccis and his worry that they would strike at Drake or Evangeline. Drake had tripled her security, even going as far as to limit her outings because he lived in terror of something happening to his wife and child. Every man under Drake had the same fear, and they were extra diligent in their protection.

When he glanced at his watch, he swore, not having realized so much time had passed. It was well beyond the time when Hayley began her practice. Dread gripped his insides but he shoved it away. He was being paranoid.

But no, Hayley was predictable. She never deviated from her schedule. Never once had she missed a session with her violin. Swearing, he got up and went into the living room, where the security cams were installed. He rewound them to one thirty and skimmed through the footage, looking for a sign that Hayley had returned home.

Nothing.

He was overreacting. She could have had to work late. She could be at a friend's house. Perhaps she even had a lover and was staying over. That brought a scowl to his face, but he quickly discounted all of his suppositions.

Like Silas, Hayley appeared to be a loner. She'd even remarked that she opened her window because the sounds of the city made her feel not so alone. She never had company over, didn't seem to have friends, and he knew enough about her schedule to know that she didn't have time for any kind of social life. When she wasn't in class she worked two jobs to late hours and then she came home and practiced the violin, sometimes not even sleeping and hurriedly leaving for class without ever having gone to bed.

His gut told him something was wrong, and his gut never steered him wrong. If she was this late, then something had happened. Fear, an alien emotion, gripped and twisted his insides. Where was she?

He knew the route she took from her late-night job. He knew every route she took, having shadowed her more than once.

Before he was even cognizant of doing so, he was on his feet, holstering his gun and sheathing his knives as he hurried toward his door. He'd backtrack her route and hope to hell he found her. Alive.

He took the express elevator that was for his own personal use and slipped into the night, taking the route he knew she never deviated from.

Hayley wearily trudged down the sidewalk, wishing she didn't still have ten more blocks to walk before she was finally home. It had been a long, frustrating day. First, she'd had another unpleasant run-in with Christopher and once again he'd acted like a spoiled, whiny child clearly used to getting his way in all things. He'd demanded to know where Hayley was living now, as though he had the right to such knowledge. He'd stomped away outside the school, a look of rage mottling his cheeks that concerned Hayley because she had a feeling he was only going to become more persistent the more she resisted his disgusting advances.

As a result of the ugly encounter, she hadn't had time to take her violin home and was forced to bring it to work with her, and she was ten minutes late, to the annoyance of her boss, Dan, who was nothing but a lecherous scumbag who thought every woman in his employ was his own personal property, even going as far as to call them "his girls."

As punishment, she'd been stuck with doing all of the cleanup at closing while he let the other women go home. Shelly, a girl close to Hayley's age, had been sympathetic and had offered to remain behind to help, but Hayley had told her to go and not to piss off Dan, or she'd be next on his list and he *would* retaliate.

She'd worked as quickly and as efficiently as possible, enabling her to clock out only half an hour late. She snorted and rolled her eyes as she punched her time card, knowing full well she wouldn't be paid for the extra time. But at least she was done and could head home.

She didn't like walking home so late in the night, or rather so early in the morning hours after midnight. But she didn't really have a choice since there wasn't a subway or bus line that ran close enough from her job to the apartment. Though the city never truly slept, it was quieter, eerie almost, the shadows from the buildings seeming to loom larger, reaching to enfold her in their embrace. She hugged the violin case closer to her chest and firmly pressed her purse between her elbow and her side even as her gaze constantly darted left and right, seeking any possible threat.

The walk home in the dark didn't usually bother her this much. She wasn't sure why she seemed so unsettled tonight. But then she had endured a less-than-stellar day, so perhaps her paranoia was merely the resulting fallout from having confrontations with two assholes.

She relaxed when she was five blocks from her apartment building and picked up her pace, despite the fatigue beating incessantly at her. Maybe tonight she'd forgo her practice session and get in a few hours of sleep, which she desperately needed. She was so lost in the fantasy of catching up on her sleep that she never heard anyone until it was too late.

Strong arms hauled her back against one of the stone buildings and out of the glare cast by one of the streetlights. When she started to scream, a hand clamped over her mouth and she gagged at the horrible smell and taste of the filthy palm.

"Keep quiet, bitch," her attacker growled in her ear.

"Ohh, we got us a nice little piece tonight," a second man said in amusement.

Her heart sank when she realized not one, but three men were preventing her escape. She stood little chance against one, much less three of the street thugs.

Her purse was yanked roughly from her shoulder and one of the men rifled through it, rage mottling his features when he turned it upside down, shaking the contents onto the street.

"Where's your money, whore?" demanded the man whose arm was now firmly around her throat, nearly cutting off her air.

Tears burned her eyelids. "I don't have any," she choked out. "Do I look like I have money?"

"A sweet piece like you?" the third man hooted. "If you don't have money, then you sure as hell have a sugar daddy who does."

"Go to hell," she yelled.

Pain exploded in her face as the one who'd rifled through her purse brutally backhanded her. She could taste blood in her mouth where her lip had split. Warm liquid slithered from her nose, over her lips and to her chin, dripping to the street.

"What have we here?" the third said silkily, wrenching the violin case from her grasp.

"No, please," she begged. "It's my violin. I'm a musician. I have to have it to play."

He opened the case and then swung the violin against the stone wall, laughing when it shattered into pieces. Tears flowed freely and a sense of helplessness and keen grief overwhelmed her. Her violin was all she had left from her father. Without it she couldn't attend school. Couldn't pursue her dream. Couldn't play the music that was so much a part of who she was.

Her head lowered, bowing as tears splattered the ground at her feet, mixing with the blood dripping from her mouth and nose.

"I don't have anything else," she whispered. "I have nothing. Please, just let me go."

The man tightened his arm around her neck until her vision blurred and spots appeared. "Seems to me if you don't have anything of value for us, then we'll have to make do in other ways," he said in a sickening voice that sent chills cascading down her spine.

His hand drifted down her neck to her breasts, roughly fondling them through the thin shirt she wore. Impatient with the barrier, he ripped the shirt and then yanked at her bra, baring one breast to his touch and the other to his friends' gazes.

"Hell, this is better than money if you ask me," the third man smirked. "I haven't had me a piece of ass this sweet in a long time. I want her first."

Hayley went wild, struggling frantically as the implication of his words sank in. She'd die before she let them rape her right here on the street. She tried to scream but she nearly blacked out when she was struck again.

Two sets of hands groped her roughly, mauling her sensitive flesh. Fingers bit into her nipples, twisting painfully and pulling until she cried out in pain. Once more a dirty hand clamped down over her mouth, rendering her silent as the other two men began tearing at her clothing.

When they went to tear her jeans open, she kicked and writhed, desperate in her bid for freedom. A fist rammed into her ribs, completely robbing her of breath. Blackness encompassed her and perhaps she did lose consciousness for a brief moment because the next thing she heard was a terrible sound of fury. Like a wild animal attacking its prey.

Suddenly she was free and she slithered to the ground, her legs too weak to hold her up. She lay huddled there, curling her legs up to her chest in a defensive position as howls of pain erupted and the sound of fists meeting flesh, the cracking of bones breaking drifted to her.

Through her hazy vision, she saw a man systematically taking apart the three men who'd attacked her. He was untouchable, dispatching them with minimal effort. She should have been terrified at the way he meted out violence as if it were second nature to him, and yet she felt . . . safe.

Then he turned, presenting just enough of his profile for her to recognize him. Her mouth fell open in shock and she winced at the pain the action caused her swollen lips.

Silas.

He'd come for her. He'd saved her. Those men couldn't hurt her anymore. How had he known?

She closed her eyes, tears squeezing from underneath her eyelids. Then gentle hands touched her tentatively, seeking a response.

"Hayley? Princess, are you all right? Open your eyes, please."

Silas's pleading tone penetrated the fog of pain that held her firmly in its grip. Her eyelids fluttered open and she moaned at the discomfort the effort caused. Hearing the worry in his voice forced her to acknowledge his plea, and gradually she blinked his face into focus.

His expression was at once savage with fury and full of relief and so much regret as he gathered her carefully into her arms.

"My violin," she gasped.

He turned from her a moment, his gaze seeking the area around them, and when he turned back, there was apology and sorrow in his eyes.

"I'm sorry, princess."

Tears flooded her eyes and she could no longer be strong. She broke into heartrending sobs, Silas's savage curses echoing as if from a great distance away.

"This is going to hurt, princess, and I'm so damn sorry, but I have to get you home so I can take care of you."

"The case," she gasped out before he could cradle her more fully into his arms. "Is it destroyed too?" She bit her lip to prevent telling him why the case was so important. But it didn't seem to matter to him. His sole focus was on her.

"It's here," he said softly, picking up the case that was broken at the handle but otherwise intact. "Be brave for me, princess. I'll get you out of here and then I'll take care of you and you'll suffer no more pain."

She was too numb with grief to pay attention to the horrific pain splintering through her ribs as he gently lifted her into his arms. He stood to his full height, carefully arranging her so her head was pillowed on his chest. Then he strode into the night, his step brisk, her weight seemingly negligible as his long strides ate up the distance to his building.

11

Silas shouldered his way into his apartment, carrying his precious bundle. He dropped the broken violin case on the couch and then cradled Hayley in his arms and took her into his bedroom.

He was shaking with fury, on the verge of becoming completely unhinged. Never was he anything but in control, but coming across those fucking bastards abusing Hayley on the street, threatening to rape her—they *would* have raped her had he not gotten there when he did—the carefully constructed control that he'd held so tightly ever since he'd killed his parents had shattered. And yet he still had the paralyzing fear that he hadn't gotten there in time. What if one of those bastards *had* raped her?

As gently as he was capable of being, he placed her on the bed, cursing when she cried out in pain. Her tears were killing him, but he was helpless to know what to do to make her stop. Every single tear was a dagger to his heart, so much so that he rubbed at his chest in an effort to alleviate the pain. Pain that went deep, so deep he hadn't a hope of touching it or removing it.

He tenderly pushed her damp hair from her face, wincing when he saw the terrible bruises already forming and the blood that ran from her nose and mouth. He wanted to go back and kill them all. Hell, they might already be dead. He hadn't exactly been mindful in his rage. Shit. He needed to call the boys and have a cleanup crew there before they were discovered. But that would have to wait a few more minutes while he tended to his princess.

"Hayley, I need you to tell me where you hurt. Where you're injured. What did they do to you?"

He knew there was agony in his voice, and guilt. He should have acted sooner. He'd known something was wrong when she didn't come home on time. He'd played it off, telling himself that she was running late, that something had come up at work or that she was at a friend's when he knew none of that could be true. She never came home that late, and if he'd listened to his gut, something he never ignored, he would have been there before those assholes assaulted her.

She opened her mouth in an attempt to speak but gasped and closed her eyes. Even breathing seemed to be torture for her.

"My ribs," she finally gritted out. "God, Silas, it hurts to breathe. I hurt everywhere."

His blood froze and he instantly unfastened her shirt, pulling it away to reveal the already darkened flesh around her rib cage.

Son of a bitch!

"Princess, this is going to hurt, honey. I'm so damn sorry, but I need to see if anything is broken. Damn it, I should have gotten to you in time!"

Her bloodied lips trembled, but she nodded bravely and a surge of pride overtook him. And then to his utter shock, before he could carefully palpate her ribs, she reached up with a shaking hand to touch his jaw.

"This wasn't your fault, Silas," she whispered. "I won't have you blaming yourself. How could you have known? I'm not your responsibility. Thank God you came at all. If you hadn't, they would have r-raped me and probably killed me."

Tears welled in her eyes again and slithered down her battered face. Rage flooded his veins and he wanted to smash his fists into the walls repeatedly, but he had to take care of Hayley. He had to calm down so he didn't scare the ever-loving fuck out of her.

"I'm sorry, princess. I'll try to be gentle. Be brave for me, my sweet girl."

She bit her lips and then nodded.

He carefully ran his fingers over her bruised and battered ribs, swearing violently under his breath when she flinched and closed her eyes, holding herself stiff. But she didn't utter a single noise. He admired her strength and resilience, knowing she was in unspeakable pain.

"Goddamn it," he swore when he felt at least two ribs that were fractured. She needed medical care, not just for her ribs but for the injuries to her face. It was likely she'd fractured her nose and possibly her jaw as well.

Already there was significant swelling to her nose and jaw. She looked like a mess and yet she was still the most beautiful woman he'd ever seen. Those sons of bitches deserved to die for daring to touch what was his. And she was his. Even if it wasn't possible in the real world. But to him, she was his, even if it was never meant to be.

"How bad is it?" she whispered, her words slurred around swollen lips.

"You have broken ribs. Not sure how bad, but I'll have a doctor come over to examine you. You're in no shape to go to a hospital. He'll need to examine your nose and jaw to make sure nothing is broken there as well."

"I hurt," she said quietly.

He knew she was in a great deal of pain to have made the admission, and the words broke his heart and made him want all the more to go back and make sure he'd finished the job. The street trash didn't deserve to live for even laying hands on her, much less brutalizing her.

But he had to get it together. She was his top and only priority. If the bastards survived, he'd track them down and avenge his princess.

When had he started referring to her as his princess? He wasn't a man prone to endearments. Evangeline was the first person that he'd used affectionate pet names with, but they were meaningless and harmless. He called her *doll* and *sweetheart*, but then all of Drake's men had done so and they were not touchy-feely men at all. But Hayley was different. She was . . . special.

"Let me get you something for pain and then I'll call the doctor to come right over. While we wait, I want you to rest and let the pain medicine settle in, and you aren't to so much as move until the doctor arrives. Do you think you can swallow some pills, or do I need to crush them up and dissolve them in a little water so you can drink it down?"

She licked her bloodied lips, wincing, and then cast him an apologetic look. "I don't think I could swallow a pill. I'm sorry."

He leaned down so their noses were nearly touching, his expression fierce. "You have nothing to apologize for. I'll be right back with your pain medicine, and then I want you to rest while I call the doctor."

She nodded wearily, her eyelids already fluttering downward. He hurried away into the kitchen and shook two pain pills from the bottle he kept for the migraines that plagued him at times. Using a spoon, he carefully crushed the pills until they were little more than dust, which he then poured into a small cup of water, stirring until it was completely dissolved.

He returned to his bedroom where Hayley lay, her expression one of utter exhaustion and her features strained with pain.

"Princess," he said in a soft voice. "I need you to drink this and then I'll let you rest while I make some calls. Can you do that for me?"

She stirred and when her eyelids fluttered he could see pain dulling her usually vibrant, sparking-with-life eyes. It enraged him that she'd been brutally attacked and that he hadn't been there to protect her.

Never again. She was under his protection even though she didn't know it.

She struggled to get upright, but he gently stopped her, instead cupping the back of her head and lifting just enough that he could place the rim of the small cup to her mouth.

"Drink all of it, my sweet girl. The pain will get better. I promise."

Slowly she sipped, making a sour face as she swallowed the contents. When it was all gone, he lowered her back down and fussed with the pillows in an attempt to ensure her comfort.

"Are you comfortable?" Then he swore. "Of course you aren't comfortable, but what is the best position to take the pressure off your ribs?"

"I'd rather lie flat and never move again," she mumbled, her pain-filled eyes already closing in exhaustion.

He arranged the pillows and blankets, cocooning her so she was as comfortable as he could make her.

"The medicine should take effect more quickly since I dissolved it in water. Hang in there, princess. You'll start feeling relief in a few minutes."

"Thank God," she whispered. "I hurt everywhere, Silas."

He had to work to control the absolute fury that threatened to explode. He turned to leave the room so he could make his calls, but her soft voice stopped him.

"Silas?"

He turned around immediately. "Is there something you need, princess?"

She swallowed, and her eyes went shiny with the evidence of tears again.

"Thank you for coming for me. For saving me," she whispered.

Her sincere gratitude only heightened his guilt. "It's my fault you were attacked. I should have been there sooner," he said gruffly.

She looked at him with faint puzzlement. "But, Silas, how could you have possibly known? It isn't your fault."

He turned and walked out, knowing damn well it was his fault.

His first call was to Drake's doctor, who ran a clinic in Drake's apartment building, and he demanded that the doctor drop everything and get over to Silas's place as soon as possible. Then he called Maddox and briefly told him what had happened and that he needed a cleanup crew, and the details and the location. Then he said he needed the rest of Drake's men to get to his place immediately to ensure that nothing like this happened again. Maddox seemed bewildered because Silas was not a man who ever got rattled, and Silas knew he sounded like he was on the edge, but Maddox didn't probe, merely telling Silas to consider it done, and that those not on cleanup duty would be over within minutes. But he didn't question Silas. That wasn't the way it worked in their tightly knit group. When a brother called with a request or a demand, no questions were asked. It was simply done. They always came, always taking each other's backs, prepared to do whatever necessary to help.

Family.

What Evangeline had made them all. And Hayley was part of it even if she had no idea she now had family or that any one of them would die for her. Just as they would for Evangeline or for one another.

While waiting for the doctor to arrive, he slipped back into his bedroom, expecting her to have succumbed to the medication he'd given her. To his shock and dismay, she was sobbing as if her heart would break.

He flew across the distance and carefully arranged himself on the bed next to her, cradling her gently in his arms so as not to jar her ribs. Hell, he hadn't even cleaned the blood from her, but he hadn't wanted to do anything for fear of hurting her or making it worse until the doctor examined her.

"Princess, what's wrong?" he said urgently. "Are you still hurting? Do you need more pain medication?"

She buried her face in his chest, her tears wetting his shirt as she shook against him.

"It was all I had left of him," she sobbed. "Oh God, Silas, what am I going to do?"

She pressed her face more firmly into his chest as if to stifle her cries, but he pried her away, not wanting to do further damage to her battered face.

"You're breaking my heart, baby. Talk to me. Tell me why you're crying. You have to know I'll do anything to fix this for you."

It seemed a stupid request, but he knew this wasn't about the attack. There was something else that had devastated her and if someone else had hurt her, he'd hunt the bastard down and kill him with absolutely no remorse.

"You can't fix this," she said dully. "I wish with all my heart you could, but no one can. No one can make my dream happen now, and now I can't fulfill my father's dying wish."

She broke off into another round of heartbreaking sobs that made his own heart ache as he shared her pain.

"Tell me about it, Hayley," he said gently. "The doctor won't be here for another ten to fifteen minutes. Tell me what's upsetting you so badly. Besides the obvious."

"They destroyed my violin," she choked out, tears streaming down her bruised and bloodied face. "And now I have *nothing*. No way to fulfill my dream. I can't afford even the cheapest violin, and while I can borrow one for classes at school, they have a strict policy about them leaving the premises, which means I won't be able to practice at home. It's over. Everything he worked so hard to make possible for me is gone, and it's my fault."

"Oh, baby, no," Silas protested. "You can't blame yourself for what those bastards did to you."

Hayley continued on, lost in her bittersweet memories.

"It was just him and me after my mom died, and we were poor, desperately poor. It was everything we could do to make ends meet and have food on the table. He worked long hours at a local paper mill. Every opportunity for overtime, he was on the job, saving to buy me a violin. He wanted so badly for me to follow my dream of playing and becoming a master violinist. But then he got sick. Cancer. I wanted to quit school, get a job so I could pay our expenses and get him the care he needed. I wanted to be with him so he wouldn't die alone. I couldn't bear the thought."

She broke off in a sob and he slid closer to her and gently stroked his hand through her hair, carefully resting the uninjured side of her face against his chest.

"But he wouldn't hear of it," she said, sorrow heavy in her voice. "I received a partial scholarship to a prestigious school of music in Manhattan, but I refused to leave him and I couldn't afford the cost of living here much less paying the rest of my tuition, but before he died, my father told me not to worry, that he had provided for me. It was so important to him that I follow my dreams. I think it became his dream every bit as much as mine, and I truly believe he held out as long as he did so he would know I kept my promise of moving to New York to enroll, because he died just after I moved here and I wasn't with him," she sobbed. "He died alone. Oh God, I left him to die alone, Silas. I'll never forgive myself for that."

"Shhh, baby," he said, running his fingers through her matted hair in an effort to comfort her. "You did exactly as he intended. It was what he wanted, and he waited, he held on just long enough to know you would be okay. You gave that to him. Peace. He didn't die alone, princess. He died knowing that his daughter was going to achieve her dream and his."

She was silent for a long moment, and then she slowly nodded. "Thank you for that, Silas. I guess I never looked at it that way."

Then tears clouded her vision, and she looked away, grief consuming her once more, but he saw something else in her eyes. Not pain, sorrow or regret. He saw unfettered rage. He was so taken aback that he could only stare in stunned silence at the abrupt change in her demeanor.

"Hayley?" he asked tentatively.

"My father wanted so badly for me to be taken care of, for me not to want for anything. He wanted only for me to attend school and not have any financial worries, so without my knowledge, he took out a life insurance policy on himself."

Her words took on a bitter note, the hatred in her eyes glowing like neon.

"When I found the paperwork and filed the claim I couldn't believe how exorbitant the monthly payments were. I can't even imagine how he afforded them or what he had to do in order to afford the payments. But the payout would have been enough to see me through school and pay my living expenses without me having to hold multiple jobs."

Her entire body went rigid even as the tears flowed in never-ending streams down her cheeks.

"I hate him," she hissed. "God, I hate him so much for what he did to my father. To me."

Silas's brow furrowed in confusion. "Who, baby? What are you talking about?"

"The slick, lying, cheating insurance salesman who took advantage of my father's desire to provide the means to fulfill my dream. He charged outrageous premiums and then filled the contract with so many confusing conditions, exclusions and fine print. God, the fine print pretty much made it possible for them not to pay the settlement for pretty much any trumped-up reason they chose to come up with. It was a scam. The salesman was a complete scam artist, and he took every penny my father had and then refused to make the payout when I filed the claim after his death. That's why I can only afford to attend school part-time and have to work two jobs as well as any odd jobs that crop up. I hate him," she said, her voice breaking on a sob. "I hate him for what he did to my father. For giving him false belief that I would be taken care of."

Cold rage filled Silas as he sat there and listened to Hayley's story, forced to pretend idle interest and sympathy when he wanted—and fully intended—to hunt down the cheating bastard and make him pay. There was no way in hell he was going to let her continue to work herself into the ground, attending school only part-time. Not with talent like hers.

Determined to track down the bastard and ensure that he paid Hayley in full, plus interest and extra for her grief, for all the weeks she'd worked herself into exhaustion, he forced his voice to sound casual as he questioned her about the salesman.

By the time the knock at the door sounded, he had more than enough information to find the sleazy asshole, who would pay dearly for fucking over Hayley and her father.

12

Maddox, Justice and Zander filed solemnly into Silas's apartment, casting curious glances at Silas's agitated state. Silas motioned them to sit on the couches in the living room and then excused himself for a moment, saying that he wanted to check in on Hayley and ensure that the doctor was doing a thorough exam.

He entered his bedroom quietly, taking in the sight of Drake's trusted physician cutting off Hayley's clothing. Rage filled Silas, as did a fierce sense of possessiveness. It didn't matter that the doctor was elderly, married and a loyal ally. Silas wanted no one to see what he considered his.

Hayley whimpered in pain as the doctor began his examination, softly asking her questions as a way to distract her from his gentle probing. Then Hayley's gaze found Silas standing in the doorway, and relief filled her face. Her silent plea beckoned him closer and he found himself at her bedside, leaning down to smooth his hand over her forehead.

He bent to press his lips to the crown of her head. "It's going to be all right now, princess. The doctor will take good care of you."

"Will you stay?" she asked, her tone desperate, her eyes wide with fear and uncertainty.

"I'll only be in the next room a few moments while the doctor finishes his exam. There are matters I have to take care of, but I'll be back very quickly, my sweet girl. I won't leave you."

She seemed to relax, her eyes glazed and dull with pain and the effects of the pain medication Silas had given her. Before he did something stupid like settle into the bed beside her and remain at her side, he swiftly exited the room, knowing his brothers had no clue why they'd been summoned to his apartment, a place others rarely encroached upon.

With no preamble and no explanation as to Hayley's place in his life or how or why he had known she was in trouble, he quickly ran down the events of the night. By the time he'd finished, Maddox, Justice and Zander looked absolutely murderous, their expressions black and filled with rage.

"Son of a bitch," Maddox swore. "I hope to fuck you killed the bastards."

Silas shrugged. "My main concern was for Hayley and her well-being. You called in a cleanup crew? I wasn't exactly . . . careful."

As Drake's primary enforcer, it was Silas's job to always be careful and thorough. The fact that he was openly admitting he'd been none of those things tonight told his brothers far more than he wanted them to know.

"Thane, Jax and Hartley are on it," Justice said grimly. "Though I think I'll place a call and tell them to finish the job and then dump the bodies in the Hudson. I doubt scum like them are going to be missed."

Silas only nodded. Then he glanced up at the only people he trusted in the world. "I have a . . . personal . . . favor to ask. I want a man on Hayley at all times when I can't be with her or looking out for her. My loyalty is to Drake and to see to Evangeline's protection. I can't be in two places at once, and so I need someone on her when I can't be there. And keep her out of sight as much as possible, your connection to her unknown. I can't afford to make her a target. Ensure you never take the same route, never take her to any of the places we primarily frequent.

No one can know about her," he said with urgency, knowing full well the consequences were their enemies ever to learn of her existence. Or of her importance to . . . him.

"No problem," Maddox said matter-of-factly. "We'll rotate. Whoever isn't assigned to Evangeline will be assigned to Hayley so that both women are covered twenty-four-seven."

"Thank you," Silas said. "I don't want what happened tonight to ever happen to her again." He paused before saying the next, making the sudden, impulsive decision even as he'd known precisely his course of action the moment he'd learned the reason for Hayley's heartbreaking distress. In a quieter tone, he put forward his request. "I will have to be away for a day, two at the most, as soon as I know Hayley will be all right. It's imperative she be protected while I'm gone, and kept tightly under wraps."

Zander lifted an eyebrow. "Anything you need help with? You know we'll do anything we can."

"It's a personal matter," Silas said, his expression darkening. "Though you can do something for me that will make my job easier."

His brothers looked expectantly at him, waiting for his request.

"I need you to find the whereabouts of the bottom-feeding son of a bitch who fucked over Hayley and her dad when he refused to pay Hayley the benefit from her father's life insurance policy, one he was charged exorbitant amounts for. As a result, she's dirt poor, struggling to make ends meet, only attending school part-time because she has to work multiple jobs just so she can eat and pursue her dream."

He saw the question in their eyes and answered before it could be vocalized.

"I set her up in the apartment next to mine. The one Evangeline used for a few days."

"But hadn't you already made it all into one big apartment?" Justice asked.

Silas nodded. "She doesn't know anything about that. I had my manager offer the place at a ridiculously low amount of rent and had a crew reconstruct the walls and furnish the place so she could move in. Otherwise she would have been homeless in a matter of days."

Maddox scowled and then swore. "Fuck. She's had a hell of a time. She gives 'down on one's luck' a whole new meaning."

"Exactly why I couldn't turn my back on someone so obviously in need," Silas agreed.

"She wouldn't happen to be young, gorgeous and single, would she?" Zander asked in a sly, hopeful tone.

Silas's features turned to ice. "You stay the fuck away from her, and don't you fucking touch her. Your only job is to make sure no one else harms her. If something happens to her on your watch, I'll have your head."

Zander only looked amused by Silas's threat. He exchanged knowing glances with Maddox and Justice, which only pissed Silas off even more. Was he that goddamn transparent? Hell, he'd practically pissed all over her and marked his territory.

"Work out a schedule and then run it by me," Silas said to Maddox. "I'll be with Hayley for the next day or two at least before I go after the bastard who fleeced her father and refused to pay Hayley what was rightfully owed her."

"You got it," Maddox said, rising from his seat, knowing the meeting had come to an end.

The three men filed out as silently as they'd come in, and then Silas was alone except for the doctor and Hayley just a room away.

13

Silas met the doctor as he walked back into the room. He opened his mouth to demand to know what Hayley's condition was, but the doctor motioned him outside the bedroom door and into the living room. Reluctant to leave her alone for a moment longer, he cast one more glance in her direction before finally conceding to the doctor's request.

"She's resting comfortably now," the doctor assured him. "I gave her an injection of pain medication, so she should sleep through the night. I've also left prepared syringes of pain medication as well as prescriptions made out in your name that you'll need to have filled quickly."

"How is she? What was done to her?" Silas demanded, impatiently cutting the doctor off.

The doctor grimaced. "The young lady will be fine, but she underwent quite a trauma. You were correct in your assessment. She has two broken ribs, but they're lower and won't cause any internal damage. I don't think they need to be wrapped, but she'll need to rest and stay off her feet for the next several days to give them time to heal."

"She won't move," Silas vowed.

"Her face is bruised and swollen, but it looks worse than it is. There is no fracture to her nose or jaw. Just bloodied. Her lip is split and her nose took quite a hit, but tomorrow if it pains her, keep ice on it to reduce the swelling. I cleaned all the blood and disinfected the cuts and scrapes to her face, hands and knees."

"Will she be able to play her violin?"

"I don't see why not. Give her a few days to rest and then I see no issue with her continuing her lessons. But she doesn't need to overdo it."

"I'll personally make sure she doesn't," Silas said grimly.

"If you need me, don't hesitate to call," the doctor said. "I'll stop by day after tomorrow unless you call before and check her over to see how well she's healing and take a look at those ribs. If at any point she has any difficulty breathing or her condition changes for the worse, call me at once. If there hasn't been any improvement in her condition or she experiences a worsening of her pain or symptoms, you'll need to bring her into the clinic so I can take X-rays and perform further diagnostic tests."

"Thank you, Doctor," Silas said gruffly.

The doctor nodded and then let himself out of the apartment, leaving Silas free to return to his bedroom.

To his surprise, Hayley was awake and lying on her side, her eyes shiny with tears. He hurried forward, sitting gingerly on the edge of the bed, and touched the uninjured side of her face.

"What is it, sweet girl?" he asked.

Her gaze flashed to his and he saw relief swell in her moisture-filled eyes.

"I thought you'd left," she choked out. "Oh God, I was so scared, Silas. Please don't leave me."

He was baffled by her response and discomfited by the need so clearly outlined on her face.

"Shhh, princess. I told you I wouldn't be far away. Are you still in pain?"

She slowly shook her head. Then her expression turned pleading. "Please stay with me, Silas. I'm so scared. Please don't leave me again."

"I won't leave you," he said soothingly. "You need to rest now, Hayley. You've been hurt very badly."

"Will you . . . will you . . ." She bit into her damaged lip, wincing.

He gently thumbed her swollen lip from her teeth and brushed the pad of his thumb over the torn skin.

"What is it you want, princess? You have to know I'll do anything for you."

Worry filled her beautiful eyes, and fear of . . . rejection?

"Will you hold me?" she whispered. "While I sleep so I know no one can hurt me? I know I'm safe with you, Silas."

He was stunned by the trust she displayed. God, when he was the very last man she should ever trust. He had no heart, no soul, and for the first time he damned that fact, because if he possessed either, he knew she'd own them.

He hadn't realized he'd stiffened until her face fell and embarrassment crawled over her face. She turned her head away, hiding her humiliation in the pillow.

"I'm sorry. I had no right. You've already done so much."

The words were laced with hurt and each one was a tiny dagger to the heart he had sworn he didn't possess.

"Of course I'll hold you, sweet girl," he said, not recognizing the husky timbre of his own voice. "I don't want to hurt you, though."

"You'd never hurt me," she denied.

He kicked off his shoes, hastily stripped out of his shirt—which was still stained with her blood—and let it fall to the floor. Then he removed his pants, leaving his boxers on, before he slid into the bed next to her, carefully arranging himself around her and pulling her into his arms while trying his best not to cause her more suffering.

She let out a contented sigh and almost before he could blink, her eyelids fluttered closed. She snuggled tightly to his body and burrowed her head into his chest, almost as if she couldn't get close enough to him. And then she was simply asleep, her soft breaths feathering over his skin.

Dear God, he wasn't a saint, and having Hayley cuddled against him like a trusting kitten was surely going to send him straight to hell. In no way did he deserve this—her. To have such a perfect, beautiful, sweet and innocent woman in his bed and his arms. But hell if he wasn't going to enjoy their forbidden night and remember every single moment of it for an eternity.

14

Silas awoke to none of his usual alert awareness. He rarely slept deeply at all, and it took very little to awaken him. But this morning fog surrounded his mind as well as a contentment he could never remember feeling. It confused him so much that he almost bolted upright, and then the warm, sweet weight against his body finally registered. *Hayley.*

As carefully as possible, he rolled her to her side so he could get a closer look at her face. As soon as he did, rage filled him again. The entire right side of her face was swollen badly and covered in colorful bruises. Though he knew those bastards were likely on the bottom of the river by now, he wanted to kill them again. Slower. More painfully. Inflict every injury that they'd left on his princess back on them tenfold. A quick death was too easy for them.

Silas reached for the control that was second nature. He didn't want to risk waking Hayley when the doctor had recommended rest. He moved slowly again until he was standing by the bed, feeling an inexplicable loss when she was no longer in his arms. He wasn't sure where these feelings were coming from and was undecided what to do about it. He had promised her he wouldn't leave, but he had some things that needed to be handled before she woke. Maybe he should . . .

He shook his head, equal parts amused and disgusted at himself. He'd never been indecisive, yet here he was almost spinning in circles over the feelings of the sleeping waif in his bed. Determination flattened both the amusement and disgust as he left his room to find her something to eat and look up some information online. He considered letting himself into her apartment to grab her some clean clothes but decided his large shirts would be easier for her to put on. He ignored the part of him that felt satisfaction at the idea of covering her in things that belonged to him. Marking her his possession. It was an idea he liked *too* much.

As he rummaged through his kitchen cabinets he considered what she might like to eat and what would be easiest to manage without causing her pain. He finally settled on oatmeal and some fresh fruit, setting the ingredients aside until she woke. He then went to his monitors and did the repeated scans of the footage from the previous night. No one had been on his floor since Maddox and the other guys left, and he relaxed a little more.

Opening his laptop, he started his search on violins, what were the best brands and who would deliver one to his apartment building. Her talent deserved the best, and he would be damned before he saw that talent wasted on anything less.

Hayley opened her eyes, immediately bereft of the warmth and comfort of Silas's presence. She emitted a low moan when she attempted the simple task of turning over. She stared out the bedroom window, trying to work up the courage to move. Judging by the throbbing already happening in her body, this was going to be excruciating, but her bladder was leaving her little choice. Gritting her teeth and bracing herself for the inevitable agony, Hayley carefully pushed the covers aside and tried to shift toward the edge of the bed. Fire shot through her rib cage and she tried not to cry out. Before she could blink the tears from her vision, Silas was leaning over her.

"What are you doing? The doctor said you needed to rest," he clipped out as he tried to settle the covers over her once more.

Though his words were sharp, there was a distinct edge of worry in his voice.

She closed her eyes. God, could she be any more pathetic?

"Bathroom," she whispered in embarrassment. To be this helpless in front of this gorgeous man, especially after crying all over him the night before, was mortifying. Worse, she'd begged him not to leave her. She'd given him no choice but to sleep in his bed with her.

Seemingly unbothered by her awkward embarrassment, he gently gathered her in his arms, his eyes brimming with apology when she let out one small squeak of pain. He carried her to the bathroom door and slowly lowered her to her feet, holding her arm the entire time to steady her and make certain she didn't do a face-plant.

"Will you be okay in there alone?" he questioned, concern clearly written on his face. "I can—"

"No," she said hastily. "I'll be fine. Thank you," she said in a more steady tone.

Looking unconvinced, he still gave her a nod. "I'll wait here for you. If you need anything, just call out, okay, princess?"

She nodded back, then ducked her head and shuffled into the bathroom as fast as her aching body would allow. After taking care of the most pressing issue, she washed her hands and drew some deep breaths as she contemplated her dilemma. She was alone in an apartment with a man she barely knew but felt totally safe with, even though she'd seen the violent side of him when he swooped in like an avenging warrior to save her. She knew she should report to the police what those men had done to her, but she was worried about Silas. He had hurt them; the crack of breaking bones and thuds of flesh meeting flesh had been hard to miss. If she reported it, would he be in trouble? She couldn't allow him to go to jail because of her.

Pulling open the door, she almost ran nose-first into Silas's chest. A solid, firm chest. Wow, he really had waited *right there*. That was a bit disconcerting. And comforting, she allowed herself to admit. Not to mention very, very . . . sexy, she thought as she eyed his bare chest. Sure, she'd dated boys in high school, but those had been *boys* and Silas was all man. Once her father became sick, the little time she'd had for dating had evaporated and she hadn't had the time or energy to focus on guys. Now, even battered and a little broken, she found she was focusing just fine. She nearly sighed. Timing had never been one of her strong points for sure.

Once again, without asking, he scooped her up and deposited her back into bed. After ensuring her comfort, he took a step back, his sharp gaze looking for any sign of pain.

"I'll get you some breakfast and your medication. I gave you another shot during the night because you looked like you were in pain, but that should be wearing off. Do you want another shot now or would you like to try oral?"

Hayley felt the heat climb up her chest at the word *oral*, and she couldn't form a word to save her life.

"Hayley? Are you okay?" He bent closer to her and she could count the thick lashes around his deep green eyes. "If you don't feel up to swallowing a pill yet, I can give you another injection of pain meds."

In an attempt to rid herself of completely inappropriate thoughts, she forced herself to meet his gaze. "A pill will be fine, I think. And there's no need to trouble yourself with breakfast. I can go home and fix something."

An uncompromising look settled over his face. "No, you won't. Stay there and I'll be back soon with your food and meds. Don't move."

Without another word, he turned and walked away. Hayley watched those thick, sexy thighs carry him out of the room and wondered if she'd lost her mind overnight.

Silas sat on the edge of the bed and watched closely as Hayley slowly ate the bowl of oatmeal and tried to figure out her odd behavior from earlier. If he didn't know better he'd swear that was desire he'd seen in her eyes as he brought her back to bed. But he did know better. An innocent woman like Hayley would want nothing to do with a man like him. She was too smart for that. What he'd glimpsed was likely gratitude and perhaps a little embarrassment, though there was no reason for her to feel either. Not with him. Not ever with him. If he'd listened to his gut and gotten to her sooner, she wouldn't be in this position.

As soon as she set the mostly empty bowl aside, he held out the pills the doctor had prescribed. Dutifully, she swallowed them down with the remainder of her orange juice. An awkward silence fell as Silas watched her, trying to decide what he should do next, since taking her in his arms and holding her now that she was conscious was out of the question, and she stared back, probably wondering how soon she could get away from him. Thankfully, his buzzer sounded and Silas excused himself.

After telling his manager to bring up the delivery, he quickly flipped through all his locks and waited impatiently for him to arrive. Hayley had put on such a brave face today, but he could see shadows lingering in her eyes. He hoped that this delivery would lift at least some of them.

Mr. Carver looked surprised to see him at the door and rushed forward, holding the package as carefully as he would a newborn baby. Silas took it from him and strode back inside, going through the ritual of setting his locks. Once that was finished, he made his way to the bedroom, hoping he'd made the correct choice.

Hayley was still sitting where he'd left her, though she looked more relaxed. Silas suspected the medication was starting to kick in and was grateful to see it. She appeared lost in thought, so he cleared his throat to let her know she was no longer alone. She blinked and aimed a sweet smile in his direction before noticing the case in his hand.

"What is that?" she asked in confusion.

He crossed to the opposite side of the bed, set the case on the bed and opened it. "I know it's not the one your father gave you, and I'm sorrier than I can say about that, but I will not allow your dreams to go unfulfilled." He extended the violin to Hayley, taking extreme care in his handling of it.

Hayley stared at him in shock, then slowly lifted the violin from its case and placed it on her lap. "Silas, I-I don't know . . ." She ran her delicate fingers reverently over the wood. "It's beautiful, but I can't . . ." As her words choked off, she raised her face and Silas could see the tears shimmering in her eyes. "I can't take this."

His brow wrinkled with confusion. Had he gotten it all wrong? Damn it, he shouldn't have even attempted to make it a surprise. He should have allowed her to choose which instrument she wanted instead of him being so presumptive.

"Why can't you accept it, princess? Did I get the wrong one? I'll get you whatever you want. Just tell me what to get."

"It's the most perfect thing I've ever touched in my life," she said softly, still gently tracing the sides.

"Then why can't you take it?" he persisted.

"Silas, it's too expensive. I can't even imagine how much it cost." Earnestness shone in her eyes.

The feeling he refused to acknowledge as disappointment loosened in his chest. She wasn't refusing his gift, nor had he fucked it up.

He gently put his hand to her bruised and swollen jaw, cupping it while making certain he didn't hurt her.

"My gift to you isn't entirely selfless. I can't describe the peace you bring to me when I hear you play. You need to share that with the world. And some punk-ass thugs will not take that away from you," he said tenderly.

He saw her sudden indecision and shamelessly used her sweet and giving heart against her. "Please don't take that from me. Giving this to you would make *me* so very happy, sweet girl."

The tears that had gathered in her eyes slid down her cheeks as she carefully set the violin back in its case and closed it. When she raised her face, a smile of pure joy beamed from her bruised face just before she leaned forward and wrapped her arms around his neck.

"Thank you," she whispered, her lips brushing his neck with every word. As she tightened her arms around him, her breasts pressed against his chest and Silas felt his dick start to harden.

Silas cursed his body as he pushed down the need to tighten his fist in her hair and drag her mouth to his. This was not what she needed or wanted, and he was a bastard for reacting this way to her gratitude. He stiffened, then gently but firmly pushed her back onto her side of the bed.

"You're welcome, Hayley," he said, struggling for control, hating the hurt look on her face. "You should rest now, as the doctor ordered."

Without awaiting her response, he turned and all but fled from the room and the temptation of those sweet, luscious lips on his own.

15

Two days later, Hayley curled up on the couch and watched Silas work at a computer. She had no idea exactly what he was doing, but this had been their routine since Silas had agreed she could finally get out of bed and move around some. She'd suggested she would be fine in her own apartment, but Silas wasn't hearing that. He'd insisted she stay, and she hadn't fought too hard to change his mind. After his rejection, she was sure he'd want her gone, but she'd been wrong. To be honest, if only with herself, she was enjoying her time with him. Though he could be gruff and bossy, it was sweet in a way. And she couldn't deny that her desire for him grew every hour she was in his presence. Staying might not have been the smartest thing she'd ever done, but she was willing to take a chance and see where this—whatever *this* was—led.

"Are you sure you feel up to going back to school tomorrow?" he asked gruffly, continuing a conversation they'd been having. "I think you need to wait at least a couple more days. Stay here until you are more healed."

The very real concern in his voice, as well as how protective and caring he'd been of her since her attack, sent soothing warmth through her entire body. She would love nothing more than to remain here with Silas another few days, but her fingers were itching to play her new violin and she didn't want to fall behind in her classes. The academy was extremely competitive, and too many missed days could very well mean the loss of her scholarship.

"I can't afford to fall that far behind. Besides, I'm sure I've long since overstayed my welcome." She wrinkled her nose and sent him a rueful glance. "I can't imagine you've enjoyed your babysitting stint."

Silas spun in his desk chair and shot her a reprimanding stare.

"You are not an inconvenience, princess. You're welcome to stay here as long as you want. In fact, I prefer it. It gives me peace of mind to know where you are at all times and that you're safe and protected. However, I do need to mention that I *will* be leaving tonight and I'll be out of town for a couple days. I've asked some of my brothers to look out for you until I get back, and now that you've decided to return to classes, they'll be driving you to and from school." He held up a hand as she opened her mouth to argue. "Your safety is not open to debate, princess. You were attacked. And when I'm unable to be here to protect you myself, my brothers will be. I won't leave you with anyone else."

Was it completely ridiculous that she promptly melted all over every time he called her *princess?* And then some of her euphoria dissipated as she processed the words after he called her *princess* and before being so adamant that she remain in his apartment. He wouldn't be there, so of course she wouldn't be a bother to him.

She had to quit reading more into the situation than what was there. Silas was a decent man and a caring individual. He would have intervened if it had been anyone. He'd made it crystal clear that he didn't return her attraction when she'd attempted to kiss him.

She sighed and then conceded, knowing she wouldn't ever win an argument with him.

"Where are you going?" she asked lightly, hoping her hurt and disappointment didn't show on her face or in her voice.

"Business trip," he said shortly, before returning his attention to the computer.

She wasn't offended by his dismissal. It didn't take a rocket scientist to figure out that Silas was an extremely private person. Careful too. Maybe too careful? His behavior resembled that of someone with deep paranoia, what with all the locks and his rigid schedule. But then his paranoia was what had saved her ass, so at the moment, she was grateful for his OCD tendencies.

Her gaze went back to Silas when his phone chimed.

"Evangeline," he answered, with warmth that until now she'd only heard directed at her. "How are you feeling?" Some time passed in silence as this Evangeline apparently answered his question. "Yeah, our date is still on. See you soon, sweetheart."

It felt like a punch in the gut. *Date?* Even if he hadn't mentioned their date, it would have been evident that Silas had feelings for whoever Evangeline was. His entire body language had changed the instant he'd answered his phone. He'd spoken to her with warmth and affection, and he'd smiled as they conversed. Silas rarely smiled at anyone, at least not in the time she'd known him. But then evidently she knew nothing about him at all. No wonder he'd gone so rigid when she'd practically thrown herself at him.

And *sweetheart?* Any warmth or pleasure over his use of an endearment with her was gone. She'd thought it had meant something since he hardly seemed like the kind of man to ever use endearments of any kind. All this time, she'd thought maybe she was special to him.

Shame, mortification and hurt bloomed in her chest. She'd forced him to sleep with her that first night, and though they hadn't talked about it, Silas had been in that bed every night since. Probably to keep poor, pitiful Hayley from begging again. What must he think of her? No matter his insistence that she remain in his apartment until she was fully healed, she realized now she was being unrealistic and too wrapped up in her own personal fantasy. She needed to return to her own apartment before she did anything to further humiliate herself. And she would. She was too attracted to him to pretend she wasn't, and never would she become "the other woman."

She nonchalantly got to her feet and grabbed her purse, which was sitting on the end table. "I just remembered I have to do laundry today or I won't have anything to wear to school tomorrow. I need to get back to my apartment, and since you're leaving, there's no need for me to remain here. I'd feel much more comfortable in my own place anyway. Have a safe trip, and again, thank you."

She flashed a too-bright smile and then walked casually toward the door and had managed to unlock three of the locks when she felt the heat of his body behind her. Her nape prickled in response, and then warm, strong hands slid over both her shoulders. He turned her so she was forced to look at him.

"Princess? Why are you leaving now?" he asked, and he was so close she could feel the words rumble from his chest.

He was staring into her eyes, a confused frown on his face, almost as if he could read her every thought—or was at least trying to. If he had any idea just what her thoughts were, he'd probably trip over himself stepping out of her way so she *would* leave.

Again she adopted the same fake smile and even put her hand on his arm, squeezing affectionately. "I just told you, silly. I have to do some laundry or I won't have anything to wear, and believe me, walking into my classes naked isn't high on my list of priorities."

She managed a teasing, lighthearted tone, but she didn't sound convincing even to her own ears. Judging by Silas's perplexed and somber expression, he wasn't buying her act either.

Praying he would do nothing further to prevent her escape, or worse, continue to interrogate her, she reached for the last of the locks and Silas stepped back to allow her to open the door. She hastily made her way into the hall, trying not to run and look like a bigger fool. She fumbled in her purse for her keys, unlocked the door and only glanced back once with a cheerful wave to see Silas standing in the hallway thoughtfully watching her.

16

The next morning, Hayley crawled out of her bed, refusing to acknowledge the pain and stiffness still plaguing her. She shuffled toward the bathroom with a frown because she could positively see Silas's smug expression that just screamed "I told you so."

And maybe she would have stayed in his apartment for another few days, but after hearing his phone conversation with his "sweetheart" and him stating he would be out of town on business, she got the message loud and clear.

She couldn't help it if his message depressed the hell out of her.

"Damn it," she muttered when she glanced at her watch.

So much for returning to classes today. After doing her laundry yesterday after fleeing from Silas's apartment, she'd been exhausted and in a lot of pain. She'd taken pain medication so she could sleep and unfortunately for her, the medicine worked too well. She'd overslept and her first class had already begun.

With a sigh, she splashed her face with some water and briefly contemplated a shower but couldn't bring herself to be that motivated. Besides, there was no one here to see her. After pulling on her loosest, most comfortable pair of sweats, she made a face at the possible choices for a shirt. Her gaze drifted over to Silas's shirt that lay discarded by the bed.

She'd worn his shirt because it was a button-up and she didn't have to contort her body to get into it and it was several sizes too large for her. She should have given it back to him, but his shirt was her guilty indulgence.

With a shrug, she pulled it on and inhaled Silas's scent. A light shiver ran over her body even as she scolded herself for torturing herself this way.

When she entered the living room, her earlier assertion of there being no one to see her was proved wrong. She stared, eyes wide, mouth open at the three very large, very intimidating-looking men draped all over her living room furniture.

Sweat formed on her brow and she couldn't seem to suck in enough air. She started backing steadily into her bedroom, her gaze never leaving the assembled men. Her chest tightened to the point of pain and her vision went blurry as she heard her own wheezing fill the air.

One of the men looked up, his brows drawn together as he studied her. Then he motioned to the others and said, "Oh shit."

Before she could turn and run and lock herself in her bathroom, a strong hand gripped her shoulder. Instantly panicking, she whirled around but then doubled over as the constriction in her chest became too much.

"Hayley, breathe, sweetheart. You have to breathe," one of the men murmured in her ear.

How the hell did they know her name?

"Fuck, didn't Silas warn her about us?"

"Evidently not. She's having a panic attack."

"Duh. Wouldn't you in her place? She's attacked and nearly raped on the streets and then she gets up to find three Neanderthals in her living room?"

Was this bizarre conversation really happening?

Hayley glanced up in utter bewilderment just as one of the men cupped her cheek, his expression softening.

"Sorry for scaring you, honey. We thought Silas had told you that we were keeping an eye on you while he's out of town."

"You're his brothers?" she croaked out.

The men nodded.

She shook her head. "He did say something about y'all, but that was when he thought I'd be staying at his apartment a few more days. I'm fine. Truly. There's no sense in all of you being inconvenienced this way. I had meant to go back to class this morning but I obviously over-slept, which means I won't be doing anything today except sitting around my apartment and practicing my violin. Tomorrow I'll be sure to get up and go back to classes."

All three men shook their heads.

"No?" she asked, perplexed by their reaction.

"Not no to everything," the one who'd cupped her cheek said. "Just the part about you being here alone at your apartment or you going back to school without us taking you. Just in case you meant that's how you were going to school tomorrow."

"Who are you anyway?" Hayley demanded. "And how did you get into my apartment?"

"Silas gave us a key. And we're here to watch over you and get you anything you want or need. My name is Maddox, by the way."

He thumbed over his shoulder to the two men standing behind him a short distance.

"Those two idiots are Thane and Jax. We won't always be with you. We will be in rotation with another team. But I'll be sure to introduce you so you never have a repeat of your scare this morning."

"I appreciate that," she muttered. "I'm going to go fix some breakfast."

"Already done," Maddox said with a grin. "You just sit down on the couch while I go fix you a plate. Silas also left your medications with instructions for which ones you're supposed to take and when."

Hayley's mouth fell open again. God, she sounded like a two-year-old dropped off at the sitter's place with detailed instructions on when to feed, change and burp her!

She shot Maddox a disgruntled look. "And how long does this go on, pray tell?"

He shrugged. "Not my call. Whenever Silas tells us to stand down and not a minute before."

She threw up her hands and stomped toward the couch. "I'm so glad I'm an adult capable of making my own decisions."

Thane and Jax chuckled, their eyes lighting with merriment.

"So who draws hot-guy duty tomorrow?" she asked dryly when she was comfortably seated. At least as comfortable as she was capable of being when every muscle in her body was stiff as a board.

Jax's eyebrows rose. "Hot-guy duty?"

She rolled her eyes. "Oh, please. Like y'all don't know you're hot."

Thane grinned. "No, but feel free to remind us frequently. I never turn down compliments from a beautiful woman."

"That ain't no lie," Maddox said smugly.

"Just do us a favor and don't call us that in front of Silas," Jax said, discomfort evident on his features.

At that she lifted one brow. They acted like Silas would be jealous or something. Or maybe they had gotten the wrong impression. For that matter, as private and as closemouthed as Silas was, maybe he didn't share personal details with the men he worked with. Like already having a girlfriend.

"Good call," Maddox said, wincing.

"Well? So who's pulling hot-guy duty tomorrow and driving me to school like I'm a kindergartner?"

"You can't fault any of us for wanting to make sure you're safe,"

Thane said in reproach. "You were attacked, Hayley. You could have been raped or killed. It's bad enough those assholes put their hands on you."

Hayley looked at Thane and then the others in disbelief. "So y'all just run around Manhattan babysitting women who've been attacked? Do you even know how bizarre this whole thing is? I've never met you before in my life and you let yourselves into my apartment and then announce to me that you're spending the day with me and you're driving me to and from school tomorrow. Am I the only sane one here?"

Maddox grinned. "Sanity is debatable. And no, we don't run all over the city protecting women we've never met. But you aren't just any woman."

As if that was supposed to make sense to her? She was beginning to think her head had been more injured by her attackers than she initially thought, because things like this just did not happen. Especially not to her.

Maddox approached the couch holding a plate mounded high with food. It smelled damn good. She eyed it suspiciously and then glanced back up at Maddox.

"You cooked this?"

All three men burst into laughter.

"Oh, hell no," Thane wheezed. "We couldn't boil water. We got takeout on our way here. Hope you don't mind but we didn't know how long you would be asleep, so we already ate."

"Oh well, then maybe I'll cook y'all dinner. It's the least I can do for messing up your schedule like this."

Thane cleared his throat and then shook his head.

"No?" Hayley asked again in exasperation.

"Sorry, doll," Jax said. "Our instructions were to make sure you rest and for you not to go anywhere alone. That means not being on your feet in the kitchen cooking."

"Do you know how ridiculous that sounds?" she asked around a mouthful of food. "I may not have gone in to class today, but I do have to go to work tonight. In fact, as soon as I finish eating, I have to call all of my bosses to make sure I even still have a job."

The thought disheartened her so much that all she could do was stare glumly down at her plate.

"Don't say it," she said in a thready whisper when she saw Maddox about to protest. "I have to work. It's bad enough I've already missed three days. I'll never be able to pay my bills, rent or the part of my tuition my scholarship doesn't cover. They were kind enough to allow me a payment plan for my tuition, but if I miss a payment, they'll revoke my scholarship and I certainly can't afford the full tuition on my own."

She was nearly in tears as the direness of her situation hit home. For the last few days, she'd stayed at Silas's and had existed in a dream world. One where she mattered to him more than any other neighbor did. And she hadn't even considered the possibility of her losing one or more of her jobs. Her bosses weren't the most understanding people in the world.

"Don't cry," Jax said desperately.

If she hadn't been so upset, she'd have found amusement in the panicked looks on the three men's faces.

Thane plopped down on the couch next to her and gently put his arm around her shoulders and then squeezed.

"Silas took care of all that, Hayley. There's no need for you to be upset. I promise everything is okay."

"Worked out what?" Hayley demanded.

"He spoke to all your bosses and to the school the day after your attack. You were in no shape to go to work or school and Silas knew how important both are to you. The school was more than happy for you to take a few days to heal, and your bosses said to take as long as you needed. They're even paying you sick time until you go back."

"What? They don't give any employee sick leave. The only leave they give you if you're sick and can't go to work is the permanent kind of leave, and that definitely doesn't come with a paycheck," Hayley said acidly.

"Apparently they do," Jax offered lightly. "They told Silas that you could pick up your paycheck at the end of the week and that you would be paid full wages."

She stared at all three men suspiciously but none of them so much as flinched.

"Which means that today you aren't going to so much as leave your apartment," Maddox said smugly. "And if you must return to school tomorrow, fine, but I'm putting my foot down about work. You have to at least take off today and tomorrow and rest as much as possible."

"Putting your foot down?" Hayley mouthed. "Who died and made you king of the castle?"

"Darlin', if you think any of us is going to face Silas and tell him we didn't follow his very explicit instructions regarding you, then you've lost your mind. Silas is not a man anyone ever wants to piss off," Thane said cheerfully.

Hayley threw up her hands. "Whatever. Y'all are just going to have to listen to me practice, then. It's not like there's anything else to do."

"We'd be honored," Maddox said. "Silas said you were very good."

Hayley flushed. Why couldn't she be attracted to one of these guys? They were definitely hot with a capital *H* and they were cute when they flirted. But she felt . . . nothing. A big fat zero—nothing. She bet money they were single, unlike Silas. It figured she'd finally start noticing men the way a woman notices a man like Silas only to discover he's off the market.

Her appetite gone, she leaned forward to put her plate down on the coffee table. She sucked in her breath sharply when pain lanced through her abdomen.

"Whoa there, honey," Thane said, easing her back onto the couch. "Better take it easy. Those ribs need to do some more healing before you abuse them further. Maybe you should think about taking a nap and practicing your violin later this afternoon? You'll need to get into bed early tonight if you plan on going back to class tomorrow."

Despite the fact that a nap was the very last thing she wanted, she got up with Thane's help and shuffled like an old woman toward her bedroom. At least she could be alone with her brooding, and she also planned to have a very long conversation with herself about falling for the wrong guy.

17

To Hayley's surprise, Thane, Maddox and Jax not only remained in her living room the rest of the afternoon, but they also spent the night sprawled all over her tiny couch and the floor. But before everyone had said their good nights and Hayley had been ordered to bed to rest, they had encouraged her to play her violin for them. After nervous hesitation she agreed. What shocked her the most was the obvious appreciation for her talent in their eyes and expressions.

Granted, no one should be judged on their appearance, but still, these men did not look like classical music fans at all. They were a rung or two above street thugs, no doubt. Not to mention a hell of a lot sexier and more badass. But they looked like they'd prefer heavy metal or hard rock over Tchaikovsky or Bach.

When they applauded her last number, she flushed to the roots of her hair and peeked shyly up at them as she bent down to secure her violin in its case. Unable to help herself, she ran her fingers over the glossy wood one more time, marveling for the one hundredth time that this was hers.

God, it had cost Silas a small fortune! She knew exactly how expensive the violin was. God knows she'd spent enough time mooning and pining over fine instruments, looking but never touching. Never in her life would she have imagined owning such perfection. What exactly was it that Silas and his partners did anyway?

Silas certainly wasn't the older retired gentleman she'd imagined owning the apartment building. And surely even owning the entire building wouldn't allow for him dropping thousands of dollars on a whim to replace her broken violin that cost a mere fraction of what her new one did.

She studied the men's manner of dress with a thoughtful expression. Definitely higher than a rung or two above street thugs. She wasn't even sure why that had popped into her mind. Their clothing was impeccable and very expensive. At first she hadn't noticed the designer clothing because the men who wore it weren't flashy in a GQ, preppy, polished manner. They were all gruff, with big bodies and bulging muscles—that just happened to be adorned in very expensive, exclusive clothing from designers she couldn't afford even in a secondhand shop.

And there was the fact that Silas had said he'd be out of town on business. After she'd awakened from her nap, Jax had gone out for supper while Thane and Maddox took turns asking her questions. One of which had been where she was from. Thane had said he'd noticed her southern accent—as if it were that hard to miss—and said that he too was from the south and hadn't realized how much he missed it until Evangeline had dropped into their lives.

At the mention of Evangeline, Hayley had gone completely rigid. Maddox had shot Thane a fierce look of reprimand that Hayley pretended not to notice but was definitely intrigued by. Did they know about Evangeline after all? This was getting more humiliating by the minute.

When she'd very nonchalantly and in a very innocent voice asked who Evangeline was and if she was from the south too, Thane had mumbled, "No one important." All the while Maddox had been glaring him down.

She'd never been so tempted in her life to blurt out, *What the fuck?* Why was everything such a huge freaking secret around these guys?

It was a big relief when she walked into her living room the next morning and saw an all-new hot-guy babysitting squad camped out waiting for her. She issued a shy wave.

"I guess Maddox, Jax and Thane have been relieved of duty. Or more likely just relieved in general that they didn't pull back-to-back babysitting gigs. I'm Hayley," she announced, determined not to react to their presence as she had yesterday when Maddox, Jax and Thane had scared the ever-loving crap out of her.

"Zander," one of the men rumbled as he rose.

Hayley stared as he seemed to go up and up and kept going. Good grief, the man was tall, not to mention barrel-chested and broad-shouldered. Geesh, and to think she'd been afraid of the others. Zander was kind of scary but in an "oh thank God he's on my side" way.

To her surprise Zander approached her and tipped her chin up with his fingers as he inspected her face.

"It's looking a lot better," he rumbled. "The others told me how bad it was. Glad to see you're recovering so well. You're a fighter."

Approval gleamed in his eyes and then, without another word, he turned and walked back to where he'd been sprawled on her too-small couch. Alrighty, then. Apparently he was almost as short on words as Silas.

"I'm Justice," one of the other men said as he stood, smiling. He winked at her and she was instantly charmed.

"And I'm Hartley," the third chimed in. "But I won't be around for long, sugar. I'm only standing in for Maddox for a few more minutes. He should arrive by the time you roll out for school."

Hayley frowned. "How come he's going to be here again? He said you all would be rotating shifts around me."

Hartley shrugged. "Silas was adamant that Maddox stick with you like glue, so unless all hell breaks loose somewhere else, Maddox will be with you until Silas returns."

Hayley's heart sank a little more. She hadn't heard a single word from Silas, and she'd consoled herself by telling herself that she doubted he would check in with anyone. He was just too . . . solitary and independent. But evidently he was checking in with his men on a routine basis. At least long enough to give them orders.

Get over it already. Not like you ever had a shot at him anyway.

She was saved their scrutiny when her door burst open and Maddox hurried in.

"Ah good, I made it on time," he said.

To her surprise, he gathered her shoulders with one arm and gave her a quick squeeze followed by an affectionate kiss on her forehead.

"I'm rolling out, then. Gotta run by and get Evangeline," Hartley said.

This time it wasn't only Maddox who glared at whoever brought Evangeline's name up. Justice and Zander both sent Hartley glacial stares that had him grimacing. Hayley's stomach churned with jealousy and she didn't even know the woman. This so wasn't like her! But they all seemed so protective of Evangeline. They spoke of her with affection in their eyes. Well, unless Hayley was around. Then they clammed up tight like they were guarding national treasure or something.

She pretended not to have even heard Hartley say Evangeline's name. Instead, she lifted an eyebrow and with complete innocence asked, "Whatever are all of you scowling at poor Hartley for? Wow, somebody didn't get out of bed on the right side this morning."

She shook her head for exaggerated emphasis and then turned as though she weren't expecting a response. But she hoped . . . Good thing she hadn't set her hopes up too high because she would have been disappointed once more as the room fell silent while she gathered her violin and purse.

"Shall we?" she drawled out. "Though I'm going on record how stupid this whole thing is. I don't need anyone to drive me to school and pick me up."

Maddox ignored her. But then what else was new anytime she said or did anything they didn't approve of?

"What time do you get out of class, Hayley?" Justice asked as he fell neatly into step beside her.

She was amazed at how easily the three men encircled her, all the while making it look completely natural and not at all planned. Maybe personal protection was the business they were in. It would certainly make sense given all the locks on Silas's door and his many paranoias, though with Silas it seemed more . . . ingrained. More a part of who he was rather than what he did for a living. All of his men wore power like a second skin and were obviously used to being in absolute control, but with Silas she sensed it extended far beyond his career choice and was a necessity. Like food, water and air were for everyone else.

"Usually by one in the afternoon. Sometimes earlier, though." She shrugged. "And sometimes later. It really depends on how long we stay and practice."

"Okay, then what time should we be there to get you today?" Maddox interjected.

"Wow, you mean you all aren't staying at the school? You know, in case there's a bomb threat?"

"Silas didn't say she was such a smartass," Zander said, amusement heavy in his voice. "I like her."

Maddox rolled his eyes. "You would. And no, Hayley. We aren't staying the entire time. We have a few things we have to wrap up, but we will be there no later than twelve thirty. If for some reason you get out before then, I want you to stay in the building and call one of us. I've already programmed all our numbers into your cell phone. Use them. And don't go anywhere without us. Got me?"

She resisted rolling her eyes again. Barely.

Instead she saluted him, which sent Zander into another round of laughter.

"Do I need to clear any side trips with y'all?" she asked as she slid into the back of a very sleek, luxurious car.

Oh heaven, but the leather was covered in the heady aroma of new-car smell. It had to belong to Silas because surely no one else he associated with was such a neat freak. She couldn't see a single speck of dust anywhere. She was almost afraid to touch anything.

"What kind of side trips?" Justice asked warily.

"Market on the way home? I need groceries."

It was a lie, but then again it wasn't. She technically did need groceries, but not the kind she planned to buy. She wasn't in the least bit domestic and her father had never minded a single bit. He did all the cooking even though she'd tried time and time again to get him to teach her so she could take over the preparation of at least some of the meals they shared in the evenings.

But twice now she'd overheard conversation between Silas's men, when they had no idea she was within hearing distance, and they'd gushed on and on about how awesome Evangeline's cooking was. How it was manna from heaven, a gift from the gods. Blech. There was only so much Hayley could stand. The damn woman, whoever she was, was perfect. The men revered her and put her on a pedestal.

And apparently Silas was dating her. Lucky him.

Her sarcasm was starting to burn even her. God, she sounded—and acted—just like a jealous bitch. It was an emotion that until now had been utterly foreign to her, and it left her bewildered by the power of the feelings Silas stirred within her.

Again, why couldn't she be attracted to any of his six business partners? Six hunky, drool-worthy alpha males. Most women would kill to be surrounded by so much testosterone on a daily basis, and yet she was pouting and sulking like a child because the one man she was attracted to obviously didn't return her attraction.

No, she might not be a goddess in the kitchen, but there was at least one meal she could kick that was guaranteed to rock their world. Then maybe they'd quit running out for takeout every single night. It made her feel guilty that they were forever paying for her meals when she couldn't afford to eat out every day.

"Hayley? You with us?"

She shook herself from her dour thoughts and retrained her gaze on Justice.

"I was asking why you needed groceries," he explained patiently.

"Because I don't have them and I need them to eat?"

He sighed, but then conceded. "All right. We'll run by the market on the way home. Although if you want, you could just tell me what to pick up and I'll run by and get it on our way to pick you up this afternoon."

She considered his offer for a moment. Since it did take a while to prepare the meal in question, it would be good if she had all afternoon to soak the fish.

"I'll text it to you," she said.

He grunted as if surprised he'd actually won an argument with her for once. As if she ever won when they had their minds set on something.

18

As soon as Hayley started down the steps of the school, she immediately saw Maddox, Justice and Zander standing by an illegally parked car. Not that they gave a damn. Someone would have to be a fool to tell them to move. Before she hit the bottom step, Justice was beside her, his hand cupping her elbow while Zander reached for her violin case.

"Seriously, guys. It's sweet of y'all to hover over me the way y'all do, but this really isn't necessary. I feel like a helpless Barbie doll with the way y'all treat me. Like I'll break or something."

"You did break something," Maddox growled as they approached the car. "Or do you forget those bastards breaking your ribs and doing their best to break every bone in your face?"

"Oh yeah. That," she muttered. Then she glared back at him. "Do you ever lose an argument or fail to have the last word?"

His smug smile told her his response without him having to say a single word.

"Y'all may be hot, but you're also annoying as hell," she said under her breath.

She heard Justice and Zander choke beside her while Maddox just laughed.

"Hot? Did she say we were hot?" Justice asked between wheezes.

"Just don't say that in front of Silas," Zander rumbled.

"What is with warning me not to talk about y'all's hotness in front of Silas?" she asked in exasperation. "First, he doesn't care who I find hot or not and second, he doesn't get to decide who I say is hot."

The three men stared at her with open mouths, and then they burst into laughter until tears rolled down their cheeks.

"Oh man, this shit's going to get really interesting," Zander choked out.

"Where are my groceries?" she demanded, sending Justice a quelling stare.

"I brought them to your apartment and put everything away."

She nodded and slid into the car. Arms crossed over her chest, she continued to stare them down all the way back to her apartment building.

As soon as she let them all into her apartment, she went into the kitchen and did inventory, making certain Justice had gotten everything she had requested. To her surprise, he'd been very exacting, as exacting as she had been in making her list. He'd gotten every single item down to the nitpicky details.

She prepared the buttermilk marinade for the fish, guaranteed to take all the fishy smell and taste from the flesh, and then set it back in the fridge to soak for a few hours. Then she laid out everything she needed for the fries, homemade hush puppies and homemade coleslaw, including homemade tartar sauce.

It was the extent and full range of her culinary skills aside from baking. Desserts, she kicked ass at. But actual meals? Not so much. So she and her dad had a deal. He made dinner and she took care of desserts. Except for her grandmother's secret fish fry recipe that had been handed down over several generations. Even her father hadn't been privy to it, and so Hayley had been forced to learn it on her own and eventually she perfected it. It was a meal her dad asked her to make at least once a week. They even went down to his favorite fishing hole to catch their own catfish. Although Hayley drew the line at cleaning them. That was her dad's job.

She surveyed the ingredients on hand and then decided on an absolutely delicious Mississippi Mud sheet cake. She would have to remember to ask if Thane would be back the following morning so she could save him a piece and see if she measured up to a Mississippian.

After popping the cake in the oven to bake, she opted to go shower and change her clothes. It had been more humid than usual today, but then tomorrow was supposed to be rain, rain and even more rain, hence the dense humidity that reminded her all too much of the constant humidity in the south.

She breezed past the guys in her living room, smiling when they called after her, demanding to know what she was cooking, accompanied by groans and comments of "whatever it is smells damn good." She hoped so. As childish as it was, just one time, she didn't want to be treated to someone's recitation of all Evangeline's virtues. And if the food didn't work and they hated it? She'd kick them all out of her apartment and no matter what Silas ordered she'd never let them back in again.

Satisfied with her plan of vengeance, she hurried through her shower, excited to get dinner started. New Yorkers were notoriously late dinner eaters, but she was too accustomed to eating early. Six was considered a late dinner where she was from. So she and her father always ate between five and five thirty.

She was delighted that she moved far easier today without the residual stiffness and discomfort she'd suffered since the night of her attack. Oddly enough, she'd suffered no nightmares. In fact, she didn't even think about that night. But then she had stayed with Silas the first few days. She'd slept in his bed, in his arms. She refused to feel guilt, because at the time she didn't know he was seeing another woman. That was for his conscience to bear because he should have told her. And well after Silas had left on his business trip, his men had rotated in and out, keeping her busy and occupied. She wondered if that was why Silas had asked them to sit on her—so she wouldn't be completely alone to deal with the fallout of her attack. She had to at least give him credit for that, because if that had been his plan, it had certainly been successful.

She flashed a smile at the three guys lounging on her ridiculously small furniture—but then they were ridiculously large men—watching a baseball game on the big-screen television mounted to her wall. The TV had amused her when she'd moved in, but after meeting Silas, it made sense that he would have furnished his apartments with things that pleased him.

"How long is it going to be?" Justice asked, his voice suspiciously whiny.

She grinned. "Not for a while yet. Y'all hungry?"

"We weren't until we started smelling whatever's in the oven," Maddox grumbled.

She flashed another serene smile in his direction and then disappeared into the kitchen, determined to torture them more.

Three hours later, the guys had obviously decided to take turns walking into the kitchen to ask her the same question, over and over. When will the food be ready? Every fifteen minutes. Each time she merely smiled and said, "Soon."

Hastily she set the small dinner table that was stuck in the in-between area between the kitchen and the living room and then eyeballed the chairs suspiciously. They didn't look like they'd accommodate men the size of Maddox, Justice and Zander. She could just let everyone eat in the living room like they had for the past two days, but cooking her father's favorite meal had made her homesick and made her miss her dad more keenly than ever. Setting the table for the others gave her the illusion of the family dinners they used to share.

As she set the table, she let her finger run over the plates, aged but still in perfect condition, that had belonged to her mother and, before her, Hayley's grandmother. Tears welled in her eyes, and she hastily wiped them away with the back of her hand when she heard the sound of one of the men approaching.

"Hayley?" Maddox said in a low voice.

"It won't be long," she said brightly. "As soon as I finish up setting the table, the food will be done and I'll have it out for everyone."

"Sweetheart, why were you crying?" he asked in a gentle voice.

To her mortification, his caring tone made her nose draw up and tears stung her lids even more sharply.

"It's nothing," she said shakily, refusing to face him. "I was just thinking about my . . . dad. I miss him so much. I know it seems silly to set the table when y'all would probably be much more comfortable in the living room, but this reminds me of my meals with him. And I guess I'm just missing him more than usual tonight."

To her surprise she found herself enfolded in Maddox's massive arms as he hugged her gently to his chest, still mindful of her healing ribs. He didn't say anything. He simply stood there and held her until she was finished sniffling into his shirt.

Embarrassed, she pulled away, wiping at the evidence of her tears.

"Do you think the others will mind?" she asked, looking back at the table.

"They won't mind at all," Maddox said softly. "I'll go round them up while you grab the food. Take your time, sweetheart. We have all night and no other place we'd rather be."

As soon as Maddox withdrew, she hurried back into the kitchen to splash water on her face and remove the evidence of her cry fest. It was mortifying enough to have been caught out by Maddox. No way she wanted the others to see her cry too.

Satisfied she had regained her composure, she dished up the food, arranging it artfully on the serving platters that matched the plates she'd inherited from her mother. It wasn't an expensive set of dinnerware for certain, but there was so much love in every single memory associated with it.

Hearing the scrape of chairs being drawn out from underneath the table, she carried the platter of fish in first, only to nearly run into Maddox, Justice and Zander. Maddox took the platter from her and then motioned for her to sit.

"We'll get the rest," Justice offered. "You've been on your feet all afternoon. The least we can do is bring the food in for you."

She smiled, nearly tearing up again, and settled in the chair Maddox pulled out for her. Seconds later, Justice and Zander returned carrying the last of the dishes filled with food, and then they all sat around the table with her.

Her smile lit up the entire room as she watched them squabble and fight over portions and who got the most, but they were also careful to pile Hayley's plate full, just giving her a stern look when she laughingly protested, saying she couldn't possibly eat that much.

"This is so damn good," Zander groaned in ecstasy.

"You got that right," Justice said around a mouthful of food. "And shit, did you see the dessert she has in there? That must have been what she's been torturing us with all day."

"This was my father's favorite meal," she said softly. "Thank y'all for making it special for me."

Maddox reached over to cover her hand with his, squeezing gently. "Thank you for including us, sweetheart. Your father was a very lucky man to have a daughter like you."

She smiled. "I was the lucky one to have grown up with so much love."

She looked at each of the men, questions burning her tongue. They all seemed private, maybe not to the extent Silas was, but still very reserved, and yet they'd embraced her quickly enough.

"What about you all?" she asked quietly. "Do you all have family here in the city or is this even where you all are from? Thane told me he was from Mississippi but never said what brought him here."

Shuttered looks folded across their faces and her pulse leapt in dismay. What a complete idiot she was for ruining what had been an otherwise perfect evening by prying into things that were none of her business.

"Most of us don't have family," Maddox said in a low voice. "Except each other. These are my brothers. Not by blood but by choice. Choice is better, if you ask me. You know the old saying that you can choose your friends but not your family? That pretty much applies to us except in our cases, we did choose our family, or rather to make our own family."

"None of us had very stellar childhoods," Zander said with a shrug of indifference. But she could see the shadows in his eyes and knew that they all still carried demons. Her heart ached for them. For what they'd never had.

"We don't talk about it much," Justice explained. "We've made our peace with the past and left it where it belongs. In the past."

"Whatever it was, however bad it was, it made you who you are today," Hayley said gently. "And who you are today is pretty damn special."

The three men stared at her with peculiar expressions on their faces. As if they'd never considered it that way. Did they, like Silas, not consider themselves good men? And what defined good? The absence of bad? No, good people had bad in them. But it didn't make them solely bad. Nothing would ever convince her that Silas or any of his brothers, as they deemed themselves, weren't the very best kind of men.

"You all are the very best kind of men," she said, vocalizing her thoughts. Then she smiled, bittersweet. "My father would have liked you all very much. You don't even know me, I'm no one at all of any importance, and yet you've all put everything on hold to help put me back together after that horrible night. I was so afraid, but then Silas was there and I haven't been alone since. I haven't even thought of that night since. Because of you all."

All three were shaking their heads. Bewildered by their disagreement, she furrowed her brow, forgetting what she had been going to say next.

"You don't think you're good men?" she demanded. "You're wrong. All of you. And I won't hear you say you aren't, or so help me I'll kick all your asses."

She was staring at them fiercely, a mutinous expression darkening her features. Then when they burst out laughing, her mouth dropped open in absolute confusion. What was she missing here?

Obviously taking pity on her, Justice winked in her direction.

"We weren't saying we weren't good men, although that point is definitely debatable. We were shaking our heads over your asinine assertion that you're no one and not important."

Maddox and Zander scowled in her direction even as they nodded in agreement.

"You're important to Silas, so that makes you important to us. Or at least that was the way it was in the beginning," Maddox said, a smile warming his eyes. "Now we think you're pretty damn important to us all for our own reasons, none of which have a damn thing to do with Silas."

She flushed and ducked her head, glowing inwardly at their statements. She bit her lip, stifling the urge to dispute her importance to Silas. Well, maybe she was important as a neighbor or human being, but not where it really counted to her. As a woman.

"I don't think Silas quite shares y'all's opinion of me," she said in a near whisper, smiling so it didn't look like she was pouting over her statement.

The men just stared at her with the most bizarre expressions on their faces. Then Maddox burst out laughing and kept laughing until she was ready to kick him under the table.

"I'm selling tickets to this show," Zander said with a satisfied smirk. "And I'm also starting a betting pool as to how long it takes Silas to correct her way of thinking."

19

Hayley put away her violin and closed the case before rising to head for the exit to the smaller auditorium where rehearsals for their spring recital were being held. She was excited to perform for the first time in front of such a crowd. It was a new experience for her, to be certain. In the last year since beginning her studies at the small but prestigious academy, she'd certainly had her share of recitals and performances, but they'd always been on a much smaller scale and never open to the general public.

But the summer symphonic production was the academy's biggest fund-raiser of the entire year. Every year toward the end of the spring semester, a select few students were chosen to perform at Carnegie Hall. It was an honor to be chosen and an even bigger honor to be awarded a solo. Hayley had been shocked when she, a first-year student, had accomplished both.

She could hardly wait to share her exciting news with Silas and the guys. Okay, so maybe not Silas, since she was certain he wouldn't care one way or another, and by then he very well could have moved on from her and their relationship. Not that he wouldn't congratulate her and even tell her how deserving she was. Silas was nothing if not completely supportive of her talent. But it wouldn't mean as much as she wanted it to mean.

Sighing morosely, she hefted up her case, nearly grinning in delight at the looks of pure envy the other students cast her way. They'd been awestruck the first day she'd brought her new violin to school and more than a little jealous. Well, and she could hardly blame them. She would have been envious in their shoes too. It was not only a gorgeous-looking instrument. It played like pure magic, capturing the essence of every note. Every time Hayley played she lost herself in the beauty of her music, letting it flow into and out of her soul as her fingers danced across the strings, her other hand sliding the bow over the violin like a caress.

A crack of thunder boomed very close by as she followed the flow of students out the door and down the long hallway to the front entrance to the school. She flinched, startled by the loud noise. And then she heard the sound of the sudden downpour unleashed on the roof of the building and grimaced in sympathy for those who had to either walk home or to the subway station.

Maddox and company would be waiting for her out front, illegally parked as always, and she grinned, lengthening her stride. She was eager to see them and share her exciting news. Maybe she would even work up the nerve to invite them, though she wasn't so certain of that. She didn't want to set herself up for rejection. God, she was such a coward. But rejection sucked. No two ways about it. She ought to know, having faced it already with Silas, though his was far more embarrassing than if Maddox, Justice, Zander, Jax, Thane and Hartley turned down her invitation.

She paused in the doorway, staring out at the rain coming down in sheets. Her cell phone buzzed and she fumbled with her purse with one hand to grab the phone. She rolled her eyes when she read the text from Maddox.

Don't come out. Give me a second and I'll come in to get you.

As if a little rain was going to hurt her. Still, she wouldn't argue, not with such an expensive violin that she did not want to get wet. She glanced out to see Maddox step from the car, opening a huge umbrella that would easily cover them both. She rocked back on her heels to wait for his arrival when a hand suddenly curled painfully around her elbow, yanking her around.

She let out a startled cry of pain that abruptly ended when she came face-to-face with a sullen-looking Christopher.

"Where the hell have you been?" he demanded. "I went to your old place, but those idiot old people you house-sat for wouldn't tell me where you'd moved to."

"Let me go, moron," she hissed. "Why do you think they wouldn't tell you? Maybe because I didn't want you to know? Ever consider that?"

"You're the one being ridiculous," he said, moving closer until he was pressing into her body.

She stumbled back, nearly tripping on the door guard on the floor. She felt an icy blast of rain douse her entire back and realized that in her haste to back away from Christopher, she'd backed right out of the open door and into the rain.

Christopher came right out with her, not backing down an inch. He was furious, his eyes so dark with rage that it was instinctive to shrink away and thrust her violin case between them in an effort to ward off his advances.

"You stupid little bitch," he seethed. "Do you not understand who I am? No one says no to me. *No one!*"

"I know exactly who and what you are, asshole," Hayley shouted. "Don't you ever touch me again. Don't even speak to me or I'll swear out a restraining order on you. Wonder what Mummy and Daddy would think of their precious little boy then?"

He drew back his hand to strike her but a much larger hand suddenly wrapped around his, stopping his blow in midair. Christopher let out a squeak of surprise and pain and just as suddenly as Maddox had prevented him striking her, he had Christopher on his knees, screaming in agony as Maddox continued to twist his wrist at a backward angle.

Maddox towered over Christopher like an avenging angel, his hair dripping wet, his eyes glacial and so intimidating that if Hayley didn't know for certain he would never hurt her, she'd be peeing in her pants about now. Judging by the terror on Christopher's face, he likely already had.

"Get the fuck away from her. Now!" Maddox barked, fury edging every single word. "You don't touch her, you don't look at her, you don't talk to her. You get me? If I *ever* see you near her, if I so much as *hear* you've been within a hundred yards of her, I'll break every bone in your fucking body and dump what's left in the Hudson for the fish to eat. You understand me, boy?"

Christopher's eyes went wide with fear and he garbled ineffectively for several long seconds before he finally found his voice.

"Y-yes, s-sir," he stammered out as tears streamed down his cheeks, his face a wreath of agony.

"You owe the lady an apology, boy," Maddox roared.

"I'm s-sorry, H-Hayley." His eyes pleaded with her to do something, anything to get Maddox away from him. But she merely stood there staring coldly back at the entitled, insolent brat. "Hayley, please! Get him off me!"

All Hayley could think about was the attack on her nights ago, when she'd prayed for the men to stop. When she'd begged them to let her go and not to hurt her. If it hadn't been for Silas then, would anyone have even found her body after they'd raped her? And now, what if Maddox hadn't been here? She'd have liked to think that Christopher wouldn't have gotten away with assaulting her on school premises in broad daylight, but things like this happened every day.

Tears burned her eyelids and she hugged her violin case to her chest, uncaring of the rain that pelted down on her head, drenching every inch of her body.

"Come on, darlin', let's get you to the car and leave Maddox to clean up the trash."

Thane's soothing southern drawl sounded just behind her, and she gratefully turned around. Then she launched herself into Thane's arms, nearly dropping her violin, but Thane caught it, transferring it to his other hand so he could wrap his free arm around her. For a minute, despite the rain, he simply held her, as her sobs mixed with the downpour. Then finally he started her toward the car, his arm solidly around her waist as they approached an enraged Jax.

"You okay, doll?" Jax asked in concern as he opened the back door for her.

She merely nodded as she slid inside the warm interior. Then she looked down in dismay.

"I'm getting the seats soaked," she said, just as she broke down into tears again.

The door opened on the other side and Thane slid in next to her, holding a towel he'd seemingly summoned out of thin air. Were these men always prepared for anything?

He gently mopped at her dripping hair and wiped the water from her face and eyes, his lips drawn tight, anger glinting in his eyes.

"Where's that blanket, Jax? Did you get it out of the back yet?"

In answer, a soft blanket was carefully wrapped around her shoulders. Thane pulled the ends together at her front and then leaned back in the seat, curling his arm around her so her head rested against his chest.

"Let's get the fuck home," Thane growled. "She needs to get into dry clothing. That little bastard can get his ass beat another time."

As if Maddox had heard Thane's demand, he slid into the backseat so that Hayley was now wedged between the two larger men while Jax got into the driver's seat. A second later, they barreled into traffic and Hayley closed her eyes in exhaustion.

"Thank you, Maddox," she whispered. "I doubt he'll ever bother me again. He was getting to be a regular pain in my ass."

"What the *fuck*?" Maddox demanded.

Hayley's eyes flew open in alarm, her gaze instantly going to Maddox.

"This isn't the first time you've had trouble from him?"

She shook her head.

"And you didn't tell us this why?" Jax demanded from the front seat.

She looked at them in bewilderment.

"Darlin', you have trouble from some pencil dick like that, you tell us. You do not show up to the same school he attends and continue to take his shit," Thane snarled.

"I am so paying him a visit later," Maddox muttered.

"No!" Hayley cried. "I don't want any of you to get into trouble because of me. Maddox, you scared the wits out of him. He won't ever get in my space again."

"Yeah, well, sometimes the message needs to be reinforced," Jax said in a grim tone.

"We won't get into any trouble, darlin'," Thane soothed. "But I can guarantee you that he won't be trouble for you ever again."

"Let's just get you home," Maddox said in a calm voice. "Silas is back. Let us worry about the dickhead trying to throw his weight around with a woman."

Her face crumbled. The very last thing she needed to hear was that Silas was back. From the guys. Not one phone call or message from him ever since he'd left, and he couldn't tell her himself when he planned to return? If she hadn't already convinced herself he had no interest in her whatsoever, this would certainly have been the last straw.

She stared moodily out the window, refusing to meet any of their gazes as they zoomed through early-afternoon traffic. A few minutes later, they pulled up to Silas's apartment building and Jax parked in one of the reserved spaces out in front. They helped Hayley from the car and hurried her toward the entrance. While the rain wasn't as heavy as it had been fifteen minutes earlier, it was still coming down at a steady rate.

They rode up the elevator in the same silence that had cloaked the interior of the car, and when the doors opened, Silas was standing in the doorway to his apartment, a black scowl on his face.

"Nice to see you too," she muttered to herself.

"Any of you ever heard of a fucking umbrella?" Silas snapped.

Hayley stared woodenly at Silas. "It's raining, in case that escaped your notice. Surely you don't expect them to control Mother Nature. I'm going to get changed."

She turned to the men who had been such great company over the past few days, sad that she wouldn't see them any longer.

"Thank you," she said quietly. "For everything. I'm going to go dry off now. I'll miss you all."

She turned and headed down the hall to her apartment, taking in Silas's look of bewilderment as she passed him without speaking further to him.

"You got a minute, Silas?" Maddox asked after Hayley's apartment door closed with a loud thud.

Silas turned his scowl on his men. "I'm going to need more than a minute for you three to tell me what in the hell is wrong with Hayley."

"She hasn't had the best day," Thane volunteered.

"That ain't all that's the problem," Maddox said.

Silas opened his door and motioned the three of them inside. He didn't like the look on Hayley's face at all. She had only acknowledged him long enough to reprimand him. And what the fuck was with her sad "I'll miss you" that she'd barely managed to even voice? There was a finality to her tone that he didn't like one fucking bit. It scared the hell out of him, especially with his men all regarding him with such grave expressions.

"Start talking," Silas bit out as soon as they were all inside.

Silas's expression grew blacker and blacker with every second of the account of the shithead who'd gotten up in her face at school.

"I hope to fuck you taught that little pissant a lesson," Silas growled.

"Oh yeah. He's scared shitless. But I plan to pay him another visit later tonight," Maddox said calmly. "Our first priority was getting Hayley out of the rain and home. She was pretty shaken up."

"So what else were you going to bring up? You said this wasn't all that was a problem," Silas said impatiently.

The three men exchanged glances before turning their collective attention back to Silas.

"Do you care for her?" Maddox blurted.

Silas reared his head back in surprise. Then he glowered at the men he called brothers.

"Before you tell us it isn't any of our fucking business, let me just explain why he asked the question," Thane said, folding his arms over his chest in a gesture of defiance.

"Get on with it, then," Silas snapped.

"Hayley seems to be under the impression that she doesn't mean anything to you or that you care for her very much."

Silas's mouth fell open in shock. Of all the things they could have said, that was the last thing he had expected.

"Not care for her?" he rasped. "Doesn't mean much to me? What the fuck kind of fucked-up shit is that? Who put that crap into her head?"

"You did, brother," Jax said calmly.

Silas stared at them, utterly baffled by this turn of events. His personal life was not up for group discussion. Ever. Whatever he felt for Hayley was between him and her and not to be shared with *anyone* else.

"Look, it was a rhetorical question if you prefer it to be," Maddox said with visible irritation. "The point I'm trying to make is that very sweet young woman has it in her head that she doesn't mean shit to you. Now, if you don't care about that and don't care to correct her assumption, which I assume is errant, then fine. You do whatever. Just don't expect us to stand by and watch you crush her in the process. But if you do care about her and you do care what she thinks and that she's hurt by your seeming indifference, then I suggest you get off your ass and do something about it before she decides you're no longer worth the effort."

"Preach," Jax said, before turning to open Silas's door.

"Fucking A, preach," Thane chimed in as he too walked out.

Maddox remained behind, though, until it was just him and Silas standing inside Silas's apartment.

"Don't make the same mistakes that you and I blasted Drake's dumb ass over," Maddox warned in a serious tone. "We saw what a good thing Evangeline was, what a good woman she was, and it pissed us off to see the shit Drake pulled with her. He nearly fucking destroyed that woman. Evangeline. And now you've got a woman who is every bit as precious, innocent and sweet as the woman you defended so staunchly, only it's you she wants. Not one of us. No one else. Just you. If you don't want her, then back the fuck off and stop giving her mixed signals. Let someone else give her the happiness she deserves. God knows she could use some in her life, as fucked up as it's been so far. But if you do want her, then I'll tell you one more time. Get off your stupid ass and correct whatever fucked-up shit Hayley has in her head regarding you. And when you figure it out, let me know, so I know whether to make my play."

Silas's rage was instantaneous. He lunged at Maddox and curled his fingers into Maddox's shirt, yanking him forward until he was in his brother's face.

"You stay the fuck away from her," Silas snarled. "You don't touch her. You don't even think about her in any way except as a woman in your protection. You get me?"

The corner of Maddox's mouth twitched and turned up into a smile. "Guess that answers that question, doesn't it?"

Son of a bitch. He couldn't believe he fell for that baited trap. He shoved Maddox away in disgust and then lifted his hand to run through his hair.

"Goddamn it. She deserves so much better than I can ever give her," he said hoarsely. He lifted tortured eyes to Maddox, the one person who knew bits and pieces of Silas's past. A past Maddox was all too familiar with, given that he'd survived very similar circumstances. "You know why I can't have her, Maddox. Do you seriously think she deserves a man like me? A man so fucked up that his issues have issues. I'll never be right. For her. For anyone."

"What I think is that it's time to cut yourself a little slack," Maddox said with quiet understanding. "Why not let Hayley decide what she deserves? Lay it out for her. Something tells me you'll be surprised. She's not a coward and she's fiercely protective of the people she loves. Something tells me that she loves you. Or that she's falling pretty damn hard and fast. But she's so convinced that you don't want her that she's made herself fucking miserable. She doesn't feel *worthy* of you, Silas. Think about that for a minute while you're torturing yourself thinking you aren't worthy of her. She thinks *she's* not good enough for *you*."

Silas's mouth dropped open in absolute shock. "Not worthy? Not good enough for me? What the fuck?"

"Hell of a note when you consider the absurdity of any woman ever thinking she's not good enough for men like you and me," Maddox said with a bitter smile.

Silas stared into Maddox's eyes and saw the same pain Silas experienced in the deepest part of his withered and blackened soul. Pain they both lived with on a daily basis, always swearing to outrun their past. To overcome, rise above it, leave it behind. And yet it was always there. Hanging over them, coating everything in dull, gray shadows.

Silas closed his eyes and swore. What if he could *never* be good enough for Hayley? Wasn't it far better to never go down that path with her than to risk it and suffer the horrific pain of having her leave once she figured out what kind of monster she gave her body to every night? How was it fair to her for him to offer false promises, promises he had no idea if he could keep even if he desperately wanted to?

"Don't fuck it up like Drake almost did," Maddox whispered in a harsh tone. "You saw what he did to Evangeline. You *hated* it. *I* hated it. Don't hurt Hayley the way Drake hurt Evangeline or you'll hate yourself for the rest of your fucking life."

20

Hayley stepped out of the shower and wrapped a towel on top of her long hair so it was out of her way. She was too tired and melancholy to worry over brushing out her hair right away. She'd pay for it later when it frizzed everywhere on her, but who did she have to impress anyway?

She pulled on a simple pair of really short gym shorts and a T-shirt, not worrying about a bra even though she was healed enough now to wear one without discomfort. True, she'd never venture out of her apartment with her boobs on full display like this, but again, who was going to see her? Besides, she didn't have the mental or physical energy to put effort into tamping down the tatas. She hated being busty and had searched high and low for a minimizing bra that actually did what it advertised and got the damn things under control. It didn't always make for a comfortable back, but it was better than bouncing and jiggling around every time she took even a small step.

When she heard the main entrance buzzer sound through the intercom of her apartment, she cursed. Who the hell would be ringing her? Had one of the guys forgotten something? Surely it wouldn't be Silas. She looked at the black-and-white monitor showing the view from the camera at the front entrance to the building and could make out a man but not his face. It must be one of the guys after all. She pressed the button on the security panel that unlocked the front entrance door and let him inside. She frowned as she yanked on her robe, suddenly regretting her decision to let it all hang out today. After making sure her robe was tied firmly closed, she headed for the door and reached it just as someone knocked. Instead of opening it immediately, she decided to be careful and got up on tiptoe to look through the peephole first.

Her mouth fell open in shock just as rage blew through her blood veins like a blowtorch. Forgoing any and all caution, she yanked the door open to face the slimy maggot who'd fleeced her father for thousands of dollars and then smugly refused to pay out the death benefit, citing an obscure clause in such tiny print that one needed a magnifying glass to read it.

"What the hell are you doing here?" she asked in an icy tone she didn't even recognize. "And how did you know where to find me, for that matter? Do us both a favor and crawl back under your rock and stay there until someone comes along to step on you."

It was then, through the red haze surrounding her vision, that she finally registered the insurance salesman's haggard appearance. She cocked an eyebrow and sent him a mocking smile.

"Looks like someone already stepped on you. More than once, I'd say."

It was a vast understatement to say the very least. His face was bruised. His nose looked like it had been flattened and his lips were split and dried blood crusted the corners. He stood there stiff as a board, his hand holding out an envelope. He was shaking so hard that the paper flapped in his hand. She could swear she heard his knees knocking together.

"Miss Winthrop," he stammered out. "I had to come in person. It was the only fair and reasonable thing to do. I owe you an explanation and an apology. Due to a clerical oversight, you were denied your father's benefits assured to him by his life insurance policy. I am here to correct that matter as well as issue you my most sincere apology for your grief, upset and inconvenience. I included an amount for your pain and suffering as well as any funeral expenses you incurred as well as a more than fair interest rate on the bulk of the benefit for the time it remained unpaid to you."

"What?" Hayley croaked.

She stared at the envelope like it was a nasty bug about to jump on her. The salesman extended it forcefully, all but shoving it into her hand. Sweat beaded his entire forehead and she could smell his body odor from where she stood several feet apart from him. She could swear he was utterly terrified of her. What did he expect her to do? Jump on him and kick his ass? He outweighed her by at least a hundred and fifty pounds, not in muscle weight either.

He carried all his excess weight in his gut. If he went down and landed on her, she was toast. But the idea of her kicking his slimy ass did hold great appeal. Unfortunately, fantasy would have to suffice, since she had little to no chance of taking him down. There was always a good kick in the balls . . .

She fixed him with the force of her glare as she began to open the envelope, warning him with a look that he better not be jacking her around. Because if he was, she'd forget about those hundred and fifty pounds, and she'd be on his ass. She might not come out the victor, but she would definitely add to that already impressive set of bruises he sported.

She dropped her gaze only long enough to look at the check she pulled from the envelope. Her eyes widened as she took in the number of zeroes in the check. She lifted her stunned gaze back to the still-heavily-perspiring salesman.

"As I said, I included above and beyond the actual benefit for your inconvenience and your pain and suffering as well as suitable interest for the time we held the amount from you," he stuttered out.

He was to the point of wheezing and she couldn't summon a single word to say to him. *Thank you*? Ha! *Go to hell* sounded better. She supposed she should be grateful that he did correct the error as soon as it was discovered, but she had a hard time believing his sudden about-face.

"What happened to you?" she demanded bluntly.

"I, uh, well, I was mugged when I got to the city," he said, backing up a few more feet.

Hayley didn't think it was possible for the man to look any more terrified than he was, but she was wrong. Hell, he looked very close to passing out at her door. Then what was she supposed to do with him?

And then it hit her. Sudden realization as she put the pieces together. The night she was attacked. Her pouring out the entire story, not only of her father giving her the violin, but also of how he was cheated by the insurance salesman. The probing questions Silas had asked so nonchalantly and then his sudden departure on a "business" trip.

She nearly laughed out loud. No wonder the man looked like he was about to piss himself. She didn't even want to know how scary Silas looked when he persuaded the man of his "clerical error."

"That's what happens when you fuck people over on a regular basis," she said softly, menace and not an ounce of regret in her voice. "Maybe you'll remember your, uh, *mugging* the next time you even think about conning another person."

He didn't say another single word. His eyes bulging wildly, he turned and fled down the hall as fast as his legs would carry him. He didn't even bother waiting for the elevator. He hit the stairwell and she heard the distant sound of pounding feet.

"Good riddance," Hayley murmured.

She glanced down at the check again, half afraid the check was nonnegotiable. But no, everything seemed to be in order. Which meant . . .

Oh God, she had to talk to Silas! She had just assumed he was likely off with his woman, Evangeline, the past few days. But he hadn't been! He'd been hunting down the insurance salesman for *her*.

She hugged herself and chanced a look down the hall toward the door of Silas's apartment. Maybe if she had been wrong about where he had been the last few days, then perhaps there were other things she was wrong about as well. Like his presumed relationship with another woman. At any rate, he deserved her appreciation and gratitude. Especially after the way she'd blown him off earlier.

She hurried into her apartment long enough to put the check in a safe, secure location, so she didn't lose it. First thing in the morning, she'd make a trip to the bank to deposit it and then pray that it didn't bounce or that payment hadn't been stopped on it.

Then, drawing in a deep, steadying breath, she left her apartment and walked more slowly down to Silas's door. When she reached it, she stood there a long moment, trying to work up the nerve to knock.

Silas paced the floors of his living room, agitated and swearing as he made up his mind and then changed it for the hundredth time since Maddox had, in a nutshell, told him what a huge, fucking hypocrite he was being. The sad thing was that Maddox was not wrong. Silas was all Maddox had accused him of and so much more.

What was he supposed to do with a woman like Hayley? She was simply too beautiful, too passionate, too . . . perfect . . . for someone like him. How long would it take her to realize what a terrible mistake she had made by allowing him into her life, and how much longer after that until she ran?

For that matter, who was to say she'd ever agree to the kind of relationship he required? He stopped pacing momentarily and let out a groan. Required? It made him seem cold and heartless, and again, he wasn't wrong. It went beyond a requirement. It was a necessity. Like eating and breathing for everyone else. Control wasn't something he enjoyed or even craved. He had to have it in order to survive each day.

But nothing he said, no rationale he could offer himself for allowing Hayley to think what she liked so she'd move on and forget about him, could erase the image of Hayley feeling hurt, rejected, unworthy by and of him! Unworthy. He couldn't wrap his brain around it. No amount of applying logic to the situation could make him forget Maddox's, Jax's and Thane's well-aimed arrows into his heart. Or what used to be his heart.

How could Hayley ever think he didn't want her? Didn't desire her with his every breath? How could she in a million years ever consider herself unworthy of *him*?

"Fuck this," Silas bit out.

He started toward the door because there was no fucking way he would ever allow Hayley to feel unworthy of goddamn anyone. He had no idea what to do about the matter of him and Hayley or if she could ever accept him for what he was, but he couldn't worry about that now. He would cross that bridge when he got there.

He was but a few feet from his door when the doorbell sounded, eliciting an immediate snarl of rage from Silas. Now of all the fucking times on earth? *Now*?

Ready to take apart whatever idiot had decided to intrude at the exact moment he finally made a decision in regard to Hayley, he threw open the door and let his most chilling glare erupt.

Hayley stood in his doorway in a robe and . . . God, was there anything on underneath that really thin robe? Her eyes rounded in trepidation as she took in Silas's obvious foul mood and took a defensive step back.

"Princess?" he managed to choke out.

"I obviously came at a bad time," she said hastily, turning even as she spoke, prepared to flee.

"No! No," he said in a calmer voice.

His pulse was beating so hard and fast he was dizzy and felt light-headed. He, who had never fainted in his entire goddamn life no matter how badly he had been beaten or how hard he prayed for unconsciousness to overtake him, was now about to do one epic face-plant right on the floor at Hayley's feet.

"Please," he asked softly. "I thought it was someone else at the door. What are you doing over here? Are you okay?"

He was sweating, another first for him. At the rate he was going, he'd soon be out of a job. What the hell kind of enforcer, the one guy in Drake's organization you did not want to cross, would it make him if he started suddenly hitting the floor and sweating like a damn pig?

"I'm fine," she said, a hint of a smile curving her beautiful, full lips.

He reached behind her to close the door. At first he opted to set the locks later, needing, wanting, his entire focus to be on Hayley. But his skin prickled the instant he turned away without performing his ritual. Even his hands were unsteady and undisciplined.

"Go ahead and lock them, Silas," Hayley said in a sweet voice full of understanding. "I can wait."

He closed his eyes and then slammed his lips shut to prevent his audible groan as he turned back to the door. Unworthy. Of him. He wanted to kick his own ass for ever treating her as if she were unworthy of him. And then he needed to figure out a way to convince them *both* that he was actually worthy of *her*.

He was so flustered that he lost count midway through and had to start from the top all over again. By the time he finished, he had managed to adequately calm his fried nerves enough to face Hayley.

He turned, immediately seeking her out, and to his astonishment, she hurled herself at him. He had no choice but to catch her or they'd both end up on the floor.

"What's this about?" he asked in bewilderment.

"Thank you," she whispered against his neck, her soft breath blowing warm over his skin. "You continue to get more awesome every single day. Just when I think you can't possibly top the latest thing you've done for me, you somehow manage to surprise me all over again."

"What are you thanking me for, princess?"

"As if you don't know," she said in amusement as she drew away and out of his hug.

He took a step toward her, not liking the sudden distance between them.

"I just got a visit from a slimy, deceitful insurance salesman who just happened to crawl out from under his rock long enough to travel all the way to New York City so he could personally deliver a check for the full amount of my father's benefit plus a substantial amount over that for things he called inconvenience, pain and suffering and funeral costs."

She stared up at him, her eyes glowing brightly. Damn it. She was looking at him like he was a fucking hero. Did she not understand what happened to the guy? She couldn't have missed the way his face looked, and yet she was thanking Silas?

"Some business trip. You certainly took care of business. I only regret not being able to land one punch," she said, her expression rueful. "I can't believe you did this absolutely amazing, wonderful thing for *me*."

He gaped at her. He couldn't help it. She was thanking him instead of condemning him? Did she not see what a monster he was? What he was capable of? He'd lived his entire life surrounded by violence only to embrace it when he was much older. But on his terms. Always on his terms.

Before he could question her or figure out what he was missing, she took a step toward him, closing the distance between them, and then she rose up on tiptoe and slid her arms around his neck. He didn't have time to think better of letting her kiss him. He wanted it too damn much.

Her lips pressed so sweetly over his that he groaned low in his throat. She licked delicately at his mouth, coaxing him to open to her. Just as he surrendered and allowed his lips to relax, he gathered his senses and placed his hands around her shoulders to pull her away.

Shame and humiliation crept into her eyes, a dull shadow masking every bit of the joy and mischief that had been there just a few seconds ago.

"I'm sorry," she whispered. "I misunderstood. Again."

"What did you misunderstand, princess?"

"Don't call me that!" she said sharply, hurt edging the words. "I thought . . . I thought you felt it too. What is between us. I thought you wanted me as much as I want you. I'm sorry. I should have never placed you in this position."

He emitted a strangled sound. "Not want you? Jesus Christ, woman. If I wanted you any more I'd be a walking idiot unable to form a coherent sentence. Don't you get it? You deserve so much better than me. I have nothing to offer you except pain and violence. And . . ."

He closed his eyes, refusing to voice the last.

"And what?" she asked softly.

"Control," he said flatly. "Total and absolute control. And what you don't understand, my beautiful girl, is that my control would not just extend to the bedroom or while we're having sex. I would control every aspect of your life. I'm not proud of that fact, but it's who I am. Sooner or later I would drive you away and I don't know if I can bear to lose you once I've had you."

"Who says you'll lose me?" she asked gently. "You act like I don't know all of this already, Silas. Granted we haven't known one another very long, but in that time, I've seen your need for control. I've seen you exercise that control. Even with me. Heck, what do you think I've been doing the past few days? I've been escorted everywhere by your men. Men you gave me no choice but to go everywhere with. Did I complain?

Did I put up much of a protest? Why don't you see yourself the way I see the man in front of me? You seem to think you're nothing but poison for me, and you know what? It's a load of crap. You are the very best kind of man, Silas. Next to my father, you are the best man I've ever met in my life. So stop with the excuses. If you don't want me, then just say so and I'll never throw myself at you again. But if you want me but you're just too afraid of scaring me or pushing me away, then I call bullshit on that too. How about you ask me what *I* want? Not what *you* think I want or need. Ask *me*, Silas."

"You can stand there and say all that after knowing what I did to that bastard who fleeced your father? I would have killed him if I didn't need to make damn certain he got a check to you. I still might," he muttered.

"I'm sure there are plenty of other people who would like to do to him exactly what you did," she said, her nose wrinkling in distaste. "If you're looking to me to throw judgment at you, then you've come to the wrong woman. I don't care about whatever horrible sins you think you've committed. I know the truth and I see the truth every time I look at you, and nothing you say will ever persuade me any differently."

"Be sure, princess," he said hoarsely. "Be very sure. Because once I claim you and possess your body I *will* own you. Body, heart and soul. All will belong to me and you will be mine to do with as I wish, anytime, anywhere, any way I want."

"Then claim me," she murmured as she lifted up on the balls of her feet once more to brush her lips over his.

With a savage cry, he lifted her into his arms and strode toward the bedroom, his blood on fire in his veins, burning from the inside out.

21

Silas's heart was thundering so hard that all he could hear was the roar of his pulse in his ears. He set Hayley gently down on the bed and then took one step back, knowing that if he didn't give himself a few minutes to get it together, it would be over in a matter of seconds. His need to claim her, to mark her, to possess her until she cried out his name was a living, breathing necessity inside him. Stronger than any other compulsion he'd felt, and his life was riddled with compulsions.

He leaned down and brushed his lips over hers. "I have to go lock up and check the monitors and turn the security system on. When I get back, I want you naked and kneeling in the middle of the bed. Make sure your hair is down but not covering your breasts. I want to see the nipples that now belong to me. I want to be able to see the sweet little pussy that also now belongs to me. Understand?"

She swallowed and nodded, desire and need glittering in her eyes. He kissed her one last time and then yanked himself away from her. He strode into the living room and mechanically went through the ritual of locking up for the night. He had perimeter alarms in every conceivable vulnerable point and cameras that not only circled the entire block but covered across the street and a radius of six blocks in each direction from his building.

After what had happened to Evangeline and her getting snatched literally feet from the front entrance to this building, there was no such thing as overkill or being too extreme in his paranoia. If it could happen to Evangeline, it could happen to Hayley. His blood froze and for a moment he couldn't breathe at the image of Hayley hurt, scared, alone.

No, she would remain in this building where he knew where she was at all times. And now that she had committed herself into his keeping, she would no longer have any use of her own apartment. She would be in his bed, his apartment, from now on. Maybe he could go ahead and do the renovations again to extend the reach of his apartment from wall to wall on the fifth floor.

Deciding he'd given Hayley enough time, he turned and stalked toward the bedroom, a sense of victory unlike anything he'd ever felt sizzling through his veins. She was courageous. He had to give that to her. She'd seen him at his worst not once but twice now. She knew things about him that should make him uncomfortable with anyone knowing, especially someone who wasn't one of his brothers or Evangeline.

But she hadn't condemned him. In fact, she got downright pissed if he even attempted to make himself out to be a monster. And as for her knowing things about him, one, he trusted her. Maybe that made him as dumb as a brick and gullible as fuck, but she was too loyal and loving to ever betray anyone who trusted her. Not without a damn good reason. Two, she was his now, which made her, by extension, his brothers' as well. They would protect her with their lives just as they did Evangeline. He couldn't very well keep all his secrets from her when she was giving him everything in return. Her trust. Her body. Her heart.

He was humbled and a little overwhelmed by what he saw in her eyes every time he caught her staring at him. Never did he imagine a woman like her looking at a man like him with those soft eyes, an even softer smile and so much understanding and warmth that he wanted to bathe in it.

Sex. Well, sex was sex. A pastime to blow off some steam. Nothing more. Nothing less. In fact, he rarely indulged in sex and when he did, he made damn sure the woman knew precisely what she was getting into and he also ensured she was more than adequately thanked.

He stopped in the doorway of the bedroom and stared in stupefaction at the image Hayley presented, kneeling on his bed, facing the door. She was so beautiful she took his every breath away. Never had he seen anything more beautiful, pure. Absolutely magnificent. And she wanted him.

Sex? Touching Hayley, sliding into her body over and over could hardly be called something so mundane as sex. It was an insult to her to suggest otherwise. And yet he couldn't bring himself to use the words most people did for the act. Making love. Never had he seen anything so much as resembling love when sex was involved. He'd learned early, the hard way, that sex was dirty, disgusting, debasing and shameful.

He was an adult now, and he could look back through the eyes of an adult and know in his heart that his experiences were aberrations. Most of the time he could separate those feelings out and not let them interfere in the present. But every once in a while, he wasn't able to, and sex wasn't even an option during those times. Even if he wanted it differently. His body simply wouldn't cooperate as long as it was trapped by the mind of a child, traumatized by a child's knowledge.

Hayley's gaze found his and she immediately smiled. It lit up her entire face, and even her eyes glowed softly in the low light. She tilted her chin upward, causing her neck to arch forward and her hair to tumble down her back in waves of silk. Her breasts thrust upward, the peaks becoming taut and puckered. His mouth watered just looking at them. Wanting to taste them.

"You're so beautiful," Silas said hoarsely.

She ducked her head shyly, color blooming in her cheeks. "So are you," she whispered.

He slowly circled the bed, trailing his hand over the comforter as he traveled up the side closer to Hayley. He wanted to be within touching distance. Glancing down, his breathing hitched as he saw the pink, delicate flesh just visible through the tufts of dark hair between her legs. Slowly he put his hand on top of her thigh and then just as slowly and delicately slid over and down, between her legs to the damp, quivering flesh.

She moaned softly but didn't move.

"Good girl," Silas praised. "That's my good girl. That's perfect. Don't move. I'm just going to touch you."

He slid his finger farther into the lush folds, going upward first, rolling over the taut nub nestled under the hood of her pussy. He played there a moment, watching as her entire body went rigid and her breaths came out in sporadic puffs. Smiling, he let his fingers drift downward to her tiny opening and traced a circle around it. She closed her eyes but still didn't move, and he knew how difficult it must be when every muscle in her body was tense. The last thing he wanted was for her to be uncomfortable. As much as he'd love to draw this out as long as possible and play with her the entire night before giving her ultimate satisfaction, neither he nor she would last that long. Not this time. There would be plenty of time later when their initial hunger had been sated.

He withdrew his hand only for her to groan in protest. Slowly, he unbuttoned his shirt, watching as her eyes followed every motion of his hands as he removed it and laid it across the chair in the corner. He unfastened his pants and lowered the zipper over his rock-hard erection, and he could see Hayley's throat work as she swallowed hard. After he was as naked as she, he crossed back to the bed and waited for her eyes to rise back to his. It took a flatteringly long amount of time. When he finally had her attention where he wanted it, he asked, "Do you know what you are going to do now?"

She hesitantly shook her head, and again he saw the uncertainty in Hayley's eyes. He realized she wasn't uncertain about *them* but about herself, and he found that unacceptable. Never had he seen a woman more beautiful than the one kneeling in his bed waiting for his possession, and before the night was over, she'd know exactly how exquisite she was. She would hold her head high in pride when he gazed at her beautiful bare body. She would know that while he wielded absolute control, it was she who had all the power over him.

"Do you *want* to know what you are going to do now?" he asked in a husky voice he didn't even recognize. When had he ever been this gentle with any woman he was about to claim? But then never had he even considered what he'd done with his partners in the past as claiming. He'd never wanted to.

When she slowly nodded, he continued. "You're going to take whatever I give you."

Her eyes flared as he climbed into bed beside her. He started with her hair, trailing his fingers through the silky strands, intentionally brushing against her nipples with every stroke. "Exquisite," he muttered. "Like the finest silk."

His fingers trailed on to her arms, continuing the movements until goose bumps covered her body. He gathered her hair in his fist and moved it across her shoulder, baring her vulnerable back to him. He couldn't wait any longer to taste her. He pressed his lips against her neck and traveled to her spine. Once there, he licked his way down to the perfect curve of her buttocks. When he gave one a nip, she startled and a whimper escaped her. He smiled in supreme male satisfaction over her response. She was fucking perfect.

His hands continued on his path and he tasted every inch of flesh he could reach. She was squirming and panting by the time he settled his chest against her back, his inner thighs pressed against her outer thighs, and his dick snugly held between the cheeks of her luscious ass. He moved his hands downward from the breasts he was caressing to the pussy he couldn't wait to claim. She was wet with desire and he used that slickness as he circled her clit. Her whimpers turned to cries and her entire body coiled, shuddered, and then she leaned back against his chest, demonstrating with more than words the trust she had in him. He caught her against him and continued to work his fingers in and out of her snug passageway while he used his other hand to rub her clit.

"Silas!"

She writhed in his arms, the glossy crown of her head falling back to his shoulder. He nuzzled his lips along the underside of her jaw and then sank his teeth into the flesh below her ear.

Her orgasm overtook her entire body. She shook, trembled and squirmed against his chest and all the while he held her tightly, her back molded to him as he felt every single shudder that racked her body.

Mine.

He wanted to roar it. He wanted to mark her, own her, possess her in such a way that no one would ever question who she belonged to. It was primitive, absolutely Neanderthal and not very progressive of him, but fuck progressive. Hayley called to instincts he didn't even realize he had. Never had he been so desperate to put his stamp on a woman. Never had he been so determined that the world know who belonged to him. He might not be very forward-thinking, what with beating his chest like an ape and grunting about owning his woman and how she belonged absolutely to him in every way possible, but never would there be a woman more spoiled, pampered and cherished than this precious girl coming apart in his arms and screaming his name. From the very first time he laid eyes on her, she had absolute power over him. He needed control, but the ultimate power was hers because he'd do anything at all to make her happy, to make her feel cherished and treasured. There was nothing he wouldn't do for this woman.

He closed his eyes as she slumped against him, her chest heaving with exertion. His dick was about to split apart at the seams. Being nestled in the cleft of her ass was simply too much temptation for the mother of all erections he was sporting. If he didn't get her in position soon, he'd be fucking her ass in another two seconds.

Unable to wait even a moment longer, he flipped her to her back, hastily slipped on a condom, spread her thighs wide and buried himself balls-deep in her tight, pulsating heat. She cried out again, this time in pain, and Silas froze. Tears swam in her eyes and discomfort was evident on her features. *Fuck.* He should have known. All that innocence went soul deep. Goddamn it, he hadn't even asked her! He'd *never* forgive himself for this. He had plowed into her with all the skill and patience of a fucking junior high boy getting his first piece of ass.

"Fuck, Hayley, I'm so goddamn sorry, princess," he choked out. "I'm such an ass. God."

He kissed the tears away from her face because he couldn't stand the sight of them shining on her skin. Tears and pain that he had caused her when he'd vowed never to cause her either. Son of a bitch!

"Easy, sweet girl. I've got you. The pain will pass soon and I'll make you feel good. I'll make it up to you. I swear to you I will."

She nibbled at her bottom lip, her gaze doubtful, but she nodded hesitantly.

He kissed her, sucking the lips she'd just been nibbling in between his teeth, and soothed the ravaged skin with his tongue. Then he kissed his way down her neck to one breast and lapped at the nipple repeatedly with his tongue.

He smiled when he sucked her nipple deep and hard into his mouth and she instantly bathed his dick in liquid honey. His princess liked having her pretty nipples teased.

Easing one hand between their bodies, he softly stroked her clit until he felt her tightening around his dick in a stranglehold that nearly had him coming on the spot. When she started instinctively lifting her hips in an effort to meet him, he knew she'd found her rhythm and the pain was turning to unmet need.

He eased his dick out of her until only the head was still nestled in her sweet heat. He continued to stroke her clit until her breaths came hard and she started twisting restlessly beneath him.

"Ready, princess?" he asked gently.

He looked into eyes shining with need as she spoke for the first time since giving him control.

"Yes," she whispered.

So much trust in that one word. His chest ached to the point of physical discomfort. It was the only word he needed. But still, he wanted to be sure she knew he wouldn't hurt her. He'd die before purposely hurting her again.

"Promise me you'll stop me if I do anything that hurts you."

She smiled and nodded.

Silas slid back inside her, closing his eyes at the overwhelming sensation of being gripped so tightly by her feminine flesh. He kept his thrusts gentle and licked his own fingers before moving them back to her clit. Her entire body bowed beneath him and her muscles locked. He groaned as she clutched him, surrounding him with her silken honey. So tight. So fucking good. Already she was on the verge of her second orgasm. He'd been worried after the way he'd ripped into her that he wouldn't be able to bring her to fulfillment again, and certainly not this soon.

He increased his pace, a sense of urgency overtaking him that they find release together. Her lids fluttered and then rested on her cheeks as she closed her eyes. Her hands slid over his shoulders, her nails digging deep as she tensed even more.

"Come with me, beautiful girl," he urged. "Right now. Together."

He began thrusting hard, deep, his hips slapping frantically against her ass. Just as her cry burst over his ears, he let out a shout of his own and buried himself as deeply as possible. He eased down onto her body, feeling her arms wrap around him and her hands caress up and down his back.

"So fucking beautiful," Silas whispered against her breast. "Never seen anything more beautiful than you."

He stayed inside her as long as he could before slowly withdrawing and disposing of the condom in the bathroom. While there, he ran a cloth under warm water then took it back to the bed. Hayley was still sprawled as he'd left her, but when she saw his intention, she tried to close her legs.

"I can do that," she whispered with a blush on her cheeks.

Silas firmly grasped her knee and spread her legs again. "Have you already forgotten who you gave yourself to? This is mine. All of you belongs to me. Mine to touch, mine to pleasure and mine to take care of."

Her eyes glittered with a sudden wash of tears as she stared into his eyes.

"Yours," she whispered back in capitulation.

He carefully ran the cloth over her puffy lips and winced when it came back with blood on it. Tossing it into the hamper, he returned to bed and pulled Hayley to his chest, wanting no space between them. His hands wouldn't stay still. Touching her was as much a necessity as control was.

As he absently ran a hand up and down her spine, he looked down at the contented look on her face.

"Why didn't you tell me you were a virgin, princess?"

She buried her face deeper into his chest and sighed. "I was afraid," she said in a barely audible whisper. "You were already so reluctant, I was worried if you knew I was a virgin, you wouldn't want me. It was just one more reason for you to reject me."

Silas fisted his hand in her hair and gently tugged her up so he could see her face. "Not want you? That's never been a problem, baby, and your virginity wouldn't have changed that."

"Why would a man with your experience want someone like me who has none and has no idea what she's doing?" she asked. "I would think that for a man of your age and experience, an inexperienced, ignorant virgin would be the last thing you wanted."

The slight echo of bitterness he heard in her voice surprised him. "Look at me, Hayley," he demanded. "No, not my chin. I want eye contact for this." When her unhappy eyes finally met his, he continued. "What you gave me tonight was the most precious gift anyone has *ever* given me, and I will always treasure it. Do you have any fucking idea how thrilled I am that no other man has ever touched you, claimed you? It means everything to me that I was your first, that you gave me that gift and trusted me with it. The idea that I get to teach you everything you want and need to know? That I get to teach you what pleases me while you teach me what pleases you? Jesus, woman. I'm a self-admitted Neanderthal, but this development might well send me back a few generations on the evolutionary scale."

She laughed softly and then hugged him with the one arm draped over his abdomen.

Silas stroked his hand through her hair and waited a moment before directing her gaze to his again.

"My only regret is hurting you the way I did," he said painfully. "If you had told me, that would have never happened. So promise me that in the future you will hold nothing back from me. Especially something that could result in me hurting you, however unintentionally. I could have made it a lot better for you, princess."

She lowered her mouth to his and kissed him. "I promise, Silas. But if it got any better, I'm not sure I'd survive. Hello? You gave me two orgasms. How is that bad?"

He chuckled and then pulled her down so her body was sprawled atop his. "It'll get even better, baby. You may not think so, but trust me. This is only the beginning of everything I have to teach you."

22

Hayley positively glowed with happiness. It was impossible not to notice the change in herself. She only had to look in the mirror to see the soft smile, the warm glint in her eyes. She was always smiling these days. Nonstop for the last week.

Silas stuck his head into the bathroom where she was standing and staring at her reflection as she let her thoughts wander. She glanced up quickly and tried to make it appear as though she were doing something except staring at herself and getting a giddy thrill over how happy this man made her.

"I'm going down to get the car. Give me five minutes before you meet me downstairs. I'll drive you to school today and pick you up so we can spend the afternoon together according to plan."

She blew him a kiss in the mirror, immediately lighting up at Silas's reminder of today's agenda. They had spent much of the last week in bed. When she wasn't attending class, she was either on her back or on her knees. She and Silas had christened every single piece of furniture in the house, and once she'd told him she was on birth control pills the morning after their very first time together, he'd become relentless, fixated on the fact he could come inside her anytime he wanted. Not that she really minded.

She was happy. Silas seemed very happy. And making him happy made her even happier. So everything was . . . perfect.

She checked her watch and then went in search of her violin case and her purse. By the time she had everything ready to go, her five minutes were up, so she headed for the door, making sure she reset every single lock, and then she used the express elevator only for Silas's use and zipped down to the first floor.

Silas was parked out front, and as soon as she exited the building, he hurried out to collect her case from her, his cell phone stuck to his ear. Not unusual at all considering he spent a lot of time on his phone. He settled her into the car in the passenger seat and then put the violin in the back before returning to the driver's side. When he slid behind the wheel, he'd evidently ended his call because he placed the phone on the seat next to him.

Hayley looked curiously at him as he pulled into traffic. It was rare to see Silas or any of his men drive. They usually had a driver unless they were babysitting her, in which case there wasn't room for an additional driver, so one of the three men always drove. What exactly did they do? She'd gotten hints, none of them very settling, but she knew Silas and what kind of man he was. Some would call her a naïve, too-trusting idiot for her unwavering faith in this man, but she knew one thing if she knew nothing else in the world. Silas and his men were good people. Nothing would ever change her mind about that.

"So what exactly do you and your brothers do?" Hayley ventured. "Does it have anything to do with security?"

Silas chuckled. "In a way, yes, and I can certainly understand why you'd think that. We do depend on very good security. Me. There are ever-present threats and danger to not only Drake but all of us. It's my job to ensure nothing happens to any of us."

Her brow furrowed in question. "You say that like there's more danger to Drake. Who is he exactly?"

Silas seemed to ponder her query a moment, his lips pursed thoughtfully. "I work for Drake—we all work for Drake. But it's not like he's our boss. It's difficult to explain. We aren't a typical business or corporation. I guess a better way of explaining it would be to say I work with Drake. I work with all my brothers. There's no dick sizing, no competitiveness. We have a job to do and we do it," he said with a shrug. "My job is to ensure no one gets to Drake or any of my brothers."

"How exactly do you ensure that?" she asked hesitantly. "Do you kill or hurt people?"

She knew how stupid she sounded. Like a complete bimbo smacking her gum, eyes wide, saying, *Oh noes! You mean, you like, make people bleed?* She wanted to smack herself and then hide her face for the rest of the day.

Silas's features became impassive, and suddenly he wore an expression Hayley was unfamiliar with. It wasn't a way he'd ever looked at her. She couldn't read a single thing he was thinking or saying. Damn it! When she screwed up, she did a bang-up job.

"Only those who deserve it," Silas finally muttered.

"Well, if they try to hurt or kill you, then yes, they do deserve it," Hayley snapped.

A glimmer of a smile curved Silas's lips and the mask slipped, allowing her to see her Silas again. He reached over to touch her hand and she curled her fingers around his tightly.

"So who was on the phone? Was it Maddox telling you the world is coming to an end and now you have to go play superhero for the day?" she teased, wanting to make him laugh again.

Instead of laughing, his lips formed a grim line and he stiffened.

"Yeah, about that. I'm afraid I have to change our plans, princess. Maddox will pick you up after school and bring you home. I have to spend the day with Evangeline. I'm sorry. I'll make it up to you, I promise."

It took every ounce of effort she possessed to keep her mouth from falling open and to keep hurt from flickering in her expression. She'd assumed that since she'd misunderstood so much already and Silas hadn't been with Evangeline when he'd gone out of town that he obviously wasn't *with* her. Especially now that Hayley was in his bed every night. She hadn't even considered such a possibility since she'd discovered how wrong she'd been about the nature of his business trip. For that matter, this was the first time Hayley had heard Evangeline's name even mentioned since Hayley's last bout of jealousy and insecurity. Hell, she hadn't even thought about the other woman. She'd forgotten Evangeline existed. And now Silas had to spend the day with this woman? Being with her was more important to Silas than any plans he and Hayley had made?

Her stomach churned even as she admonished herself for once again jumping to conclusions. She'd been wrong about Silas's business trip.

But had she been wrong about everything else?

"Who is Evangeline?" she asked tightly. "I've heard you and the guys mention her, but no one has ever said who she is."

Or what she was to all of them. What she was to *Silas*.

Her stomach churned more violently when Silas's face softened with obvious affection at the mere mention of Evangeline's name. Silas, who so rarely softened around anyone. This was a Silas that Hayley had waited for, had fought for. She'd despaired of him ever looking that way about her.

"She's Drake's wife. I thought you knew that. You'd like her. She's a complete sweetheart. Has all the guys wrapped around her finger. And she cooks like a dream."

To add insult to injury, Silas *groaned* his appreciation.

"Everyone eats until we make ourselves sick any time she makes dinner for us. It's quite a madhouse," he added with a chuckle.

Drake's wife. Okay, was that really supposed to make her feel better when Silas obviously had so much affection, and God only knew what else, for her? Jealousy sucked. Evangeline was probably a wonderful person. Certainly all Silas's brothers liked her well enough. No, they *loved* her. That much was obvious. Yeah, Drake's wife was probably gorgeous too. And had apparently enslaved the entire male population with her culinary expertise. But the simple truth was, Hayley had no desire to ever meet the other woman. Especially if it meant watching the rest of the men fawn all over her all night. An entire day or night or occasion for Hayley to have shoved in her face all the ways she didn't measure up? After such a promising start to the day, Hayley was calling it. Today officially sucked. While Silas was off spending the day with the epitome of perfection, Hayley was relegated to being foisted off on whichever poor brother drew the short end of the stick and had to pick her up from school.

God, could this get any more embarrassing? She felt like an elementary kid being collected from the bus stop by an annoyed older sibling.

She swallowed hard, doing everything in her power to maintain her composure and not allow Silas to see the disappointment and dismay on her face or hear it in her voice.

"So you're spending the day with her, then," she said lightly.

She'd give anything to be able to rub her throat, but she left her hand in her lap, determined not to let Silas see the insecurity that was eating her alive.

Silas shot her a quick glance. "Yeah. Sorry, princess. It's not my usual day for my lunch date with her, but something came up and she's priority over everyone, Drake included, so I don't have a choice."

Hayley nodded and then fixed her gaze out her window, careful to keep her expression neutral.

It's not my usual day for my lunch date with her.

Usual lunch date? As in a regular occurrence? Obviously it was. Suddenly Hayley was thinking back over her time with Silas, searching for a window of time when Silas would have been with Evangeline and not her. She almost didn't suppress the breath she wanted to blow out in frustration. Three days a week her classes went beyond normal lunch hours. Was that what he was doing while she was in school? Having his date with Evangeline?

Priority over *everyone*? What the hell did that mean?

It means she's more important than you, dumbass.

It meant Evangeline would *always* take priority over Hayley. Could she live with being second on the list of priorities of the man she loved with all her heart? For that matter, was she even second? Or third?

No. No way. But what choice did she have? Over her dead body would she ever be one of those women to throw out an ultimatum. *Her* or *me*. Yeah, yeah. That always worked out so well for everyone involved. Not. Then there was the fact that she was just too cowardly to stand there and watch as Silas *didn't* choose her.

And, well, Hayley knew in the deepest part of her heart that Silas would never choose her over his brothers. Or Evangeline. So she needed to decide if she could accept that, live with it, and if she couldn't, then she needed to get out before she was completely destroyed. Before her confidence and sense of self-worth were whittled away to nothing, before she *became* nothing.

She breathed a sigh of relief when they pulled up in front of the school. Hayley immediately opened her door, prepared to hop out, when Silas caught her hand. She leaned back in and rolled her eyes.

"There's no need to walk me in. Besides, you'll be late for your day with Evangeline," she said, her voice cracking just a bit.

"There is every need," he bit out. "Do you forget that little punk-ass shithead who can't take no for an answer still attends this academy with you?"

She sighed in exasperation. "As if he'll ever mess with me again after Maddox got finished with him."

And then before he could press her, she slipped from his grasp, hopped quickly from the car and then opened the back and grabbed her violin. She even managed a cheerful wave as she hurried toward the school before Silas decided to get out and punish her for her blatant disobedience right there in front of the entire city.

She was running late, having gotten out of practice fifteen minutes after the class was usually over, but she couldn't bring herself to hurry out and then apologize for her tardiness. They weren't even supposed to be responsible for her today.

And then an unwelcome, completely fucked-up thought came to mind. No, not fucked-up, just *fucked*. Because it was a very good point. If Silas wasn't even supposed to be with Evangeline today and something came up that *required* someone to be with her, then why couldn't one of the *three* men picking Hayley up go babysit Evangeline for the day? Unless Silas was only too happy to volunteer his time and services.

So what if she was Drake's wife? Not like having a thing for another man's wife was anything new or uncommon. So what if Silas worked with and for Drake? Again, nothing new about being in love with your brother's wife either.

This was beyond fucked up. She'd be damned if she'd sleep in a bed where Silas was secretly fantasizing about another woman. Oh God. She placed a palm to her stomach as it lurched. Was he imagining she was Evangeline when they made love?

"Stop the hysterical train, Hayley," she muttered in disgust. "Reaching much?"

The problem wasn't that she was reaching, or rather jumping to conclusions now. The problem was she should have done a hell of a lot more reaching before she decided she'd misunderstood the situation in the first place and then jumped into bed with Silas. A man who made it clear where she lay on his list of priorities.

When she walked into the circular foyer at the front entrance with three halls branching off in different directions, she couldn't help but smile. Maddox, Thane and Justice were standing there joking around and looking completely out of place.

As if sensing her stare, Maddox lifted his gaze and immediately found her and grinned broadly.

When she approached, he scooped her up in a hug and nearly broke her ribs all over again. He planted a sloppy kiss on her nose and then set her down between him and Thane.

"How you doing, darlin'?" Thane asked, wrapping his arm around her shoulders and squeezing.

"I'm good. What about y'all?"

She didn't have to force a smile. As down as she was before, seeing three of her favorite people in the world was definitely the cure-all for the "feeling sorry for myself" blues.

"You ready to head home?" Justice asked as he opened the door for her.

"Yeah, but hey, think we can stop at the market on the way?"

They eyed her mischievous grin and then Maddox groaned.

"Seriously? You're going to torture us by having us take you to buy all the stuff to make the best damn food I've had in forever when we all know Silas hasn't left that fucking cave of his in a goddamn week and the chances of us getting to eat any is slim."

"I have it on good authority that Silas won't be there," she said, in her sassiest voice.

Thane and Justice glanced at one another, their expressions suddenly serious. Even Maddox looked perplexed.

"If he isn't going to be there, then why wouldn't he have us stick around after we drop you off?" Maddox demanded. "What the fuck?"

"Unlike the rest of you who are so quick to believe the opposite, I do not need a babysitter, much less a horde of hot-guy babysitters."

"Where the hell is he?" Maddox persisted.

"He had a pressing engagement he couldn't miss. Top priority, according to him," Hayley said with only a slight bitter twist to her lips. "Hey, guys, what's the holdup? Are we buying food or what?"

The three once again exchanged glances and Justice shrugged. "Let's go buy her some food."

"Oh, and you're all invited to dinner," she announced as they neared the car. "That is, if y'all don't also have a pressing engagement that is top priority."

"My top priority is feeding myself," Thane said.

"Amen," Justice said fervently.

"I never turn down a gorgeous woman's cooking," Maddox said cheekily.

"And said woman would never turn down the opportunity to cook for her hot-guy babysitting squad."

They all burst into laughter and Hayley valiantly tried to shove aside all thoughts of Silas and how his day was going.

23

Silas inserted a different key into each lock as he went from top to bottom. He let out a long breath when the last lock came open and he pushed open the door to his apartment. All day he'd done nothing but think of Hayley. He'd missed her. He'd been distracted, and he was *never* distracted from his primary object. Evangeline had been worried sick that something was wrong, and the last thing she needed was yet more worry and stress piled on her when she was so heavily pregnant.

He felt a surge of guilt. He'd dumped Hayley after Drake had called asking Silas to stay with Evangeline. He could have asked Maddox or any of the other guys but because Drake called him, he felt obligated to step in. But he couldn't keep shitting on Hayley this way. It wasn't fair to her when she was the most unselfish person he'd ever known and never asked him for anything at all.

His absolute loyalty had always been to Drake and the rest of his brothers and by extension anyone who belonged to them. For the first time he was questioning his priorities. And now, of all times, when the risk and danger to Drake, his wife and child, and his brothers was at its highest, he could ill afford to be distracted from their protection.

He frowned when he heard male voices and then Hayley's rising above them. It sent a shiver of pleasure straight down his spine, and then he shook himself from that moment of euphoria to concentrate on who the fuck was in his apartment, with *his* woman, making *his* woman laugh.

He was almost to the kitchen when Hayley, bearing an armload of serving dishes, darted across the walkway to the dining table on the other side. She didn't even see him until she'd placed one of the platters on the table and turned to dash back into the kitchen.

She came to an abrupt halt and then her smile lit up her entire face as she took in his presence. Warmth snaked through his chest into regions so solidly frozen with layers and layers of ice. Places that had never felt warmth in his life. God, would she always light up this way for him? Only him?

"You're home," she whispered, launching herself into his arms.

He caught her and gathered her tightly against him, burying his face in her hair. For a long moment he simply held her there, inhaling her scent and savoring the feel of her warm, fragile body against him.

"Good day?" she asked when he set her back down on her feet.

He nodded. "You?"

She wrinkled her nose. "Same old, same old. Practicing for the recital. Didn't get out until fifteen minutes late so I thought I'd make it up to the guys by making dinner. I wasn't sure if you'd make it home on time."

He glanced at the table, surprised to see so many places set. When he returned his gaze to Hayley, she was looking anxiously at him.

"I invited Maddox, Justice and Thane to stay for dinner. Is that okay?"

He put his finger to her lips, a peculiar fluttering in his stomach. "You inviting my brothers to eat will always be okay, princess. They need this. I need this. I had no idea you could cook, though."

She narrowed her eyes. "I'm not the chef *some* people are, but I get by in the kitchen. You never *asked*. The guys can vouch for this particular meal since they ate it while you were out of town on your *business* trip."

She'd cooked for his brothers while he'd been out of town? Maybe them staying with her twenty-four-seven hadn't been the best idea. She was young, beautiful and so very loving, caring and effervescent that who in the world wouldn't be charmed by her in a matter of seconds? Only a man missing a dick could look at her and not get ideas. Ideas that could get them killed. By Silas.

He held up his hands in mock surrender. "Hey, I've always said you were a woman of many talents. Many, many talents," he murmured as he closed in on her again. "I have no doubt I'll be wowed."

Her eyes sparkled mischievously. "Bet your ass you will."

He patted *her* ass when she turned away and returned to the kitchen. She threw him a saucy wink over her shoulder and then busied herself with the remaining food.

"Soup's on!" Hayley bellowed from the kitchen.

Silas grinned at the feisty little minx and how she had every single one of them trained to obey on command. Hell, he wasn't excluding himself either. He'd already acknowledged that he might have the control in their relationship, but all the power rested with her.

Well, just until after supper. The little temptress still had to be punished for her earlier blatant defiance, though he had a good idea he would enjoy her punishment every bit as much as she would. He nearly snorted at the idea of actually hurting her. He'd cut off his right arm before allowing anyone to hurt her, much less inflict physical harm on her himself.

As he heard his brothers making their way to the table, Silas stuck his head into the kitchen.

"Need any help, princess? You shouldn't be carrying so many heavy dishes at the same time."

She turned, her arms loaded down with the platters in question, and gave him another smile that caused him to melt on the spot.

"This is the last load," she said. "Go ahead and take a seat with the others. I'll be right there."

Ignoring her invitation, he stepped forward and relieved her of two of the heaviest platters, ignoring her eye roll. That would get her another punishment when the others left.

He sniffed appreciatively as his gaze wandered over the trays piled high with food.

"Smells wonderful, princess. I can't wait to try it. This must have taken you hours."

He frowned slightly as he said the last. Then he glanced back up at her.

"Don't think I don't appreciate the fact you cooked such a wonderful meal for me and my brothers, but you already put in a long day between your classes and the extra practice when you get home. There's no need for you to be on your feet all afternoon when any one of us could go pick something up."

Her smile was soft and she did not roll her eyes this time. "You're so good to me, Silas. But the truth is, this is honestly the only full meal I'm any good at making. As a result, I don't cook it often. In fact, the last time I made it apart from when you were out of town that time was for my father before he passed away. I'm more of an improvise-and-make-do-with-what-I-have-on-hand kind of girl."

His heart twisted at the sudden flash of pain in her eyes at the mention of her father, and a scowl worked its way over his features before he could call it back at the image of her getting by on the little to nothing she'd had before she'd moved in with him.

"Never again will you go without," he vowed.

The thought made him physically ill, and he had to shake the images off before the trembling in his clenched fingers caused him to drop the dinner she'd prepared all over the floor. Here was a woman who deserved so much better than what life had handed her. She was so loving and giving and life had shit on her at all turns. That shit was over. He'd make sure she always had the means to live easy and free. Even if it was without him.

"Silas," she said softly. "Everyone is at the table and I don't want the food to get cold."

"Right," he said, turning swiftly in the direction of the table.

Silas was quiet even for him throughout the meal, only half listening to the conversation around him. He was utterly conflicted about his feelings for Hayley, and his motivation for that matter. Logic and instinct guided his every thought and action, and yet his relationship with her defied both. Was this how Drake had felt about Evangeline? Was this why Drake had been a complete and utter wreck since the moment he met her? And why he'd made such a complete muck of things again and again?

He hadn't questioned his reasons or even what he wanted short *or* long term when he'd responded so impulsively to Hayley. How was it fair to her that he didn't even know where this thing between them was headed or how long it would last? He was in so far above his head that he was drowning, and it was a sensation completely unique to his adult life. It was a feeling of helplessness he hadn't felt since he was a child living under the authority and control of abusive parents.

How long would she be content to give, for him to take, without receiving in equal measure? He dropped his utensils and slipped his hands to his lap, curling his fingers into tight fists so he didn't betray the fact that they were trembling violently. He could feel the clammy sweat on his forehead and neck and prayed no one else took notice.

It took him a moment to realize he was exhibiting the initial signs of a panic attack, something else he hadn't experienced since he was a child cowering in a hiding place hoping with all his might he wouldn't be found that night.

And yet for all the guilt, and yes, uncertainty he felt about his self-ishness when it came to Hayley, the mere thought of *not* having her made the panic rise even more sharply. It was something that didn't even bear thinking about.

Damned if he did and even more damned if he didn't.

What a fucking situation to be in. Never in a million years had he ever even contemplated having this particular dilemma. A relationship was something he'd sworn he'd never involve himself in for hundreds of reasons. And yet he'd given not a single one of those hundreds of reasons the briefest consideration before plunging so recklessly headfirst into the one thing he would have laughed himself silly over the mere mention of just a few months ago.

At least now he could look back at Drake's psychotic, uncharacteristic behavior over Evangeline with a more objective eye. He could even summon sympathy, where before his two primary judgments of Drake had been that the man was out of his fucking mind and that he'd acted reprehensibly and unforgivably toward Evangeline numerous times.

Silas blinked when he realized Maddox had been saying something to him. Apparently many times, judging by Hayley's look of concern and his brothers' frowns of reprimand.

"Earth to Silas. Anyone home?" Maddox asked in exasperation.

"What?" Silas asked irritably.

Maddox shook his head. "I was saying how delicious the dinner is that Hayley made for us. Wouldn't you agree?"

Fuck. Not only had he tuned everyone out, completely lost in his own little world, but it appeared he hadn't jumped in at the right moment to give Hayley the praise and appreciation she was due.

He gathered her hand in his and lifted it to his mouth to press a kiss to her silky soft skin.

"It was absolutely wonderful, princess. Best damn meal I ever ate."

She flushed, but pleasure and happiness over his compliment glowed warmly in her eyes. His gut tightened. He'd do whatever it took for her to look at him like that every goddamn day.

"I was hoping there'd be leftovers," Thane said morosely as he surveyed the empty platters. "I was already drooling over tomorrow's lunch. Sure beats the hell out of takeout or whatever the hell's currently in my fridge."

Hayley's eyes sparkled with mischief and she donned an innocent smile. If she had any idea of its effect and that it would get her any damn thing she wanted, she would likely use it a lot more often.

"I may have just set aside enough for you to take home."

Thane did a fist pump. "You're my new favorite girl, Hayley. Your wish will forever be my command."

"Back off," Silas growled. "Any wish she needs fulfilled will not be by you."

Maddox and Justice sent her an honest-to-goodness pout that had Silas staring at them both in disgust.

Hayley rolled her eyes and then laughed. "I made enough for all of you to bring home leftovers. Why do you think it took me twice as long to make dinner as it did the first time I cooked for y'all?"

At that Silas's frown deepened. "You shouldn't have been in the kitchen on your feet all afternoon. You've been working way too hard practicing for your recital."

She heaved a sigh of exasperation. "You forget that not so long ago I was working two steady jobs and any other work I could pick up. Trust me. Standing in the kitchen for a few hours is a lot less taxing than being on my feet in a crowded bar serving drunk customers until two in the morning."

Silas's lips tightened at the reminder of just how hard she'd been forced to work.

"I'm glad you're no longer working those ridiculous hours," he said gruffly. "You were running yourself into the ground."

"Yes, well, now I don't have to, thanks to a *clerical oversight* being found and corrected," she said with a perfectly straight face. But her eyes sparkled with amusement at the private joke they shared.

Silas's jaw clenched at the mere reminder of the man who'd done so much damage to his princess.

His attention was diverted when his brothers began rising from the table, picking up the dishes to take into the kitchen.

"You outdid yourself, babe," Justice said, letting out an exaggerated groan. "It's time for us to get on out of here. We've taken up enough of your time as it is, and as Silas said, you shouldn't have spent all afternoon slaving over a hot stove when you've been so busy with school and practice."

They paraded into the kitchen, insisting Hayley remain seated while they cleared the table. When they were finished, they all dropped affectionate kisses on top of her head and said their good-byes. Hayley beamed and gave them all a wave as they exited the apartment. Silas was close on their heels, securing each of the locks behind them.

When he turned back to Hayley, he was barely able to voice his command around the excitement and need mounting in him.

"Go into the bedroom and completely strip. I want you belly down on the bed, feet planted on the floor. Do not move. Wait for me. I'll be in as soon as I've taken care of cleaning the kitchen."

"Oh, but—"

He arched one eyebrow that silenced her immediately. "Do as I told you," he said in a dangerously soft voice.

She shivered, chill bumps erupting on her arms. Without another word, she rose gracefully from the table and hurried toward the bedroom. Only then did Silas allow himself to smile as he anticipated what he had in store for his princess.

24

Hayley warred with nervousness and excitement as she hurriedly complied with Silas's command. Though it had been softly worded, there had been nothing soft about his eyes or expression. There was a feral light in his gaze and his features had been rigid with purpose. He had looked almost . . . savage. She shivered at the memory and rubbed her palms rapidly up and down her arms in an attempt to warm herself before she settled into position on the bed.

His brooding intensity should scare the wits out of her but she couldn't bring herself to ever truly fear the man she'd given herself wholly to. She knew in her heart he would never hurt her. He'd been nothing but fiercely protective of her, and he had also made her feel so very cherished and treasured. What woman wouldn't melt into a puddle to have a man like Silas be so focused on her every need and comfort?

She bit her lip. Then what had been in his eyes tonight and why did she have the distinct feeling that she was about to see another side to Silas? Not that she was fool enough to think she knew everything there was to know about a man with more secrets and shadows than her entire hometown. She would probably continue to be surprised and see something new from him twenty years from now, if she was so fortunate as to still be in his life.

Her eyes widened with the realization of just what she'd just admitted. Permanency. A life with Silas. She wanted to roll her eyes at herself and mutter a loud *Duh!* Why should the thought of wanting to be with him twenty, forty, sixty years from now surprise her? She was so wrapped up in him that she never wanted to work herself free. He was everything she'd ever wanted in a man. The only question mark looming over her was . . . Evangeline and just how and where she fit into Silas's life and why another man's wife took absolute precedence over Hayley's importance and role in Silas's life. It made her unsure and insecure, and neither was a welcome or comforting feeling.

If Silas truly cared for her the same way she cared for him, he wouldn't constantly place the needs of another woman—a *married* woman—over Hayley. Hayley wouldn't be relegated so far down the list of Silas's priorities, ranking at least fourth—if not lower. She knew his loyalty was to Drake, Evangeline and his brothers above all others, and those were just the ones she knew about. Who knew who else rated higher?

Maybe she was just a distraction. A passing source of entertainment and an outlet for sex. Convenient. Maybe he didn't have any intention of keeping her around for any length of time, and if that was the case, she was the biggest fool ever for putting him first, for giving him her absolute loyalty, obedience and submission.

She didn't doubt that Silas was a good man. He wasn't an asshole, at least not on purpose. He'd never given Hayley any indication that he didn't value her, and he always looked out for her best interest and protected her from any perceived threat. But if she didn't have his heart, if she didn't have his absolute commitment, what did she really have?

He owned every piece of her, body, mind and soul. Could she say the same about him? And did she even want to know the answer to that question? Sometimes the truth hurt. It cut as deeply as the sharpest blade, and sometimes ignorance truly was bliss. At least if she didn't know the truth she could continue to create her own reality and remain unaware of Silas's true feelings for her.

She closed her eyes, angry that she was ruining what promised to be an exciting, pleasurable night because no matter what Silas planned, no matter the uncompromising set to his features, she knew he would take care of her and ensure her pleasure before his own. If she knew nothing else, she knew this to be the one steady truth in their relationship.

If she would only stop overanalyzing and picking apart every aspect of his personality and stop letting her insecurities and fears overrule all else and just relax and live in the moment, then she'd be a hell of a lot happier for it. She couldn't predict what might happen tomorrow, next week, next month or five years from now. But what she could do was enjoy each and every minute she and Silas were together, and no matter what the future held, she would hold close and savor and cherish every single moment she had with him. The only thing she could control was the here and now. Nothing else. So why torture herself endlessly on the *what ifs* and *maybes*?

Feeling marginally better after the stern lecture she'd administered to her deeply held fears and insecurities, she relaxed and instead focused on what Silas had planned for her and just what he'd do to her tonight.

Just the thought sent a warm flush over her entire body, and an electric tingle skittered up her legs to her torso and to the roots of her hair. Her fingers that had been splayed wide, planted on the mattress on either side of her head, dug into the bed and curled into tight fists, the material of the luxurious comforter gathered in her grasp.

Her body was suddenly restless and a low moan slipped past her lips as she fought the urge to writhe and slip one hand down between her legs to stroke over her highly sensitized clit. She fought off the temptation, knowing Silas wouldn't be pleased, and pleasing him made her happy. She loved the approval that warmed his gaze when she willingly did his bidding. It made it sound like she was a child desperate to please or gain the approval of a parent or adult. It would no doubt make her appear needy and pathetic to other people, but she didn't give one fuck about what anyone except Silas thought about her. Making him happy—wanting to make him happy—was something she did for her every bit as much as she did it for him. And if something satisfied her and filled the hollow places in her heart, then that was all that mattered. She owed no one explanations, nor did she have to justify her decisions to anyone but herself.

She breathed in sharply and went completely still, letting her fingers uncurl and relax when she registered Silas's presence in the bedroom. Her pulse sped up and a flutter began deep in her belly, traveling to the many erogenous zones at the apex of her thighs. Her vagina clenched in greedy expectation of what was to come.

She nearly flinched when his huge hand covered her ass cheek, offering a caress as he petted her.

"That's my good girl," he said huskily, approval laced in every word. "You're my very good girl. So obedient and mindful of my instructions."

She flushed with delight, warmth shooting through her veins at his praise.

"However, you weren't so obedient or mindful of my wishes earlier today. My princess must be punished for such blatant and willful disobedience. I won't tolerate you ever ignoring matters concerning your personal safety."

Her eyes flew open at the unexpected reprimand. *What?* She barely managed to keep from voicing the shocked *What?* aloud but bit into her lip just in time. Her mind raced frantically, perplexed and trying to understand what he meant. She'd ignored matters concerning her personal safety?

"More than the fact that you disregarded my wishes," he continued as he kept caressing the plump swell of her ass, "is the fact that you put yourself at risk by placing yourself in danger and prevented me from being in a position to protect you if the need arose. And that, my beautiful girl, is something I will never allow. Your safety, your well-being, is not just important. It's *everything*. This is one area I will tolerate no defiance, and you *will* obey me when it comes to your welfare. Is that understood?"

"Y-yes," Hayley whispered.

Understanding finally registered. He'd been angry that she hadn't waited for him to walk her into the building when he dropped her off at school. She hadn't even considered it because so much else had consumed her thoughts since then. A part of her heart melted at the stern gruffness that did nothing to disguise the very real concern in his voice.

"Yes, what?" he prompted.

"Yes, Silas."

"Promise me."

"I promise, Silas."

"Now, as your punishment you will remain positioned exactly as you are except I will bind your hands behind your back. You will receive twenty lashes from a flogger and after each one you will thank me for punishing you and keeping you safe. You get me?"

Stunned, she tried to respond but nothing came out. When she finally could formulate a sentence it came out choppy and nearly inaudible.

"I get you, Silas."

"Repeat back my instructions so I know you understand."

"After each lash I am to thank you for punishing me and keeping me safe," she said, her breath hitching in her throat.

His hand traveled up and then back down her spine in a loving caress that was in direct contradiction to the steel in his voice.

"That's my princess," he praised.

His hand left her and she nearly cried out her protest. There were muffled sounds and then he was back. He captured one of her hands and very gently brought it around to the small of her back before retrieving the other and positioning her wrists in a cross. Then he began winding rope around her wrists, taking care not to make it too tight or abrade her skin.

He hadn't administered the first blow and she was already violently aroused, her entire body tense, expectant, her nipples taut, her clit tingling with anticipation. She closed her eyes, sinking her teeth into her lip. Oh God, she'd never last the twenty lashes he'd sentenced upon her.

Would he fuck her when he was finished, or would withholding her pleasure be part of her punishment? She went moist as images of him spreading her, her arms still bound, thrusting deep and hard over and over into her willing body bombarded her senses.

This time the moan escaped her lips and she twisted restlessly in an attempt to alleviate the burning need that gripped her so relentlessly.

He moved away from her again and she strained to hear any sound he made, trying to track his movements and anticipate when he'd administer the first lash.

It came out of nowhere, taking her completely by surprise. Fire erupted on the fleshy cheek he struck and raced over her skin, turning quickly to heated pleasure that hummed through her veins, bathing her entire body in the euphoric aftermath of the initial pain.

Never had she experienced anything to rival the sensation of the crop across her bare ass. By the time she'd blessedly remembered to thank him for punishing her and keeping her safe—very nearly forgetting after the initial blow—she was mindless with edgy need, pleasure and a haze of euphoria that settled over her like the thickest cloud.

When he reached the halfway mark, he paused and she very nearly cried out in disappointment and had to stifle her pleas for him not to stop. He petted and caressed every inch of flesh he'd marked with the flogger and then leaned down to cover the same area with kisses.

She let out a whispered sigh of sweet contentment, wondering how something that felt this good could possibly be called punishment.

When his lips left her, she tensed in expectation of the next blow, even arching her buttocks eagerly as if begging for the kiss of the flogger.

"My beautiful, sweet girl," Silas murmured in obvious approval. "So perfect. So obedient. I'm so fucking lucky."

Tears pricked the edges of her eyes as the precious words seeped into her very soul. Silas wasn't a demonstrative man by nature. She'd observed how he was with others. Quiet, reserved. And very private. And yet with her he was so much more open. Affectionate. Approving. That she got to see a side so few rarely witnessed gave her a measure of satisfaction unlike any she'd ever known.

She jumped when the next blow fell even though she'd been expecting it at any second. It was harder than the first ten and she had to battle through the initial burn before the exotic bliss finally followed on its heels. He stepped up his efforts for the remaining lashes and with each subsequent flick of his wrist, the intensity grew until she was no longer cognizant of any thought or rationale. She could only feel. Experience. Give herself wholly to wave after wave of exquisite, earth-shattering pleasure.

She was panting when the last blow was administered, and her thank-you was a barely audible whisper. Once more Silas leaned down, and this time he pressed his lips to the small of her back just below where her bound wrists rested. It was like a benediction. Full of praise, admiration and approval. She had pleased him and that gave her indescribable pleasure.

To have brought even a measure of happiness and satisfaction to a man who'd seen little of either in his dim, gray life gave her a sense of peace she hadn't felt since she was just a little girl with no worries except what game to play next. Before the days of her father's illness and watching him slowly waste away and become a shell of the man he used to be.

Perhaps she gave Silas something he rarely experienced, but he too gave her something she'd long gone without. Protection. Affection. Being needed by someone. Love . . .

She blinked rapidly as the last word rolled through her mind, glowing brightly. Oh yes, she loved him. She'd loved him from the very start, of that she was certain. Why else would she have reacted to him as she had? Why else would she give him something she'd never give to another man? Her absolute submission. Control. Her body, her heart, her very soul.

Slowly and with great care, Silas loosened the bonds around her hands and in turn brought each wrist to his mouth and kissed every inch that had been touched by the rope. This big, beautiful man was so very good to her and he was all hers. Except maybe he wasn't.

She immediately closed the door on that wayward thought, refusing to allow anything to ruin this moment. She wouldn't think of Evangeline—or what she was to Silas. Not tonight. She wouldn't believe such a thing of him. He was too honest and blunt, always saying what was on his mind, and she couldn't conceive of him betraying her in such a horrible fashion. She had to be wrong. There was no other explanation.

Letting go of her hands, he gently turned her over and then pulled her to her feet, wrapping his arms around her. He fed hungrily at her mouth like he was starving for her. Every bit as ravenous for her as she was for him.

She went a little crazy, her need to touch him, to bring him the same pleasure he gave her consuming her to the exclusion of all else. She ripped at his clothing, desperate and impatient to remove any barrier between them, wanting to be skin on skin.

He didn't utter a single protest or admonishment, seemingly as mindless as she was, needing her every bit as much as she needed him. His shirt went flying, minus at least three buttons, lost in her haste to undress him. His jeans followed and then his underwear slid to the floor, leaving him naked, his erection scorching her sensitive flesh.

She started at his mouth, kissing him with as much fervor as he'd kissed her merely seconds ago. Then she worked her way to his neck, nipping and biting, marking his beautiful male skin. The idea of marking her territory, of giving him a visible sign of her possession, aroused primitive instincts within her.

She kissed, licked and sucked over his muscled chest and lapped at his flat nipples, causing them to become rigid beneath her tongue. Gripping his hips, she licked her way lower, swirling her tongue around his navel and teasing him until he growled and circled her shoulders in his strong grasp.

Her final destination was just inches away. His erection jutted upward magnificently, every vein exposed, the dusky color of the head evidence of the extent of his arousal. She wanted to lick and suck him until he begged for mercy. Each time in the past that she'd intended to pleasure him with her mouth, to take his huge cock as deeply into her mouth as possible, he'd always been too impatient and had interrupted her before she had the opportunity to give him as much pleasure as he gave to her on a nightly basis. Tonight she wouldn't be deterred.

Lowering her hands and bending her knees, she wrapped her fingers around his massive girth and flicked her tongue out to lick at the bead of moisture forming at the tip of his cock. Before her tongue touched him, he let out another growl.

"No!" he said harshly.

She was immediately lifted and tossed down onto the bed. He loomed over her, his features drawn into a savage expression of need and intense arousal. Before she could so much as utter a word, he spread her wide, baring her completely to his possession, and he was above her and then inside her in one forceful lunge that robbed her of all breath.

It was too much. Already hypersensitive and violently aroused, she shattered into a million tiny pieces as soon as he completed one brutal thrust. She cried out and latched desperately onto his powerful arms, needing an anchor in the ferocious storm of her orgasm. It went on and on, seemingly endless, until she sobbed with need, hunger, a little frightened at the intensity of their passion and her body's reaction to Silas's invasion.

"Shhh, princess. I've got you. Just hold on to me and trust me. Let yourself go. I'll never let you fall."

With another cry, she completely unraveled, shocked and terrified by the power of her second release so quickly after the first. She felt as though she were held together by only the thinnest of threads.

"Trust me," Silas whispered against her ear as he hugged her close to his chest.

"Always," she whispered back.

She floated on a sea of the most beautiful pleasure she'd ever experienced as she registered Silas following her over the edge. He slumped down over her body, blanketing her with his warmth and strength. This was what she loved and craved most in the aftermath of their tumultuous lovemaking. When he was as boneless as she and he gave her his full weight while still buried deeply inside her. The sense of peace in this moment was the most beautiful thing she'd ever felt. Here and now there was no room for doubt or insecurity. There was just her and Silas, and in his arms, nothing could ever hurt her.

"Have to say, princess. You might have to disobey me more often," he said between ragged breaths. "Although I might not survive it if you do."

She laughed softly, joy filling her heart. "If this is your idea of punishment, then I hate to be the one to break it to you, but you don't exactly provide incentive to be a good girl."

He nipped at her lobe and then licked the mark to soothe it. "You're *my* good girl, though."

25

Hayley rubbed the last of the wetness from her hair after drying off from the shower she'd laughingly begged Silas to let her take and then walked back into the bedroom. Her stare was immediately drawn to Silas, who was still naked and sprawled lazily against the headboard. God, this man was magnificent.

His gaze immediately locked onto her and he smiled, a spark in his eyes that made her shiver. The muscles in his arm flexed as he raised his hand to crook his finger at her. He chuckled when she crawled onto the bed next to him.

"I don't know why you insisted on a shower when I'm just going to mess you up all over again," he drawled, a wicked glint to his eyes.

His statement elicited a full-body shiver, chill bumps of anticipation prickling over her skin. Licking her lips, she hesitantly slid her hand over the top of his muscled thigh, brushing the tips of her fingers over his testicles. She held her breath, waiting for his inevitable rejection, bracing herself for the hurt and confusion over why her touching him so intimately seemed abhorrent to him.

Maybe the other times were just a coincidence. She did have a history of jumping to conclusions, and those instances had been at times when his patience and control had been thin. But now after being initially sated, the mood was more relaxed and she was determined to show him her love and give him as much pleasure as she was capable of.

When he didn't move away or redirect her attention, she relaxed, relief bubbling up inside her. Emboldened by his acceptance, she wrapped her hand around his now-hardened flesh and then lowered her head, her hair splashing over his thighs like a curtain.

Before her mouth could close around him, he fisted his hand in her hair while gripping her arm with his other hand, and he hastily dragged her up his chest so that her thighs straddled his hips.

She opened her mouth to ask him why when his lips melted over hers, his clever fingers simultaneously stroking over her clit while he used his other hand to tease one of her nipples. With a soft moan, she surrendered, melting into his body as he continued his delicious torment. But this time, she wouldn't forget to question him later. No longer could she tell herself that it was all in her head.

One of his hands left her and she heard the nightstand drawer open, then felt something cold press against her clit. She gasped and tried to pull away from the sensation, but Silas clamped down on her hip to prevent it.

"Reach down and put my dick in that sweet pussy," he growled, and Hayley hurried to obey. "That's right," he hissed as she slid down his length. "Now don't move until I say so. Not one twitch, princess, or I'll redden your ass again."

Hayley stared at Silas with uncertainty, not at all sure what to make of their current positions. She gave him a half smile and adopted a teasing tone. "Wow, I'm never in control. I have no idea what to do here, Silas."

Amusement was thick in Silas's voice. "It's adorable that you think you'll be in control because you're on top." He tweaked her nose affectionately. "I assure you that at no time will you be in control, sweet girl. Now put your hands on my shoulders and keep them there."

She leaned forward to follow his command and as soon as her hands were in place, the hard coldness pressed against her clit again. "Silas, what—?"

A cry of shocked pleasure escaped her as the coldness started to vibrate. The sensation shot from her clit to her nipples, then continued to spread. Her nails dug into his shoulders as she fought the urge to impale herself on him over and over. *Don't move. Don't move.* Oh God, she needed to move.

Just when she knew she was going to defy Silas's order, he moved the toy from pressing in one spot and began circling her clit. Her strained breathing eased slightly and just as she thought she could handle the sensations, he once again pressed it firmly to her clit, holding it in one place. Her world narrowed to that buzzing object and the enormous erection stretching her trembling muscles.

She made a desperate sound of need. "P-please, Silas. Please. I need to move."

"Are you sure that's what you need? Positive?" he whispered against her trembling lips. "Beg me prettily and I'll consider granting my princess's request."

As if he would ever deny her. Hayley almost gave him a smug smile until she remembered he *had* denied her one thing and she had no idea why. She wasn't experienced enough to understand the intricacies of male sexuality, and she was completely puzzled by Silas's reaction to her. Maybe it was just a stereotype that all men liked for women to go down on them.

"Please," she said in her most husky, enticing voice. "*Please* let me move. I *need* to move."

His hand shifted lower and his eyes glittered as he stared at her. "Go," he said in a harsh, needy voice as he pressed the toy against his dick, sending a shock wave of vibration through her pussy. "Ride me hard, princess."

Her eyes nearly rolled back in her head at the electrical surge that made his engorged cock quiver and stimulate her highly sensitized tissues. Desperate for the pleasure he promised, she rose and fell, trying to hold back the orgasm that was precariously close to erupting over her.

No. It was too soon. Calling on discipline and restraint she didn't think she possessed, she fought to keep her release at bay. She wanted to make this as perfect for Silas as it would be for her, and to do that she had to keep moving but not end it before it had barely begun. She increased her pace but kept a very tight leash on the edgy, clawing need that was all-consuming. In response, Silas's fingers dug into her hip as he began to arch his hips, no longer content for her to do all the work. He seemed determined to drive himself as deeply as possible into her welcoming body, and she wanted that every bit as much as he did. But when he once again moved the toy and began a relentless assault on her swollen clit while pumping forcefully into her, she could no longer hold back the inevitable. He dragged her lips to his, and her scream was swallowed up by his mouth, his tongue plunging inward, mimicking the action of his cock. A mere second after she came screaming and writhing wildly in his arms, his entire body grew taut, his muscles tensing, a look on his face that could be interpreted as either intense pleasure or pain marking his features, and he followed her into the chaotic swirl of ecstasy. Her heart clenched when he shouted her name and then he gathered her in his arms, nearly crushing her with the strength of his hold, and he whispered so very tenderly, "My princess. My precious girl."

Never had she felt so cherished, like she was the most important person in Silas's rigid, disciplined world. She could spend forever like this, soaking up his tender endearments. Exhausted, completely sated and spent, she snuggled deeply in Silas's arms, nestled against his chest, a sigh of deep contentment escaping in a long breath. Silas seemed as content as she was for him to hold her in the ensuing silence, rubbing his hand up and down her back as she burrowed even deeper into his embrace until there was no space between them and they were joined physically, mentally, soul deep. No longer were they two separate entities but one single being. She was so deeply in over her head. If Silas didn't feel the same way as she did, she would be utterly destroyed. She closed her eyes and shook off those thoughts, knowing she was on a path that potentially led to heartbreak.

"I don't think I can move," she murmured ruefully.

"That's okay, princess. I like you right where you are. Just let me hold you for a little while and then I'll take care of my girl."

She sighed again and allowed her mind to drift, enjoying the euphoric haze that seemed to envelop them both. She could so easily imagine this being their future. Their forever. As soon as she registered that thought, some of the glow dissipated and her lips turned down in unhappiness. Why couldn't she just be happy with what she had? Why set herself up for potential disaster? Why did she have to risk damaging her relationship with Silas by being a clingy, insecure twit? She knew without a doubt Silas would never tolerate or accept a woman trying to make demands, conditions or *ever* calling the shots when he was abundantly clear on his position when it came to him having absolute control and his demand for complete submission.

She was jolted from her thoughts when Silas stirred beneath her, and it was automatic to clutch him in an effort to prolong the moment and preserve the intimacy they'd shared. Silas affectionately kissed the top of her head.

"Time to take care of my princess."

He gently eased her off him and onto the bed, where she curled up, still boneless. He ran his hand gently down her side before leaving the bed to get a cloth to clean her up. Hayley watched his muscular ass flex as he walked away and made a sound of feminine appreciation because her man was the definition of perfect. She'd never seen a man built the way he was. Broad shoulders and chest, lean waist and arms and thighs rippling with muscle with not so much as an inch of spare flesh to be found. She loved his body, loved snuggling up to him, but she loved his heart the most and how dedicated he was to her comfort and care. He indulged her every whim and spoiled her shamelessly. What more could a woman ask for? He was the total package.

Despite her best effort, reality intruded as she recalled that, once again, Silas had blatantly rejected her attempts to pleasure him with her mouth. And it wasn't the first time. Or the second. No longer could she chalk it up to heat of the moment, coincidence or even her imagination, and though the last thing she wanted was to incite any discord between them, it was too important to her to know if he didn't want her or if he simply found her too inexperienced and inept.

Hadn't he promised to teach her everything she needed to know? How to please him? He'd seemed genuinely delighted by her inexperience and had reassured her more than once that he was glad he was the only man who'd ever made love to her, just as he had expressed enthusiasm for being the source for anything she needed to know or learn.

When Silas returned to the bed to clean her up, she felt shy and nervous and suddenly very unsure of herself.

Ever in tune with her every mood, he sent her a seeking look as he tossed the cloth in the hamper. He settled on the bed and tucked her into his side as he kissed the side of her head.

"What's wrong, princess?"

Should she bring it up? God, this was so awkward. And what was she going to do if the problem really *was* with her or he simply didn't want her that way? Silas wasn't the type to pacify anyone. He wouldn't evade her question or lie to make her feel better. Suddenly she wasn't so sure she *wanted* to know the truth.

She briefly closed her eyes and silently inhaled a long, fortifying breath. Oh, please don't let her be making the biggest mistake of her life. She turned slightly toward Silas, tilting her head to peek up at him from beneath her lashes.

"Can I ask you something, Silas?"

Silas tensed as he saw uncertainty and obvious discomfort flash over

Hayley's face. She looked vulnerable and *scared*. Automatically he reached out to touch her face in an attempt to ease the lines of worry. What could possibly have her so anxious about asking him anything? Was he that rigid and imposing? He wanted her to trust him and never hesitate to come to him for *anything*. Had he done something to make her feel as though she couldn't?

"I hope you know you can ask me anything, my sweet girl," he said in a gentle tone.

She glanced down a moment before lifting her gaze once more, color staining her cheeks. "Why don't you want me to touch you ... there ... to pleasure you like you pleasure me?" she asked in a low voice.

Silas's brow furrowed in confusion, not immediately understanding her question. She always pleasured him. Hell, being in the same room with her pleased him. Looking at her pleased him.

"Why won't you let me touch you with my mouth? Do you not want me that way? Is it because I don't have any experience? Am I that terrible at it?"

Her flush deepened, and her expression became more distressed as understanding flashed painfully in Silas's mind. He closed his eyes, tormented by the thought that he'd made her feel unwanted. Not good enough. As if she didn't please him. When nothing could be further from the truth. Dear God, how did he explain? How could he tell her of his shameful, degrading past and why the mere thought of having anyone perform oral sex on him sent him to dark places in his past he never wanted to revisit again?

He desperately scrambled for something to say, an explanation. Something that would reassure her without having to delve into the sordid details that would horrify her and forever change the way she looked at him. How could she possibly ever want to be near him again if she knew the awful truth? What if she no longer wanted him?

He slid his hand down to tuck his fingers beneath her chin, nudging upward so she was forced to meet his gaze.

"Hayley, you trusting me to be your first lover, the gift of your virginity, is the single most precious gift anyone has ever given me. I said this before and I absolutely meant it. In no way does your innocence and inexperience affect my absolute desire for you. I *love* that I'm the only man who has ever touched you so intimately, the only man who has ever made love to you, and I love even more being the one you discover your passion with and being the man who teaches you anything you want to know. Nothing will ever change that."

Her eyes and expression very clearly showed her confusion and uncertainty. Her doubt.

"Then *why*?" she whispered. "Why don't you want me to pleasure you in that way? You can show me how if I'm doing it wrong. I want to give that to you, Silas. It's important to me."

Silas closed his eyes as awkward silence fell over them and pain slashed through his heart. To withhold the truth from her would only feed into her insecurity and she would forever perceive it as a rejection of her, and he'd die before ever making her feel that way.

And yet if he lost her by confessing who and what he was, a part of him would die anyway. Bracing for her inevitable horror and rejection, he sucked in a tortured breath, his expression going as bleak as he felt.

"It's not you, princess," he said in barely above a whisper. "It's never been you. You're so fucking perfect and I'm . . ." He closed his eyes again and looked away as unfamiliar emotion and vulnerability gripped him.

Beside him, Hayley shifted, going up on her knees as she slid her hands into his, holding tightly.

"You're what, Silas?"

"Damaged. A monster. A killer," he said dispassionately.

Her sudden intake of air was audible, and he tensed.

"I'll *never* believe you're a monster," she said in an angry voice. "I don't care what you believe. What you've been told. You are *not* a monster and I won't have you say it."

"I killed my own parents," he said bluntly, his eyes going to her face to witness her reaction.

She didn't so much as blink. "Then I'm thinking you must have had a pretty good reason," she said softly, her hold on his hands never loosening.

For a moment he was completely robbed of speech as he stared at her in astonishment.

"Tell me, Silas," she gently prompted. "Tell me why you killed them."

"They were abusive. Obsessed with money, though neither of them ever worked a day in their lives. One night when I was nine years old I was hiding in one of the bedrooms, as usual, while my parents were throwing one of their parties where the goal was to get as drunk and as high as possible and then be hungover for days after. Though I feared the parties, I actually looked forward to the aftermath, when my parents would be too strung out and hungover to even notice me. Those were the only times I wasn't subjected to their abuse. Any other time I was their outlet for their frustration with their own pathetic, miserable existences."

Hayley made a sound of distress but said nothing. Her only other reaction was the instant tightening of her hands around his. He couldn't bear to look at her, to see the sympathy and compassion shining in her eyes.

"So there I was, cowering under a bed, only aware of the sounds and smells of sex, alcohol, drugs and the too-loud music that always blared through the piece-of-shit house my parents had found abandoned and moved into. One of the men they were partying with stumbled into the bedroom just as I had decided to risk leaving my hiding place and escaping out a window because things were getting bad, much worse than usual, and I just wanted to escape.

"When I saw the way he looked at me, I knew something was very wrong. I was so scared that I was frozen in place, unable to move, much less run. At that moment my fear was as strong as the hatred I had for my parents, their constant abuse, their nightly parties, the never-ending uncertainty I lived with. He dragged me to the middle of the room, shoved me to my knees and unzipped his pants. I was so terrified and shocked that I didn't even fight him. But when he squeezed my jaw so hard I thought it was going to break to make me open my mouth and then shoved his dick down my throat, I went crazy. I bit him . . ."

Silas broke off, the memories of that night crashing over him, battering his senses. God, he hadn't thought about that night in years. Hadn't allowed himself to. He chanced a look at Hayley and flinched when he saw tears rolling down her cheeks. He shuddered, determined to get it all out and then deal with the consequences.

"When I bit him, he hit me so hard I almost passed out. Then he pulled a gun I hadn't even noticed he had on him and put it to my head. He gave me two choices."

The shame was suddenly as sharp as it had been that night, and Silas couldn't go on. His throat was closing in on him, rendering him incapable of speech. Then Hayley leaned forward, burying her face in his neck, the warmth of her tears on his skin as she pressed soothing kisses against the side of his neck. Feeding on her strength and loving support, he sucked in several breaths to steady his frayed nerves and forged ahead, knowing it was best to get it over with and not delay the inevitable.

"He told me I could suck him off or he'd blow my fucking brains out."

"Oh Silas, no!" Hayley said in a stricken voice as she lifted her head from his neck.

He closed his eyes, too ashamed to look at her when he made his humiliating, cowardly confession.

"God help me, I thought about it. I knelt there on my goddamn knees in that filthy fucking house and contemplated refusing just so he would shoot me and end my miserable existence. I wanted to die. I saw it as a way of finally escaping. Then he laughed at me and tossed his gun on the bed and to my everlasting shame, I panicked, because I'd taken too long. I hadn't been man enough to just tell him to do it. So I begged him to kill me. I called him every name I'd ever heard my parents call me, trying to piss him off enough to shoot me in his rage. And the son of a bitch laughed, and he kept laughing the entire time he forced his cock down my throat. If I hadn't been such a fucking coward I would have gotten the escape I had fantasized about every waking minute of every day," he said bitterly.

"You are *not* a coward," Hayley hissed fiercely, tears running openly down her face. "I will not sit here and have you think it or say it."

Silas attempted a halfhearted smile at her staunch defense but failed miserably.

"After he came all over my face and forced me to lick him clean, my mother and father stumbled into the room, as usual high as kites and drunk off their asses. To this day I don't know why but for one second I actually had hope that they'd help me. That they'd be pissed that this fucking stranger just sexually assaulted their child. It was a stupid thought because they'd never done a damn thing to help me before. But worse than the fact that they stood there laughing—they actually laughed!— was the sudden spark of excitement and . . . greed . . . in my old man's eyes. I knew then that I had fucked up by not having made the man shoot me and that I'd regret that decision for the rest of my life. Because now my parents had a new source for the money they coveted but refused to get off their lazy asses for. They began prostituting me out to men who didn't give a shit about the age or sex of the person sucking their cock."

"I hate them!" Hayley said viciously, tears still running in never-ending streams down her beautiful face. "God, I wish *I* had killed them. They *deserved* to die."

She leaned forward again and wrapped her arms around him, holding him with all her strength as she laid her head on his shoulder, but he was so numb and frozen and lost in the past that he didn't feel her reassuring heat or the comfort she offered.

"For two years, I endured the worst. Forced to blow anyone who forked over enough cash. Then one night when I was eleven, my dear old mom and dad came home from a meeting with a prospective 'client.' They calmly informed me that I could make them more money by doing more than suck cock and that they had several clients interested in fucking a young boy. To this day I still don't know what happened. Something inside me just broke loose and it was like I was no longer in my body but outside it, passively observing as, for the first time, I openly defied them. I told them to go to hell.

"My parents lost their shit. They beat me over and over with their hands, fists, belts, a pool cue, whatever they could grab on to, and the detached part of me accepted it, that I was finally going to die, and I embraced it. All I could think was that I would finally be free and at peace.

"But then I seemed to step back into my body and I couldn't even feel the horrific pain that I'd felt just seconds before. I didn't feel anything at all except overwhelming, horrible rage. I took them both apart with my bare hands. All the pent-up fury, pain and grief that I lived with ever since I could remember erupted, and I was utterly unstoppable."

He stared down at his open hands, now so much larger than those that had ravaged two adults, and he could still see the bright red blood staining them. He curled them into fists, refusing to feel remorse for killing two soulless monsters.

"The cops showed up just seconds after I killed them. Found out later an elderly neighbor had watched the whole thing, since my dumbfuck parents didn't bother to close the door. He was disabled and couldn't help me, but he did call the police. I can still see the look on those cops' faces. They were horrified. Not by what I'd been through, but by what I'd done."

His jaw clenched as he remembered one of the cops whispering to his partner. *He has death in his eyes. Poor kid never had a chance. They've turned him into a monster and now it looks like what they ended up with is a savage killing machine.* They weren't wrong. He *was* a monster. There was no fighting genetics.

"They knew it was self-defense, without a doubt. That was obvious. But they'd seen what I was capable of, even at such a young age, so I was deemed a threat. Instead of being sent into the foster system, I was placed in a juvenile detention center to keep me out of trouble and to protect the public. They thought it would curb my 'violent tendencies.' They were wrong, but I did learn how to work the system. By the time I turned eighteen, I'd learned everything necessary to create and live the life I wanted."

He shrugged indifferently, but on the inside his heart was hammering so hard he felt dizzy.

"So you see, Hayley, the man you gave your innocence to is a remorseless killer who gets sick to his stomach if a woman goes near his dick with her mouth. Quite a winner you chose."

He continued to stare at the wall, not wanting to see the disgust that was surely on Hayley's face.

She raised her head from his shoulder, and he waited for the inevitable judgment.

"Are you fucking *kidding* me?" she shouted.

Despite his determination not to, he glanced at her, taken aback by her vehemence.

There was no disgust, pity or condemnation on her face. Just pure, unadulterated . . . rage. *For* him, not *at* him.

For a moment he couldn't breathe for the hope that welled unbidden from the depths of the soul he hadn't thought he'd possessed anymore.

"What was *wrong* with those people? What kind of an asshole sees a horrifically abused child and puts him in juvenile detention instead of getting him the help he deserves? What the *fuck*, Silas?"

Bewildered by her adamant defense of him and not at all certain what to do with the woman who'd shed tears for him, had held and supported him while he confessed his sins and then damn near screamed her outrage loud enough for the people one floor down to hear, he brushed at her still-damp face with shaking fingers, clueless as to how to respond. This was the very last thing he'd expected.

"Baby, I *was* a danger to society," he said in a low voice.

She snorted and then fixed him with a ferocious glare. "Danger to society, my ass. Quite frankly the world needs more people like you." Her tone gentled as she wrapped her arms around him. "Protectors. People who care and who stand for what's right when no one else will. You saved *me*, Silas. My own guardian angel."

Silas held her tight and dragged her down to the bed, an unfamiliar burning at the edges of his eyes. What was he supposed to do with her? In no way did he deserve this precious woman who was so pissed over the cards he'd been dealt as a child. He'd never tell her this, but for the first time, he had no regret for his tormented past, because everything he'd endured, all the ugliness and violence, had led him to her so many years later. And any amount of torment was worth it if the end result was her in his arms right now.

He hugged her even more fiercely, overcome and humbled by her passionate defense. He buried his face in her hair because he didn't trust himself to look at her without succumbing to the tears that burned like acid in his eyes.

26

Hayley spent a sleepless night nestled tightly in Silas's arms. His grip around her had been fierce and he never once loosened his hold on her, almost as if he were afraid that he'd awake and she would be gone. It devastated her that he had looked at her with dull eyes, hopelessness etched like stone on his face as he'd bared his most horrifying secrets, just waiting, expecting her to condemn him and walk away.

The rest of the night, what he'd told her weighed heavily on her mind as she battled indecision over an idea that had formed and taken root. She was awake when he first stirred, but she closed her eyes and adopted the peaceful look of sleep, not wanting him to know she'd lain awake in his arms agonizing over whether to act on her idea.

So much rode on her successfully pulling it off. This was one case where it would have been far better to have left things alone and not ever have attempted it than to go ahead with it and have it backfire in her face. She had so much to gain . . . and *everything* to lose.

She felt lips on her forehead and then her cheeks and finally her lips. She allowed her eyelashes to flutter open and smiled up at Silas.

"Good morning, princess."

Instead of answering, she lifted the upper half of her body and rotated over him, kissing him hotly as she pressed him back onto the pillows.

His eyes gleamed with amusement and a smile curved the hard features of his mouth.

"What's this?" he murmured.

She put her hand on his chest to make known her desire for him to stay exactly where she positioned him.

"Just let me," she whispered against his mouth as her tongue delved inward to explore every inch of his mouth.

"Never let it be said I denied my sweet girl anything. Especially when she says good morning like this."

She continued her gentle exploration of his mouth and face, leaving no part of his skin untouched. Finally, she drew away, staring earnestly down at him as she gathered her courage for the risk she was about to take.

"Do you trust me, Silas?"

He frowned at that, obviously surprised by the question. "Of course I do, princess. Apart from my brothers, you are the only person in the world I trust without reservation."

He seemed startled by his own admission and wonder crossed his face, almost as if he hadn't considered the matter before and his answer had been automatic but now he realized it was true. A strong sense of satisfaction sizzled through her veins, but still, she had to make absolutely certain.

"No, Silas, I mean do you *really* trust me," she said with complete seriousness.

His brow furrowed and he slid his hands over her hips and up her sides before pulling her down over him so their faces were mere inches apart.

"What's wrong, Hayley? What has you so worried and uncertain? And the answer is yes. I trust you in a way I've never trusted another, including my brothers. How could I not when I told you my most shameful secrets, things I haven't even shared with my brothers much less another living soul, and you never once judged me or condemned me? Hell, you wanted to go kick everyone's asses, from my parents, to the degenerate child molester, to the cops who tossed me in juvie. You make me whole, my darling girl. You've given me something I've long lived without. Hope."

Tears blurred her vision and her breath hiccupped from her mouth as her chest worked up and down with the effort of trying to calm her breathing. And her nerves.

"I need you to trust me *now*," she said, touching her fingers to his cheekbone. "I lay awake all night thinking about what happened to you, and as a result of such terrible abuse you not being able to bear the thought of someone performing oral sex on you. And I understand. Believe me, I understand. I can't imagine anyone in your situation who wouldn't react in exactly the same manner."

His expression was still puzzled as he stared at her, discomfort evident in his eyes.

"Just tell me what's on your mind," he said quietly.

She took a deep breath. "Your only experience with oral sex was abhorrent, humiliating and degrading. But no one has ever touched you that way with . . . love. All they've done is taken from you. Let me show you the difference, Silas. Let me show you *my* love. Let me give that to you. If at any time you're uncomfortable or if it brings back too many painful memories, I'll stop immediately. I would never force you to do anything that caused you pain. But let me try. Let me show you the difference between someone who is only forcing and degrading you and someone who only wants to *love* you."

He was silent for so long that she thought she'd made a huge mistake. His expression was brooding, his eyes distant and seemingly a million miles away. She averted her gaze, biting her lip to keep her tears at bay.

Silas cupped her chin in his large palm and rubbed his thumb over her cheek in the softest of caresses.

"Look at me, princess."

Reluctantly she complied, and a burst of hope erupted from her heart when she saw the tenderness reflected in his eyes.

"I don't even know what to say. No one has ever offered me such a selfless gift. No one has ever tried to make right the wrongs of the past. No one has ever cared enough. I'll try, sweet girl. For you, I'll try. But please know that if I can't . . . if I can't do it, it has nothing to do with you and it will not be a rejection of you. I don't want to hurt you, my darling. I wouldn't hurt you for the world and I don't want you to be disappointed in me if I can't go through with it."

She flung her arms around his neck and held on for dear life. "Never," she vowed. "This isn't about me, Silas. It's about you. Only you. My feelings have no place in this. And I will never be disappointed in you. It's enough that you trust me enough to let me try this for you. I only want to make you happy and whole."

He buried his face in her hair as he gripped her every bit as tightly as she held him.

"You already do, my beautiful girl. You already do."

She drew away and kissed him passionately, pouring her heart, her soul, her love into every kiss they shared. She framed his face in her palms and made love to his mouth, mimicking exactly how she would make love to his cock. She sucked lightly on his tongue, stroking over it with the tip of hers, giving him a taste of what was to come.

Then she straddled his hips and began nipping, biting and sucking at his neck, first on one side and then the other. Her hands were splayed wide over his broad chest as she worked lower still, her hair falling over his skin. Silas gathered the long strands in his hand, bunching them into a fist so he could see her face as she lavished love and attention over his chest and abdomen.

She could feel his heated gaze on her, could feel his cock at the juncture of her legs. It was stiff and so rigid, a fiery brand against her skin. She prayed with all her heart that he wouldn't retreat to his past and lose all his desire the moment she turned her attention to his beautiful erection.

She took her time, taking a leisurely path down his gorgeous body, wanting to slowly acclimate him and not trigger a negative response by rushing things. She paused at his groin, pressing kisses to the wiry hair just below his abdomen, and, using her hands, she parted his legs, moving inch by inch so he was open to her. She took heart in the fact that his erection was still hard and bulging, every vein distended and visible as it strained upward toward his navel.

Still, she bypassed direct contact with his cock and instead licked and kissed the insides of his thighs while lightly scraping her nails over his testicles. She alternated light, fluttering kisses up and down his thighs while she grew a little bolder with her hands, cupping his balls and fondling them in her palm.

Every time she instigated something new, took things further than before, she held her breath, waiting for the inevitable stiffening and him pulling her away, but he remained relaxed beneath her, though she could see the strain on his face and his own worry that he wouldn't be able to overcome the demons of his past. It broke her heart that this proud, strong man had been so cruelly treated by the very people who should have sheltered and protected him with their last breaths. He should have been their top priority over all else, not loud parties and getting drunk and high and using him to vent their own deep-seated unhappiness over their own choices. It made her sick to her soul because he more than anyone did not deserve the betrayals and many injustices heaped on him by people who should have protected him.

Her pulse sped up and her chest tightened with dread as she ran her tongue over his balls, replacing the gentle touches of her fingers. She was acutely in tune with every nuance of his body language and would instantly know if she'd gone too far. To her relief, he didn't tense as her mouth moved lovingly over his sac, sucking lightly at the puckered flesh just below his burgeoning erection.

She continued her tender ministrations, licking, sucking, caressing his thighs with soft touches, and to her delight a low moan of pleasure escaped his lips. She chanced a glance up to see his head thrown back, eyes closed, his expression one of complete bliss. Captivated by the pleasure outlined on every contour of his face, she continued to stare for a long moment, emotion knotting her throat.

Not wanting to interrupt the moment or give him time to dwell on the past, she returned to her lovemaking, only this time she licked the underside of his cock from base to tip, bolstered by his reaction to her actions.

He went rigid, his hips flexing upward in an almost violent motion. Cursing herself, she immediately withdrew and stared up at him anxiously, near tears for pushing him too hard, too fast.

"Do I need to stop?" she asked in a discouraged tone.

His eyes flew open. "God no, princess. If you stop now I might die."

His denial was so passionate, his face so flushed and eyes glittering with harsh need she nearly cried her relief but did as he asked and immediately returned to lavishing love and affection on his most intimate parts.

She applied suction to the outside, paying special attention to the plump vein that ran the length of his cock on the underside and then ran her tongue delicately around the head, tasting the salty drops of pre-cum that beaded the tip.

"Please," he said in a strained voice. "Take me inside your mouth, princess. Make love to me."

She wrapped her fist around the base and stroked up and down as she once more looked up at him with uncertainty.

"I've never done this before, Silas. You have to tell me if I do something you don't like. Tell me what you like. How to please you."

He let out a tortured groan. "If you pleased me any more I'd pass out. There's no possible way for you *not* to please me, baby. And if it makes you feel any better, I don't know any more about this than you. I guess we'll learn together."

She sent him a shy smile and then lowered her mouth, slowly sucking the head inside her mouth and then continued on, taking more of him, inch by delicious inch. Determined to take every last bit until no part of him wasn't completely engulfed by her mouth, she breathed through her nose and refused to give in to the urge to gag. He bumped against the very back of her throat and unintelligible sounds of agony whispered harshly past his lips.

More small spurts of pre-cum splashed the back of her tongue, and she swallowed them greedily as her movements became more confident and aggressive. She might not have a clue what she was doing, but instinct and her determination to give this man ultimate pleasure made up for her lack of experience. She sucked and swallowed, taking him to the back of her throat until her nose pressed against his groin. Then she curled her hand around the base and gripped him tightly, pumping up and down in sync with the friction of her mouth.

"Hayley, princess, I'm going to come," he gasped in wonderment.

He tried to pull her away, fisting his hand in her hair, but she was having none of that. No way she would ever reject any part of Silas. She wanted all of him. Never would she have him feel as though she were repulsed by anything to do with him. For the first time, she blatantly disobeyed him and refused to let him pull her away. She tightened her grip and increased both the friction and momentum as she propelled him over the edge.

This was all hers. He jetted forcefully into her mouth, hitting the back of her throat and coating her tongue. He filled her as quickly as she could swallow and she refused to allow even one drop to spill from her lips.

He was giving her something he'd never given any other woman, and that sparked a primitive, savage sense of satisfaction within her. Now she understood how Silas felt about being her first lover. That he'd touched her and filled her in places no other man had ever seen, much less touched. Because this, giving this to Silas, being the only one to receive this from him, was all hers.

She continued to swallow as he gave her the last few surges of his release and then she lovingly licked and sucked, bringing him down from his orgasm and cleaning every drop of cum from his still-rigid cock.

When she finally allowed his penis to slide free from her mouth, he reached down and hooked his hands underneath her shoulders and dragged her up his body until she lay atop him.

His eyes glittered with so much emotion, so many varying reactions that it was impossible to decipher them all. He put a hand to her cheek and stroked, tucking her hair behind her ear as he continued to stare at her in awe.

"I have no idea what to say right now, Hayley," he said in a choked voice. "You have no idea what this meant to me. For you to do this for me, for you not to be disgusted after hearing everything I told you . . . I don't even know what to do with you right now."

She smiled. "Well, if I have to tell you then that certainly takes all the fun out of it."

He laughed and she marveled at the sound. So joyful, light, carefree. As if the weight of the world had been lifted off his shoulders.

"You messed up, my darling girl," he said, a mischievous glint in his eyes.

She lifted one eyebrow and cocked her head to the side in question.

"I'm afraid you've created an oral sex addict. Blow jobs are now my new best friend. You're going to have to do that more often now. A *lot* more often."

She grinned and then dissolved into laughter. "And that's a problem why?"

He groaned and then hugged her to him fiercely, burying his lips in her hair as he kissed her over and over.

"What did I ever do to deserve you?" he asked hoarsely. "I still wake up every morning and wonder if it was all just a dream. And then I look over at you, lying there in my arms, and I marvel at the fact that, not only are you very real, but you're also mine."

"I will always be yours for as long as you want me," she said with absolute sincerity.

He held her there for several long minutes, neither disturbing the quiet. Then he sighed as if in regret.

"You should be practicing today, princess. Your recital is just a short time away."

She lifted up so she could look at him. "I know, and I'm terrified. I'm so worried about panicking or just freezing on stage and having all those people stare at me while I sit there unable to perform."

He squeezed her. "Not going to happen. You have incredible talent."

"You're going to be there, aren't you?" she asked anxiously.

He smiled and leaned up to kiss her on the nose. "I wouldn't miss it for the world, princess."

27

"Now?" Silas asked, making no effort to hide his irritation. "What the fuck? This can't wait?"

Sitting beside him in the car, Hayley cast a curious look sideways at him. He had just picked her up from the school and had planned to take her to lunch and do as much as possible to get her mind off tonight's performance. Now that wasn't going to happen.

Goddamn it.

His lips thinned but he also knew he couldn't ignore Drake's summons. He'd said it was important and he was calling all his men in as soon as they could all get there.

He swore a blue streak over the phone, letting Drake know what he thought of his timing.

"Okay. I'll be there, but I have to run Hayley home first."

He tossed his cell phone into the center console and looked at Hayley, allowing his sincere regret to show in his expression.

"I'm sorry, princess. I'm not going to be able to make lunch. Drake called an important meeting. I have to get there as soon as I run you by the apartment."

She smiled and reached over to squeeze his hand. "It's all right,

Silas. I'll grab something to eat at home. I'm not sure I'm up to eating anyway, and I'd like to get in at least one more practice session before tonight's performance."

"Okay, but don't leave the apartment without me. I'll be back in time to take you to the concert hall. We'll do dinner afterward to celebrate. Sound good?"

She flashed him another smile that had him precariously close to melting.

"I like that idea much better than eating before," she said ruefully. "At least then I won't worry about throwing up everywhere."

Pride shone brightly in his eyes as he squeezed her hand in return. "You're going to do great," he said softly.

He drove faster than usual to his apartment and insisted on walking Hayley up before reminding her to set the locks behind him, and then he hurried back down, an intense scowl on his face because of the fucking meeting Drake had called. Now? Today of all days? He'd promised Hayley lunch and then he'd intended to spend the afternoon taking her mind off tonight's performance. Whatever bug was up Drake's ass, he better get over it before it was time for Hayley's recital.

When he arrived at Impulse, the nightclub Drake owned, the other men were already present and Drake glanced up at Silas's arrival in relief.

"What's so urgent?" Silas demanded as he sank down into a chair close to where Drake was seated.

"Something's going down with the Vanuccis," Drake said in a grim tone. "I need you to call your informant in the Vanucci organization and see what he knows and have him put his ear to the ground and ask him why the fuck he isn't reporting what the hell's going on over there. The Luconis claim to have very time-sensitive information, news of an imminent threat, not to them, but one of us. They've asked me to meet with them tonight."

Silas arched an eyebrow. "You think my guy's turned on us?"

"That's what I want you to find out, and if so, deal with him accordingly," Drake said pointedly.

"You're not going to this meeting alone," Silas said in a flat, uncompromising tone.

Drake might call most of the shots in the business, but when it came to matters of security, Silas's word was absolute.

"I'm not," Drake, a resigned look on his face. "Maddox, Zander and Jax will accompany me. Evangeline has a doctor's appointment she can't miss followed by her Lamaze class. I need you to take her, Silas. It's imperative she not have any upset. She will hardly suspect that I'm in any danger if you're not with me."

"So you're going to lie to her?" Silas asked, blinking in surprise.

"No!" Drake barked. Then he rubbed his hand over his hair in a tired motion. "I'm simply not giving her the details and I'm damn sure not telling her we have an unverified, unspecified threat to us. She loves you and feels comfortable with you. If I can't be with her for her doctor's appointment and Lamaze class, then I want you with her. I know you'd never let any harm come to her."

Silas curled his fist, his features growing tight with anger. A sense of helplessness swept over him, further enraging him. What the fuck was he supposed to do? He could never turn his back on Drake or Evangeline or any of his brothers, and yet he was expected to do so with Hayley?

"What's the problem, man?" Maddox asked quietly.

Silas refused to look at any of them. "Hayley's recital is tonight and I promised her I'd be there."

A round of curses went up.

"I'll take Evangeline," Maddox said calmly, looking to Drake for confirmation.

Drake hesitated, a look of regret tightening his face. "Fuck. Under any other circumstances I wouldn't hesitate to put you on Evangeline. Silas *has* to do it. Evangeline knows his role and as long as he's with her and not me, it will never cross her mind that I'm meeting with the enemy I'm in bed with."

"I won't leave Hayley unprotected," Silas said in a steely voice, his jaw clenched so tightly that his entire head was beginning to ache.

"Of course not," Drake agreed. "I won't leave someone important to you unprotected any more than you would. Okay, new plan. Maddox, you take Justice and Zander and cover Hayley. Make sure she never leaves your sight and you take her to the recital and back home immediately after. Stay with her until Silas returns. The rest will accompany me. The club manager will just have to cover Impulse for a few hours tonight. It's more important that we be elsewhere."

He hesitated and sent a look of genuine regret and apology in Silas's direction. "I know what I'm asking and I'm sorry. I would never ask this of you if it weren't absolutely necessary," he said quietly.

Silas nodded, his jaw still clenched. What Drake was saying was that Evangeline came first. Before Hayley, Silas would have absolutely agreed. But now? Evangeline had to come first with Drake, yes. But not Silas. Nor any other man who had a woman of his own to protect. Evangeline was *not* more than Hayley, and neither was she more important. He'd never felt more helpless in his life, and it infuriated him that he was in an untenable position.

After tonight, when they had more time and so much wasn't riding on the safety of them all, Silas would have a long talk with Drake about Silas's priorities going forward. For now, Silas had a phone call to make, one he dreaded making with all his heart. He owed it to Hayley to give her an explanation to her face, but there wasn't time. He just hoped like hell she'd forgive him like she had so many times before, and that she would give him one more chance to prove to her that she was everything to him.

. . .

Hayley stood backstage, wishing she felt the excitement her fellow students displayed over their first recital. She *had* been excited. The thought of being onstage, sharing her music with hundreds of people hadn't thrilled her as much as the idea of knowing Silas would be sitting in the front row, his eyes glowing with pride as he watched her perform.

But Silas wasn't there—wouldn't be there—since, once again, he was spending the evening with Evangeline. How could he have canceled on her at the very last moment when he'd *promised* her just earlier that afternoon that *nothing* would keep him away?

I wouldn't miss it for the world, princess.

Tears stung her eyelids and she blinked furiously, determined that no one witness her pain and humiliation. He couldn't make it.

And his big, important reason he wasn't attending? *Evangeline.* She hated the jealous woman she was becoming but couldn't find a way to stop it. Every time she discounted any possibility of Silas having some sort of relationship with Drake's wife, something happened to make her realize she had been stupid to ever deny it.

She was such a fool. A gullible, trusting, naïve fool.

"Earth to Hayley." Maddox's deep, amused voice sounded beside her.

She turned, praying her eyes and expression didn't betray her grief. "I'm sorry, Maddox. What were you saying?"

Maddox studied her closely. "Hey, are you okay? I was asking if you needed anything."

She shrugged. "I'm fine. Really. Just nervous, I guess."

Zander and Justice moved from the shadows where they'd been propping up a wall as they waited. "No need to be nervous," Zander rumbled. "You'll go out there, kill it and be back home in less than an hour and a half."

"I won't be going home right afterward," she said flatly. "I was invited to a post-performance party by one of the other students. I'm sure Silas won't be home anytime soon anyway, and it beats spending the evening alone in an empty apartment."

She silently cursed when she heard the bitter tinge of her last words.

Her eyes narrowed in confusion when the men exchanged grim looks of discomfort.

"Uh, sorry, Hayley, but that won't be possible," Justice said with a grimace. "Silas gave us strict instructions to get you back to the apartment as soon as the recital was over. We're needed elsewhere tonight and we can't be out at a party with you."

Hayley's lips thinned in anger. "Let me get this straight. Silas *ordered* you to take me straight to his apartment as soon as the recital is over when he doesn't even know when or if he'll be home tonight?" she snapped. "But it doesn't matter because I don't recall inviting any of you to the party, so you don't have to worry about me interfering with the important stuff y'all have to do. In fact, I see no reason for y'all to be at my recital. It's not important or anything, so feel free to go attend to more pressing matters. I'll get a ride home after the party. Call Silas. I'm sure he won't care," she said, sarcasm dripping from her words.

Maddox cleared his throat. "We, uh, can't do that either. I'm sorry, honey, but Silas is to be disturbed only in the event of an emergency, and there's a lot of shit going down tonight, so it's best if we take you back to the apartment where you'll be safe."

Hayley's mouth fell open and this time, despite her best efforts, she couldn't control the surge of tears that welled and burned like acid. The situation was only worsened when she saw blatant sympathy reflected in Maddox's eyes.

Zander's expression resembled a thundercloud, and Justice's lips curled into a snarl.

"Bullshit," Justice bit out. "There's a lot you don't understand,

Hayley, but you need to get this if you don't get anything else. You are important to all of us. Especially Silas. And I won't have you thinking what you're currently thinking, and I damn sure won't have you looking at us with tears in your eyes."

"Give us tonight, honey," Maddox said gently. "I swear to you that everything will be explained, but right now you have a solo to rock."

"If she doesn't get an explanation as soon as all this shit's over with tonight, I'm going to kick Silas's fucking ass," Zander snarled.

She rapidly turned her face away so the thin streams of tears wouldn't be visible. "I got all the explanation I needed when Silas told me he wouldn't miss this for the world and then called me to say that Evangeline was more important."

"What?"

"What the fuck?"

"Hayley—"

The outbursts were simultaneous and so forceful that she didn't even know who said what.

"I have to go," she choked out, grateful that a stagehand was calling for the musicians to take their places.

She fled, running onstage, sliding into her chair. She picked up her violin and sucked in huge, steadying breaths as she valiantly tried to regain her composure. She couldn't blow this. She couldn't allow her emotions to rattle her performance. Desperate to clear her mind and give the performance of her life, she focused on her father, his pride in her and his determination for her to be exactly where she was right now. Peace instantly descended as she struck the first note and the haunting strains of the violins rose from the orchestra. She wouldn't let him down. Not now, not ever. For him, she would do this.

When the last echo of her violin slowly dissipated and Hayley's solo signaled the end of the concert, the crowd erupted in applause, giving her and the entire group of assembled musicians a standing ovation.

Tears glittered brightly on Hayley's face as she rose and took her bow. As soon as the curtains fell, she hurriedly left the stage, dodging the many congratulations and excited celebration of her fellow students. She paused just offstage to hastily wipe away the evidence of her emotion and bent to put away her violin.

A strong hand squeezed her shoulder and she stiffened, pausing a moment before rising to meet Maddox's gaze.

"You did amazing, sweetheart. You absolutely nailed it."

She offered him a weak smile of thanks as Justice and Zander pushed in to create a barrier between her and the stampede of people chattering excitedly and high-fiving madly.

"Come on, let's get you home," Justice said gently. "We'll talk later. Promise."

She said nothing as she allowed Zander to take her case, and she followed Maddox's lead as Zander and Justice flanked her in the direction of the nearby exit.

"Hayley!"

Hayley turned briefly and offered a small wave and a halfhearted smile in the direction of Kara, the first-chair cellist who was throwing the afterparty. She didn't refute Kara's joyful "See ya there!" She was too embarrassed to explain that she wouldn't be attending and definitely not why.

As soon as the cooler evening air hit Hayley's face, her stomach curled into a knot and she hesitated, her step faltering as she bent over to control the surge of nervous energy as it tried to find an outlet. She'd pushed it and all her rioting emotions down for her performance, but now reaction was setting in and her knees were shaking violently.

"Hayley? What's wrong?" Justice asked sharply. "Are you going to be sick?"

She wiped her mouth with the back of her hand and jolted back upright. "I'm fine," she said stonily.

Zander, who had paused just ahead of her, turned in her direction, and to Hayley's horror, she saw a car roar precariously close to the small group heading for Maddox's car. Simultaneously, the front and back windows on the passenger side slid down and two guns appeared. Before she could shout a warning, shots sounded.

She lunged toward Zander as her violin case went skidding across the ground. Desperately she tried to push him away, but when her body slammed into his, his arms wrapped around her like steel beams and they both went flying to the ground, Zander landing atop her with a sickening thud.

She was screaming his name. She knew she was and yet she couldn't hear anything. All she could feel was the warmth of his blood as it soaked into her clothing and the absolute limpness of his unconscious body.

28

Hayley huddled in the corner of the waiting room, head down, knees drawn to her chest in a tight ball as she rocked back and forth. The police had questioned her incessantly, but there was little she could tell them. It had all happened so fast. She couldn't even provide a description of the vehicle because all she'd seen were the windows sliding down, guns aiming in her direction. She could only remember the terror and certainty of Maddox, Justice or Zander being killed. And then Zander covering her. Taking the bullet that should have hit her.

Hayley had become extremely frustrated and increasingly more agitated to the point of hysteria that she couldn't recall much at all about the gunmen. Only that they'd worn masks covering their entire faces except for their eyes. When it'd become apparent that as a result of their questioning, she'd only become more distraught, the police had turned their attention on Justice and Maddox. They'd been rigid and angry, more worried about Hayley than they were about cooperating with the investigating officers. Only when a witness at the scene had been able to give the authorities a lead on the vehicle the shooters had driven had the police finally stopped their inquisition.

Never fully aware, even during her questioning, Hayley had with-drawn even further, the feeling of Zander's weight over her, the warmth of his blood covering her skin the only memories that overwhelmed and tortured her.

Several times a tentative seeking touch registered on her shoulder or arm but she flinched away, refusing to be drawn from the fog of worry, torment and guilt. She hadn't been allowed to ride to the hospital with Zander, though she screamed his name and fought tooth and nail as Maddox and Justice both pried her away from Zander's unconscious, bloody body. She'd refused to allow anyone to examine her, saying that Zander was the one who'd been shot. It was he who needed their attention. And she'd been furious with the police and their repeated attempts to distract her from her vigil.

She went still when she heard Maddox a few feet away on his cell phone as he apprised Silas of the night's events.

"You need to get down here immediately," Maddox said quietly. "She's severely traumatized. She won't let anyone near her. No, I don't think she was hurt, but she's not doing good at all, man. She needs you right now. She was devastated that you weren't at the recital. She wasn't herself after we told her that we had orders to take her directly back to the apartment. She wanted to go to some party she was invited to because she was under the impression you wouldn't even be home tonight. She doesn't understand the danger or the threat, or at least she didn't. Damn it, Silas, she's hurting and I don't know how to make her stop."

Fresh tears streamed down Hayley's buried face, and her shoulders shook with sobs. She didn't want Silas here. Not when it was so obvious she meant so little to him. Zander should have never been at her recital that night. He should have never been shot.

If he died because of her, she'd never forgive herself. Never would she be able to look any of the men now gathered in the waiting room in the face.

A furor of activity and sound echoed from across the room, and she dimly registered the arrival of more of Silas's friends. Then she heard an unfamiliar man's harsh demand to know what had happened, and when she realized who he was—*Drake*—it only caused her to tear up all over again. What had happened? Did he know where his wife was and that Silas was with her and not with Hayley as he'd promised?

"Is she all right?" Drake demanded. "What the hell happened? *How* did this happen and who the hell is responsible?"

He raged on, but Hayley shut him and everyone else with him out. Everyone was there except the one person she most wanted—or had wanted. At the moment she didn't think she could bear to face him.

"Who is with Evangeline?" Drake demanded hoarsely.

Hayley flinched and shifted so that her arms were now covering her ears in addition to her head.

"I sent Thane over so that Silas could get here as fast as he could," Maddox said calmly. "I've kept him updated every few minutes. He's one pissed-off man right now. Last time I spoke to him, he was just five minutes from the hospital, so he should be walking in any time now."

So Drake did know that Silas had been with his wife all night, and was apparently unbothered by it. But then it was hardly likely that he knew the depth of his brother's devotion to the woman he'd married.

Hayley curled into an even tighter ball, ignoring the pain, the guilt, her overwhelming worry for Zander, knowing that the very last thing she could handle right now was facing the man who'd broken his promise—and her heart.

Silas threw open the doors to the emergency room and immediately scanned the waiting area for Hayley, his heart lurching in fear when he didn't immediately spot her.

"Where is she?" he demanded hoarsely.

Drake and Maddox both stepped toward him and then turned in

the direction of a faint, blood-covered figure huddled into a barely visible ball in the far corner.

"Hayley!" he cried, immediately shoving Maddox aside.

But Drake and Maddox held restraining hands on both his arms.

"Just hold up a minute," Maddox murmured.

"What the fuck?" Silas raged. "Why hasn't she been taken care of? Let me go, damn it!"

"She hasn't spoken to anyone except the police when they questioned her, and even then she was pretty out of it. She won't let anyone near her," Maddox said in hushed tones. "She said she wasn't hurt and screamed at everyone to take care of Zander. She tried to shove him out of the path of the gunmen but was too late and Zander took her down with him to protect her. She's freaked-out, man. You're going to have to take care with her."

Silas's face was a wreath of torment. Oh God, this was his fault. He never should have left her care to others. She was his responsibility. Not Evangeline. Not anyone else. Hayley was *his* and he'd failed her and his brother unforgivably.

"Let me go," he choked out, finally shaking loose from the restraining hands.

He hurried to where Hayley was hunched down on the floor, her arms covering her head entirely. His heart hammered violently as he took in the amount of blood—Zander's blood—on her clothing.

He reached out, his hand shaking, and touched her hair.

"Princess?" he whispered. "Are you okay? Are you hurt? Say something to me, my darling girl."

She reacted violently, wrenching away from his touch, her eyes wild as she scooted backward, bumping into the chair at her side. Pain instantly flashed over her face, but what she said stopped him in his tracks.

"Don't touch me!" she hissed, shrinking farther away from his outstretched hand. "Don't ever call me that. I'm not *your* anything."

His mouth fell open in shock and then he glanced over his shoulder to where the rest of his brothers were gathered, looks of extreme worry in their eyes. In Maddox's and Justice's, though, he saw faint pity and understanding. What the hell was going on and what hadn't they told him?

Something Maddox had said to him on the phone only just registered. At the time he'd been frantic with worry over Hayley, fearing that she'd been seriously injured.

She was devastated that you weren't at the recital. She wasn't herself.

He closed his eyes as sorrow gripped him. And so much regret.

"We need to get you up, Hayley," he said in a soft voice. "I need to make sure you weren't injured. I can't tell what is Zander's blood and what could be yours."

It was the wrong thing to say. A haunted look filled her eyes and tears welled, sliding soundlessly down her cheeks.

"Is he dead?" she whispered.

"No, princess! He's going to be okay. I swear it. They're taking him to surgery, but nothing vital was hit. He lost a lot of blood and he'll need time to recover, but I swear to you he's going to be all right."

"I'm not your princess," she said tearfully. "I don't even *matter* to you."

His heart nearly exploded out of his chest. He wanted to cry like a baby, but he held it together by the thinnest thread.

Then she suddenly began pushing herself up, ignoring the protests from his brothers that she shouldn't move. She pushed his hands away as he reached to steady her, but as his hand glanced over her bare leg before her dress fell back into place, fear lanced through his entire body, temporarily paralyzing him.

His palm came away bright red with fresh blood. Terror seized his veins, turning his own blood cold. His apology for missing an event he'd sworn to her he wouldn't miss would have to wait. Everything would have to wait until it was determined how badly she was hurt.

She stood to her feet, her hand immediately clutching her side as she swayed precariously in front of him. Pain and confusion registered in her eyes, making her look even more vulnerable than she had when he'd first seen her huddled on the floor covered in blood.

"Hayley," he said in a soothing voice one might use when trying to calm an injured wild animal. "Listen to me, sweet girl. You've been hurt. I think you may have been shot. You're bleeding, baby. Let me get a doctor to look at you. I swear to make things right just as soon as you've gotten the care you need."

"You'll never make this right," she whispered in a voice strangled by tears and emotion.

Devastation was written all over her face and she seemed to not even register anything else he'd said other than he would make things right. She was in fierce denial of her injury, her sole focus only on Zander and his well-being.

When she took another wobbly step back, another savage round of objections rose sharply from his brothers, and Maddox suddenly appeared at Hayley's side, his eyes bright with concern.

"Hayley, sweetheart, listen to me," Maddox pleaded. "Honey, you're hurt. You're bleeding badly. You have to let us get you back to an exam room."

She shook her head adamantly, her eyes going wild once more. She was obviously in shock and only partly cognizant of her surroundings and completely unaware of the danger she was in. Seeming to forget that Silas was still in front of her, in her haste to move away from Maddox and his entreaty for her to submit to medical care, she bolted forward.

Silas lunged for her as her knees gave way and collapsed beneath her. She dropped like a rock and he barely managed to catch her before she hit the floor.

"Get me a doctor!" he roared as he surged to his feet, clutching Hayley to his chest in desperation.

He watched in horror as her blood dripped to the floor, and then he glanced back to where she'd been ever since she was brought into the ER, and he nearly lost his mind when he saw the bright smear of blood all over the area where she'd huddled.

Impatient, he charged through the swinging doors that led back to the treatment area. He was immediately met by a nurse who stared at him in shock.

"She's been shot," he said hoarsely. "Please help her."

The nurse went into immediate action, yelling for a stretcher. As soon as one was hastily wheeled over by an orderly, Silas gently laid her down and the nurse took over, shoving him back. But Silas refused to leave her. The nurse argued furiously that he was impeding in her care and it finally took the efforts of four of his brothers to wrestle him back to the waiting area, where he began his long vigil.

Forgotten was Drake's meeting with the Luconis, determining what the potential threat to them was or even apprising Drake of his conversation with the mole planted deep within the bowels of the Vanucci organization. All Silas could focus on was Hayley and the fact that she had been shot, and every minute that no one came out to give him an update on her condition, he died a little more.

29

Silas sat in the darkened hospital room holding Hayley's limp hand, exhaustion taking its toll on him. It had been the longest night of his fucking life waiting for word on her condition. And then the ER physician had come out and reported that she had indeed been hit by one of the bullets that had riddled Zander's body, and she was being taken straight to surgery to remove it from her lower abdomen.

Maddox had painfully recounted to Silas and the others how Hayley had seen the car—and the guns—aimed in their direction before he, Justice or Zander had and that she'd launched herself at Zander in an effort to protect him. Maddox and Justice had been grim and pale upon learning she'd been shot, and Silas knew well the guilt they felt for thinking they hadn't been able to protect her, because Silas shared it.

His brothers remained in the waiting room until Hayley was brought out of surgery and into recovery and waited still until she'd been moved to a private room, still groggy and out of it from the anesthesia. Every single one of them had filed in to see her and ensure for themselves that she was alive and breathing.

As soon as she'd come around, her respirations immediately increased, her blood pressure rose and she became diaphoretic. The nurse had been quick to administer IV pain medication and Hayley had been out ever since, resting peacefully and pain free.

His brothers had urged him to get some rest, even volunteering to take turns sitting at her bedside while he slept a few hours, but he'd refused, adamant that he be with her every moment and that he be at her side when she finally regained consciousness and was aware of her surroundings.

He stroked her fingers and the inside of her wrist, then lowered his head, closing his eyes to remove the images of her bloody and falling and his haste to catch her before she hit the floor and injured herself further. The same images that had tortured him all night.

His head jerked upward when he felt her twitch and then heard her restless movement followed by the whisper of her ragged breath. He surged to his feet, leaning over the bed so he could stare into her eyes the moment she awoke. Her eyelashes fluttered sluggishly and the tip of her tongue darted out to rub over dry, cracked lips.

When her eyes finally opened, they were unfocused and dazed. A small gasp of pain escaped her, her eyes growing bright.

"Princess, are you in pain?" he whispered urgently. "Should I call for a nurse?"

Even as he posed the question, he reached for the call button and depressed it. As he waited for the nurse's arrival, he stroked a hand through Hayley's hair and then lowered his head to press his lips against her forehead.

She moaned again and he could see her open her mouth, trying to speak. He gently hushed her.

"Wait for pain medicine, sweet girl. It hurts you too much to speak right now. Wait just a minute and then you'll feel much better," he soothed.

Her gaze finally became focused and when it settled on him, recognition flashed and just as quickly her eyes filled with tears. His gut clenched tightly and his throat knotted thickly with emotion.

"Please don't cry, princess," he choked out. "You're breaking my heart."

The door swung open and Silas glanced up in relief to see a nurse approaching the bed with a cheerful smile.

"I see you're awake, Miss Winthrop. Can you tell me how you're feeling?"

"H-hurts," Hayley rasped.

The nurse gave her a sympathetic look and then deftly inserted a syringe into the IV port of her hand. She checked Hayley's vitals and then told Silas that the doctor would be making his morning rounds soon and would give an update on her condition as well as how long he expected her hospital stay to be.

As soon as the nurse left, Silas turned his attention back to Hayley, who was lying on the bed, eyes fluttering closed as she sighed with relief.

"Better?" he asked as he gathered her hand in his once more.

Her eyes came open and settled painfully on him. He knew he'd have to apologize quickly and hope she forgave him for completely failing her.

"Who is she?" Hayley demanded bitterly.

Silas reared back, surprised and puzzled by her question. "Who is who, princess? I don't understand."

"Evangeline," she hissed.

His eyebrows went up even further. "Drake's wife. I told you that, remember?"

Hayley turned her gaze upward, refusing to meet his stare any longer. Her lips were trembling and he could see the moisture welling in her eyes that had nothing to do with her physical pain.

"No, who is she to *you*?" Hayley said scornfully. "You don't go on regular dates with the wife of a man you consider a brother and refuse to offer any sort of explanation to someone you claim is important to you unless that brother's wife means more to you than she should. Why do you constantly drop everything on a dime for Evangeline?

Why do you and your men refuse to even speak about her around me, like she's some huge damn secret and all of you are so protective of precious Evangeline?"

She broke off with a choked sound of pain that ripped his guts right out of him. Before he could even collect himself to respond to her deep upset, she forged relentlessly on.

"But most of all, why do I get pawned off on your men and shoved aside and completely forgotten for another man's wife? If she's so precious and everyone loves her so damn much, then why couldn't one of the others go do whatever it was you did with her so you could come to an event you not only promised me you would attend but knew how important it was to me? I kept telling myself I was being hasty and jealous and too fast to jump to conclusions. I gave you the benefit of the doubt over and over again when it's obvious that I was right to be suspicious all along. Last night showed me in exacting detail exactly where I stand on your list of priorities and it's not very damn high," she said so low he almost didn't hear.

But he had heard. Every single word. And now he watched as endless streams of tears slithered down her pale, ravaged face. At first he'd been shocked at the conclusions she'd drawn. He'd felt immediately defensive, angry even, his instinct to correct her very bad opinion of Evangeline, but then he realized she was exactly right. Furthermore, she didn't know Evangeline, because as she'd said, he and his brothers had shut her down at every turn out of duty and loyalty to both Evangeline and Drake, never recognizing the fact that the two women should have absolutely been introduced. His relationship with Evangeline explained. The lack of trust both he and his brothers had demonstrated toward her was appalling and unforgivable.

Looking at the matter from her perspective, he cringed. *Fuck.* All the times he'd left her so he could handle Evangeline's detail. The phone calls. The "dates." Missing tonight's recital, when he knew how important it was to her, and as she'd so aptly said, pawning her off on his men, making her their duty instead of his. What a complete fucking idiot he'd been. How she hadn't walked out on him a long time ago, he'd never know, but he was extremely grateful for her generous and forgiving spirit and the fact that until now she'd always given him the benefit of the doubt.

He was gutted. He'd put his loyalty to Drake above his commitment to Hayley, and in the process bruised the heart of this beautiful woman. He should have gotten Drake's permission to tell her the full situation from the beginning and if Drake had refused, told her about Evangeline anyway, but he'd never in a million years thought she would believe another woman was more important to him. All the years of secrecy were so deeply ingrained, a huge part of the man he'd become, and it might have cost him the one woman he'd ever bared his deepest secrets to. The only person who made his past bearable and most of all, the only person to have ever made him forget and make peace with it.

He shattered completely on the inside, his devastation surely as evident on his face as it was on hers and in her eyes. He gathered her gently in his arms, taking extreme care not to jostle her. Ignoring the fact that she went rigid the moment he enfolded her in his embrace, he pressed his lips gently to hers and then rested his forehead against hers.

"I am so sorry, my beautiful, sweet girl," he said around the knot in his throat. "Never in a million years would I try to hurt you or make you doubt me in any way, though I can see now how very careless I was and why you feel as you do. I not only owe you my sincerest apology, but also a very belated explanation as well. I hope when I have fully explained that you will find it in your beautiful, loving heart to forgive me for ever causing you so much pain."

He lifted up just enough that she could see into his eyes, his heart, and recognize his absolute sincerity when he, for all practical purposes, got on his knees and begged her forgiveness.

Her eyes lifted to meet his, hope flaring in her beautiful gaze. She looked so hopeful and sad at the same time that it broke his heart all over again, and he wished with everything he had that he could go back and undo all the damage done to this precious woman.

He gathered her hands in his and lifted them to press a kiss into each soft palm and felt her tremble softly beneath his mouth.

"Evangeline is Drake's very beloved wife. He met her less than a year ago and she was the first woman to ever soften any of our hearts. No, my precious girl, don't look like that," he said when her gaze grew somber at his words and immediately lowered. "Hayley, look at me, please," he begged softly.

Reluctantly, she did as he asked, and he gripped her hands a little tighter.

"None of us had ever dared become involved with a woman. Not with the ever-present threat that exists to us and anyone or anything we value. Drake fell hard for Evangeline from the start, but he fucked up quite badly with her. More than once. He didn't trust her and as a result, she suffered greatly for his mistake. Maddox and I formed an unbreakable friendship with Evangeline, but nothing remotely romantic ever evolved from our friendship. Maddox and I offered her support and a refuge when Drake very cruelly tossed her out of his life without any means of survival. Unbeknownst to us at the time, she was pregnant, and once Drake realized his mistake, Evangeline wasn't so forgiving of him. It was a rough time for them both and when she came back, I continued to be a steady source of support and friendship to her. My absolute loyalty has always been to Drake and his protection and by proxy anyone important to him or anyone who could be used to manipulate or hurt him."

Silas sucked in a deep breath, realizing he was making a complete muck out of things.

"The world my brothers and I exist in is a very dangerous one as I'm sure you're well aware, judging by the amount of security we always use and the fact that you and Zander were gunned down less than twenty-four hours ago," he said painfully.

"As such, I am routinely called upon to guard Evangeline when Drake or one of the others can't. We rotate shifts, but when Evangeline was in the early stages of her relationship with Drake, I started a routine of bringing takeout to her apartment once a week, something that continued upon her return to the city and has carried on especially during her pregnancy. By necessity she lives a very isolated life with few friends and little contact with her family save Drake and the rest of us. She's sacrificed much to remain in Drake's life, and so the rest of us try to do what we can to make her isolation more bearable.

"When I met you, I had never imagined being in Drake's situation. Of being made vulnerable by another person, especially a woman. I admit, I handled things poorly and I didn't factor in the changes it would mean for me and the fact that I now owed anyone but Drake and myself an explanation for my actions or choices."

He sucked in another long breath and looked pleadingly at her, knowing he was to the part of the apology and explanation where he had to beg her to overlook his many mistakes and be willing to give him another chance.

"Never once have I even looked at another woman since before or after meeting you. Not in the way I look at you. I've never felt this way about another woman. I care for Evangeline, yes, but as a little sister and nothing more. I look out for and protect her as I would a sibling, but I've never felt for her—or any woman—what I feel for you, and I am so deeply sorry I let you down, princess. Since Drake asked me personally to be the one who went with Evangeline to her doctor's appointment and then to her Lamaze class, I didn't feel as if I could say no. But I should have. And I'll never make that mistake again if you'll forgive me and give me another chance to make you happy, my beautiful girl."

Her eyes swam with tears again as she stared up at him, her chin and mouth trembling. A single tear slipped down her cheek, and he leaned forward to kiss it away, no longer able to bear the sight of her tears.

"Forgive me, princess," he whispered against her damp skin. "Please come home with me so I can take care of you and spoil you ridiculously."

"You already spoil me ridiculously," she choked out.

She ended her statement in a sob and then tears gushed down her face and she clutched at his chest with her hands, pulling him downward.

As soon as he lowered himself enough, she circled him with her arms and buried her face against his neck, her tears wet against his skin. He stroked his hand over the back of her head, threading his fingers through her tangled hair.

"I-I'm sorry," she sobbed.

"No. No! You have nothing to be sorry for, my darling."

His own throat tightened and he felt the threat of answering tears. So much worry, pain and ultimate relief, both that she was going to be all right and that she was giving him another chance. It was more than he'd ever hoped for.

"Shhh, princess. You have to stop crying. I can't stand it. I'd do anything at all to keep you from ever crying."

"Is Zander really going to be all right?" she asked fearfully, her words muffled against his neck.

"Yes, I promise," he soothed. "I don't want you to worry about anything except getting better and coming home to me. Okay?"

"Okay," she whispered as she clung fiercely to him.

He closed his eyes, his heart suddenly free of the horrible weight it had borne since the day before when he'd had to tell his princess that he couldn't attend her recital.

30

Hayley came sluggishly awake and rolled very carefully from her uninjured side to her back, cringing when her stiff back protested strenuously. Her wound was healing quite nicely and the surgeon had told her how fortunate she was that the bullet must have deflected off some other object before becoming embedded in her lower abdomen. As a result, it hadn't penetrated deep enough to cause any injury to her internal organs, and most important it hadn't jeopardized her future chances of having a child.

The main source of her discomfort stemmed from the fact that she could only lie or sleep on her uninjured side and she was well accustomed to a very random, haphazard sleeping style that resulted in her sleeping on both sides in turn, her back and her belly. And since being released from the hospital a week ago, Silas had been strict in not allowing her up for any length of time, which meant she spent most of her time either on the couch or in bed lying on the same side.

Lucky for her, Silas had gotten up before her this morning and had yet to come check on her and carry her—yes, carry her—into the living room, where she typically ate breakfast with him. This morning she was going to propel her own self into the bathroom and bypass the mortification of Silas's daily trip with her to perform her bodily functions. She wouldn't push attempting to bathe on her own yet, because no doubt, he would hear the water and come running and then she'd receive a stern lecture and she'd be returned to bed, and if she had to spend another minute lying in an uncomfortable position she was going to scream her head off.

Getting up was surprisingly easy once the muscles in her back ceased their bitching and moaning. She stood cautiously, her hand on the mattress just in case she wasn't as balanced as she thought she was. She trudged toward the bathroom and smelled the scent of frying bacon. For some reason, her temporary upswing in mood after getting out of bed on her own came to a crashing halt as she was assaulted by a rush of memories from over a week ago.

Her heart ached fiercely and swelled in her chest, causing an uncomfortable tightening. Sweat broke out on her forehead as she recalled in vivid memory the shooting. Zander covered in blood. The agony of waiting to know if he'd live or die, and then the discovery of her own bullet wound, completely overlooked by her and everyone else in the ensuing chaos.

Tears burned the edges of her eyes. It wasn't that the memory was new or unexpected, but it mostly haunted her sleep, when she dreamed of that horrible night. Every single night since her release from the hospital she'd awakened in terror, her skin hot and clammy, and Silas's arms around her, his lips pressed to her hair as he rocked and soothed her through the horror of her nightmares.

She hadn't even been allowed to visit Zander yet because Silas was adamant that she take things easy and make a full recovery, and he also wanted her to remain completely out of sight. It was thought that the intended targets had been Justice, Maddox and Zander and her association was still unknown. She would live under constant threat were it known for certain she had anything to do with Silas or his extended family. A family steeped in danger and violence. She wasn't ignorant of the kind of "business" Silas and the rest were in and even with Silas once admitting, when questioned about whether they hurt people, that they only hurt those who deserved it, Hayley had lived in a bubble of denial, never having been exposed to any element of their profession.

All she knew was that because of her a man was in a hospital bed with at least three bullet wounds, all because he'd been tasked with the job of protecting her. And that wasn't something she could live with. Especially if Silas discovered who had shot her and Zander and retaliated. She would not be the cause of anyone else being so seriously hurt, or God forbid, killed. Nor would she ever allow anyone to use her to get to Silas. He'd had enough pain in his life. She refused to be the source of even more.

It was a decision she'd made while lying in the hospital, watching the guilt, exhaustion and desperation on the faces of Silas and his men. But she had yet to share it with Silas and she knew it was wrong of her to drag it out, basically using him as a crutch until she recovered, only to walk away afterward. Time was of the essence and before things resorted to violence again, she needed to be gone.

She had to fight back the tears as she finished her business in the bathroom and then slowly trudged into the kitchen to find Silas, her heart silently shattering the entire way.

Silas was at the stove preparing the breakfast he intended to serve to Hayley in bed when he felt a prickle of awareness at his nape. He sensed, not heard, her presence behind him, and he swiftly whirled to see her standing a short distance away, dressed only in one of his button-up shirts that dwarfed her much smaller frame.

The dullness in her eyes bothered him. Though she was rapidly healing—physically—she hadn't shown any signs of her former sunny disposition in all the time she'd been home from the hospital. And though she was here every single day and wrapped in his arms every night, he was frustrated by the sensation of her retreating from him and slowly slipping away. Only the fear he'd felt the night of her shooting was sharper than his current fear.

He couldn't put his finger on why, but he had a very bad feeling, and his gut never steered him wrong.

"You shouldn't be out of bed, princess," he gently reprimanded. "I was bringing you breakfast in bed this morning. You haven't been resting very well and I thought it better if you slept in today. Maybe take a nap right after you eat. You haven't been eating enough either. You need to get all your strength back."

She took a few slow steps toward the bar, her lips quivering softly as her wounded eyes searched his.

"How is Zander?" she asked quietly.

He went to her, no longer able to stand the distance between them. He carefully enfolded her in his embrace and she buried her face in his chest. He stroked her hair, trying to give her as much comfort as he could, and he rushed to reassure her of Zander's recovery.

"He's just fine, princess. He's back to his usual grumpy self, bitching and yelling at everyone in sight, demanding to know when he can go home, because in his words, he's fucking fine and a few pussy-ass bullets aren't enough to keep him down."

He said it in exaggerated fashion in a light and teasing manner, hoping to make her laugh or at least cause her some relief. Instead she shook silently in his arms and he felt the warmth of her tears against his neck.

Silently cursing, he held on to her, not saying anything more, just holding her as tightly as he could without causing her pain. But she didn't wince or flinch. He'd noticed that as of several days ago, the only discomfort she seemed to suffer was from the stiff and sore muscles in her back, unused to sleeping in only one position.

When she finally drew away, her eyes were puffy and swollen and she ducked her head, refusing to meet his gaze. She pushed slightly away from him and he reluctantly let her go, a sense of helplessness gripping him. She seemed to have fallen into a deep depression, and it showed no signs of lifting no matter how often he gave her good news regarding Zander. She gave little thought or notice to her own injury. Her only concern through it all had been for Zander.

She took a position on the other side of the bar, almost as if purposely putting a barrier between them. He turned back to the stove so she wouldn't see his deep frown. Or the deep grooves of worry on his forehead.

He dished up the last of the bacon and then seasoned the eggs and took the biscuits from the oven.

"Silas?"

He turned back to Hayley at her hesitant, uncertain-sounding call. He studied her, not liking the dark shadows that seemed much more prevalent in her eyes this morning. Suddenly he dreaded responding, not wanting her to say whatever was weighing so heavily on her.

"Yes, princess?" he finally managed to get out.

She fidgeted nervously, looking down at her hands before finally meeting his gaze once more.

"Before, when I asked you about what you and the others do, you weren't honest or not completely honest when you answered me, were you?"

He tensed all over, the dread in his heart increasing with every breath. He'd known it was only a matter of time before she got beyond the initial shock and horror of the shooting and began to ask questions about it and his connection or rather how his lifestyle entered the picture. He'd tormented himself over the fact that once she put all the pieces together, she'd no longer accept the inherent risk to herself, and she would walk away.

"And then when you explained about Evangeline, you mentioned how she was used against Drake—how she could still be used against him," she continued on without waiting for him to respond. "It stands to reason if anyone important to Drake or to any of you could be used against you, then that same threat exists to me, doesn't it?"

Fuck.

While he knew this conversation was inevitable and that she deserved nothing but the full, ugly truth, he'd hoped to delay it until she was fully recuperated and in a much better frame of mind.

"Yes, princess," he said in a low voice. "That's exactly what it means."

"And the reason you've always had your brothers with me when you couldn't be wasn't because of your need for control and absolute order in your life but rather because you perceived there to be a legitimate threat to me or to all of you at any time."

Again, he nodded and grimly said, "Yes."

He realized he was holding his breath, and as tears filled her eyes as the knowledge was confirmed, the ugly truth there to see in her expressive eyes, his dread increased a hundred times over. The sensation of her slipping away from him hadn't been his imagination or a manifestation of his worst fear. It was very real and now was the moment she saw him for the monster he truly was and he lost everything.

"I can't do this, Silas," she said painfully, tears streaking down her beautiful face.

He closed his eyes, knowing he had no right to demand or even beg her to stay. She was in danger every single day by virtue of her association with him. How could he do anything but let her go when her life could very well depend on it?

"I never claimed to be a good man, princess," he said gruffly, emotion thickening his voice. "I've done things . . ."

She lifted her head, her eyes sparking, her mouth falling open in shock.

"Not a good man?" she asked hoarsely.

His brow furrowed, bewildered by her reaction. Wasn't the reason she was even now prepared to leave him because now she knew him for what he was?

"Silas, you're the very best man I know. Your brothers. They're all good men. You want to talk about the things *you've* done? Do you forget that I'm the reason your brother is lying in a hospital after nearly dying because he was protecting me? I'm a liability to you all, Silas, and I won't have that. I will never allow myself to be used against you or your brothers. To hurt you or any one of them. I could never live with myself if the next time we weren't as fortunate and someone or God forbid, you, *died* because you were protecting me. I can't do it. I *won't* do it," she cried.

After her impassioned outburst, she turned and fled the kitchen, disappearing into the bedroom, leaving Silas utterly stunned and speechless.

What the *fuck*?

Realization was slow in coming, and when it did it had the effect of a lightning bolt. She wasn't leaving because of him or who he was. She had seen the heart of him, the very essence of the man he was, and she wasn't repulsed or disappointed. God. She was leaving *for* him. To *protect* him.

Oh *hell* no.

It was *his* goddamn job to protect *her*. And the job of every one of his brothers. They'd lose their shit every bit as much as he was about to lose his if they heard all she'd had to say.

Then he realized she'd just told him she was leaving him and was likely in the bedroom packing when she was in no condition to even be up and moving around. He let out a roar and charged after her, catching her before she even made it to the closet.

He grabbed the arm on her uninjured side and whirled her around, ever mindful of hurting her. But at the moment he wasn't backing down. He was practically snarling, baring his teeth as he seethed in rage at the idea of her *leaving* him because she was worried she was a liability to him, for fuck's sake.

She stared at him, worry bright in her eyes. "Silas, what—?"

"Not. A. Word," he said, cutting her off.

Her expression was a whirl of confusion and faint shock over his vehemence, but she'd unleashed the deadly predator that always clawed so close to the surface. If she truly couldn't accept him, then he'd have no choice but to let her go, but he'd fight her tooth and nail over the ridiculous notion of her walking out of his life in order to protect him and his brothers.

He heaved a breath, the words, protests and denials swirling like a tornado in his mind, and tried to compose himself enough to make damn sure she understood that he would not tolerate her making such a drastic decision.

He carefully wrapped his hand around her throat, feeling the reassuring thud of her pulse, how it leapt in response to his fingers circling her delicate neck. His eyes narrowed as he stared intently at her.

"I was willing to let you leave once you knew the type of man I am. It would have taken the last piece of my black soul, but I would have let you go. But if you think you're leaving me for my own good, as a way of protecting me or my brothers, you're out of your fucking mind. You're mine, Hayley, and I will not let go of what is mine. I protect what's mine. You do not and will not ever protect me. You get me?"

Her eyes widened in shock and her lips trembled. "Y-Yes."

"Yes, what?" he prompted.

"Yes, Silas," she whispered.

"Get undressed and go get on the bed. Make sure you're comfortable and that your legs are spread wide so I immediately see what is mine and only mine."

Her eyes widened further and she opened her mouth but then closed it promptly and bit into her bottom lip as if stanching the flood of questions and her protest. He smiled to himself, ensuring it didn't show on his face or in his eyes. He had to make sure she got his message loud and clear.

He uncurled his hand from her neck, unable to resist caressing the soft skin just below her ears. Then he dropped his hand away and gestured toward the bed.

"Go," he ordered.

She hurried to do his bidding and he watched in avid fascination as she shed his shirt, leaving her in just the lacy scrap of her panties. She pulled them down her legs and let them fall to the floor, and he nodded his approval that she hadn't tried to bend down, hurting herself in the process.

When she got on the bed and after a few cautious movements settled into a comfortable position, she shyly parted her thighs, splaying them open to bare the glistening pink flesh of her pussy.

"Wider," he said huskily.

Once more she complied with his command. Satisfied that she was positioned as he'd directed and that she was going nowhere, he ducked into his closet, stripping away his clothing and then rummaging for what he needed. When he walked back into her sight, her cheeks darkened and her eyes went cloudy with arousal and desire.

He made no effort to hide the soft wrist cuffs from her view as he closed in on her, suddenly looming over her slight body. Her nipples were erect and turgid, begging for his touch, his mouth, his tongue.

Slowly and with great care, he lifted her arms over her head and then secured her wrists together with the cuffs. She gasped softly when she realized she was utterly vulnerable to whatever he wanted to do with her.

Once she was exactly as he wanted her, he walked around to the other side of the bed, where her legs were splayed wide, and then he crawled onto the bed between her thighs and leaned forward, planting his hands down on either side of her head.

"Now, we're going to have a conversation all about the honesty you're so fond of. I'm going to ask you questions and all I require is a simple yes or no. Nothing more. You with me, princess?"

"Y-Yes, Silas."

His eyes gleamed with satisfaction. He leaned down, adjusting his body lower down hers, and sucked one taut nipple into his mouth and kept suckling until she was gasping and writhing beneath him.

"Do you want to be with me?" he asked in a silky voice.

Frantic need registered in her eyes when his mouth let go of her nipple and he stared expectantly, waiting for her answer.

"Yes," she breathed.

He let out a growl of appreciation and levered his mouth to the sensitive skin of her neck, nuzzling and sucking, leaving his mark on her fair skin. He worked his way down her body, pressing gentle kisses to her bandaged wound before moving even lower between her thighs, and he nipped the inside of one hard enough to elicit a moan as she began to thrash beneath him again.

"Be still," he said harshly, issuing a light slap to her clit that caused her body to go rigid, but she became still once more. "That's better," he praised. "I don't want you hurting yourself, my beautiful girl. Now tell me, is this your home?"

"Yesss," she said in a long, harsh hiss.

He delved between the succulent lips of her pussy and lapped greedily at her entrance, pushing his tongue inward as more sounds of sweet agony rose from her.

"Am I your home, Hayley?"

"Yes!" she said desperately.

Once again, he feasted on her, sucking and lapping at her like a man starved. She began trembling, her legs quivering uncontrollably as she hovered precariously close to her climax. She let out a wail of protest when he lifted his head abruptly, and he saw the harsh lines of need engraved on her face and knew she was right there. One more touch was all she needed.

He continued to survey her calmly, soaking up the sight of her below him, hands cuffed over her head, willing and submissive to his every desire. Captive to whatever he chose to do to her.

"Promise me you'll never try to take what is mine, what I own, from me again," he said in a biting voice full of dominance and absolute possessiveness.

"I promise!" she said in a strangled voice. "Please, Silas," she begged. "Finish it. I need this . . . you . . . so much."

At the thickening of her voice, so close to tears, he could no longer bear to delay her ultimate pleasure any longer. He was satisfied that she knew exactly who she belonged to and that he'd removed any ridiculous notion she had of ever trying to protect him when she was his to cherish and protect.

He lowered his mouth and began delicately eating at her throbbing, pulsing flesh, adoring her with every lick, suck and nip of his teeth. After a few seconds of working her slowly back up again, he registered the signs of her impending climax once more and this time he didn't stop.

He began sucking at her clit while using his fingers to plunge deeply inside her. He pushed his finger over the rougher part of her canal where her G-spot rested and he was instantly bathed in her silken heat.

"Give it to me," he growled. "Right now. All over my mouth, princess. Give me what is mine to take."

He sucked hard, stabbing his tongue repeatedly over her pulsing clit, and added a second finger inside her pussy, stroking fast and hard. She let out an unintelligible sound that was garbled and then she screamed his name as he slid his mouth down to her entrance and thrust his tongue into her, over and over, coating it with her heated honey. He let out another growl and clamped both of his hands around her hips, holding her in place as he continued eating her mercilessly.

As quickly as one orgasm overtook her, he could already feel the telltale convulsive tightening that signaled another rapidly consuming her. He drew back and she threw him a desperate, pleading look, begging him with her eyes not to leave her hanging.

"Shhh, my princess," he soothed as he positioned his dick at the mouth of her entrance.

He pushed in with one thrust, burying himself deeply into her swollen channel. He closed his eyes as he reached total depth and then he locked himself there, remaining utterly still.

"Silas, please, please move," she pleaded. "I'm burning up!"

"Look at me," he commanded. "Eyes on me, my sweet girl. Do you trust me? Do you know that I'll always, always see to your pleasure above all else? Do you remember your promise that you would willingly give yourself into my absolute care and keeping, my ownership of your body, your heart, your soul?"

Tears glittered in her eyes as they softened with love and complete, unconditional acceptance.

"Yes, Silas. Always."

"I need you to be very still. You're still healing and I will not do anything to cause you pain or to damage your recovery. Lie as still as possible while I take care of my princess."

Slowly she relaxed around him until he could feel the throbbing pulse of his dick embedded deeply within her body. His hips were flush against hers, and no part of his erection remained unengulfed by her sweetness.

Then he began rubbing his thumb over her clit in a firm circle. Her pussy clenched and spasmed around him, nearly squeezing the head of his dick right off. He closed his eyes and concentrated on breathing through the need to empty himself inside her.

He increased the pressure and the speed of his manipulation of her clit, finding just the perfect rhythm that had her gasping and clutching at him like a greedy fist. Her eyes widened and then blanked, a startled "Oh" spilling from her lips.

"That's my girl," he purred. "Come for me now, Hayley. Let go. I've got you, sweet girl. Let yourself go."

He never left her clit, milking every bit of her orgasm until she lay utterly spent on the bed, her eyes closed, a light sheen of sweat covering her body. Gritting his teeth, he eased out of her and then began pumping hard at his erection, aiming his release onto her pussy and then her belly, watching in satisfaction as it splattered over her skin, marking her in a carnal, primitive manner.

"Who owns you, princess?" he asked in a silky voice.

"You do, Silas," she said in a sleepy, sated voice.

He lowered himself to her uninjured side, gathering her into his arms as he reached up to unfasten the cuffs around her wrists. He made no move to clean her up. Not this time. It suited him perfectly for her to rest with his brand of possession all over her.

"Never try to leave me for my own good again, my sweet girl. Next time I won't be so lenient in my punishment."

She cuddled against his chest like a contented kitten and sent him a sleepy smile.

"Got news for you, honey. If this is your idea of punishment, then you're a walking advertisement for willful disobedience."

"Don't get any ideas," he warned.

"Oh, but I do love your punishments," she said dreamily.

31

"I need everything you've got," Silas said quietly into the phone. "Shit's about to get deep, Ghost. You've been buried in the Vanucci shithole for too long. It's time for you to come home. Do this for me, get every piece of information they have on us, especially any hits they're planning, and I'll get you the fuck out of there."

"I'm doing my best, Sye," Ghost said in a weary voice. "You know this takes time. If I raise any eyebrows, if I give the Vanuccis any reason to question my loyalty to them, then I fuck us all. You know that."

"Call me the minute you have anything," Silas said. "I won't have anyone else in this family hurt and especially not killed. If I have to take out every last one of the Vanucci scum, I will."

"Not without me," Ghost said in a tone that suggested no argument. "You're not going on some fucking suicide mission, Sye."

Silas nearly smiled at the adamancy in his brother's voice. It pained him that Ghost had spent the last fucking three years living in filth and being a diligent general in the Vanucci army. All to keep his brothers safe. It was time for him to come home. Ghost was every bit as stubborn and devoted to his cause as Silas was, and he was the only one who dared to ever argue with Silas, something Drake didn't even do.

"Just make sure it doesn't *have* to come to that," Silas said, before ending the connection.

He turned to see if Drake was finished with his phone call yet. Maddox was working on one of the desktops that had three twenty-six-inch monitors, giving him as many vantage points as possible as his fingers flew over the keyboard. Thane was slouched on the couch, a weary look on his face. He'd spent the last night at the hospital, sitting on Zander and making sure he didn't walk out of the hospital before the doctors thought he was ready. Hartley had relieved him first thing this morning and Justice had been assigned to Evangeline. Everyone else was gathered in Drake's offices waiting to hear any incoming news and awaiting the time when they would hit back at the Vanuccis.

"The Luconis are scared shitless that it's only a matter of time before the Vanuccis go after them. They believe the hit on Zander is nothing more than a distraction so the Luconis will relax their guard, thinking that the bigger threat exists to us. Whatever information they glean from their informants and the people they have on the streets, they'll pass along immediately to me."

Thane sat up straight on the couch, fully awake now. "You trust them?"

"On this? Yeah," Drake said indifferently. "They want their families safe and they know we can make that happen. For now they aren't going to do anything to piss us off, which means we can expect their full cooperation. One of the cops who raided Impulse New Year's Eve was found dead in an alley this morning. Makes me believe even more that the Vanuccis had dirty cops on their payroll and those dirty cops went after Evangeline, and they're also the ones who got to Hatcher and got him to turn."

"The dead cop one of the dirty cops? Or is it a good cop who saw or heard the wrong things in his department?" Silas asked. Unsaid was the fact that if the cop was dirty, the likelihood he was on Vanucci's payroll was good and Silas could possibly pin his murder on them. Killing a cop, even a dirty one, would bring down a hell of a lot of heat on the Vanuccis' empire. If they had cops crawling up their asses at every turn, it wouldn't leave them any time to perform hits on Silas's brothers or the people they cared about.

"I'll get on that," Maddox said. "I'll see what I can dig up and get back to you in a few hours."

From the corner of his eye, Silas saw Jax lean in, staring hard at one of the security screens he was monitoring, a scowl on his face.

"Yo," Jax called. "I got something here. Black car with tinted windows has passed the back lot three times in the last half hour and now they're fucking pulling in."

Everyone hurried over to look over Jax's shoulder. But he suddenly shot out of his chair, a grim look on his face.

"Fuck! They just tossed out a body!"

Silas hit the stairs, not daring to wait for the elevator. His brothers pounded behind him, their guns drawn, as was Silas's.

Fucking Vanuccis. What had they done now? More importantly, who was the body?

Fear was stark in his chest. Sweat beaded his forehead and he realized he was holding his breath as he stopped just outside the door leading to the employee parking lot. He kicked the door open and stepped out, Maddox at his side, their guns trained in opposite directions as Jax went low, taking the middle.

"Clear," Silas barked. "Car is long gone. Anyone see the body?"

He eased out, making sure he was first. Always first. The enforcer. Ultimate protector for Drake and all of his other brothers. It was who and what he was. He'd give his life for any one of them. Just as he would for his princess.

When he caught sight of the huddled female figure, her face completely hidden by a veil of long dark hair, his stomach bottomed out and he broke into a run just as a tortured cry erupted behind him and Thane burst by him like a demon from hell.

"Gia!" Thane cried out in agony, his voice breaking under the weight of more emotion than Silas had ever heard in the man's voice.

He and the rest of his brothers stood a few feet away, staring in shock as Thane dropped to his knees and gently cradled the broken woman into his arms and held her close against his chest. Thane buried his face in the woman's hair, his shattered moans making every man present wince and flinch at the terrible sound and the appalling sight of the bruised and bloodied woman.

"I've fucking had it with the goddamn scum-sucking, bottom-feeding Vanuccis and their propensity to beat up defenseless women because they're too fucking cowardly to take us on face-to-face," Maddox said, fury replacing his usual absolute stoicism.

Maddox definitely had a tender spot for Evangeline and now Hayley as well, and he demonstrated extreme gentleness and care with both women, but otherwise, he was always reserved, emotionless, and if he had ever been remotely involved with a woman for any length of time, no one, not even those closest to him, knew about it.

But the sentiment he expressed was equally shared among them all. Especially Drake and Silas, since both their women had been victims of the pansy-ass motherfuckers. Expressions of rage and also hardened resolve shone on every single one of his brothers' faces.

"It's time for us to stop sitting on our asses worrying about their next move," Jax growled. "I vote we take the fight to their front door and wipe the earth with their sorry asses. We'd be doing the city a service. Trust me, no one, not even their wives or children, would shed a tear at their fucking funerals."

Drake held up his hand to stanch the rebellion before it got out of hand, but no one looked happy with his silent dictate. Including Silas, who much preferred straightforward action over plotting in office

chairs and playing a goddamn chess match with their opponent. He
sent a meaningful look in Jax's direction and Jax nodded in satisfaction, understanding what Silas was telling him. Even Drake didn't dare
to presume to tell Silas what or what not to do. Silas was absolutely
loyal to Drake and his brothers, but he was a lone wolf and when he
decided on a course of action, Drake wasn't stupid enough to think he
would hold any sway over his enforcer.

Silas dropped to one knee beside Thane, nearly looking away at the
terrible grief in his brother's eyes. His gaze drifted over the unconscious woman and rage built even higher within him when he took in
her battered features and the fact that there didn't seem to be a place on
her body that wasn't bruised or bloodied. He reached between her
body and Thane's to gently press his fingers into her neck, feeling for
her pulse. He breathed a sigh of relief when he felt the faint patter in
return.

"Bring a car around," he called back to no one in particular. "We
need to get her to Drake's clinic so the doctor can treat her off the
books."

Then he turned his attention back to Thane, who was still holding
her solidly against his chest, rocking her back and forth as he whispered urgently into her ear.

"Thane," he said in a low voice. "Who is she?"

Thane lifted his head just enough to look at Silas, and Silas was
shocked at the tears shimmering in his brother's eyes.

"She's mine," he said hoarsely. "My family. She's all I have left."

Silas glanced sharply up at Drake to see that Drake was as stunned
as Silas and the rest of their brothers were. Thane *had* no family. Or so
he'd claimed. No one had ever questioned him further on the matter.
All of their pasts weren't pretty, and only peripheral details about anyone's had ever been discussed.

Jax knelt on the other side of Gia and brushed her hair away from her face, baring the damage. "One of the club's security guys is getting the car now, brother. We'll get her taken care of. You have my word." He paused a moment and then carefully wiped the blood from one of her eyes before glancing inquiringly back up at Thane. "Where did she come from? You said you didn't have any family."

A shudder shook the big man's body and more agony creased his face. "She's my stepsister. When she was just a kid, she followed me around everywhere. She was the sweetest little girl I'd ever known. I kept her safe from my bastard father, making sure he never put a hand on her, but just before I turned eighteen, the abusive son of a bitch finally pissed off the wrong person and ate a bullet that took off half his face. After that I left because she and her mom would be much better off without me around as a constant reminder of my old man. But I always made sure they had what they needed. Sent them money and checked in when I could."

He broke off, his hands trembling as he closed his eyes in a visible effort to maintain his control.

"Two years ago, Gia's mom passed away and she had no one. No money for college and no job options that I would ever entertain her having. She's better than that and I was determined she would have better. So I brought her to the city. Told no one. Set her up in a nice place, made sure she was enrolled in college and put enough money in a bank account for her so she'd never have to worry about working and she could focus on school and living her life. I was such a fool," he whispered, his pain and guilt shaking Silas's entire foundation.

"She's perfect and innocent and so fucking beautiful and smart. I didn't want to expose her to my life or put a target on her by anyone ever knowing of my connection to her. I wanted her to be happy, to have all the goodness in life she deserved and not the shit we live every goddamn day. Look at Evangeline."

Drake immediately bristled, a low growl sounding from deep within his throat as he stepped forward. Thane ignored him and continued his bitter diatribe.

"Evangeline lives in complete isolation. She has no friends in the city. Her only family lives hours away and she rarely gets to see them. She can't even go for a fucking walk because we're too terrified someone will put a bullet in her. She doesn't go anywhere. She stays all day in that fucking apartment and never complains, and the only people she ever sees or interacts with are us. And she and the rest of us will live in fear every single goddamn day, especially after she has her baby, that something will happen to her, and so we put a shorter and tighter leash on her all the time, and that's a hell of a way for a woman to live just because she fell in love with one of us. I never wanted that for Gia, and in my arrogance I thought I could be careful enough and give her all the things I wanted her to have and let her live close enough that I could see her from time to time, take her to lunch or simply sit with her at her place and talk and see her smile, and now she's the one who's paying for my stupidity and my inability to keep her safe. We have no business bringing women into our world, no matter how much they love us or we love them," he bit out. "Because if we loved them, really loved them and weren't so damn selfish, we'd put them as far away from us as possible so they don't live every single day in fear of being beaten, raped or killed. No one we love or care about will ever be safe, and you're deluding yourselves if you ever think otherwise."

The car roared up, cutting off Thane's bitter words, and without another glance in his brothers' direction, Thane lifted Gia into his arms and hurried to the waiting car. He got into the backseat, cradling Gia in his lap, and as soon as he was settled, the car tore off again, heading toward the clinic.

The others silently filed back into the club, tension so thick in the air that it was stifling.

"This means fucking war," Jax ground out as soon as they were back in Drake's office.

He stared at his three remaining brothers as if daring them to argue.

Silas merely nodded his agreement, too numb and devastated by the painful truth that Thane had leveled at all of them. But especially Silas.

"As soon as we know how Gia's doing, I'll go over what security measures Thane had in place for her and then figure out a way to beef things up so this shit doesn't happen again," Maddox said in a surly, pissed-off voice. "But he's a paranoid bastard. No fucking way he just left her in the wind without adequate protection. Hell, none of us even had the slightest fucking clue about her, so how the fuck did the Vanuccis tag her when we didn't even know about her?"

Drake's face was so rigid a rock would break if it hit him in the face. "One moment of inattention. That's all it takes. Evangeline is going nowhere until she has our baby and then I'm taking her away on an extended vacation so she can get out and be a normal human being. She's going to hate having her freedom taken until our child is born, but she'll understand. She'd never do anything to put our child at risk. I won't give them another chance at her."

"Fuck," Maddox said in a weary voice. "We're stretched too goddamn thin! With Zander in the hospital we can't afford to leave him vulnerable. We have to have men on Evangeline at all times and now we have to protect Gia. Silas, what about Hayley and her classes? How long before she finishes this semester? She can't go out every day without as much protection as we can throw at her. Fuck it all, we don't have enough men to put on Zander and the women, and I don't want any of us going anywhere alone, for that matter."

"I'm pulling Ghost as soon as he gets his hands on information pertaining to the Vanuccis' planned hits," Silas said tightly. "He has two men loyal to him in the Vanucci organization as well who will come with him. He's very good and he'll be useful in pulling a security detail. We'll manage. We always do."

"And what about Hayley?" Maddox persisted.

Silas curled his fingers into tight fists at his side. "I'll handle things with Hayley. I know what has to be done."

"I'm heading home and sending Justice back to you, Silas," Drake said. "Jax, can you go relieve Hartley at the hospital and fill him in on what's going on? Have him report in with Silas and tell him and Zander to be on alert at all times. That goes for all of you."

Drake left, Jax on his heels, leaving Maddox and Silas alone in the office. Maddox turned and stared at Silas, his gaze peeling back Silas's skin until he felt completely dissected and scrutinized.

"I don't like the way you said you were handling things with Hayley and that you knew what had to be done," Maddox said in a low voice. "Don't be stupid, Silas. Don't do something you'll regret for the rest of your fucking life."

Silas turned his back, effectively shutting his brother out, then pulled out his phone and put it to his ear. "I have a phone call to make," he clipped out, effectively dismissing Maddox.

Maddox swore a string of curses that would have a grown man paling. Silas closed his eyes and finished punching in the number and started the process of giving Hayley what Thane wanted his sister to have. The good in life and not the shit he and his brothers lived in every day. Thane had been right about that much. Theirs was a life that no woman should ever be forced to live.

He closed his eyes as sorrow swept over him such as he'd never felt. *Forgive me, princess.*

32

Hayley walked to the side exit of the school that Silas and the others had told her to use from now on and peeked out the door, surprised when she saw not one, but two cars parked close by the entrance. Maddox and Justice stood by one, arms folded over their chests, looks of utter seriousness etched into their features. Silas stood alone by another and when he saw her, he gave her a quick motion for her to come to him.

She dashed for the car, surprised when suddenly Maddox was there to open the passenger door for her. To her further shock, before she got in, he suddenly enfolded her in a bone-crunching hug that stole all the breath from her. Grateful her wound was completely healed, she returned his hug, uncertain of what else to do.

"You have my number," Maddox said in a somber voice as he loosened his hold. "If you ever need anything, you call. Got me?"

She nodded, her mouth open as he turned and stalked back to the car where Jax waited.

"Get in, Hayley," Silas ordered shortly, galvanizing her into action.

She slid in and shut the door, putting on her seat belt, and then glanced curiously in Silas's direction. "What on earth was that about?"

His gaze was shuttered, and that sent a shaft of hurt streaking through her. Eyes that had always been warm and open to her were now replaced by the cold stare he gave everyone else. The one encased by impenetrable ice.

What in the hell was going on?

Not answering her puzzled inquiry, he pulled into traffic, never once looking her way or speaking to her. Not even asking about her day. Nothing.

Dread settled into her chest. Had something else happened? Had Zander taken a turn for the worse?

"Is Zander all right?" she asked anxiously.

"He's fine," Silas snapped.

She shut her mouth, unable to hide her reaction to his coldness. She turned away, not wanting him to see the sudden tears that sprang to her eyes. Okay, so he was having a bad day. She could deal. She just wouldn't speak to him until he was over whatever was up his ass.

She leaned her head against the window, careful to keep her gaze averted from Silas. She was so lost in her thoughts that several minutes later, she realized they weren't driving to his apartment. She lifted her head, studying her surroundings in confusion.

"Silas, what's wrong?" she demanded. "Where are we going?"

"You'll know when we get there," came his short response.

Okay, he was seriously pissing her off now. Whatever his problem was, it had nothing to do with her or anything she'd done. How could it have been when she'd been in class all day and hadn't seen him since she'd arrived at school that morning?

She glared at him, but he never acknowledged her or diverted his gaze from the windshield.

A few minutes later they pulled up to a high-rise building in midtown, and she arched her brow but didn't bother to speak since Silas was giving her the silent treatment. He merely got out and motioned for her to do the same. He didn't even touch her as they walked into the building, and each time she moved close to him he purposely distanced himself.

By the time they got into the elevator, she was so pissed she was ready to take his head off. He drummed his fingers impatiently against the rail as they soared upward and she could swear he emitted a sigh of relief when the elevator stopped on the twenty-seventh floor. He got off and left her to follow as he strode down a hallway to a door at the very end. To her surprise he produced a key and inserted it into the lock, opening the door and motioning her in.

As she cautiously entered, her eyes widened when she realized this apartment contained the furnishings from her old apartment she lived in before she moved in with Silas. She turned to look at Silas, confusion clouding her mind.

"Are we moving?" she asked.

"We aren't moving," he said icily. "You are. I've had all your things moved here. The apartment is in your name and the utilities have been prepaid."

Panic and heartbreak shattered her attempt at maintaining her composure.

"What?" she whispered. "Silas, I don't understand. What is wrong?"

"Nothing is wrong," he said in a bored voice. "We're done. Finished. Over."

Utter devastation rendered her motionless. Only her knees and then her hands began to shake in reaction. *What?* He might as well have been speaking Mandarin for all the sense he was making. Over? No. They had made love this morning and he'd left happy. When they texted during her lunch break, they'd made plans for this weekend. Now it was *over*?

"I don't understand. Did I do something wrong? Silas, just tell me what—" His harsh laugh cut her off.

"My God, Hayley. You can't be this naïve. Where did you see this going? Marriage, two kids and a minivan in the suburbs? That may be what happens in a podunk town in Tennessee, but not here, at least not with me. I wanted you in my bed and I got you there. And you were good, babe, no doubt. But I'm done."

Babe? The utter condescension in his tone was her complete undoing. He hadn't once called her *princess*. His sweet girl, darling girl or beautiful girl. Just *babe*. As if she were some chick he'd once flirted with and then laughed with his friends about later.

Tears welled and ran in rivulets down her cheeks, and she made no effort to hide them or wipe them away. *Done?* Maybe she *was* that naïve. No, she hadn't envisioned a minivan in the suburbs, but she had thought she'd spend the rest of her life with this man. As his wife. As his cherished submissive. And now he was *done?*

Finally, the pain and loss bubbled up and found a voice as tears streaked her cheeks. "What is *wrong* with you? You're done, and I have no say in it? I *tried* to leave! I *tried* and you wouldn't let me. You told me this was my home, that *you* were my home. That I didn't have to be alone anymore. And now you're *done?* Was this some kind of fucking game to you? Was I just a game? Why the hell would you refuse to let me leave if you were planning to dump me? Why go through such an elaborate charade, or is it just that no one dares to leave you and you're the only one allowed to do the dumping?" she asked bitterly.

"Think what you want, Hayley," he said with a bored-sounding sigh. "But it is what it is. I'm leaving and I don't want you in my life—or bed—any longer. Don't embarrass yourself by making a scene, Hayley. *I don't want you*. Do I need to spell it out?"

Numbness had completely overtaken her as she absorbed the dispassionate way he stood there shattering her as though she were nothing. Had never been anything to him.

"No," she whispered. "No need to add to my humiliation more. I loved you, Silas. I gave you *everything* and I never once asked you for a damn thing and certainly not a fucking minivan, children or a house in the suburbs. The only thing I'm guilty of is being too stupid to live by believing someone like me could ever matter to someone like you. I hope the next woman will make you happy, since apparently I was a miserable failure in that regard."

For the briefest of moments, she thought she saw shards of pain splintering in his eyes, but just as quickly he donned that unflappable, emotionless look, and he turned and walked out of the door and out of her life, leaving her in pieces all over the floor of the place he expected her to live in.

It took every bit of willpower she possessed not to call after him, not to go after him and beg on her knees if that was what it took. To ask him what she had done that was so wrong that he'd treat her so callously and with such a lack of regard. He'd discarded her like yesterday's trash, and maybe that was what she was to him. Certainly no one worthy of a place in his life.

She sank to her knees, covering her face with her hands as sobs escaped her numb body.

33

The next week was interminable for Hayley. She went through the motions of each day like a robot programmed to do its master's bidding. She didn't eat, didn't sleep. Instead, she lay awake in her big bed, alone, hot tears making her nose swell and head ache vilely as she replayed every moment she'd spent with Silas.

She trudged to the subway station two blocks from her new apartment building and rode it to the stop a block away from the school and walked through the crowded streets with unseeing eyes.

It was the very day after Silas had so cruelly shattered her heart that she discovered something else was every bit as absent as her soul was. The passion and zest she had always felt for her music was utterly gone. Even she winced at the flat, uninspired notes pulled lifelessly from the magnificent violin Silas had bought for her.

By the fourth day, one of her professors had pulled her aside after class, his expression one of bewilderment and concern as he questioned what was going on with her. She hadn't known what to say. She just didn't care. About anything. The one thing that had always brought her joy in life was now the source of unending pain because all she thought of when attempting to play was Silas and how much he'd loved listening to her perform.

Making an instant decision, she'd informed her professor she was done and was going to her advisor at once to withdraw. Her professor had begged her to complete the semester so she wouldn't have to retake it all over again, but she wouldn't be swayed. It was the first decision in a week that brought her any relief or peace.

Two hours later, utterly exhausted, she trudged her way through the lobby of her apartment building after an emotionally draining meeting with her advisor, who, like her professor, had implored her to think about what she was doing and that her scholarship would most certainly be revoked if she simply withdrew from classes. Hayley had merely shrugged and left, opting to walk the entire way instead of taking the subway.

After getting off the elevator, she walked listlessly to her door and shoved it open, having not even bothered to lock it on her way out that morning. She went rigid as soon as she was inside, loathing floating through her entire body. She hated this place. Despised it and everything it stood for. Silas buying her off after casting her aside.

Fuck that.

He'd treated her no better than a discarded whore. She glanced down at the violin case she carried and suddenly couldn't bear to even look at it anymore. She stormed into her bedroom and tossed it onto the still-made bed and then went to her closet and began yanking out the items of clothing that truly belonged to her, and she made damn sure she left every single thing that Silas had ever given her in its place in the closets, the drawers and the apartment.

Yes, she'd made the worst mistake of her idiot, young life by trusting a man who didn't deserve either her trust or her love, but that didn't mean she had to spend the rest of her life paying for that mistake. And the very first thing she was doing to climb out of her shell of misery was cutting ties with everything having to do with Silas Goodnight.

This wasn't her apartment. Nothing in it was hers except the few threadbare items of clothing and her mother's dishes. Everything else could rot or burn to the ground. She didn't give a shit about any of it.

She wasn't without options. She still had every penny of the insurance check as well as the substantial amount given to her above the promised settlement, and if she was careful, it would last her a long time. Not in the city, but anywhere else that the cost of living wasn't so prohibitively exorbitant.

Nothing was holding her here now. She no longer had a scholarship to a prestigious academy of music. Her father would most assuredly understand her heartbreak and her inability to continue pursuing his dream for her. All he ever truly wanted was for her to be *happy*. And staying here was making her decidedly *unhappy*.

She would move to someplace temporary and she wouldn't shell out a ridiculous amount in the process. Not when she planned to leave this fucked-up place in her dust just as soon as she formulated a sound plan and figured out where best to go. She was tired of living in the past and she had no one and nothing to go back to in Tennessee. She needed a fresh start in a place where she was just another face in the crowd and nobody knew of her pain and betrayal.

There were a lot of big cities in the south, even ones with schools of music. With the amount of money she now possessed, she could afford to rent a small apartment or even a house and pay her own way through school.

Exhilarated to finally have a plan of action, she made short work of packing her things and used a few articles of clothing to protect her mother's dishes as she reverently packed them in one of the empty boxes left behind from when Silas had so hurriedly cut her loose and hadn't wasted a single moment in moving her out of his apartment and his life.

The minute she was finished, she hoisted the box in her arms and then tossed her large gym bag over her shoulder. She glanced around the room, ensuring she was leaving nothing of herself behind before gathering her purse and heading for the door. She stopped, realizing she was still holding on to the keys, and then she turned, launching them toward the kitchen counter, watching as they skidded across the smooth surface before coming to a stop right in the middle, where they'd be easily found.

That's what I think of your parting gift, Silas. And fuck you too.

She would splurge and spend tonight in the cheapest hotel she could find and use this night to search for vacant apartments in the not-so-great parts of the city, where her money would go further.

As she rode the elevator down, tears threatened as grief and a keen sense of loss sliced through her, cutting her and making her bleed more fiercely than a bullet ever had. But she fought them off, biting harshly into her lip. Never again would she waste another breath or tear on a man who didn't deserve to breathe the same air she did.

"Are we boring you, Silas?" Drake asked dryly from behind his desk.

Silas looked up from his phone, where he'd been watching the surveillance footage of the hallway in front of Hayley's new apartment. She'd left just after returning home from class, carrying what looked to be a large box and a bag and her purse thrown over her shoulder, and he wanted to know where the hell she was going.

"What did you say?" he asked, not masking his irritation with being interrupted.

"We were just discussing strategy for dismantling the Vanuccis' entire organization. You know, nothing terribly important," Drake muttered sarcastically. "Anything you'd like to contribute?"

Silas shook his head in frustration. "Not yet. I told you that you had to give me extra time with Ghost now that we not only need names and details of their planned hits but also if Gia was their doing and if so how they tagged her. He has to tread very carefully or it could mean his life plus those of the two men he has in the cesspool with him. What about Gia? Has she said anything yet? Provided any information we can use?"

Maddox leaned against the desk and scrubbed his hands down his face. "I talked to Thane a few minutes ago. He said she's still heavily medicated, and the few times she's woken up she's been terrified so they immediately sedated her. She's a mess. Hell, *he's* a mess. We don't need to get to the bottom of this just to keep our loved ones safe, we need to do it to keep Thane from burning down the entire fucking city in vengeance."

"If they come near Evangeline again, I'll light the fucking match," Drake snapped. "Find that goddamn info. I don't care who you have to threaten, bribe or kill. Just do it."

After looking around the room at his brothers, he let out a sigh and said what everyone else was likely thinking or had at least briefly entertained. "Is it possible that we have another traitor in our organization? None of us even knew about Gia, so what's the possibility of an outsider knowing?"

Grunts and what sounded like growls filled the air and Silas acknowledged that no matter how expensive their suits, his brothers were damn close to fucking feral. If one of them had turned on the family, the rest would rip him to shreds. And Silas would lead the pack.

Jax broke the silence that followed, his fury a living, breathing entity. "No fucking way it's one of us. We made a mistake with Hatcher, and Evangeline paid the price. We learned a lesson from that in the most painful way possible. It *won't* happen again. We'll find this motherfucker, end him, and our family will live happily fucking ever after. End of fucking story. Unless someone has something relevant to add, I'd suggest we get on with this shit and stop planting doubt in the minds of our goddamn family." Jax paused and looked around. "No? Okay, then. How about we stop talking about what we're doing and actually get off our asses and get it done." He shot up from his seat, a savage pissed-off storm brewing in his eyes, and stalked out of the room, slamming the door behind him with enough force to knock it from its hinges.

The remaining men looked at each other, unsure what to make of the usually taciturn Jax being so . . . verbose. Silas hated the sliver of doubt that crept in as he considered why Jax was so adamant. Hatcher's betrayal had left them all a little dented when it came to unwavering trust. And while he hated it, it cemented his decision to remove Hayley from his life. If he felt he couldn't trust his brothers, then being alone was the only choice he had.

"Gotta say, he has a fucking point," Maddox said in disgust. "We'd get a hell of a lot more accomplished if we actually took some goddamn action and stopped all the fucking finger pointing. That shit's about to piss me the fuck right off."

Drake cleared his throat. "Jax spent the morning with Evangeline. She's upset. Zander's shooting hit her hard. But I promised to stop hiding things from her, so she knows about Gia too. She's . . . not handling it well. Her blood pressure is up and the doctor has said if it doesn't stabilize soon, he'll have to put her on bed rest. And I'm telling you right now, if that happens, I'm moving up our vacation plans and I'm taking her to an island in the middle of the fucking ocean as long as it has adequate facilities for her to give birth in, and I won't be coming back until she and the baby are both strong, happy and completely recovered."

Questions about Evangeline's health flew from the other guys, but Silas cut through them all. "How serious is this, Drake? Does she need to be in a hospital? Maybe you should take her away now and leave us to handle this shit. With you out of the country, you'd have one hell of an alibi and no way you'd take any heat for what we do."

"Right now the doctor doesn't believe she or the baby is in any danger, but she is being monitored. And I'm not abdicating my responsibility to my brothers any more than I am to Evangeline and our child," he said fiercely. "So shut the fuck up. I'm a big boy and I can take any heat that results."

Silas knew arguing with him would be pointless, but he couldn't resist needling Drake just a bit. "Whatever she needs, let me know. I'm actually surprised you're so calm about this."

Drake's dark, burning gaze fell on him. "Calm? Lit matches, Silas. Get that goddamn information from Ghost *now*."

Drake slowly stood, grabbed his phone and headed out the door, undoubtedly heading home to Evangeline. Silas motioned for Hartley to fall in behind Drake. He'd made it very clear that no matter what Drake said about it, he was never to go anywhere alone and he was never to be without protection any more than Evangeline would be.

"You heard the boss," Silas drawled. "Get me something I can work with. I'm going to yank Ghost's chain and tell him I need his timeline moved up and him out of the fucking Vanuccis' pile of shit yesterday."

Silas would put his own plans into motion just as soon as he figured out where the hell Hayley was and why she still hadn't returned home to her apartment.

34

Silas was out of his *mind* with worry. Hayley was missing. She hadn't returned to her apartment since the night he'd seen her leave with a fucking box and a bag slung over her shoulder. He knew because he'd sat up all hours of the night, watching and waiting for any sign of her on the security cameras he'd so meticulously installed so he could keep apprised of her comings and goings. So he'd know she was... safe. Out of harm's reach. At least until they finally took out every last fucking member of the Vanucci family. It could take months. Far longer than he could expect Hayley to sit around waiting on him, especially after he'd cut her loose in such an unforgivable manner. But he couldn't allow himself a single break in his icy exterior because if he had, it would have all come out and then Hayley, as fierce as she was in her absolute devotion and loyalty, would have never *allowed* him to push her away. The only way he'd had any chance of pulling it off was by making her believe he no longer wanted her.

As fucking *if.*

The heart he never knew he possessed lay in pieces, as did the tattered remnants of the soul that was already as black as death and so stained that he could never hope for redemption. Or of having something so precious and pure as Hayley was. She deserved so much better than the man he was, than the man he'd been. The man he'd always *be*. But no one, *no one*, would ever love her as much as he did. That was little consolation to him, especially now that he had no fucking clue where she was or if she was even safe, the very reason he'd so coldly cut her from his life but *never* out of his heart.

Forgoing his daily check-in with Drake and his brothers, he went radio silent and drove like a man possessed to her apartment building, trembling with impatience and in dread of what he'd find when he let himself into her apartment with the spare key he'd kept so he'd always have access.

When the elevator finally stopped on her floor, he ran down the hallway like a maniac, fumbling to insert the key into the lock. He hadn't had time to install more than the one deadbolt and regular key lock above the knob that came standard with the apartment, but he should have returned the very next day as soon as Hayley left for class and ensured she was absolutely safe in the place he'd moved her to. But fearing she'd read far too much into that action and knowing she'd know precisely who was responsible for the new locks, he'd made himself stay away.

Not so now.

He shoved the door open and walked in, bellowing her name in a voice riddled with fear that he didn't recognize. He *never* allowed emotion to rule him, to unhinge him as it did now. His knees began to shake so badly he could barely remain upright as he stumbled through the empty living room and into the equally empty bedroom.

His gaze immediately found the violin he'd bought her, nestled in the open case lying in the middle of her bed. When he went to her closet, he frowned upon seeing it still full of clothes. Fear gripped him. Had she meant to come back after all? Had something prevented her from returning?

As he flipped through the items, some still with the store tags unremoved, recognition hit him as did the jagged slash of pain that flayed open his chest. She *had* left. She just hadn't taken a single thing he'd given her or bought for her. The only items of clothing missing were the inexpensive, threadbare shirts and jeans that had belonged to her before she met him. She'd made it so he no longer existed, had no part in her life, just as he'd done to her.

He closed his eyes and walked out of the bedroom before he fell completely apart. Grief and regret consumed him as he walked into the kitchen and saw that her mother's dishes were gone but everything else had been left neatly stored in the cabinets. Even the food he'd made sure was stocked was exactly as it had been left by him.

Then his gaze fell on the set of keys lying in the middle of the counter and he made a grab for them, counting them. He curled his fingers around them until the hard metal cut into his palms. Not a single key was missing from the set he'd left with her. She'd left and he had no fucking idea where she'd gone, if she was okay, if she was hurt, in pain, if she was even *alive*.

The city was huge and she could be anywhere—if she was even still *in* the city. She could be anywhere in the goddamn *country* for all he knew.

He hurled the keys against the wall and turned and stalked from the apartment, slamming the door with enough force to shatter the sturdy wood. Her school. What about her classes? Her violin was here, so what was she using to play?

He ran back to his car and drove like a crazed lunatic, swerving through traffic, running red lights and narrowly avoiding pedestrians. He didn't let up on the accelerator until he came to a skidding halt outside Hayley's school.

After scaring one of the meek, pimple-faced paper pushers out of his mind, Silas managed to discover that Hayley had dropped all her classes just two weeks before the end of the term, resulting in the revocation of her scholarship. Silas left the terrified young man before the cops arrived to haul his surly ass to jail and returned to his car, where he buried his head against the steering wheel and closed his eyes.

Tears burned the corners of his eyes as he realized the extent of the damage he'd done to his beautiful, darling girl. He'd ruined her life by trying to save it. What a hell of a trade-off. She'd lost her scholarship, her dream, had broken her promise to her father all because the man she loved was a raging asshole who deserved to be shot in the fucking head *after* his nuts were cut off and shoved down his throat.

She was the most talented young woman he'd ever had the pleasure of knowing, along with the honor of having her gift bestowed on him each time she played for him. No matter how often or what hour he asked her to play for him, she always willingly complied and transported him to another place where there were no Vanuccis, no Luconis and no threat to the people he called family. She brought him the one thing he'd never known in his entire life until he met her. Peace. And he'd repaid her by ripping her to shreds and taking everything from her. Her talent, her hopes, her dreams, her entire life.

Forgive me, beautiful girl. My princess. I love you so goddamn much it hurts. I'm bleeding without you. I can't live without you and I can't bear to ever have you hurt or killed because of me and the man I am, the life I lead.

He had to find her. He wouldn't sleep, wouldn't eat until he knew she was safe. He would find her. And then what? He'd taken her apart as ruthlessly as a man had ever savaged a woman. If nothing else, he'd find out where she was and he'd put a dozen men on her if that's what it took. He'd put surveillance cameras to catch every sight line possible so that no threat would go undiscovered. If he couldn't be with her, then he'd damn sure protect her even if from a distance.

He drove toward Impulse, only one thing on his mind. He'd use their extensive database and hack into anything that would aid him in his search for Hayley. If he was lucky, she was still in the city and he'd be able to track her through utility companies, apartment rentals, hotel rentals, telephone, whatever he could avail himself of. He wouldn't stop until he found her. Nothing else mattered until he could be assured of her safety.

When he rolled in to Impulse and hurried up to the office, he was relieved to discover that Drake had already been in and, not knowing when Silas would make it in, had left to return to Evangeline. The only two currently in, finalizing plans for their first offensive move against the Vanuccis, were Maddox and Justice.

Silas went straight to his desk, muttering to the others that he was following up an important lead. He just didn't specify what lead or that it was far more important than the fucking Vanuccis.

An hour into poring over utility records, apartment rentals and hotel records, he still hadn't found a goddamn thing, to his never-ending frustration. His concentration was broken when his burner phone rang and he swore, knowing he couldn't ignore Ghost's call.

"What you got?" Silas demanded shortly.

"I have it all," Ghost said just as shortly. "I'll take photos and send them to your phone. Could take me a bit because these files are seriously thick. Judging by some of this shit I've found, a lot of it came directly from a leak at the cop shop. Confidential police business stamps on some of it. Fuckers are in bed tight with the cops, which is very bad news for us if we carry out our strike against them."

Silas was already motioning to Maddox and Justice as he simultaneously fired off a text to Drake on his other phone.

"Forget taking photos. I want all of it. We may need it to cover our asses. Meet me at Impulse as soon as you can get here."

"I can't walk out of here with an armful of the Vanuccis' private files. Use your head, man. I'll be no good to you dead."

"I want you and your two guys out of there permanently," Silas said in a grave tone. "Shit's about to start going down and I want to make damn sure you don't go down with those fuckers. Pull your two guys immediately and bring everything you've got directly to me."

"You sure?" Ghost asked skeptically.

"I'm positive. Now move!"

"I'm on my way as soon as I let my guys on the inside know." There was a moment of silence and the sound of papers rustling through the phone. "Whoa, wait, Silas? You still there?"

"You still got me," Silas said impatiently.

"There's an open file on the desk. Looks like Vanucci's newest reading material. Think she might be one of yours. Dark-haired woman, looks to be in her early twenties, named Hayley Winthrop? There's an address on the front as well. I'd say they've already chosen their next hit."

Silas froze to the very core. His heart was screaming in denial. Not Hayley. God, not Hayley. Don't let him be too late to save her. If only he hadn't pushed her away, she'd still be with him and not out there somewhere he couldn't protect her with the Vanuccis breathing down her neck.

"Give me the address right now," Silas said hoarsely. "Then grab the files and get the fuck out of there now! Your departure just got moved up to yesterday. I can't be responsible for what happens to you or your guys if you stick around for longer than five more minutes."

He was already standing and steadily strapping on his entire arsenal as Ghost relayed the address, confirming Silas's worst fear. It wasn't her previous address but one unknown to Silas, which meant that the Vanuccis had already tagged her while Silas had been sitting with his thumb up his ass scouring countless records looking for any clue as to her whereabouts.

Silas tossed the phone down and turned to run from the office, when a strong hand wrapped around his arm.

Baring his teeth, Silas snarled, "Let. Go. Now."

"I've got some info you need to hear," Maddox said, refusing to let Silas go.

"It can fucking wait!"

"No, it can't," Maddox said hoarsely. "It's about Hayley."

Silas froze. Oh God. Don't let them have already gotten to her. He stared at Maddox with his heart in his throat.

"Make it quick," he said savagely. "She's been missing for fucking *days* and I only just figured out where she is because Ghost found a file on her open on Vanucci's desk. They're already planning their next hit. *Her!*"

"Jesus," Maddox whispered. "I'll tell you on the way. Let's go. Justice, you're with us."

"You packing?" Silas asked grimly.

Maddox sent him a baleful look. "Hell yeah!"

Thirty seconds later, they jumped in Silas's car and Silas tore out of the parking lot as Maddox input the address into the GPS unit.

"What about Hayley?" Silas demanded.

"Fuck," Maddox said, closing his eyes. "Zander called me from the hospital pissed as hell because before he could only remember bits and pieces of the shooting. It happened so fast. But he remembered it all in exacting detail a few hours ago. We assumed that we were the targets of the shooting, and it appeared that way because Hayley got hit when she tried to run up to Zander and push him out of the way. But Zander says that's not what happened."

"What did, then?" Silas shouted. "Spill it already. We don't have all goddamn day!"

"Zander said that Hayley saw the guys pull up. We didn't. But he saw her face and when he turned around he also saw the guys and they didn't immediately shoot. They *hesitated*. It wasn't until Hayley gave them a clear shot by moving from *behind* Zander and running to push him out of the way that they opened fire. Zander was able to get in front of her, mostly, and took most of the damage except for the rico-chet that hit Hayley. *She* was the target, not us, which means they tagged her a long time ago and had been waiting for an opportunity."

Silas felt the blood leave his face, and he started sweating from head to toe. He'd been so fucking arrogant from the very start. So certain he could keep Hayley off the radar and that no one would know he was involved with her. When all along those sons of bitches had known. He was extremely fortunate that Hayley hadn't already been killed, and if he didn't get to her in time, that was exactly what was going to happen to her.

"Rein it in, brother," Justice said quietly. "You have to keep a cool head or you're no good to her. We go in and do this the right way and no one gets killed. You with me?"

Silas gave a clipped nod, but his pulse was thundering so loudly in his ears that he had no clue what Justice had said.

"Hartley's with Evangeline, and Drake will meet us there. Jax is on his way as well. Let's go get your girl, Silas. And this time, try to keep her, okay?" Maddox said in a tight voice.

35

Hayley forced herself out of bed after yet another sleepless night and sat with her legs over the edge, her arms wrapped tightly around her waist. She lifted her head and grimly surveyed the interior of the shabby apartment she'd rented. She couldn't remain here another night. She'd chosen it because she could pay by the week and in the daylight it hadn't looked too bad. But it was in a crime-infested slum that was overrun with gangbangers and drug dealers.

Just last night, she'd sat huddled in her apartment in the corner after hearing shots beneath her window and when she'd finally looked out, she's witnessed in startling clarity a drug deal going down.

After that she'd taken the Colt her father had given her before she left for the city, the same gun he'd spent many a day teaching her to shoot from the time she was a little girl, and she'd placed it, loaded, underneath her pillow, within easy reaching distance. He was determined his baby girl would always know how to defend herself, but until now she hadn't felt she needed it.

She let out a harsh-sounding laugh. Hadn't needed it? It damn sure would have come in handy the night she'd been mugged and especially the night of the recital and Zander's shooting. If she'd had it then she could have given those bastards a dose of their own medicine and they would have never seen it coming.

Never again would she be without it at all times. She'd kept it, yes, but she'd always kept it safely stored. Now, however, she didn't leave her apartment without it in her purse and she didn't move an inch inside her apartment without the reassuring metal pressed to her palm.

She pushed herself out of bed, knowing it was extremely late, but it had been past dawn before things had settled enough for her to drift into an uneasy sleep. She dreaded even leaving the relative security of her apartment, but she refused to become a prisoner here. She was packing her stuff today and leaving. She didn't know her final destination. Yet. But by the time she got everything ready, she'd at least have an idea.

Easing the gun from beneath her pillow, she secured it in her purse and then, so eager to get out of there and put the whole ordeal behind her, she didn't even bother taking a shower. She hurriedly packed her meager belongings and then splashed cold water on her face, brushed her teeth and pulled her hair back into a ponytail.

She carefully pulled back the dingy curtains to peek out her window, sighing sadly as she saw the faint outline of the city in the distance. Despite the grief and despair so heavy in her heart, she would miss the city with all the flash and flurry that had swallowed her up whole from the very first day she'd stepped into it.

To a small-town country girl like her, Manhattan had seemed so full of glitz and glamour, so sophisticated when she was anything but. She'd made the adjustment in no time at all thanks to the kindness of the elderly patrons of the school who'd asked her to apartment-sit for them while they toured Europe. It had been her first real taste of independence, and she'd flourished and even enjoyed her new life.

Now it was time to pick up the pieces and move on and become the independent, self-sufficient woman her father had raised her to be. She just wished she knew where to begin or how to get over the one man she knew she'd never stop loving.

Finished with her packing and fully dressed and ready to face her future, a future without the man who'd given her such hope, she secured her purse over her shoulder and went to the door, placing her ear to the aged wood. When she heard a faint scuffle and the routine shouting her neighbors indulged in on a daily basis, she stepped back and decided to wait a few minutes before she headed out the door. The last thing she wanted was to walk right into the middle of a domestic dispute.

After what seemed an interminable wait, the yelling settled into complete silence. She stood a few more moments, making sure they'd gone back into their apartment, and then went to crack her door to have a look before she dragged her heavy bag down the stairs and walked to the nearest subway station. Even taxis didn't dare come into this neighborhood. She had yet to see a single one in the days since she'd moved in here.

She had her hand on the handle when the door suddenly exploded inward, knocking her back several feet, where she landed painfully on the floor. She let out a scream as a huge man loomed over her, and as soon as she opened her mouth to scream again he lashed out and backhanded her so hard she fell over, hitting the floor with the other side of her ringing head.

Two men came rushing in and grabbed her as she yelled hoarsely, refusing to give in to their demands for her silence. The next moments came in a confusing blur as everything she'd been taught as a little girl by her overprotective single father came rushing back. Things she had been too shocked and frightened to use the night she was rescued by Silas.

This time she wasn't terrified and unable to defend herself. She was pissed. She'd had enough of being bullied, knocked around and shit on by men she didn't trust and men she had trusted. She might very well be signing her own death warrant by not meekly abiding by their demands, but at this point, bring it on. She wasn't going anywhere without a fight.

She kicked, punched, clawed and continued to scream until a large fist slammed into her cheekbone, sending her sprawling back to the floor. Dazed and confused for a moment, she heard a harsh voice whisper, "Shut the bitch up," before that same hand covered her mouth.

Not willing to just give up and accept her fate, Hayley resumed her fight. Her nails dug into flesh as a fist connected with her ribs, robbing her completely of breath. Shit! Those were the same ribs cracked in her mugging, and by the pain scorching through her midsection, she'd bet every penny of her bank account he'd just cracked them again.

Her free hand fumbled for the cheap lamp beside the couch and she brought it down on whoever, and whatever, she could reach. A hand tightened in her hair and slammed her head against the floor, leaving her vision blurry. She blinked rapidly, trying to bring her attackers into focus, but it was nearly impossible with the way he held her to the floor, using all his weight to press down on her.

She felt cool air against her chest and knew her shirt had been ripped open. The man who was currently straddling her had blood trickling from his temple and her nail marks on his cheek. "Our father doesn't like a lot of fight in his women. We'll have to take care of that," he snarled as he ripped the button from her jeans.

Oh hell no. She wasn't letting this pencil-dick asshole rape her. She'd gladly choose death before allowing him to violate her and rob her of what little dignity she had left.

Knowing what they planned, she redoubled her efforts to escape. The second man, who greatly resembled the man straddling her, and whom she assumed was his brother, limped over to help subdue her as her flailing legs kicked over the coffee table and sent the glass top shattering to the floor. From a distance, she heard banging and her neighbor's voice yelling, "Keep it down over there or I'm calling the cops!"

Ironic since he made every bit as much noise on a routine basis fighting with his old lady.

Both of her attackers froze and exchanged quick glances, and then the man atop her pulled a gun from nowhere and pressed it to her forehead. "I've had enough out of you, bitch. Move again and I'll blow your brains out here and now. My father just wants to talk to you, and I'm the man who's going to deliver you to him so he can see that I'm perfectly capable of running the family business. Now, are you going to be a good girl and come with us or does this have to get messy?"

Hayley knew they were lying. There was no "talk" to have, but she also knew that he was dead serious about the gun at her head. She would give them what they wanted until she could blow *their* fucking brains out, or die trying.

The younger of the two brothers dragged her to her feet while the older one kept his weapon trained on her. The pain screaming through her ribs made it hard to breathe and her vision was still blurry from the repeated blows to her head, but adrenaline was keeping the worst agony from her injuries at bay.

They made their way out her door and down the hallway, not passing another soul. As Hayley stumbled down the stairs, her purse, which she'd somehow held on to, banged against her hip and reminded her she wasn't down and out yet. She quickly glanced at the piece of shit who'd threatened her with a pistol through one rapidly swelling eye and noticed he no longer held his gun in plain view. Must not have wanted to alarm anyone in case any of her neighbors actually gave a shit. The idiot obviously wasn't familiar with this particular section of town.

She was led to the trash-strewn back alley behind the building where she'd watched drug deals happen from her window. There was a black town car waiting.

Never let them take you to a second location.

The instructor of the self-defense courses she'd taken as a teen had drummed it into all his students' heads. If she got into that car, she knew she was dead. If she put up a fight, she'd probably still be dead. Either way, she died, but fighting at least gave her a chance that, once inside the car, would disappear with every minute they got closer to wherever they were taking her.

As her kidnappers carried on a low-voiced conversation on either side of her, she slowly slid her hand into her purse and wrapped her fingers around hard steel. Her last remaining link to her father. And if this didn't work, she knew she'd be seeing him soon.

Hayley faked a stumble, putting a few feet of space between them. The men spun around, both reaching inside their jackets for their weapons. As her back slammed against a nearby Dumpster, she pulled out her father's Colt. Everything she'd learned as a young girl at her father's side on a hilltop in Tennessee came back as she sighted down the barrel, exhaled and squeezed the trigger.

36

As the navigation guided them deeper into one of the seedier areas in the underbelly of the city, Silas felt Maddox's glare boring into him.

"Just say what's on your mind," Silas hissed impatiently.

"What the hell is Hayley doing in this neighborhood, Silas? You said you set her up with another place. *This* shit is what you meant? What the fuck is wrong with you?"

"Goddamn it! You know me better than that. I never intended her to be living like this." He couldn't keep the sharp pain or the overwhelming fear out of his voice, despite his best efforts. "I set her up in a nice place not far from her school, but she hasn't been back home or to school in days. I . . ." He closed his eyes, saying the last in a whisper. "I lost her. I spent all fucking morning trying to track her down. Then Ghost's call came and I can only pray to God I make it in time."

Justice made a sound of disgust and Maddox just looked pissed as hell.

"It never occurred to you to ask for help? Like when she first went missing? She's not just yours, Silas. She's ours too. Just like Evangeline is ours. We're your fucking brothers."

"This shit isn't right," Justice bit out, clearly in agreement with

Maddox's furious statement. "Yeah, Hatch fucked us over. Sold out to the goddamn cops. But if we can no longer trust one another, we may as well hand the city over to Vanucci because we'll all be feeding the fish in the Hudson and then where will Hayley, Evangeline and Gia be?"

Silas knew they both spoke the truth, but he couldn't worry about them or the issue of trust now. Not when his entire world was hanging by a thread. Later, when he was certain of Hayley's safety, he'd work on repairing what Hatcher had destroyed.

The GPS informed them their destination was approaching on the right and as Silas pulled to the curb, gunshots filled the air. Diving out of the still-running car, all three men pulled their own weapons and raced toward the sound.

Not Hayley. Don't let it be her. I can't be too late.

Feet sliding, he flew into the alley, then shock stopped him in his tracks and for a split second he was rendered immobile by the gruesome sight that greeted him. Beside him, he heard Maddox whisper, "Sweet Jesus."

Hayley was sitting on the ground in front of a Dumpster, bloody and bruised. Again. She held a gun in unwavering hands, dry-firing into two obviously dead bodies. Her eyes were blank and the only other sound in the eerie silence apart from the incessant click, click, click as Hayley robotically continued firing was the sound of her harsh, terrified breathing.

Silas heard running footsteps behind him but still couldn't look away from the horror in front of him.

There was an audible inhale and other sounds of complete shock, and then Drake's voice drowned out any sounds Hayley was making.

"What the fuck happened here?" Drake roared.

The question jarred Silas from his stupor and he ran to Hayley, his legs so shaky that he collapsed to his knees as soon as he reached her.

"Hayley!" His tortured cry spilled from his lips. "Oh God, baby. Let me look at you. Can you tell me what happened and how badly you're hurt? Where you're hurt?"

She didn't even acknowledge his presence. She just continued with the steady click, click, click as she fired over and over, her eyes dull with pain and terror and so cloudy that he knew she was no longer even aware or cognizant of her actions.

Maddox leaned over her other side and gently eased the Colt out of her hands. Behind Silas, Drake was issuing orders for cleanup. He hadn't looked at Drake even once and had no idea who had come with him.

Silas ran his hands over her body, trying to determine the severity of her injuries. Most of the blood appeared to be from her face, where her nose was busted and the corner of her mouth was cut open and bleeding steadily down her neck, but her shirt and pants were both open, leaving him to fear the worst. That he hadn't gotten here in time to spare her the pain and degradation she'd suffered at the hands of Vanucci's men. Dear God, what had they done to his sweet girl?

"Hayley? Baby, I need you to talk to me. Where are you hurt? I'm here. You're safe now. Just talk to me, princess. Please," he begged.

Silas pushed Maddox away so he could gather her gently in his arms and lift her off the filthy pavement. But as soon as she left the ground, she became a wildcat, struggling and swinging but still not saying a word.

"Hayley! Stop before you make your injuries worse. It's Silas, I've got you, sweet girl."

If anything, his words made her fight harder until he was forced to lower her back down. Restraining her would only cause more damage. He would just have to keep talking until she came back to herself and recovered from the initial horror of her attack.

Easing back a little, he slid his hand around her slender throat, caressing the tender skin in hope that the familiar act would calm and steady her.

"You're all right now, princess. I promise."

Her hand came up and slapped his away, and her eyes finally met his.

"You promise? You *promise?*" Her harsh whisper sent chills down his spine. "We both know what your *promises* are worth. Don't touch me," she said, recoiling from his hand.

This time Silas didn't care that tears stung like fire and threatened to burn a path down his face. Her words were like the sharpest knife, slicing directly through his heart. She was absolutely right. His promises meant nothing to her. He'd made her many and had broken every single one. He wanted to beg her forgiveness here and now, but the most important priority was to get her to a doctor so the severity of her injuries could be determined.

Maddox edged closer to Hayley. "We need to get you help, Hayley. You've got one hell of a bruise on your face and with the way you're holding your side, I can tell you're hurt." He took in her disheveled clothing and the blouse she was now gripping closed. The rage and pain on his face was obvious. "What did they do to you? Did they..." He trailed off, probably not able to voice the word that Silas hadn't allowed to truly cross his mind until that moment. *Rape.* Had these men raped his beautiful sweet girl?

"No," she whispered raggedly. "They tried..." Her gaze bounced helplessly around, finally landing on the bodies a few feet away. "Are they dead?"

Her voice trembled and tears began silently trickling down her ashen cheeks. Silas wanted to howl and vent his horrible, all-consuming grief. She'd suffered terribly because of him. Not once, but three times, because in each instance he had failed her when she'd needed him most. How could he ever hope to gain her forgiveness when he would never forgive *himself?*

Drake was squatting next to the bodies, carefully going through their pockets, when he heard Hayley's barely whispered question.

"Yes, honey," he said in a soothing voice. "They'll never hurt you or anyone else again."

Using his foot, he rolled one of the bodies over.

"This is Vanucci's oldest son. Stupid fuck can't take a shit without Daddy telling him how. I don't even want to know why he was allowed out of the house, but he's an inept little chickenshit, and we have that to thank for Hayley being alive right now. The other is Vanucci's second-oldest son. My guess is they were making their move and trying to prove themselves to the old man."

Maddox held up the gun he'd taken from Hayley. "Not the usual firepower carried by these assholes. A revolver? They don't leave their houses without assault weapons or a gun capable of carrying at least a dozen rounds."

"It's mine," Hayley said dully. "I want it back."

Silas's muscles twitched as he held back the overwhelming urge to pull her into his arms and hold her forever. She wouldn't accept that from him and it was no less than he deserved but it still killed him. Then her words sank in and the panic he'd been fighting bubbled back up. "What?" he roared, then spun toward Drake. "She can't even legally carry that gun here. This will never go down as self-defense with half the fucking cops on Vanucci's payroll and the fact that if the Vanuccis grease enough palms they'll easily pin this on her and claim they were the victims."

"Easy, Silas. A cleanup crew is on the way. This will all be taken care of and there will be no blowback on Hayley. We'll cover her. I promise. Just get her to our doctor and have him look her over. This part is handled."

Silas reached once more for Hayley, but she went rigid and turned away from him, curling into a ball in front of the Dumpster.

"Princess, you heard Drake," Silas said in a soft voice. "I have to get you to a doctor. I swear we'll work everything out just as soon as I know you're all right."

Holding one hand out to ward him off, Hayley used the Dumpster to push herself to her feet. Once she was up, she straightened as much as she could, still holding her ribs, and stared him down as tears splashed onto the ground, mixing with her blood.

"I have two words for you, Silas." She barely managed to get it out through stiff, swollen lips. "*Fuck. You.* And your promises. I'm no longer your responsibility. That was *your* decision. You were *done.* Now *I've* made *my* decision. *I'm* done."

Silas absorbed every verbal blow, knowing he deserved them and so much more. He stood there, soul shredded, as Maddox talked to Hayley in a low voice, easing closer as he might with a spooked horse.

"Sweetheart, listen to me, please. You've been badly hurt. You and my brother aren't in a good place right now. I get that. But you do need a doctor. Let me take you there. If you go to the hospital, it might get reported. No one can know you were here, honey. You'll end up in prison for that gun. Do this for me. Please. I can't just leave you here alone and hurt."

Hayley's shoulders slumped and she closed her eyes. "I'll go," she conceded. "But only if *you* take me."

As she pushed away from the Dumpster, her legs buckled and Maddox was there before Silas, sweeping her up against his chest. Maddox met his eyes briefly, and then Silas watched him stride quickly from the alley, carrying Silas's entire world in his arms.

"Silas?" Drake called. "I need your help. The guys are almost here. Let's get your girl covered, and then you can start digging yourself out of the hole you made. I've been there, man. It'll be one of the hardest things you've ever done, but crawl if that's what it takes. It's worth it. Because nothing is harder than living without the other piece of your heart."

37

"Where the fuck is Hayley?" Silas roared over the phone. "I just went by the clinic and no one's there."

Maddox sighed and there was a momentary silence that made Silas even crazier.

"Hayley refused to go to the clinic. The only way I could get her to agree to allow the doctor to see her was to take her to a hotel room and call the doctor from there."

"Where?" Silas asked in an icy voice.

"Uh, I don't think—"

"Where, goddamn it?" Silas shouted.

Maddox blew out his breath and then related the name of the hotel and room number. Silas accelerated and drove as fast as was possible, pulling up to the hotel fifteen long minutes later. He strode past the reception area and got onto the elevator, punching the number for the thirtieth floor.

Moments later he was banging on the door and growled menacingly when Maddox answered, his big body filling up the doorway so Silas couldn't push by.

"You can either let me see her or I'll go through you," Silas said stonily.

"She doesn't want to see you, man," Maddox said, sympathy in his eyes.

"Then she can tell me that to my face. Now *move*."

Reluctantly Maddox allowed him by and Silas strode into the suite, his gaze locking onto the bedroom door, which was slightly ajar. He paused at the door and peeked through the crack to see Drake's doctor finishing his exam of Hayley's battered body. Silas closed his eyes, the sight of all the blood and bruising more than he could bear. How much longer would she have to suffer for who and what he was? For all the mistakes he'd made with her from the very beginning?

He pushed open the door just as the doctor was giving Hayley the last of his instructions, and he walked swiftly toward the bed, motioning the doctor out.

Hayley lay against a mound of pillows, her dark lashes resting on her pale and battered cheeks. He slid onto the bed, sitting so he faced her and gently picked up her hand, lifting it to his lips. Staggered by the emotion welling in his chest, he felt a peculiar wetness on his cheeks.

As soon as he touched her, Hayley's eyes flew open and she snatched her hand back so quickly that it rocked her midsection and she emitted a pained gasp. She held her hand to her chest, covering it protectively with her other one, and tried valiantly to scoot away from him.

"Careful, princess," he said in a low voice. "Don't hurt yourself. You need to be as still as possible so you don't cause yourself any more pain."

"You're the one causing me pain," she said in a ragged breath.

He sucked in his breath and looked away as more tears slid silently down his cheeks.

"I have so much I want to say," he said. "I'm so sorry, my beautiful girl. I've made so many mistakes. I never meant to hurt you time after time. I can't do anything right when it comes to you. You knocked me on my ass since the moment you entered my world, and then you became my world."

She held up a trembling hand to stop him. "Don't bother," she said scornfully. "You have nothing to say that I want to hear. I can't trust anything that comes from your mouth. I've been nothing but honest with you, Silas. I've kept all my promises. Can you say the same?"

"I—"

She shook her head. "No, don't say anything. I don't want to hear it."

"Princess, please. Let me explain," he begged. "Things were heating up and there was so much danger to you—to all of us—and all I wanted was for you to be safe and happy. To have the kind of life you should, and not one where everything is so fucked up with me. That's why I sent you away and made you believe that I no longer wanted you. And oh God, that killed me, baby. That's the only lie I've told. When I told you we were over and pretended you weren't someone I wanted to be with when you are the only person in the world I want to spend my life with."

"You are such a hypocrite," she seethed, effectively cutting off his impassioned plea. "Do you remember when your brother bled all over me? When he and I were both shot? I tried to leave you. Because I only wanted you safe. I never wanted to be a liability to you or a way for your enemies to get to you. But you wouldn't let me. You made me stay and you made me love you and then you made the unilateral decision to push me away. No one made that for you. You could have been honest with me and told me what was going on. Did that ever occur to you? That I have a mind and a brain of my own and that I should have been allowed to decide for myself whether I wanted to accept the risk of being with you?"

Silas's mouth fell open, wincing at the unvarnished truth. Every single word she spoke was a truth arrow that struck with pinpoint accuracy.

She shook her head, plunging ahead before he could summon something—anything—to say that would change her mind.

"You think I'm weak and helpless. That I can't so much as take a piss without you telling me how and when. Here's some information for you,

Silas. I'm not weak. I'm not a brainless twit. Giving you my love and my submission was my *choice*. I can live just fine without it, and quite frankly I've lived this far without a man controlling every minute of my day. I gave that to you because I wanted to and because it made you happy, and making you happy made *me* happy. But I don't *need* it and I don't need *you*."

He sat motionless, bleeding on the inside as he stared at the determined set of her face, read the truth in her eyes. There was no going back. He'd pushed too far this time, and he'd lost the one thing in his life he'd ever truly cared about.

"Please leave," she whispered. "I hurt enough, Silas. Please, just leave me alone. Is that too much to ask of you?"

Slowly he shook his head and stumbled to his feet. "No, princess. It's not too much to ask. I just want you to be happy and safe. It's all I've ever wanted. If you want me to leave, I'll go. I . . ."

He choked back the words of love that threatened to strangle him. They were of no use to him now, and what did he know about love in the first place? With one last, long look at the woman who held his entire heart and soul in her hands, he turned and walked away, shuddering with every step.

It wasn't until the door softly closed behind him that Hayley fell apart, burying her bruised and battered face in her hands as sobs painfully racked her thin frame.

"Honey, you're breaking my heart," Maddox said nearby, as his arms suddenly went around her. "Cry all you want to. I know it hurts."

She buried her face in his shoulder as her entire body shook with pain that wasn't just physical.

38

"I've been over every single file that Ghost brought us from the Vanuccis," Justice said. "Reports from Hatcher, a list of all the dirty cops on Vanucci's payroll and a list of hits. The good news is it's all accounted for, which means no mole in our organization. Bad news is I still have no fucking clue how they knew about Gia."

Silas frowned. "And Hayley?"

"They must have tagged her early on, man. Sorry," Justice said with a wince. "You know how careful we all were about being seen with her, the hoops we went through each time we went out to ensure we didn't have a tail. Never taking her to any of our regular places. You keeping her in the apartment most of the time. Maybe it was dumb luck on their part. It may have just been a case of them being in the right place at the right time."

"Hatcher overheard a phone call." Thane's gruff voice came from the doorway.

Silas and Justice both turned to see Thane push off the frame where he'd been leaning, the five-o'clock shadow looking more like a five-day growth, pronounced fatigue and stress evident in the deep grooves of his face.

"I was talking to Gia here when no one was supposed to be around. When Hatcher showed up unexpectedly, I promptly ended the call, but he must have been listening for a while before he made his presence known. It's the only possible explanation."

Justice swore and Silas's scowl deepened. Fucking traitor had been the source of unending grief to them all.

"Hey, man," Justice called softly to Thane. "What's the latest on Gia?"

Thane slumped on the couch and put his face in his hands, rubbing wearily. "In and out of consciousness. Every time she wakens for any length of time, she has panic attacks so bad they have to sedate her again. No one has even been able to question her yet, so all they have to go on are the physical findings of the exam they did on her," he said bitterly.

"Why don't you let one of us stay with her tonight," Justice offered. "You look beat. You need to get some rest. You can't keep up this pace."

Thane cast a meaningful look in Silas's direction. "Don't think I'm the one you need to be worrying about. How long's it been since you got any sleep, Silas?"

Silas stiffened and rose from his seat. "Got shit to do," he muttered, ignoring his brothers' knowing looks.

As he walked away, he heard Thane mutter, "I think I'm going to pay someone a little visit."

Silas walked mechanically to his car and drove to his apartment, thinking about a fifth of whiskey—or three. Then maybe he could forget his pain and the overwhelming sense of loss that accompanied his every waking hour. And perhaps for the first time since he'd pushed Hayley out of his life, he could actually sleep.

Hayley sat curled up in the comfortable chair in the hotel suite after downing one of the painkillers the doctor had left her, more for the pounding in her head than the pain in the rest of her body. The ache in her heart she didn't even bother trying to fix. Some hurts you just didn't get over and there was no medicine or quick fix. No magic cure-all, except time and distance. Yeah, well, both happened to suck.

For two days after Silas had walked out that final time, she'd been sequestered in this hotel room, grief and sorrow overwhelming her. She'd cried herself to sleep more times than not, and she moped around like someone who'd lost all hope. Her only visitors were Silas's brothers, a steady rotation through her room, and after the first mention of Silas when she'd vehemently made it clear his name was not a welcome topic, no one else had brought him up.

She sagged to the side, her brain processing things a bit slower now that the medication had taken effect, and just as she'd closed her eyes in an attempt to forget everything for just a little while, a soft knock sounded at her door.

She cursed under her breath, not wanting to move from her comfortable position. Thankfully, before she had to, the door opened, and to her surprise, Thane stuck his head in. She squinted in his direction, unsure if she was seeing him properly or if the drugs had muddled her perception, because the man looked about how she felt.

He gave her a lopsided grin as he came in and shut the door behind him.

"Hey, kiddo. You up for some company?"

She shrugged. "If you don't mind that I'm a little loopy at the moment."

He strode over, his long legs eating up the distance between them, and settled in the chair across from hers.

"How you feeling apart from loopy?" he asked softly.

She shrugged again, angry that she only wanted to cry.

"I'm sorry I haven't been by before now. I didn't find out all that went down until after it occurred. I've been spending all my time at the hospital with Gia."

She frowned. "Who's Gia?"

"My stepsister."

"What happened to her? Is she going to be okay?" Hayley asked in concern.

Thane's mouth dropped open. "That giant idiot didn't tell you what happened?"

"If the giant idiot in question is Silas, we haven't had much of anything to say to one another," Hayley said stiffly.

Thane shook his head. "Gia is my stepsister, but no one knew about her. I had hoped to keep her away from the kind of shit we deal with on a daily basis, but the Vanuccis got to her and beat the hell out of her. Nine days ago, they dumped her out of a car in the back parking lot of the club. It wasn't a good day for any of us, and I said some pretty nasty things about the fact that no one any of us cared about would ever be safe and would never live free and happy. Silas took it harder than most."

Hayley sucked in her breath as comprehension dawned. "That was the day he showed me the door."

Thane grimaced. "Yeah. I wish now I had kept my mouth shut."

Anger seized her as a whole lot more suddenly made sense.

"That moron," she hissed. "God save me from idiotic men. *Giant idiot* is far too nice of a description for him."

Thane lifted his eyebrow, obviously perplexed by her reaction. "Uh, I didn't mean to get you all riled up, kiddo. I just thought you should have all the facts."

"Oh, I know the facts," she said in disgust. "Believe me, I get the picture. I swear, men so incredibly *stupid*."

As she said the last, she struggled up out of her chair, wobbling unsteadily. Thane was on his feet immediately, his arm going around her to steady to her.

"Whoa there, sunshine. Where do you think you're going?"

"I'm going to go knock some sense into a dumbass's thick head."

"Uh, not that I don't firmly believe he needs it, but I'm not sure you should be going anywhere at the moment, honey. You're about to take a header."

"Look, you can either take me over to his apartment or I'll get a cab, but either way I'm going," she said stubbornly.

"I'll drive you," he said instantly. "But you might want to think about getting dressed first."

Hayley glanced down at the shirt Maddox had buttoned for her to keep her from having to pull anything over her head, and she made a face. Then she turned her pleading look at Thane.

"This is embarrassing," she muttered. "But I don't have anything but this. And I need help because I can't lift my arms over my head. Maddox had to help me into one of his shirts and I can't exactly go anywhere in only his shirt and my underwear. A bra is out."

Thane looked as if he'd swallowed his tongue and she could swear he paled a little. The look of desperation on his face was almost funny if she hadn't been so pissed off at her own boneheaded man.

Then he closed his eyes as if praying for deliverance. "I'll make you a deal," he said, wincing as he spoke. "I'll run down to the hotel gift shop and see about getting you some sweats and a decent shirt if you swear never to tell Silas I had to help you get dressed. I like my face just like it is."

Hayley pursed her lips and glared in his direction. "Wuss. Whatever. Just hurry up before I fall asleep."

39

Hayley waved over her shoulder as she stepped off the elevator on Silas's floor, leaving Thane to ride back down. He'd wanted to walk her to Silas's door, but she'd refused. She wasn't leaving without one hell of a fight and she'd rather not air it all out in front of witnesses.

Squaring her jaw, she marched up to Silas's door and knocked sharply. She winced when she heard a thud, followed by the sound of breaking glass and muffled cursing. Then there was silence. She lifted her hand and knocked more loudly. If she had to stand here knocking all night she'd do it.

Finally she heard the sound of Silas fumbling with the locks, and she held her breath until finally the door opened wide and Silas stood before her, blinking fuzzily. She wrinkled her nose when she caught a whiff of the alcohol that seemed to encompass him.

His face scrunched up in confusion as his bleary-eyed gaze swept over her.

"Princess?" His voice was barely audible as he stared at her in bewilderment. "You're here."

She put both hands on her hips and glared at him. "Oh, that's just great. I came over here to tell you exactly what I think of your noble gesture and how self-sacrificing you are and you're so drunk you won't even remember me giving you a piece of my mind in the morning."

He looked so sad that it was all she could do to stand firm and not wrap her arms around him and hold him close. Then she glanced down to see shards of glass glittering on the floor all around him.

"Silas, you have to be careful. You're barefooted and there's broken glass everywhere. Let's go inside before you fall over."

He followed her like a lost puppy and when she saw blood smudges on the floor she realized he hadn't missed all the pieces. Placing a cautious hand on his chest, she eased him around and led him to his couch. His eyes never left her.

"Prop your feet up on the table. I'm going to grab the first-aid kit."

She was almost to the bathroom when his whispered, "Miss you," reached her.

After grabbing the kit, she sat on the coffee table and began pulling the tiny slivers from his still-bleeding feet. Once again, his gaze followed her every move. He was treating her as if she were an apparition, afraid if he looked away she might vanish. "Miss you so much," he whispered again. "All day, all night. All I do is miss you."

Tears stung her eyes as she blinked to keep them from falling. He was breaking her already-broken heart. She cleared her throat. "I can yell at you later, honey. Let me clean up your feet." She uncapped the antiseptic. "This is going to hurt. I'm sorry," she said quietly.

He never flinched as she dabbed the liquid to his cuts.

"Hurts all the time. Didn't used to. Felt nothing and that wasn't a bad thing. Then you came along. Felt peace. Felt fuckin' happy for the first time in my life. Then I fucked it up. Now it hurts. Should, though. I deserve it. Didn't deserve you. Never did. Knew that but I took you anyway. And brought you into hell with me."

Hayley lost her battle with the tears as she wrapped his feet in gauze. God, so much pain in his voice. He didn't know what he was saying and would likely hate himself in the morning if he remembered baring his soul this way. She'd been prepared to yell at him. To stomp around and make her point and then tell him what she thought about him tossing her out for her own good.

She went to the bedroom, grabbed a pillow and brought it back to the couch. "Can you lie down for me, Silas? I need to clean up the broken glass."

He reclined back onto the pillow, reaching up to trail his fingers down her damp cheek. "Don't cry, my Hayley. You have to know I'd do anything for you." He slowly lowered his hand back to his chest, his gaze still locked on her face.

She looked away, no longer able to meet his eyes without succumbing to the temptation to curl into his arms, where she'd finally feel warm and safe again. But she wouldn't take advantage of him. He might not want her when he sobered up. Not after she'd told him to fuck off, not once, but twice.

By the time she finished sweeping up all the glass, all she heard from Silas's direction was his light snore. She tossed the glass in the garbage and then picked up one of the comforters and gently covered his unconscious form. Then it was she who trailed fingers down his bristly cheek.

"What am I going to do about you, Silas?" she whispered. "We're both so miserable. Are we going to keep pushing one another away until it's too late?"

The light shining against his lids caused jackhammers to start up in Silas's head. With a groan, he tried to roll over and almost fell off his . . . couch? Cracking open one eye, he confirmed that yes, he was on his couch. And yes, he had killed the fifth of whiskey in his cabinet. And a second one. He'd been working on his third when the doorbell rang and . . .

Ignoring the pounding in his head, he bolted upright. Hayley had been there. He looked to the right and discovered Hayley was *still* there. Curled up on the opposite couch with his comforter wrapped around her, raven hair spread across his pillow. His pulse ratcheted up about a hundred more beats per minute. Jesus, but she took his breath away.

Moving as quietly as possible, he eased to his feet and had to bite back a hiss. *Fuck.* Half the bottle he broke in his rush to get the door open the night before must have been stuck in his feet. When Hayley should have been home resting and tending to her own injuries, she'd been *here* taking care of his stupid, drunken ass. He wished he could be one of those drunks who had complete amnesia of the previous night, but he had perfect recall. He clearly remembered the tears streaming down her face as she wrapped his feet. He really was the lowest motherfucker to ever walk the planet.

He went to the kitchen and started the coffee, downing some ibuprofen dry. He'd let her sleep as long as she wanted, and then when she was up he'd fix her breakfast and find out why she had come over when she'd made it clear she never wanted to see him again. He frowned. She'd said something about wanting to yell at him. If the pounding in his head ever eased he might be able to figure it out for himself, but he doubted it. Her words and the resolve on her face at their last meeting had made it clear there was nothing he could offer that she would want.

The coffee had just finished brewing when he heard Hayley start to stir. He fixed her a cup just the way she liked it and brought it to her. As she sat up, a grimace crossed her face and her breath hitched.

He set the cup down so quickly, it sloshed up over the rim. Then he reached for her to help her sit up, making sure his hands were as gentle as he could make them.

"Careful." Realizing how gruff he sounded, he cleared his throat and tried again. "Easy, princess. Do you have your pain medication?"

Slowly adjusting her position, Hayley shook her head. "No. I didn't think I'd need it."

Setting the cup near her within easy reach, he went into the bathroom and found the painkillers in his medicine cabinet. Bringing them back, he set them next to her cup. "Take these, baby. I know you don't like the way they make you groggy, but every movement is causing you pain and I can't bear to see you hurting."

She swallowed the pills, then took a sip of coffee before looking back at him. Then she averted her gaze, staring down at her cup.

"I came over here to yell at you and give you a piece of my mind and now . . ."

His heart slammed hard against his chest and he tried so hard to quell the sudden flash of hope that attempted to flutter upward.

"And now *what*, princess?" he whispered.

Tears filled her eyes and it was all he could do not to haul her into his arms and kiss every single one away.

"I'm so mad at you, Silas," she said hoarsely.

"Why shouldn't you be?" he asked bitterly.

"Why didn't you tell me about Gia? Why didn't you trust me enough to let me decide whether you were worth the risk? Because you are— were. Why did you never ask me if I thought you were worth everything to me? I would have never left you. Why did you leave me?"

He closed his eyes, his heart hurting so much it felt like he was dying.

"It was never a matter of me not trusting you, princess. It was me I didn't trust. I failed you over and over. I've caused you nothing but pain and misery and I refused to be the reason you died. You deserve so much better than I can ever give you. You're so beautiful, so precious, so . . . good. Everything I'm not and everything I'm not worthy of."

Her eyes grew stormy and she scrubbed furiously at her tears as she glared at him.

"Only I get to say who's worthy of me and my love," she said fiercely. "You don't claim that right, Silas. No one does but me. You understand?"

He blinked at her vehemence.

She closed her eyes, pain and sorrow so evident on her pale features.

"How did we come to this, Silas?" she whispered. "How did we go from being so happy, so perfect for one another, to you sitting so far away and me being so afraid to reach for you? Can you promise me that if I reach out, you'll meet me halfway? That if I take the risk, it'll be worth it? That you'll never throw us away again?"

Her voice cracked on the last word and Silas could stand no more. Not meet her halfway? Oh hell no. He was going all the way. She'd never have to make a single damn move again. He was beside her in an instant, pulling her gently onto his lap until she was cradled in his arms, her head resting on his shoulder. He buried his face in her neck and plunged his hand deep into her silken tresses, gathering the strands until they wrapped around his fingers.

"Never, sweet girl," he whispered against her neck, feeling her pulse beating wildly against his lips. "Never again will you doubt my absolute love and adoration for you. My devotion and commitment to you. You are everything to me, princess. My life, my world, my reason for living. You will never know how sorry I am for the hell I've put you through, but if you'll give me the chance, I'll spend my life making it up to you."

He rubbed up and down her back as her tears soaked into his T-shirt.

"Seeing Thane's sister lying there on the pavement, all I could see in my mind was you. That could've happened to you, and I'd rather die than have that happen. I panicked. I just wanted you safe and I thought pushing you away was best. I was wrong, princess. So fucking wrong. You are the best thing that's ever come into my life and I was a fool to let you go. I love you, Hayley. I thought by watching Drake and Evangeline I knew what love was. But again I was wrong. This feeling . . . God, baby. It's worth fighting for. Worth dying for. Please give me a chance to prove it."

Hayley lifted her head and stared deeply into his eyes, and he was humbled by what he saw so clearly reflected in hers. Love. Forgiveness. Understanding.

"I never stopped loving you, Silas. I tried. God knows, I tried. I'm so scared. I'm terrified. But I want to try. But only with you. Always with you. I'll never love anyone else but you."

Silas squeezed his eyes shut to hide the betraying tears as Hayley lowered her face to nuzzle *his* neck this time.

"Living with me won't be easy." His voice was gruff again but he didn't care. "With my control issues, combined with the dangers surrounding my job, you'll never have a normal life. Are you sure you want to sign up for that?"

"Fuck normal," she answered with a watery laugh. "What has normal ever brought us anyway?"

"Not a damn thing," Silas murmured against her lips.

40

"Fuck," Silas groaned as Hayley's mouth closed over his rigid erection once more. "My princess loves my cock."

Hayley smiled and sent a sultry look upward. "That's not all I love."

His eyes softened and the harsh strains of arousal that lined his face disappeared as he reached down to softly caress her cheek. Then, as he continued to stare, a gleam appeared and his eyes glittered with the promise of something guaranteed to make Hayley erupt in a full-body shiver.

"I want my mouth on you," he said gutturally.

She huffed around his length, allowing it to slide all the way out until just the tip balanced precariously on her lips before she sucked him deep again, eliciting another groan of pleasure from him. He tapped her cheek in warning.

"Either I get your pussy while your mouth's around my dick, or you lose my dick and I get my mouth on you. Choice is up to you."

The way she saw it, in either situation she was the clear winner, but she was determined to see her seduction through. Silas allowed her control so seldom, and she wasn't about to give it up now, even if she had to compromise.

"Oh, all right," she said with an exaggerated pout.

In about three seconds, her body was yanked up and rotated, her pelvis lowering to his wicked tongue as her knees settled on either side of his head. Oh God, how could she possibly focus on blowing his mind when her mind was currently mush?

She licked and teased as Silas did plenty of licking and teasing of his own, and soon they were both making earthy sounds of intense pleasure as they pleasured each other with their lips and tongues.

She smiled in satisfaction as she took him to the back of her throat. This was all hers. No one had ever given this to him before. Never had he allowed anyone else to pleasure him this way. This . . . like him . . . was all hers, and no one would ever have what was hers again.

His tongue shot out, circling her clit before lapping downward to plunge inside her. She wiggled atop him, breathing through her nose as she tried valiantly to get him off before she went off like a rocket. She could feel his smile of triumph on her most sensitive flesh, and she redoubled her efforts to bring him to completion before she lost all her senses.

Ever since the first time he'd allowed her to love him, to use her mouth on him, it had been like a dam bursting. He seemed ravenous for her mouth and demanded it often. When she woke up in the mornings, he'd guide her head downward, saying without words what he wanted. In the shower, he'd push her to her knees and lose himself in her mouth before yanking her upward and fucking her from behind against the shower wall. And then there were the times when she'd wait for him to come home, on her knees, so she was the first thing he saw when he entered their apartment. He'd stride over, already loosening his fly, before thrusting deeply into her mouth. As much as he loved it, she loved it even more. He'd jokingly said that he'd created a monster. A cock monster.

She closed her eyes, using every bit of her concentration to ward off her impending orgasm so she could force him to his own first. He was close. Very close. Already she could taste the tiny spurts of his pre-cum and feel his hardness swell even larger, signaling his imminent climax.

Tightening her mouth around him, she sucked him as deeply as she could take him, until her lips wrapped around the very base of his cock. He trembled beneath her and she heard—and felt—his muttered "fuck" between her legs. Determined to get what she wanted, she sucked, lapped and licked, applying firm pressure with her mouth until finally, finally she heard his guttural cry and he arched upward, exploding into her mouth, filling it with his essence.

She was so close to her own orgasm and now that he was coming down from his, he pushed her even harder, and she hurried to reverently cleanse every inch of his cock before she became mindless.

"Give it to me," he growled.

He gently sucked at her clit, then flicked his tongue over the throbbing bud until her legs quivered uncontrollably. She threw back her head, his name a cry on her lips, and then his tongue stabbed deeply within her. Her orgasm flashed hot, wild, nearly painful in its intensity as she bucked and writhed over his mouth. He held her hips tightly, refusing to allow her to escape the swirls of his tongue.

She slumped down on him, panting softly, her eyes closed as he continued to lick and softly nuzzle her. Then his hands palmed the globes of her ass and caressed before gently lifting her up and rotating her so he held her in his arms, her head pillowed on his shoulder.

He kissed the top of her head and held her closely, possessively, just as he always did, and she sighed in utter contentment.

"Love you," she whispered.

His entire body tightened and then trembled in reaction. Just as it had every other time she'd said those words over the last two weeks, two glorious weeks they'd spent holed up in Silas's apartment, completely cut off from the outside world while she'd healed and their relationship had been cemented. He'd spent every moment making it up to her, apologizing, not only in words but in actions, for the pain he'd caused her.

"Love you too, sweet girl," he said gruffly.

Then he hoisted himself upward and sat up, hauling her with him so she now sat astride his lap, his back resting against the headboard. There was hesitation in his eyes and he looked . . . nervous. Hayley was astounded because Silas never looked nervous.

After a moment, he said, "There's something I want to ask you, princess."

For some reason she felt the strong need to reassure him. To remind him he hadn't lost her, that she loved him and that she wasn't going anywhere. She put her hand to his cheek and looked at him with all the love in her heart.

"You know you can ask me anything, Silas."

He gathered her hands between them and then stared into her eyes, and she'd never seen him look so vulnerable and unguarded.

"I—"

His cell phone rang and Silas swore long and hard. Then he looked at her, apology in his eyes. "I'm sorry, princess. I've got to take this. It's Drake."

Hayley nodded. "Of course. Should I leave you to talk in private?"

His hold on her hands tightened and suddenly she found herself pressed against his chest as he reached for his phone with his free hand, his other arm wrapped firmly around her.

Well, she guessed that answered that question.

"Yeah," Silas said into the phone.

There was a brief hesitation and then, "What? Wait—isn't it too soon?" Once more Silas was silent a moment. "Okay, Hayley and I will be there as soon as possible."

Silas tossed his phone aside and then turned his worried gaze on Hayley. Dread splintered up her spine and she tried to swallow the large knot forming in her throat. Silas's gaze immediately softened and became remorseful.

"Sorry. I didn't mean to scare you. It's Evangeline. She's in labor and

Drake's about to go out of his mind. She's not due for a bit yet but the doctors have assured him that the baby has an excellent chance of survival at her current gestational age, but they're attempting to stop her contractions to give the baby as much time as possible in the womb before delivery."

Hayley fidgeted uncomfortably and sat up, prying herself away from Silas.

"Um, shouldn't I stay here?"

Silas looked at her like she'd lost her mind.

"Princess, where I go, you go. Period. I'm not leaving you alone until the fucking Vanuccis have been dealt with for good. Hell, even after that I'm not ever going to want you where I can't see and touch you at all times."

Hayley's face burned with embarrassment and shame. "But I thought and said some terrible things about her," she said in a low voice. She glanced down at her hands, no longer able to look at Silas. "I don't imagine she or Drake would want me there right now. Only family."

Silas's firm hand closed around her chin. "Look at me, baby."

His voice was soft and sweet, and when she finally found the courage to meet his gaze, his eyes were full of understanding. And love.

"First of all, no one but me knows anything of what you thought or said. I'd never betray you by repeating anything you said. Secondly, had I explained fully about Evangeline in the first place and not put her higher in my priorities than you, then you would have never had cause to think or say the things you did. And thirdly, you *are* family. My family. My brothers' family and most definitely Drake and Evangeline's family. Evangeline will love you. She's a very sweet woman and about your same age. She's led an isolated existence since becoming involved with and marrying Drake, and I have no doubt she would welcome having you as a friend. Who couldn't possibly love you, my darling girl?"

Hayley's smile was tremulous. "You think so?"

He cupped his hand behind her head and pulled her to him so he could press his lips to her forehead. "I know so. Now we need to get to the hospital before Drake does something really stupid like tear the damn place down or hurt one of the doctors."

Hayley's eyes widened but she quickly got out of bed and rummaged in the closet for a pair of jeans and a nice shirt. She did a quick hair and makeup job because she didn't want to look like she and Silas had spent the entire two weeks in bed. Even if that was precisely what they'd done. If Silas hadn't routinely gotten up to cook, they would have starved.

Thirty minutes later, she and Silas strode hurriedly into Evangeline's hospital room, and despite Silas's assurances, nervousness overcame Hayley, and she hung back, standing behind Silas's large frame.

She swallowed when she saw that all of Silas's brothers were there filling the unusually large hospital suite. But then Drake could certainly afford the best, and she couldn't imagine him allowing his wife to be in anything but the best.

To her bemusement, when she entered behind Silas, his brothers all surged in her direction, ignoring Silas's warning growl, and they each in turn hugged her affectionately, asking how she was doing, ruffling her hair or dropping kisses onto her cheeks.

Maddox enfolded her in his arms and pressed a kiss to her temple. "How you feeling, sweetheart?"

She blushed, warm pleasure suffusing her veins. "I'm good," she said shyly.

"Silas taking good care of you, kiddo?" Thane asked as he pulled her away from Maddox and gave her another fierce hug.

She ducked her head bashfully. "Yes," she said huskily. "I'm fine, you guys. Promise."

"Get your hands off my woman," Silas grumbled.

His brothers chuckled.

Drake left his wife's bedside and folded his hands over her shoulders, his gaze tender as he stared down at her.

"I'm glad you're feeling better, honey, and I'm sorry you were dragged into our fight. I'll regret what happened to you for the rest of my life. It should have never happened, and if we'd done our job better, you would have never been nearly killed."

Silas's expression became pained, and guilt surged on his features, a bleak look entering his eyes.

"It wasn't your fault," she said softly.

Drake didn't look convinced. In fact, he looked every bit as guilty and remorseful as Silas.

Hayley peeked around the men and her gaze skittered to the woman propped on the hospital bed as she took her first glimpse of Evangeline, her own guilt soaring.

Evangeline's face lit up with warmth as she smiled at Hayley. "You must be Hayley," she said sweetly. "I've been dying to meet you. I'm Evangeline, Drake's wife."

Silas wrapped his arm around Hayley's waist and urged her toward Evangeline's bedside.

"Evangeline, I want you to meet someone very special. This is Hayley Winthrop. I should have introduced the two of you much sooner," he said in chagrin.

Evangeline stared balefully at Silas. "Yes, you certainly should have." Then she shook her head. "You men. I swear you're so stubborn and thickheaded."

Hayley laughed, charmed by Evangeline's sweet demeanor. "Boy, you said a mouthful, Evangeline."

"It's very nice to finally meet you, Hayley," Evangeline said sincerely. To Hayley's surprise, moisture rimmed the other woman's eyes and they shone with happiness as she stared back at Hayley. "You can't possibly understand how happy I am that Silas has someone like you. He's been so alone for so very long. You've made him so happy and for that you have my everlasting gratitude."

With those words, any doubt over Silas and Evangeline's relationship immediately evaporated. It was obvious that Evangeline cared deeply for Silas and only wanted him to be happy, a trait both women shared.

Impulsively, Hayley took Evangeline's hand in hers, concern flooding her. "Are you all right?" she asked anxiously. "Is the baby all right?"

Evangeline smiled and rubbed the mound of her belly, pure joy flooding her features. Drake was immediately at her other side, his eyes so full of love and tenderness that it made tears well in Hayley's eyes at witnessing something so beautiful.

"Oh yes, our baby girl is just fine. A little impatient, but she's been convinced to stay in her mama's womb for a little longer. The doctor has been able to stop the contractions, and as long as I take it easy, he believes I'll carry her until much closer to my due date."

"And that's precisely what you're going to do," Drake said gruffly.

Evangeline rolled her eyes and Hayley laughed as the two women shared a brief moment of camaraderie at having such overprotective, hovering men.

"Are they going to release you then?" Silas asked, concern edging his voice.

"Not until she's no longer having a single damn contraction," Drake growled.

Everyone's attention went to the door when it opened and a tall, gruff-looking man strode in. Hayley gulped as she stared in awe. As with all of Silas's brothers, this man exuded power in his every movement. His stare was piercing, his eyes dark and brooding. He was as big and as muscled as Silas, which was saying a *lot*.

More surprising was Silas's reaction. He jerked, emotion flaring in his usually unreadable expression.

"Brother," Silas whispered.

And then Silas met the other man and yanked him into a fierce hug.

"It's damn good to see you again. Welcome home," Silas said in a suspiciously choked voice.

The room erupted as every single one of the men assembled greeted the newcomer. It was obvious the man meant much to Silas and his brothers. Hayley and Evangeline exchanged puzzled glances as they waited for an introduction.

"It's over," the man said quietly to Silas. "The Vanuccis are no more."

Hayley and Evangeline both flinched as the men explosively reacted to the bombshell. Hayley slipped her hand into Evangeline's and squeezed, unsure of what this—anything—meant. Tears glimmered in Evangeline's eyes but relief was evident in her expression.

Drake held up his hand for quiet, and silence immediately descended. It astonished Hayley that in a room full of dominant, alpha men, Drake wielded so much power and respect.

"You are Ghost no more, brother," Drake said, emotion filling his own voice. Then he turned to the two women still looking on with confusion and trepidation, his expression softening with apology when he saw their obvious worry. "Andre, I want you to meet two very special women."

Warmth spread through Hayley's entire body at the sudden sense of belonging. Acceptance. No longer did she feel like an outsider to this tightly knit group. It was in the expression of every man present how important she and Evangeline were to them. She swallowed back the knot of emotion and blinked to keep the sudden surge of tears at bay.

Drake slid his hand tenderly over Evangeline's cheek. "This is my wife, Evangeline." Then he directed his focus to Hayley. "And this is Hayley. She belongs to Silas."

To Hayley's surprise, Andre walked over to her and gently enfolded her hands in his, his eyes softening, losing the hard edge he'd worn when he'd entered the room.

"I'm very glad you're okay, Hayley. I couldn't have lived with myself if I had been too late uncovering the information the Vanuccis had on you. I hope you'll forgive me for the ordeal you went through. Silas is a very lucky man to have a woman as fierce as you."

She gaped at him in astonishment, having no clue how to respond.

"I think we all know that it was my fault she was without protection and forced to fight off her attackers herself," Silas said painfully.

"Bullshit," Hayley said fiercely.

The others chuckled and then once more Drake held up his hand for silence.

"Tell us about the Vanuccis," Drake said urgently.

Andre cast a look of admiration toward Hayley. "She took out the old man's two oldest sons. The youngest is a pussy and disappeared, afraid for his life. The old man is dead and his empire is in shambles. The women and children fled the country because with the organization destroyed they're now easy pickings, and the Luconis moved in and took out anyone who had any position of power in the old man's army. Quite simply, the family business is no more and the vultures have swooped in to take over the connections and alliances that Vanucci once held, and the Luconis know better than to fuck with us. They would be signing their death warrant and they know it."

"It's over," Silas murmured, looking to Drake.

There was so much relief in Drake's expression and suddenly he looked so much less burdened. He stared at his wife, a glitter of moisture shining in his eyes. She stared at him with answering joy and relief and then simply held out her arms, and he immediately enfolded her in his embrace, burying his face in her hair as he rocked her back and forth.

"Thank God," he choked out. "Nothing will ever hurt you again, Angel. I swear it on my life."

Silas stepped behind Hayley and wrapped his arms completely around her, his lips in her hair. His body shook against her as he gripped her tighter.

"Nothing will ever harm you now, princess," he said, echoing Drake's vow to Evangeline. "I'll always keep you safe and I'll never let you go. I need you to believe that."

She turned in his arms and hugged him as tightly as he held her. "I know, Silas. I love you. I trust you. I always will."

Uncaring of the roomful of people, he crushed his lips to hers, kissing her urgently, his tongue sweeping into her mouth, tangling with her tongue. He pressed his forehead to hers and simply held on to her, relief stark and raw on his face.

"Let's get out of here," he said gruffly.

She smiled. "Take me home, Silas."